Vengeance Is Mine

Vengeance Is Mine

Daniel McClure

McClure

For and In Memory of
Margie Nell and Thomas Mark,
My first critics and fans,
who read the earliest pages and wondered how it would end.
I wish you were around to read the finished product.

Cover art by Janis Anderson

CHAPTER ONE

Clack Collins was drunk. The deputy was mad. And the preacher was nervous. The occasion that formed this trio was the drunk's wedding anniversary, although Clack was the only one of them who knew that. And he was drinking to forget. On this thirty-ninth anniversary of the Collins' nuptials, Clack's wife would not be attending the day. Truth be known, Jennifer and Clack Collins had not celebrated an anniversary together in three years. And Jenni had no intentions of sharing in any of the events that would be part of her husband's commemoration of that *dreadful* occasion. Clack's drinking had been on the increase for the past seven years, but over the last three, he had experienced only occasional binges of sobriety. The question Jenni, and all those who knew him well, wanted to ask was had he been sober at any point since New Year's Eve? Everyone guessed no, and that was ten months ago.

It was a vicious cycle. For those last three years, Clack said he drank because Jenni was mad at him, which was not entirely true, and Jenni stayed angry at Clack because he drank, which was absolutely true. No one knew which was the catalyst for their current set of circumstances, and most of their friends were tired of trying to sort it out and even more tired of caring.

Primetime, the senior adult monthly luncheon at South Mill Baptist Church, was just ending when Lanie, the church secretary, appeared in the fellowship hall to summon Pastor Matt to an urgent telephone call. Pastor Matt was winning friends among a couple of blue-hairs, talking about a rutabaga pie and a six-layer cake with chocolate icing when he was interrupted. In an old, southern town, and especially in a small, southern church, one thing was certain – the women could cook. There were those who were known for this dish or that, a dessert or a casserole. There was always the occasional belle who overestimated her culinary abilities, but for the most part, sweet goodness abounded at any event provided by the ladies of South Mill. As the pastor excused himself to the church office, Mrs. Linda McIntire promised she'd wrap up some cake for Matt to take home to his wife. Miss Mabel Ginn covered her rutabagas with a used piece of tinfoil, handed the aluminum pan to the pastor, and promised to make some for his family and have them over for Sunday lunch soon. Pastor Matt flashed a dimply smile, and said, "I'm holding you to that." An admirable gesture for someone who had just tried rutabagas for the first time and discovered that he hated the vile roots.

Matt Hardy was the new pastor at South Mill. He and his wife, Abigail, and their two children, Maggie, the six-year-old, and M.J. (Matthew Jr.), the four-year-old, had come to South Mill in June, just four weeks after he graduated from seminary at the ripe old age of twenty-eight. Matt had the boyish charm that came with his age. He was a few inches shy of six feet tall, a goal he had hoped to achieve back when he was a high school athlete. The ten pounds he added during his years in graduate school actually complimented his lean figure. Feathery brown hair arched over his face, calling attention to his beautiful blue eyes, his best and favorite feature, the only one he ever came close to bragging about. Abigail loved her man certainly for all of his physical appeal, but she loved his heart too. She was his brown-eyed beauty, only an inch or so shorter than him, and the couple looked good together. He, too, loved everything about her - especially her love for God and for people, and her favorites among people were their children. Youthful and passionate, Pastor Matt was like a young racehorse out of the gate for the first time – enthusiastic and awkward – but seemingly unprepared for the treacherous race ahead. Seminarians are eager to be called to a church, and oftentimes the history and track record of the church itself is overlooked out of sheer need for a job and the prospect of heroically bringing revival to the church and town. And this little South Carolina town certainly was in need of revival.

The church was twenty-three years old and had come into existence in 1987, when Central Baptist split right down the middle over the issue of ordaining women as deacons. The theologically moderate leadership of Central really did not find themselves impassioned on either side of the issue, but the prospect of getting some of the *old farts* out of their hair was promising enough to persuade a vote in favor of letting the ladies in. The conservatives, under the leadership of a prematurely-retired pastor, the Reverend Stephen Heath, would not stand for what he called a "femi-nazi" movement. On a Sunday morning, Central Baptist Church voted to ordain women as deacons, and on that same Sunday evening, South Mill Church was birthed on the sun porch of Stephen and Dorothy Heath's home, with forty-five people in attendance – eighteen men, nineteen women, three teenagers, and five children (three of them the grandchildren of the Heaths). By the time Matt arrived in the summer of 2010, the church had grown from forty-five to 233 people, a pattern marked more by births and marriages into the South Mill family than by new believers coming to faith and joining the church. In that same quarter of a century (almost), eight new pastors had been called by the church, some lasting as long as two-and-a-half years. No one minded losing pastors so often since Brother Heath was always so willing to step in as interim-pastor. He had now done so seven times, and each go-round he assured the church that they did not have to pay him for his service to the Lord, yet he never hesitated to deposit the checks they wrote him twice a month just the same.

When pastor number eight arrived, Brother Heath did what he had done seven times before – took the new pastor out to eat at the K&M Cafeteria, chauffeured him to the nursing homes and hospitals to show him around, and led him almost by the hand into the home of every elderly and so-called homebound member of the church. The elder pastor was a portly man with broad shoulders and an even broader belly. He had the coiffed hair that signaled to everyone who met him that he was either an evangelist or a used car salesman. He towered at least six inches above the new *kid* even with the slight stoop he had developed in recent years. At each stop, Brother Heath, as he preferred to be called, would smile his toothy grin and rub Pastor Matt on the head, pat him on the back, poke him in the ribs, or find some other gesture to make the new minister appear and feel much more youthful than he already was, each time referring to the pastor by the term "little fella." Then, he would chuckle in the most condescending way as he assured the most senior members that he would be helping to make sure *this* young pastor did his job. Pastor Matt did a great job of faking gratitude.

Breaking free, finally, from the clamor of little old ladies each trying to fatten him up with her own favorite dish, Pastor Matt secluded himself in his office to take a phone call that sounded much more pressing than rutabagas and chocolate cake.

"Hello, this is Matt Hardy," he began.

On the other end of the line was Eric Pressley. Eric was one of the deacons at South Mill Church, one of the younger ones. He was a good man with a heart of gold. He worked as a construction supervisor for Sawyer Industries, a contract company that was building the new Tri-County Medical Center, a regional hospital that would, upon completion, offer 600 beds for patients from the three counties represented in the name, and at least five more from the region north of them who would choose to go to South Mill rather than the larger cities that were just as close. Eric had a crisis and needed the help of his new pastor.

"Hi, Matt, this is Eric."

For the last five months, Matt Hardy had insisted that the church folks call him by his first name. Titles seemed to be quite important to the membership there at South Mill, but the new pastor felt they were wordy and awkward. "Please, just call me Matt," he would say when others would address him as Brother Hardy, Pastor Matt, or Reverend anything. He did make exception and allow the children in the church to call him Mister Matt because he agreed children needed to respect their elders. So, when Eric greeted him with, "Hi, Matt," he couldn't help but to celebrate a little in his heart. It may have been the first time the pastor felt like someone considered him a friend.

"Hey, Eric."

"I'm sorry to interrupt your luncheon, but there's a situation involving one of the guys here at work. I'm hoping you can help."

"I'll certainly try." A phrase Matt would learn to quit saying soon into his pastorate.

"You remember Clack Collins? Big man. He's come to the church a few times, usually on Wednesday nights for dinner."

South Mill was still small enough that on Wednesday nights, before Prayer Meeting and choir practice, the church got together for supper. In fine southern fashion, the church had, for the last twelve years, paid two black ladies to do the cooking. Matt innocently assumed they were there simply because their food was, in his words, "flat out amazing." It was, after all, 2010, and a black man was leading the country. Each week the congregation feasted on the delectable home cooking for the low price of three dollars for each adult, two dollars for children, and a family maximum cost of twelve dollars, certainly an affordable dinner and a price fixed by one of the former pastors who had six children.

"Yes, I know Clack. What's wrong, Eric?"

"Well, I helped Clack get on out here with Sawyer, and he's done real good work. You know he used to own his own construction company? Anyway, for the last three days, Clack hasn't shown up for work, and this morning one of the girls that works with us called him and got an answer."

Matt was intrigued at the story so far and said *"uh huh"* a couple of times just so Eric knew he was listening.

Eric continued, "Pastor, Clack's drunk, and he told the girl here that he has a .38 that he's gonna use to kill himself. I don't know what to do. He lives there in South Mill, about three miles from the church, on Boggus Drive, in a white mobile home with silver trim, about a quarter of a mile down on the right. I hate to ask you, but do you think that you could..."

"Eric, I'm on my way," Matt cut him off. "Thanks for calling. I'll keep you posted." With that, Pastor Matt hung up the phone and sprang into action.

Pleased that one of his deacons recognized his giftedness at reaching out to hurting people, Matt bounded from his desk and headed for the door. Two thoughts rushed through his mind as he crossed the floor. One – he should stop by the sheriff's office and get a little help saving this man's life, and two – did he have what he needed to save this man's soul? Patting his backside, he found that he did indeed have his pocket-sized Bible tucked in his pants. He kept a small version of the Good Book between the waistband of his pants and his tucked-in shirt where it fit nicely in the small of his back – and pulled it out for impromptu readings to hospitalized church members and families of dying saints, as well as for sharing God's promises with lost sinners like the one he was headed to see.

As he departed the office, he asked the secretary and one lone, straggling senior adult to be in prayer – he was going to... He fumbled to finish the thought. *Prevent a suicide* was a little too presumptuous and way too much information to just throw out there. "I'm going to *rescue the perishing*," he quoted an old hymn. They assured him they would pray, and since he knew they wouldn't, he made sure he did. From the door to his 1996 Chevy S-10, he threw up a quick prayer for Clack Collins, that he would see the possibility of a peaceful solution to his temporary troubles that pulling that trigger would not bring.

Clack had not always been a drinker – mostly because his early experimentation with alcohol had proven to be the shortest route to personal humiliation. Not long into their relationship, a group date with college classmates, including Clack's roommate Jed and Jenni's roommate Lori, led to Jenni's insistence that Clack abstain from the bottle.

At a downtown tavern about ten minutes from Jenni's campus, Jed and Clack had consumed enough spirits that their speech was somewhat slower and noticeably louder. Jenni and the other girls didn't mind and actually encouraged the immaturity because the boys seemed to be much more relaxed and affectionate as they drank. The jollity of the evening came to a screeching halt for Jenni, though, when Clack, turning to call for another round, came face to face with the voluptuousness of the waitress. Clack couldn't help himself at that point - the alcohol had to comment.

In the most sincere and polite way a drunken college boy could, he placed his order for another pitcher, calling the waitress by a name that did not belong to her - Dolly Parton! His reference to the busty country-music singer did not please Jenni. Jed led the howling laughter, and the other boys joined in cheering for *"Dolly! Dolly! Dolly!"* With that, the date was over.

Beginning to sober on the ride home and realizing the offense he had caused, Clack attempted to apologize to Jenni. His brain, how-ever, was still swimming, and all he managed to come up with was, "Jenni, I'm sorry that waitress had bigger boobs than you." And though they were in Jenni's car and she was driving, Jenni walked back to campus – and took the keys with her. Clack slept in the car.

They moved on from the awkward events of that encounter, and Jenni tried to forget it. Clack, on the other hand, did not forget and chose to apologize for it again, this time more drunk than the last. The apology came at Clack and Jenni's wedding reception in the form of an inebriated toast to Jenni's breasts saying, "Jenni, I think your tits are the perfect size. Hell, anything more than a handful is a waste anyway."

First nights of a honeymoon are seldom as lonely as that one was for Clack.

CHAPTER TWO

When the cop and the cleric arrived, Clack was outside of his rented double-wide under a canopy carport that was much too cluttered with lawnmower parts, fishing gear, and piles of old clothes than his six-month separation from Jenni should have provided. Lighting a cigarette, he staggered from under the canopy into the gravel driveway that was more sand and dirt than gravel, a common landscape for the Palmetto state. In his inebriated condition, Clack was happy to see his preacher show up at the chain-link gate in front of the trailer. Ignoring completely the uniformed companion that was just exiting his patrol car, Clack motioned for the preacher to come inside the gate shouting commands to the two large, fuzzy, white dogs in the yard. Clack barked orders to the dogs that were unintelligible to the human ear and, judging from the wagging tales and friendly romping of the canines, just as meaningless to them. As the preacher approached cautiously, not knowing whether *suicidal* might also mean *homicidal*, Clack fell on him in a full embrace and began to weep on his shoulder, a scene Matt had not rehearsed on the drive over. For an uncomfortable minute-and-a-half, no words were spoken except by the pastor who whisperingly comforted a very drunk, very sad, and very large man by repeating over and over, "Clack, Jesus loves you." The giant seemed to become peaceful in the clutch of the young pastor. It was, however, the quiet before the storm.

The deputy had held his peace now for ninety seconds, and it was time to demand some action. Stepping through the gate, the gangly, middle-aged officer disturbed the peace.

"Mr. Collins! I'm gonna need you to step away from the pastor now," came the order.

Alcohol again calling to mind famous people, Clack erupted in response, firing back, "Hey, Barney Fife! Where did you come from? What do you think you're doing coming onto my property?"

It wasn't really Clack's property. Instead, he had found out about it from an engineer on the job site whose heart had gone out to Clack when he heard about his separation from his wife. The engineer had bought the property and parked a double-wide trailer on it when his own daughter had escaped a doomed and abusive marriage six years earlier. It had been a real blessing to her and her two-year-old, a good hiding spot while she divorced the jerk. She had since remarried a wonderful Christian man and no longer needed the place. He rented it out to Clack month-to-month at a much cheaper rate than Clack was paying to stay in a local motel while working at the hospital site.

Barney Fife! Even in the tension of this hostile episode, the minister had to admit that the deputy accompanying him did bear a striking resemblance to the Andy Griffith sidekick. Even the little town they lived in was very Mayberryish, especially so for the twenty-first century. He thought it funny that, as intoxicated as Clack was, he had a keen sense of his surroundings. Trying hard not to laugh, the minister tried to put his hand on Clack's shoulder, but Clack was already charging toward the deputy.

"Mr. Collins, do you have a gun?" asked the deputy.

"Hell yeah I've got a gun! I've got a lot of guns, but I ain't tellin' you where they are."

"Mr. Collins, I'm going to ask you again – do you have any weapons on you?"

Seemingly drunker than just moments before, Clack flexed his arms like a body builder, kissed in the direction of each bicep, and said, "here's my weapons, Barney Fife. I'm a trained killer."

"Are you threatening me, Mr. Collins?"

"Noooo sir, officer!" came a mockingly disrespectful response. "But you need to know that I was a colonel in the United States Air Force." Pastor Matt wondered why Clack felt the need to offer up that piece of information at that particular moment. It seemed like an odd thing to say. Maybe it was just the alcohol talking.

"Well, Colonel...can I call you Colonel?"

"You can call me Colonel, and I'll call you Barney Fife," Clack slurred as he staggered closer.

"Well, Colonel, that's not my name. My name is Sergeant Andrews, and I want to help you out today."

"Well, Sergeant, I outrank you, and I don't need your help. Just get on outta my yard, and leave me and the preacher here to work things out."

"I can't do that Colonel Collins. When I leave this yard, I'm going to have to ask you to come with me."

Again, seeming to become drunker by the minute, Clack threatened the deputy with an attack from the dogs that were now lying beneath a shade tree about fifty feet away. Insisting that the dogs were trained to become aggressive on command, Clack began another rage that again made the preacher stifle laughter.

"Sho-Sho-Hut!" Clack yelled in the direction of the dogs and then began a series of arm gestures that looked a lot like a baseball coach signaling a runner to steal third. These, evidently, were the secret commands to which these trained canines responded. The dogs did not move.

Nevertheless, with one eye on the dogs, Deputy Andrews again urged, "Colonel Collins, I'm going to have to ask you to come with me. Please put your hands behind your back."

"You aren't gonna arrest me! Sho-Sho-Hut!" Again, the hand signals. "Why would you arrest me? I'm drunk at my own house. I ain't hurt nobody...yet (aiming that comment at the officer). You can't arrest me."

"I'm not arresting you, Mr. Collins. I'm only taking you into custody for your own good."

"Well, for your own good, Barney Fife, you'd better get the hell off of my property! The dogs are waiting on my last command, and then your ass is theirs. Is that what you want, Barney Fife?"

"No, Colonel, it isn't, and I don't want to have to shoot your dogs, so you just don't give that last command, okay?" the deputy implored, certain now that the dogs would not react anyway.

At that, as if some cerebral switch had been flipped, Clack broke. Tears, real ones, began to flow again, and the angry, massive figure doubled over and began to weep.

"Oh, please, Barney, don't hurt my dogs. They're all I've got. My wife filed for divorce. Today's our anniversary, and they served papers to me this morning. Today! Can you believe the bitch? If you shoot my dogs, I won't have anything left."

Anyone would have immediately felt pity for the poor man, and with an unexpected tenderness, Deputy Andrews apologized to Clack for saying he would shoot the dogs. He again pleaded with Clack to ride with him to a place where they could talk and get Clack some help before he did hurt himself. The place of which he was speaking was the East Carolina Psychiatric Hospital, where they would evaluate Clack for both his alcoholism and his suicidal behavior. This time, Clack agreed to go along with the understanding that he was not being arrested. As the deputy helped him into the patrol car, he looked again at the dogs and asked the preacher if he would feed them until he got home. Pastor Matt's head instinctively began to nod as he pondered how he was going to stop being so quick to say "yes" to people. As the deputy closed the back door to the car, Clack, choking back tears, said, quite calmly, "I really was in the Air Force. I flew Black Ops in Vietnam." With unmatched empathy, the deputy said, "I was a linguist over there. I understand."

"You were in Nam?"

"Air Force, Colonel. First Lieutenant, so you still outrank me."

Clack laughed through his tears, but that was all he needed to hear. Immediately, he was in the company of a brother. He actually enjoyed the ride in the patrol car to the hospital. It was tranquil to be with someone who, at least partially, understood some of the demons Clack faced daily.

No siren, no lights. Pastor Matt watched in silence as the patrol car slowly faded down the narrow, country road. He noticed an old wooden swing and suddenly felt exhausted from the tension of the last half hour. As he collapsed onto it, the creaking of the chain roused the canines who impulsively vaulted in his direction. The recall of Clack's insistence that these were trained attack dogs sent the preacher into a moment or two of sheer panic wondering if the squeak from the chain could be misinterpreted as that final command. Then, having no other line of defense, he reached into his back waistband, pulled out his Bible and aimed it at the two dogs as though he might shoot them with it. He shouted the only scripture that came to mind, *"Peace! Be still!"* Maybe the words of Jesus that halted a raging storm at sea could work on two orphaned animals.

The larger pooch, unfazed by the rebuke, leapt into Matt's lap, and the smaller one sidled up to him on the bench seat of the swing.

Both began to lick the hand still holding the Bible, and though he wanted to give credit to the power of the Word of God, he laughed as he realized they were licking Miss Mabel's rutabagas that were now dried and stuck to the heel of his hand. He hadn't noticed that that the aluminum pan had drippings of the gross vegetable on the bottom as he promised to take some home to the family.

"You like rutabagas, boys?" he asked. "Well, wait 'til you see what I have in the truck for you!" After all, he did tell Clack he would feed the dogs, and Clack hadn't specified what to feed them.

Matt dropped his Bible on the ground, just to protect the leather from the slobber of the two gigantic tongues, and it fell open to a page with a bright, florescent pink line across it. Without stooping to see the highlighted words, Matt knew what they said. From the gospel of Luke, the tenth chapter, *"Go; Behold, I am sending you out as lambs among wolves."* It had been the main text of the sermon that was preached at Matt's ordination service just seven months earlier. He glanced quickly at the wolf to his left and the one in his lap, and sort-of half laughed and half prayed, "Thank God!"

They shared the rutabagas, and then each made his way to the back deck of the trailer to his own personal bowl that Pastor Matt was filling with the IAMS® dog food he found in a bright metal trash can, about half the height of a normal one, on the back porch. He knew where to look because his parents used to keep his pets' food in cans just like those when he was growing up. He filled their other bowls with fresh water and promised the fur balls he would be back soon.

He closed the chain link gate, checked the latch twice, and then got in his Chevy and headed back to the office. On his way, he decided to stop at the sheriff's office again just to find out where they had taken Clack. He was still new in town, and the East Carolina Psychiatric Hospital was not yet on his radar. The dispatch clerk told him how to find the ECPH, nothing more than a three-story annex attached to the backside of the main hospital, The South Mill Medical Center. She assured him that they would be keeping Clack for at least forty-eight hours, after which Clack could, and probably would, sign himself out AMA (Against Medical Advice). That gave the pastor tomorrow to convince Clack to stay put. As much as he wanted to call the dog incident a miracle, he knew keeping Clack in the hospital was going to take a real one.

Back at the church office and after jotting down a few notes in preparation for Sunday's sermon, Pastor Matt packed his backpack, a relic leftover from college that had served him well in seminary, too, and was now the closest thing to a briefcase he had ever thought to carry, and he headed home. The ride was short – five blocks, one that could easily be walked, but if five months in town had taught him anything it was that church people expected to see his car in the parking lot as they drove by during the day...a sure sign that he was at work, earning the salary that their tithes and offerings provided.

At home, M.J. and Maggie met him at the door with hugs and kisses, but the sweetness of their affectionate welcome was spoiled by a pungent aroma that wafted through the living room, from the kitchen, and into the foyer. Abigail met him just inside the front door and said, "Miss Mabel called telling me how much you enjoyed her rutabagas at lunch today, so I ran to the grocery store and tried her recipe for supper tonight."

He kissed Abigail on the lips. He loved doing this in front of the children because of the way it made them grimace and shriek. He also kissed her like that because he was madly in love with her, and he hoped and prayed he would never have to spend an anniversary alone like Clack did. After eight or ten seconds or so of "eeewww grosssss!" from his kids, he interrupted their silliness by announcing they were going out to dinner. The kids began rattling off which fast-food establishment they preferred, and Abigail, secretly relieved they didn't have to eat the putrid things, asked what to do with the rutabagas.

"Bring them with us," he instructed. "I met two new friends today that love Mrs. Mabel's rutabagas! I'll stop and introduce you to them."

CHAPTER THREE

Locked up in a hospital room that felt more like a jail cell, Clack toasted his anniversary with his tears. Drunk, he was mad at Jenni and blamed her for everything. Sobering now, he knew everything could and should be blamed on him. Nurses and family members visiting other patients were serenaded badly by his repetitive rendition of Jimmy Buffet's lament, "Some people claim that there's a woman to blame, but I know…it's my own damn fault." He couldn't remember any other "Margaritaville" words, so he just sang those over and over again. When the monotony got to him, his memory made sure he remembered that it was, indeed, his own fault.

Clack had graduated first in his 1967 high school class back in Wilmington, North Carolina. He looked like a politician, with broad shoulders, eyes that looked like bluish steel, and swooping brown hair that was shorter than most other guys were wearing theirs in the late sixties. At a height of nearly six-foot-four, when he gave his valedictorian address, he spoke with grand gestures that accentuated his full wingspan and extra-large hands. Everyone assumed he would become president one day or at least a well-renowned senator.

Hoping to be a walk-on for the basketball team, Clack chose to attend the University of South Carolina, in Columbia. But a moving and patriotic speech at freshman orientation by the Recruiting Flight Commander from the Air Force ROTC motivated Clack to pursue military service over collegiate athletics. He immediately changed his registration card, dropping a music appreciation course and adding AERO 101 to his schedule. Once in the program, Clack was evaluated as highly qualified for scholarship and enlistment in the Air Force ROTC Detachment 775 at the University of South Carolina.

As a scholar, he pursued his degree in Mechanical Engineering, earning a consistent 4.0 throughout his academic career. As a conservative who supported the U.S. involvement in the conflict going on in Vietnam, he soared to the heights of his ROTC class. Clack was on his way to becoming a very important man in American military service and politics, at least that's what his parents told all of their friends at work back in Wilmington, as well as other members of the Collins family. And from all outward appearances, they were right about their impressive son. Clack's number had surprisingly not been called in the draft in 1969, allowing him the opportunity to graduate on time. Then, in the fall of his senior year, his commission delayed only by the fact that he hadn't graduated yet, he was assigned with three of his comrades from DET 775 to present colors at various government and social events in and around the Palmetto State.

Though the arts community was laden with anti-war sentiment, the South Carolina College of Art and Design, located just south of Columbia, was not. The school, after all, was in the south, the Bible belt, the first state to secede from the union. So, in November each year, the school held a Veterans' Day Patriotic Festival, complete with artwork commemorating great moments in U.S. military and political history, most of which centered around the valiant efforts of the Confederate Troops in the Civil War. The event was capped off with a grand dinner concert in the cobblestone courtyard of the school.

The school's symphony always honored the veterans and those presently serving in the military by offering beautifully arranged pieces of patriotic music, including "The Star-Spangled Banner," "America the Beautiful," and the most emotion-filled piece of all...."Dixie!" In the fall of 1970, South Carolina's School of Art and Design featured at its Veteran's Day Patriotic Celebration a budding new pianist, vocalist, and composer by the name of Jennifer Hart Grimes.

Clack Collins called the cadence as the color guard presented, and "The Star-Spangled Banner" began. Clack stood at attention, saluting a flag he loved. For some reason, though he had never been in battle, he fought back tears almost each and every time he heard that song. He could just imagine his father's generation, bloodied and tired through the night on European battlefields, hunkered down in fox holes, waiting to see what the new day brought. And the idea, the lofty idea of freedom's banner still waving in the first light of morning just melted this mountain of a man. Clack always had been a crier – and he felt no shame when it was over his country's flag.

After the presentation of the flags and the Pledge of Allegiance, the Color Guard was usually dismissed to drive back to campus in Columbia. That night, however, the four guard members did not hurry back. Instead, at Clack's insistence, they took a seat on a red-brick planter at the very back of the courtyard and watched and listened. As the team had about-faced to parade out of sight, Clack had caught a glimpse of the featured pianist. Now, out of the spotlight and at ease, he refused to leave until he met her face to face. He became mesmerized as she played riff after riff on stirring anthems. And, when she abandoned the keyboard to sing the solo in "Dixie," and the spotlight fell on her shoulder-length, feathered, auburn hair, he fell in love with the biggest alto sound he had ever heard. How could someone so petite bolster such a powerful sound? He would not leave until he knew her phone number and asked her out on a date. His buddies were quite patient, all anxious to see him succeed in this mission.

Collins had never had a date that they knew of, never asked a girl out in the three years he was on campus with them. Rumors spread; jokes were made. But Clack had dreams, big ones, of decorated military service and prominence, and his standards for whoever would be on his arm as he pursued those plans were quite high. That night, sitting on the bricks, the three other officers-in-training were captivated by their quiet, calm, reserved captain. It was as if Clack had waited all this time, calculating precisely the moment in which he would finally strike. This was it! His patience had paid off, and they felt certain he would soon return with his prize. If he didn't, though, they were prepared to laugh and make fun of him the entire ride back to school at the epic rejection.

With the conclusion of the annual concert, Jennifer Grimes had proven to be all that the musical arts department claimed she was. Still in college, Jennifer possessed all the talent and poise of a seasoned performer. That was, in part, due to her upbringing. Her father had been a United States Congressman. Her mother was once a Home Economics teacher, a career she abandoned immediately upon her husband's election to the House of Representatives. If there had ever been a southern couple custom made for each other, Congressman Jameson Grimes and his wife, Mary Ellen Hart Grimes were that couple. Their commitment to their church was rivaled only by their devotion to the social calendar of Cardelville, South Carolina, a town in which the Congressman had once been king.

His political career began with election to the Cardelville City School Board, from which he resigned to run for mayor of Cardelville. His mayoral race was so successful that after just one term he ran for the State Legislature. The party he and Mary Ellen threw to celebrate his victory was the largest gathering of the town's elite that had ever been held. It was surprisingly lavish and eccentric, and to the best of anyone's knowledge, the party was the grandest celebration ever thrown by an unopposed candidate.

Jameson always knew he could make more money at politics than if he had to work a real job. He was an accountant by trade, though he had somehow managed to only work a year-and-a-half at his father's accounting firm after he graduated from college before entering the world of politics. Mary Ellen had come from money, so the financing of his political career did not require that Jameson spend much time preparing tax forms or working a balance sheet. He served the state well, gaining road improvements and no small amount of state education money for the school system that had launched his career. He finally became the Lieutenant Governor in 1958, and in 1960, announced his bid for the Sixth Congressional seat for the great state of South Carolina.

The Sixth District elected him in a landslide over a liberal who wanted South Carolina to set the pace for desegregation in the public schools. Grimes served two terms before the unforgiving people of the district brought him back home to Cardelville. They let him slide when Congress passed the 1964 Civil Rights Act which banned segregation. But when his affirmative vote was revealed over the 1965 Elementary and Secondary Educational Act which offered millions of dollars in federal aid to school districts that increased their enrollment of black kids, Mary Ellen flew to Washington to start cleaning out his apartment.

Jennifer dutifully greeted the patrons who showered her with accolades and then shared a quick but public moment kissing her father on the cheek and hugging her mother. She then headed back to the conservatory to file her music away and grab her *Baroque History* book so she could squeeze in a few moments studying for the next morning's exam. Being careful, as she left, not to catch a high heel in the cracks between cobblestones, Jennifer Grimes did not notice the military escort she had acquired along the way. When the sense hit her that someone was staring at her, she turned quickly and was startled to see the four uniformed men close behind. The one in front, though, had the most disquieting effect on her of them all – not in a frightening way. His eyes were serene – what she could see of them in the shadows of his cover. As she faced him full on, he removed his hat and spoke with a kind, mellow voice.

"Miss Grimes, my name is John Claxton Collins, and I must say that your performance was the most beautiful salute to our country that I have ever heard." Such formality coming from such a young face made Jennifer giggle a little, half struck by how empty compliments usually were and how awkwardly sincere this one seemed. "You're sweet. Thank you!"

Jenni blushed at herself, partly for responding so quickly but mostly for what she didn't say but surely thought. Clack couldn't help but notice that the freckles on her nose, half hidden already by her stage makeup, kind of vanished as she blushed and reappeared as she regained her composure. It took a strong will to not lose his cool when he saw the moonlight play in her bashful blue eyes. John Claxton Collins was the most princely figure she had ever envisioned, let alone seen. He was noble, like the knight in the fairy tales that had forged her earliest dreams. "Are you...a musician?" She was searching for words.

"No, ma'am, but I am an admirer."

"An admirer?"

"Yes...of yours...of your music, I mean."

With a quick dig to the sassy roots from which Jenni was raised, she pressed the young airman, "Well, which is it?"

"Both," he shot back, through a solid smile and a confident twinkle flashing from his steely-gray eyes.

They both laughed, having completely lost sight of the three other cadets standing just a few strides away. They, however, were glued to the scene. If this superhero was nervous, not one of his sidekicks could tell.

The van ride home was celebrative. Clack was a hero coming home from a victorious night. He had a telephone number for her dorm room, her parents' home address in Cardelville, their phone number, and a date next Saturday evening. It had taken a little convincing, and Jenni tried to make the excuse that she was going home for a quick visit the next weekend (something she did almost every weekend – but that was none of Clack's business – at least not yet). Finally, Clack prevailed. Going home, no problem. He'd go there. It was a date! Dinner at Dusty's, a Cardelville favorite, owned by Jenni's aunt, but again not something Clack needed to know. If things went badly, she'd have her family there as backup ready to swoop in and save her.

Three weekends later, Clack was becoming a mainstay in the small town. Stopping at Jake's Grocery just off of Main Street on his way into town, clerks were beginning to call him by name, and Jake, himself, had given him the royal tour of the storefront establishment. He regularly stopped to pick up flowers or candy for Jenni. Once, he had even been sent to the little market by Mary Ellen to buy a bag of sugar – something the housekeeper had, evidently, overlooked on the weekly shopping list. Clack was glad to oblige, especially for the key ingredient in Mary Ellen Grimes' sweet tea. It was the best in the south, and Clack was sure Mary Ellen would need the entire five-pound bag to sweeten a single gallon. It was syrupy good, and Clack pronounced it so the first time he drank it by suggesting that they heat some up and pour it over pancakes the next morning. Mary Ellen was not sure it was a compliment, but she laughed along with everyone else.

Those three weekends in Cardelville were filled with family lunches at the Grimes home, moonlit strolls by the lake, and even one Saturday afternoon matinee movie. The courtship was as charming and elegant as novels about the "old south" make them out to be. The Congressman, as he still preferred to be called, was both frustrated by the amount of time Jenni was spending with Clack and pleased by the prospect of his only daughter marrying such an impressive soon-to-be airman. He said yes reluctantly when Jenni asked if Clack could join them for Thanksgiving.

Thanksgiving was a very big deal for the Grimes family. Aunt Janice, who owned the restaurant, and her husband, Trey, and their three sons, ages eleven, fourteen, and seventeen, usually joined Jameson, Mary Ellen, and Jenni at the Grimes family's beach home on Edisto Island. There, they would be joined by Jameson's brother, Jeffrey, and his wife Lisa, their college aged twins, Justin and Kelli, and, for that one holiday only, Kelli's boyfriend from Maryland, a Yankee in the opinion of everyone there, and a bur under the saddle of The Congressman in particular. The twins were sophomores at Clemson University, whose engineering program had attracted this Yankee – along with too many more. Each occasion Jameson had to spend with the transplant was quickly followed by a letter to the state legislature and a phone call to his cronies about limiting those out-of-state college acceptances.

Clack was especially grateful for the blessing of that fall and also accepted the invitation to join the family for the holiday festivities at the beach. He would join his family at home by Thursday evening, but first he would experience a Thanksgiving like he never had.

They had arrived at Edisto on Saturday, and Sunday afternoon they traveled by caravan coupes and station wagons to Charleston to see a musical theatre company's matinee performance of *The Sound of Music*, in a small theater that had been converted from an old church building just off of Citadel Square. Jenni had played Liesl in the production her senior year in high school, traveling to Charleston for weekend rehearsals and missing school during production weeks. As the family walked along the battery that afternoon, shadows were setting on Fort Sumter. The congressman looked at Clack and said, in what Clack hoped was a joking manner, "I guess if we'd have had us an Air Force when we (as though he had been there) fought the Civil War, it might have ended a lot differently." Clack searched the deepest corners of his mind to formulate a response, but words would not come. Clack found the entire statement ridiculous and his usual creative impulse incapable of crafting any sort of respectable response. He smiled, wrestled with it in his head, and asked no questions lest any portion of the absurdity be repeated. Things were progressing well with Jenni, and he did not want to say or do anything to spoil it.

That very afternoon, in the presence of her entire family, as they watched *The Sound of Music,* when Captain von Trapp and Maria kissed on stage, Jenni reached for Clack's hand and gently let her head fall onto the soft firmness of his shoulder. Jenni was pretty sure she was in love; Clack was certain that he was.

The Grimes family called it a Low Country Thanksgiving, and folks from the South Carolina coast knew the meal well. Shrimp, sausage, red potatoes, and corn-on-the-cob, all boiled together in The Congressman's secret seasoning and dumped onto newsprint laid across the blue and white checkerboard table cloth for the family to devour was a new experience for Clack – but a welcomed alternative to turkey and dressing. As soon as Jameson gave thanks to the Lord for the feast and the prosperity they all enjoyed, everyone said "Amen" and dug in. Clack shook his head and stifled laughter as the socialites lost all dignity and began eating with their hands, tossing shrimp shells into a bucket in the middle of the table. It was a tradition he would grow to love.

Following the noontime feast, Jenni, with her father's averse approval, left with Clack for higher ground to do Thanksgiving with his family. Things were moving forward for the young couple.

The weeks between Thanksgiving and Christmas were a blur, as those weeks usually are. When exams were completed, each headed home for the holidays. On break, Clack had time to declare his love for Jenni to his parents. Clack's dad even surprised him by loaning him money to buy an engagement ring. A small emerald cut was the selection, and Clack spent $750 on the purchase. The gold band and the quarter carat looked tiny in Clack's hands, but the color of the diamond was perfect, almost blue, and Clack felt that euphoric knot in his stomach – the same one he had felt in high school before a big game – the same one he felt on the drive home that night from presenting colors at Jenni's concert. It was almost Christmas, and he was a little kid who could hardly wait for the big day.

Christmas Eve was the big occasion for the Grimes family, and no one was expecting Clack to be there – except for Jameson, who had protected the secret for seventeen days now. Clack had asked for a private meeting with him the day before Jenni finished exams. The congressman gave his blessing and went all out to play the part of someone who did not know any secrets – a craft he had mastered in his political career. Clack left Wilmington at noon, driving what was normally a four-and-a-half-hour drive in about three hours and fifty minutes, a fact about which he would brag to Jameson and Jeffrey because men crow about things like how fast they can make a trip. That day he included it in his conversation just to have something to talk about to keep his mind, and perhaps any suspecting family members' thoughts, off of what he hoped was not too obviously his real reason for showing up so unexpectedly.

Once in Cardelville, Clack needed a way to kill some time. The Christmas Eve service at the Methodist Church was at 5:00, and if he arrived too early at the Grimes' home, he knew he stood no chance of faking it that long with so many family members around. He stopped at Jake's, but the grocery store had closed at noon. It was, after all, Christmas Eve. In true Cardelville fashion, though, Jake had set up a table out front under the awning complete with a few bags of sugar, flour, yams, Karo syrup, vanilla extract, fruitcake, and a few other odds and ends...just in case someone had forgotten some of the essentials. A note said, "LAST MINUTE GROCER-IES: Help yourself, but write a ticket and drop it in the box. We'll settle up after Christmas! Merry Christmas! Love, Jake."

By 4:30, it was time to face the music, literally. He arrived at the house just in time to get into the car with Jameson, Mary Ellen, and Jenni to go to church. He had planned it that way so there would only be time to talk briefly before the service began. Clack would make sure to keep up the conversation with topics like his superb driving skills that brought him there in record time, as well as the nice gesture of the town's grocer. That should occupy everyone and keep too many questions from coming at him about why the Christ-mas Eve surprise. As his Pontiac, a 1966 Grand Prix, came to a stop, Jenni bounded from the front porch and ran and wrapped herself in his arms. Jameson opened the doors of his Cadillac, a Sedan de Ville, bought new just a month earlier, a 1971 model. He grumbled about the hugging going on in his front yard and how it was going to make them late for church. Truth be known, though, Jameson wanted to be a tiny bit late. It would be very pleasing for him if all the eyes in the church service were on his elegant wife, his talented daughter, and his soon-to-be military hero son-in-law.

Following the Christmas Eve service, the Grimes family had Christmas. The meal was superb; the desserts were delicious. Clack ate little and tasted less...he was as nervous as he had ever been. He looked at his watch. A quarter 'til nine. It was time.

On cue, Jameson cleared his throat and asked, "What brings you down on Christmas Eve, Clack?"

Fighting the lump rising from his gut to his throat, Clack made his response with the coolest poise he could muster.

"It's Christmas, and I have a few gifts I wanted to share."

He first turned to Mary Ellen, gave her a beautifully wrapped box in which she would find a wind chime she had admired as they walked in Charleston at Thanksgiving. To the congressman, he presented another wrapped gift in which two confederate bills, a five and a one, had been framed with a miniature version of the rarely seen Palmetto Guard Flag, a replica of the one first raised over Fort Sumter by the Confederates. Each parent was pleased.

Then, Clack turned to Jenni. Her box was the biggest of all. She opened it gently, and laughed when inside it was a smaller box. She rolled her eyes when she came to yet another box, even smaller inside. But when she got down to the last box and absorbed the trimness of its size and the likelihood of its contents, she fought back tears. The dam broke, though, when Clack knelt on one knee and watched her open the tiny box. His great hands had never seemed so gentle as they took the ring from the box and placed it on Jenni's finger and said, "Jennifer Grimes, my name is John Claxton Collins, and I am in love with you. Will you marry me?"

"YES! I will marry you, John Claxton Collins!" Jenni almost screamed her response at him.

Tears and hugs all around were followed by the sound of another car outside - a Pontiac Bonneville with North Carolina plates. The Collins had arrived at the invitation of Jameson Grimes, a plan he had contrived himself and kept secret from everyone, including Clack. John and Rebecca Collins were welcomed with gusto. More hugs and congratulations and welcomes to the family. The guest house was ready, and Clack and his parents would celebrate Christmas there as a family the next morning and then join the Grimes for the rest of the holiday celebrations. Mary Ellen escorted them to the kitchen, and Clack followed, finally able to eat and enjoy the magnificent spread set before him.

lines and congratulations and welcome to the family. The next morning was Jenni, Clack, and his parents would celebrate a bit more sensibly the next morning and then join the Grimes for one of the holiday celebrations. Mary Ellen escorted them to the kitchen, and Clack followed. Finally, Phil arose and eyed the magnificent spread set before him.

4

CHAPTER FOUR

Winter came and went almost unnoticed by the Grimes girls. Mary Ellen was in her element planning what felt like, at times, one colossal party stretched over several months. Wedding plans intertwined with spring recitals and graduation in May. The date was set for June fifth, a little earlier than Mary Ellen thought it should be, but Clack was to report to San Antonio early in July for training, and the thought of a groom halfway across the country just sounded like chaos to Jenni and her mother. Even if Clack would not be making any of the important decisions, they still wanted him close by. The ceremony would take place at First Baptist Church instead of the Methodist one because it could accommodate more guests. The Baptists, however, did not accommodate alcohol or dancing at a reception, so a more tolerant venue had to be chosen. The Grimes' home was the selected site, and it would be donned with three large, lighted tents where the party could go on late into the night. The Langdon Art Center would be the rain plan, though it was much too small.

Turns out it did not rain in June at all, much to Mary Ellen's glee. Vocal and piano recitals, graduation for Jenni and for Clack, and the grand wedding day were all dry. Had days been available in the Sears & Roebuck catalog, the Collins-Grimes wedding party could not have ordered a more beautiful day for a wedding or a more perfect evening for an outdoor reception. The day was replete with politicians, relatives, friends, and a few enemies. Jameson always said you needed to keep your enemies close and completely unaware of how you really feel about them – so a dozen or so made the guest list for the ceremony and reception.

Clack's dad was his best man even though they had never been exceptionally close. Clack's dad worked hard and held tightly to all that he earned. Clack had been surprised when his dad loaned him money for the engagement ring. And it came as a big shock to Clack, when he and his dad were dressing in their tuxedos, for his dad to say, "Don't worry about repaying me for the ring money. Your mother and I love you and are very happy for you and Jenni."

Clack knew his parents lived tight, but he also knew that they had a nice savings account and were not hurting for the money, so he didn't feel guilty about just saying, "Thanks! I love y'all, too." He suddenly felt better about having his dad standing beside him on his big day.

Truthfully, Clack's best man would have been his college roommate, Jed. He'd not known a better friend in his life, and though Jed was a bad influence on Clack, according to Jenni, Clack felt like he was a better man because of the shenanigans Jed roped him into. Clack leaned toward the introverted, serious side of social engagement, whereas Jed tended to be the life of the party. Neither had pursued the fraternity scene in college mainly because they had in one another the only brotherhood either needed. The other guys from Clack's small circle of friends were there, too, including the other three honor guard members.

There was great alarm and loud disagreement about whose fault it was that Clack had too much to drink at the wedding reception and embarrassed Jenni again. She blamed Jed, the bad influence. He was insistent that they drink to old times, and Clack had readily agreed Friday night, after the rehearsal dinner. He couldn't see Jenni that night anyway, and who knew if they'd ever have the chance to just be boys together again...so might as well get tanked; they did. At the wedding reception, however, Clack knew he should not drink. He was inexperienced, and he wanted the night to be perfect. Jed, though, again reminisced with his roommate about pranks and professors and weekend trips to the beach they had taken as under-classmen. When the conversation turned to upcoming training and possible deployment to Vietnam, Clack toasted his best friend, and one drink led to another shot and things got out of hand fast. Clack was, for his linebacker physique, quite a lightweight when it came to alcohol. Of course, Clack's parents, who were in a hurry to get back to their motel and prepare for the early trip home the next morn-ing, blamed the Congressman for letting the reception go on so late into the evening. Clack's mother reasoned that anyone who drank would be drunk by the time that party broke up. Clack was willing to let any of them take the blame – as long as it wasn't directed solely at him.

What should have been the last toast of the night was from Jed, who wished the couple well. Holding an unsteady glass of cham-pagne up above his head, sloshing a little out as he waved it back and forth, Jed offered the ghastliest blessing Mary Ellen had ever heard when he said, "Clack and Jenni – here's to a long and happy life to-gether – may all your ups and downs be between the sheets." Ladies shrieked; the college men howled; and the grown men tried not to laugh and appear undignified.

Clack, not wanting to end the night on a note like that, took the microphone and offered a toast to his new bride. He began with niceties, but, as the alcohol kicked in, he became emotional about the blessing of meeting such a wonderful, talented, sweet, kind, beautiful...and...rich. He didn't mean to say that – and covered his mouth saying, "oops!" He went on and on, and then began apologizing for not being a better man and not doing enough to help her get ready for the wedding. Looks of pained consternation set in on the faces of their wedding guests as the groom lamented on. Then, it dawned on him that he was drunk, and he apologized for that. And as one memory led to another, he remembered the fretful night barhopping with Jenni, Jed, and Lori, and offered another drunk apology for his fascination with that waitress' bosom. And with that, Jameson took the microphone, thanked everyone for coming, and asked them to all drive home safely, though he knew that was a long shot for some of them.

Clack sucked up coffee while Jenni packed the car. She drove from Cardelville to Jacksonville, Florida, on their way to Daytona Beach. Clack all but slept it off in the car, and when they stopped at a Holiday Inn, Jenni went in and checked into a room with two double beds. She did help her husband into the bed, and she crawled into the other bed and spent her first night of wedded bliss separated from her husband by a night stand. By morning, she was more committed to enjoying what was left of the honeymoon than fighting with Clack about his drinking. She couldn't resist, though, making use of the Gideon Bible she saw in the nightstand drawer. She raised it to chest level and dropped it on Clack's snoring head and told him to get up and get a shower – they had a honeymoon to get started. Clack thought getting started must mean morning sex. She meant get a shower, and let's drive to Daytona, and we'll see what happens then.

The rest of the honeymoon was picture perfect. They arrived just after lunchtime at the condominium Jameson had arranged for them. Just south of Daytona, on Ormond Beach, they sunned and sailed and did all the things that honeymooning couples do. They even sipped a small glass of wine at night under the stars, and they truly were in love. Clack was the perfect husband without the booze, and Jenni was perfect in every way according to Clack. When the week was over, they returned home to the Grimes' compound, staying in the guest house for the two weeks before the move to Texas.

You couldn't see the seats inside the Pontiac for the pillows, dresses, boxes, dishes, and music books. Jenni and Clack darted from the car to the house and from the house to the guest house for one last look around to make sure they weren't leaving anything important behind. Goodbyes were held in the kitchen, the patio, and then finally beside the car. Jenni fought back a tear or two, but Mary Ellen never fought. She boohooed as her only child left. The assignment in San Antonio was only six months, but no one could guess where they would go from there. Deployment was almost a certainty, so Jenni and Clack felt sure she would return to Cardelville while he was in Asia. Jameson hugged and kissed Jenni, then hurried around the car to shake hands with Clack. Seemingly, any disdain leftover from the wedding reception had vanished with a sincere apology from Clack and the assurance from Jenni that he was just not used to the effects of alcohol. The congressman, Mary Ellen, and the rest of the family all seemed to be willing to forgive and forget - another skill quickly perfected when you have a family member in politics. Drunk at a wedding reception was a small infraction when Washington scandals broke daily for families like Jameson's. Emotion was not something to which Jameson was prone. He had not cried at the wedding—showing only joy for the couple's future together. As he closed the door to the car with Clack in the driver's seat, he caught a glimpse of Jenni smiling at Clack, and it triggered a memory of a little girl smiling at him as they loaded up for the first Thanksgiving spent at Edisto years earlier. He managed a "be careful!" Then, he turned quickly and retreated to the house - a lump in his throat and a knot in his gut. Worry overcame him as he watched his only child leave with a man who might die in combat someday – and he wished he could stand between her and any pain. His voice broke in a whisper as he said privately what he wished he had said to her, "You can always come home, baby girl." He spent the rest of his day in his study. Mary Ellen went shopping.

5

CHAPTER FIVE

Clack and Jenni arrived in San Antonio late on Saturday afternoon. They checked into a Ramada Inn near the base. Dinner was followed by a little romance, and they slept as well as the first night in a strange place goes. Sunday, they set out to discover The Alamo. Monday, they checked in at Lackland Air Force Base, where Clack would train with the 37th Training Wing. They were escorted to the furnished base housing apartment that would be theirs for the next twenty-six weeks. Clack began his training on Tuesday, mostly in classrooms at first, and then later in helicopter field training. With only a handful of nighttime flight instruction courses, Clack was mostly in class only from 7:00 a.m. until 4:00 p.m., a seemingly easy schedule. Each afternoon, Clack and Jenni went on walks together, had dinner that Jenni cooked in their apartment, went shopping at the commissary, and enjoyed being husband and wife. On Saturdays, they would go out to dinner and see a movie. On Sundays, they slept in. They viewed the time at Lackland as a gift of twenty-six weeks to get to know each other better than they knew anyone else in the world. And they loved each other!

At the end of almost twenty-two weeks, Clack and Jenni flew back to Columbia, where Jameson and Mary Ellen were waiting at the airport for them. Thanksgiving had never seemed so sweet to any of the Grimes family – primarily because they had never had anyone *home for the holidays.* The idea made the Perry Como song much more personal to each of them. The Collins family was invited, too, but they chose to stay in North Carolina. Clack and Jenni drove up for a day and visited his family, but the bulk of the long weekend was spent between Cardelville and the Edisto house. The decision had already been made that Jenni would stay home until after Christmas. Clack was being relocated to Sheppard Air Force Base in Wichita Falls to train with the 80th Flying Training Wing. The congressman thought that was odd, since the 80th trained fighter pilots and Clack flew helicopters. He kept his thoughts to himself, though, around the family.

Thanksgiving dinner was festive and entertaining. The twins were there, but this year Kelli did not bring her Yankee boyfriend. Clack was glad – he had felt so sorry for him the year before. Kelli indicated that things were not so peachy between them these days, and she spoke as though they might break up soon. Justin chimed in and said, "He thinks our family is crazy!" Everyone laughed, but Kelli's falling eyes indicated that Justin was telling the truth. Who could blame the guy, though? Clack was just thankful he was born in a southern state.

One night was spent back in Cardelville before Clack had boarded a plane back to San Antonio. It would have been nice to have a few minutes alone with Jenni before they spent the next four weeks 1200 miles apart, but Jameson and Mary Ellen drove them to the airport in Columbia. Jenni had not spent more than one night without Clack since the wedding, and she was sure she was not going to like it. Being home would be nice, but she was not the little Grimes girl anymore – she was a college graduate, a military wife, and an independent woman. Thinking it did not go a long way in convincing herself of it.

At the airport, Clack carried his one bag, which he would not need to check for the flight – a brown leather satchel that was much lighter on the return flight since it no longer held Jenni's hair products and the two pairs of shoes she could not fit into her own suitcase. He realized how light it seemed when he hoisted it over his shoulder at the car. It felt quite empty. He was happy to have been free to dress in jeans and a sport shirt for a few days. Back in uniform, though, for the flight, he felt pride and a strong sense of duty as he anticipated the training he would begin receiving in just a few days. Strangely, though, he felt a lump in the pit of his gut – like the lightweight satchel, he knew he was leaving some part of himself behind. He could not remember feeling that way ever before. Jenni felt it too, but with nothing exciting to balance the weight of it, she carried the ominous feeling all the way to the gate. Clack kissed her goodbye and then hugged her parents. As he made his way to the gate, he turned back and returned to kiss her again. He didn't say anything – he couldn't. It was to be only four weeks, but he choked back emotion without knowing why. Jenni would describe it in a letter to him later that evening as *a feeling like my brain had been wiped clean – I could think of nothing but you, but I could not think of anything about you either.* Perhaps they both worried that four weeks of being apart might become a more enduring farewell. Clack boarded the plane; Jenni boarded the sedan; both drifted off to sleep and dreamed of nothing but one another.

Clack tried to call when he arrived back at Lackland, but the phone line at the Grimes residence was busy all afternoon. Jenni knew that Clack would call, but she also knew her father was busy on the phone – up to nothing, she presumed, but working hard at catching up on gossip from his politician cronies. Supposedly, the heavy hitters from the local committee were scouting him out for another run for Washington. She did hear him raise his voice once, but all she could make out was something about *the 80th* and *stealth*. There he was, she surmised, boasting again about his son-in-law. Finally, as supper time was rolling around, the phone rang and Jenni grabbed it. An operator said, "I have a collect call from John Claxton Collins." Jenni laughed at the full name. "Will you accept the charges?" the operator continued. Jenni, on behalf of her parents, consented to the long-distance tolls. They talked for about five minutes, mostly about how much they were going to miss each other and then said good-night. Clack left for Wichita Falls the next day.

For the next four weeks, Clack only called twice each week, and Jenni found the times that Clack called to be a little bizarre. She was accustomed to him being in training until 4:00 each day, but while at Sheppard, he would call anytime between 1:00 and 3:00 in the afternoon – sometimes even as early as 8:00 a.m., which was an hour earlier in Kansas. The one time she inquired, he told her they got out early some days and that he had the day off when he made that early morning call. Jenni thought that she should have gone with him if he had that much time off during the day and even suggested that she come for a visit. He told her that the Air Force wouldn't allow it. He wasn't lying. He was, however, being untruthful about his work schedule. It was random. Sometimes, he trained all night, and when he called Jenni early, he was just coming in and getting ready to sleep a few hours before going back out on maneuvers again. What she did not know would be better for her peace of mind. If she knew what Clack was being prepared to do or what her father suspected was the case, she would worry – and Clack, oblivious to Jameson's investigative work, was worried enough – no need for her to join in the fun.

<hr>

Clack's drive down Memory Lane was hijacked when a nurse barged into his hospital room. "Time to check your vitals!"

Clack's first thought was to yell at her to get out, but he quickly reconsidered thinking that maybe the nurse was a smoker and would share one of her cigarettes with him. He asked, but she looked offended, so he backed off. She checked his vital signs, which Clack thought was a dumb thing to do and told her so. He wasn't sick or dying – it wasn't his heart or his blood pressure or some virus that had landed him in the hospital. It was his drinking – and he didn't know why she needed to check his temperature and pulse. Was there some illness going around that elevated your fever, increased your heart rate, and gave you an insatiable craving for Kentucky bourbon or Scotch whiskey? If so, his condition was critical, and the family should be called in immediately.

She finished her checks and left without chit-chat, as Clack was not the most pleasant patient she had ever attended. He would get angry about them keeping him there against his will – then he would soften and become weepy and apologize for being so rude. She had seen it all before, and she knew he would not be there any longer than the law required him to stay. There had been hundreds, if not thousands, of his kind in and out of the substance abuse floor of the psych unit. When she took the job, she had hoped to make a life-changing difference, but two-shifts-and-then-they-were-gone proved to have little or no impact on the drunks and addicts that came her way. She resigned herself to getting in and out of the room without them vomiting or urinating on her – and even that was wishful thinking at times. At least Clack was in control of his bodily functions. As she left, Clack thanked her. The sentiment caught them both by surprise. She did not, however, turn back to acknowledge his gratitude.

As though the entrance to his hospital room was a revolving door at the Ritz, the traffic flowed in and out. The food cart lady came in to retrieve his breakfast tray, and Clack had cleaned his plate. An orderly came in to pick up the trash and soiled linens. Then, another face – one Clack knew, but momentarily could not piece into the puzzle of his circumstances. It was Pastor Matt.

Matt came in with a big grin – but not like a televangelist or used car salesman so often associated with his kind. His was a genuine smile, like he was truly happy and enjoying the interaction with another human being. Clack wanted to be mad, at first, since this was the joker that had brought Barney Fife his way and, consequently, landed him in this hospital cell. As much as he desired to be angry at the minister, he found himself feeling like he was watching a close friend from his past enter the room, though he barely knew the South Mill community and its clergy. He managed not to return the smile and to remain stoic as the young minister offered a bubbly *good mornin'!*

"Do you remember me, Mr. Collins?" asked the preacher. As he uttered the question, the very thought of asking it seemed silly to Matt Hardy. Just nineteen hours earlier, he had held this man like a baby, had patted him and whispered words of peace and hope into his raging ears, then, shortly later, had assumed temporary custody of his dogs. Now, with him in his right frame of mind, he wondered if the man even remembered him. Clack did. "Are you my ride home, Preacher?"

"Well," Matt replied, unprepared for such a suggestion, "I might be, but not right now."

"Why? What are we waiting on? I don't have a ride. You can just take me back to the church with you, and I'll walk from there. I'm sober. I'm clean. There's nothing wrong with me now. I just had a bad day yesterday, and you and your sheriff friend made it even worse. So, take me home. I gotta go to work."

Matt had to think quickly.

"Well, Mr. Collins..."

"Call me Clack. You drug my ass to the hospital...you can at least call me Clack."

"Well, Clack, I have three other church folks to visit in the hospital before I can go back to the church. I can go make those rounds and then come back to check in on you, but I think you might want to stay up here another day." Clack didn't feel like arguing, and no one was more surprised by that than Clack himself. Matt tried to make pleasant conversation. "How was your night, Mr. Clack?"

"It was hell!"

"Well, I'm sure it couldn't have been that bad, and it looked like you had a good breakfast. This is a good place to be while you do some thinking."

Correcting him, "Mr. Clack? I said just call me Clack! And the only thinking I am doing is about how much I want a cigarette, and wouldn't you know the bitch nurse assigned to me doesn't even smoke 'em." Matt was at a loss, but he trudged right into the mess.

"What brand do you smoke?"

Clack hesitated before he answered *menthol*. That wasn't even a brand name, and he wasn't even sure why he said that. He hated menthol anything. That minty smell and taste was not one that he enjoyed with tobacco. To Clack, smoking menthols was like biting into a chocolate brownie to find that someone had laced the mix with mint. *What kind of a sick joke is that?* Menthol...it was one of those things you say when you're mad that you really don't mean – and Clack was definitely agitated. What did it matter to the preacher, anyway? The last thing he wanted was to make small talk over something like cigarettes with this kid preacher. But he still asked, ""What about you, preacher? What's your brand?" He couldn't help himself.

"I prefer to chew," Matt said slyly.

"What's your brand?" Clack sounded demanding.

"Oh anything you've got...Bubblicious®, Big League Chew®, Hubba Bubba®."

Clack smiled but did not laugh. Matt tried to look innocent, but suppressing a chuckle, he almost choked on the gum he just happened to be chewing at the moment. Clack almost laughed at that.

"I'd really like to go home, Preacher!"

"Let me go make some other visits, Clack, and I'll come back by this afternoon."

It wasn't the response Clack had wanted, but for some reason, hearing it from Reverend Hardy, it felt right to stay at the hospital. He agreed and shook the hand of the preacher. As the preacher grasped Clack's mammoth hand, he instinctively started praying out loud for Clack. Clack was struck by it, uncomfortable and unfamiliar – yet strangely peaceful. He tried to pull his hand away, but there was a grip in that skinny, frail hand that would not easily turn loose. Clack froze in an awkward stance and just held on until it was over. When Matt said *Amen*, he actually released before Clack did.

As Matt said goodbye and headed for the door, he assured Clack he would be back that afternoon. There was no doubt he was sincere. Only a crack was left as the door was shutting when Clack suddenly remembered and called out, "Did you feed my dogs?"

Matt felt guilty about the rutabagas, but nodded and smiled. "They're well-fed, Clack." No one had to know what he fed them. Clack seemed pleased, and as the pastor exited the room, Clack felt calm, almost hopeful – although he did not know of anything in his life about which he should feel that way. Again, the notion came over him that there was a connection between himself and the young minister. Peace was hard to come by, so Clack took a nap while it lasted.

Pastor Matt was honest. He did have three other hospital visits to make. The first would be an attempt to crawl out of a hole he didn't know he had dug. Larry Grogan, a retired school teacher and no-longer-active deacon at South Mill, was recovering from triple bypass surgery. Rumor was that Kay, his wife, was really lambasting the new preacher because he had neither come by the hospital nor called during Larry's ordeal. No one from the Grogan family, though, had called Matt or the church office to tell him about it. Even Larry's son, Billy, came to church Sunday, ushered, and even prayed the prayer right before the offering. Not only did Billy not mention his father's heart condition to the family's pastor, but he didn't mention it to God either. It was Miss Vergie Mays, the oldest member of the church, who had called the church office to tell Lanie, the secretary, how upset the Grogans were that no one from the church had been by to visit. Matt found it hard to believe that *no one* had been by – and he found his suspicion confirmed when he arrived and found that Brother Heath had been there the entire day of the surgery and had returned at least once each day just to see how Larry was progressing. Matt wondered why Brother Heath had not let him know – Southern folks expect their pastor to have ESP and to be at the hospital whenever they are ill. No one could know that better than a man who had spent his lifetime working the hospitals, nursing homes, and funeral parlors. *Why hadn't he shared this news?*

The second stop was one that Matt dreaded just as much. Sister Ethel Hughes had personally called the Hardy's residence the night before to let *Brother Hardy* know that her sister Mildred was going to be having knee replacement the next day. She wanted the pastor to be sure and go visit her in the hospital and threw in, "but you'd better tell her who you are, 'cause she says she ain't seen hide nor hair of you since you got to South Mill." Matt found that humorously asinine. If Miss Mildred had come to church even once since he had become the church's pastor, she would have seen both his hide and his hair. In fact, the only reason Sister Ethel had seen either was because she never missed a free meal the church was hosting, and she had attended the covered dish dinner held in Matt's honor his first Sunday at the church – without covered dish in tow. Matt remembered her because, before she left, she went back through the line scooping up as many leftovers as she could fit onto two or three Styrofoam plates before covering them with aluminum foil that she had helped herself to in the church's kitchen pantry. Matt had his eye on a chocolate layer cake that day, but Ethel took all that was left of it – balancing the smaller dessert plate on top of her aluminum foil stack – before he could even get a taste. Visiting the backsliders was not on his *top ten* list of things to do that day. He would much rather make a difference in someone's life than attempt to pacify and placate those who were, what he called, genetic church members. Their families were part of the church for generations. They, therefore, assumed the right to be heard, and in this case seen, whether they ever came to church or not.

While he had good ole Ethel on the phone, he did take an opportunity to dig at her a little. He shared with her how much he'd missed seeing her at church and inquired as to when she might be back. With a tone only slightly snarkier than the one she'd been using, she explained to him, again, how she had had to take care of her sick and dying mother and that had kept her out of church on Sundays. Matt had read the history and had the scoop on most things South Mill, but he went for it anyway – "Oh, I'm so sorry to hear about that. How long ago did she pass away?"

A long pause. Then, "It'll be eight years this September." Matt magically turned a laugh into a sympathetic breath. He knew that she never came to church before her mother got sick either, but he would let it go. He was not in the practice of begging people who claimed to be a Christian to act like one.

The final visit of the morning was important to Matt, though many of his church folks would never even know he made the stop. The Wellers, a family who had moved to town from somewhere in Pennsylvania, just after Matt and his family did, were at the hospital that day, too. Their oldest son Jacob was having a tumor removed from underneath his shoulder blade. Right after their move, he had come down with pneumonia, which turned out to be a short-lived case. The chest x-ray, though, revealed a much more troubling condition. Biopsy results said it was benign, but the doctors wanted to take it out just to be on the safe side. The Wellers had visited the church only twice, and they clearly were not your typical breed of southern Baptist church-goers. In fact, Matt wasn't sure they were church-goers at all. This, however, was his strong suit, targeting and then homing in on *outsiders* and building relationships with them. He really believed he could help them believe. Introducing people to Jesus – that's what he had long since understood to be his life's purpose and mission.

The Wellers were so surprised to see the preacher they'd met twice come through the waiting room doors. When he spotted them and made a beeline, they were visibly moved by his presence. Christopher, the youngest, crawled out from under a blanket, where he was watching an episode of *Clifford the Big Red Dog* on an iPad, to see who was there. He smiled big and said, "Aren't you the guy that says the prayers and stuff?" Matt laughed, rubbed his head, and said, "Yes, I guess that would be me." The family looked embarrassed, but Matt was so comfortable with the interaction that no one bothered even explaining who he was to little Christopher. The pastor reached to pick up a large Macy's bag, the paper kind with woven paper handles on it to carry large purchases. He had sat it down as he came in the room and pulled from within it a basket filled with treats.

"My wife put together a little snack supply for you all just in case you end up having to stay a couple of days. I know it can get expensive living off of vending machines and cafeteria food, so maybe this will give you guys a little something to munch on." Christa and Toby Weller, Jacob's parents, eyed the display of candy, crackers, fruit, and what looked like some homemade brownies. There was a card attached that said *Praying for your family as you walk down this road with Jacob! Your friends, the Hardys.*

Matt spent a few minutes asking casual questions about ordinary things. *What moved y'all to South Mill? What was the town like y'all moved from in Pennsylvania? How are y'all enjoying the south? What sports teams do you follow?* That last question was for Toby. After a good and relaxed visit, a doctor appeared to share with them that everything had gone as planned – that Jacob was in recovery and that they had no reason to think the tumor was anything but a benign mass that should not give him any more trouble. They would keep him overnight just for observation because they did make a larger incision than they had planned, but, otherwise, everything went flawlessly. Everyone breathed a sigh of relief. When the doctor excused himself, Matt took opportunity to say he must be going.

"Before I do, though," he ventured in, "would you mind if I prayed with you all and thanked God that everything went so well for Jacob today?"

Christa wiped a tear, and Toby simply said *please*. Matt prayed a brief, sweet prayer, thanking the Lord for making such a bad day turn really good. When he finally did leave, Toby spoke for the family and said, "We'll see you Sunday!" Matt smiled and went on his way wondering what their faith might be. He was satisfied that he would find out soon enough.

It was still early, not yet 11:00, and he needed to pray and think and maybe make a phone call or two about Clack before he showed back up expected to take the man home. He called Lanie, asked her to search out a few phone numbers, and drove south. He called home and asked Abigail to fix him a sandwich – he'd run by quickly to grab it and go. Of course, he'd have a quick smooch, too, just to gross out M.J. He loved his little family!

CHAPTER SIX

There was little time for chewing, so as Matt more or less swallowed his lunch, Abigail recounted to him the unsettling events of her morning. Her story began with how he had forgotten Maggie's lunch as they left the house. Matt always dropped Maggie off at school in the mornings on his way into the church office. On more than one occasion, the two had made a mad dash out the door to avoid the tardy bell at South Mill Elementary School. That morning, Abigail had been forced to get dressed, put on makeup, and coerce M.J. to get ready to go - all before Maggie's class went to lunch at 11:10. Matt laughed without feeling sorry for Abigail. She was probably dressed nicely to begin with, and the need to put on more presentable clothing before driving almost one-quarter of a mile to the South Mill Elementary School was more about vanity than it was about necessity, so Matt just smiled big on the inside. His amusement, however, waned as the story continued.

On the way home, Abigail had swung by the drugstore to pick up Maggie's allergy medicine and ran into Dorothy Heath, who was accompanied by Shirley Wallace, a homebound member of the church. If anything about the vast number of shut-ins who were part of South Mill Church frustrated Pastor Matt, it was the fact that they were only "homebound" on Sundays. Most of them, Shirley Wallace included, could break free from the shackles of their ailments to go to the bank, the post office, the mall, the downtown cafeteria, and, apparently, the drugstore. It was evident to Matt that Abigail was flustered as she told her husband how smug Dorothy had seemed as she pointed her out to Shirley, insisting that they knew one another. Matt had met her once at a funeral, but Abigail had never had the pleasure. Abigail lamented the encounter and admitted that she was made to feel quite guilty.

"You know the *newest* pastor's wife, don't you?" Dorothy had goaded.

"No. I've never even seen *this* one," came the loud and brash reply.

"Well, get to know her, Shirley. Stephen's training this one right - says he's planning to be here a while."

Shirley took that as an opportunity to tell Abigail how, where she came from, preachers visited the elderly and sick. Abby took the bait.

Sweet and innocent, almost in a whisper, "Oh, I didn't know you were sick."

"Well, dear, why else would I be at the pharmacy?"

Abigail laughed it off but was secretly hurt. Who was this old woman, and why was she so snarky toward her? She vowed inside herself to fix some food to take to her house, but as she shared that oath with Matt, he vehemently forbade her from doing so. He didn't normally begrudge the elderly for their austerity, but seeing his wife dishonored prodded him to abandon, if only momentarily, his typical docile demeanor. Wishing he could stick out his tongue and wrangle the words back in as soon as he put them out there, Matt asked, "What else did Dorothy have to say?"

"Nothing else, really, except something about how you were really going out of your way to try and reach the outsiders. I wasn't really sure how to take that - but I thanked her and told her that was your passion." *Outsiders* was the term used by long-time South Mill parishioners to refer to visitors, back-sliders, and non-churchgoers. They made no distinction between the various groups - they were just *outsiders*. Matt chuckled once, under his breath and from his throat, as he gulped one more swig of tea. Matt was committed to investing his life into people who would not naturally slide into church on Sundays. And though he knew Dorothy Heath, probably speaking for her husband, was not complimenting him, he celebrated it as a victory anyway that she and Brother Stephen had actually noticed.

The thought of outsiders jogged Matt's memory. Wondering if Clack had conned anyone into taking him home from the hospital yet, he remembered his promise to return. Integrity was important, even when dealing with a suicidal drunk, so he headed back. As he drove to the hospital, he couldn't help but heat up a little over the interaction his beautiful, devoted wife had experienced that morning. Had Abigail misunderstood? Surely those ladies weren't aiming their fangs at her? She's sweet and wonderful. He reasoned within himself that it was just a misunderstanding and that Abigail had wrongly taken any of it personally.

He called the church office from his cell phone just to check any messages. There were three. Lanie read from her duplicate copies of the phone memos she had written and spread out on Matt's desk. A Clack Collins had called twice – didn't leave a message though. The third message was that Brother Heath had called, and though Lanie told him the pastor wasn't in, he dropped by a few minutes later anyway. "What did he want?" Matt cringed as he asked.

"He just said he wanted to go over some things with you. Do you need the number?"

"No. I know *that* one. If he calls back, tell him I'll call him this evening, from home."

Brother Heath, Matt's seven-time predecessor, called or dropped by often to "go over some things." There was no guarantee of the subject matter for those conversations. Sometimes he wanted to talk about how Matt's sermon was too long the previous Sunday. Other times, he relayed messages laden with strong opinions to Matt from various inactive members – all of whom Brother Heath seemed to be in weekly conversation with. Matt had wondered from these experiences if, perhaps, that was somehow part of his job as the new pastor. Making the rounds that his predecessor seemed to make would take an exorbitant amount of time – time that Matt Hardy could not imagine having. There were enough *active* members of South Mill, not to mention all of the prospects, to which he felt called to minister. Neglecting his pastoral and preaching duties to them for the sake of keeping up with the attitudes of those who no longer attended seemed fruitless.

On the occasions when Matt would venture to say so, Brother Heath would say something like, "Well, he still gives to the church," or "She's got a lot of family still here." Matt often smiled in amusement at the strange notion that *The Church*, established upon relationships and fellowship, somehow evolved to an organization for which sending a check once-in-a-while or having a grandson or cousin who sometimes showed up for Easter services had anything to do with being entitled to membership privileges – especially privileges like criticizing the pastor or the budget or perhaps even the preacher's wife.

In the recesses of his thoughts, Pastor Matt found it curious that Brother Steven seemed to know whether or not members, active or otherwise, gave money to South Mill. He certainly did not know who did and who didn't. He was very careful to stay away from information like that. He had been taught in seminary that such information was best kept within the ranks of the church treasurer and finance committee so that there was never a temptation to show favoritism to big givers. He believed in treating everyone the same, and he never wanted to be faced with the burden of catering to one member over another because of the size of his or her tithes and offerings.

He would talk to Brother Heath that night, and he might just explain to him the inappropriateness of the interaction between their wives earlier in the day. Then, he remembered the advice he had been given by so many mentors along his journey into ministry, *you have to choose your battle. Most of the hills climbed in ministry are not hills worth dying on.* Matt would keep quiet.

Parking in a space marked "CLERGY" at the hospital, Matt stepped out of the truck and tucked the Good Book into the small of his back then grabbed a small brown paper sack from the passenger seat and said a little prayer as he walked the sidewalk toward the door of the hospital. He halfway expected to see Clack camped out on the cracked, white marbled steps smoking something he had conned off of another *inmate*, but through the front doors and lobby and past the information desk of the main hospital, he breathed a sigh of relief that the man was still, evidently, in the annexed psychiatric wing. On the elevator, he looked down at the brown paper bag, shook his head, and chuckled at what no one else would ever know he had done. Knocking on the door, he received no answer, but ventured in anyway.

Matt always hesitated before entering anyone's hospital room. He had literally seen *more* of some of his church members than he had ever anticipated seeing while they were laid up in their sick beds. Just weeks earlier he virtually swore off hospital visits altogether. The ban came as the result of an incredibly awkward visit with Carrie Jarrard, a sweet old widow who, under normal circumstances, would never motivate such a vow. She was eighty-seven years old and had no family close by. She had been checking her mailbox and, on the way back up the driveway to her house, noticed a rosebush that needed some pruning. Independent and invincible, she grabbed an old chair from the front porch, steadied its four legs in the mulch in her flower bed, and climbed up to reach the wild stems. She maneuvered up and down the chair successfully, but stepping out of the garden, she caught the heel of her shoe on a brick that lined the bed and fell on her shoulder. It wasn't a long trip down for the four-foot, eight-inch granny, but the 230 pounds she sported did a number on her that required surgery followed by some heavy-duty pain killers. High on the meds when her minister came to call, she exposed herself to him from multiple vantage points, none of which he enjoyed. If he stood on the side of the bed where there were no monitors or IVs, he had full view of a large left breast that hung out of her loosely draped, hospital gown. If he stood, instead, at the foot of the bed, he had to deal with her uncovered and sprawling legs - and though he hadn't looked long or with any trace of interest - sweet ole Carrie wasn't wearing any underwear, and her gown was hiked up much too high to serve its purpose. Attempting to see no more than he had already caught good glimpses of, Matt awkwardly looked out the window, at the florescent bulbs above his head, at the television mounted high on the wall that was playing some daytime courtroom show, and even at the lady in the hallway delivering food trays from the cafeteria to the patients. Oh how he hoped she would bring one in to Ms. Jarrard's room. She didn't! A nurse, though, did come to draw blood and, sensing Matt's discomfort, covered up the inevitable focal points in the room - but Miss Carrie quickly threw off the covers declaring that it was too hot for them, and Pastor Matt once again began his game of looking at anything and everything but the patient he came to visit.

With the memory still fresh enough to exercise caution when entering the room, Matt felt certain he would not find Clack Collins bearing all. When Clack saw the preacher, he jumped up from the bed and rushed him, bracing himself and gripping the pastor by both shoulders. Matt could not tell if he was clutching him in anger or in gladness. Clack's greeting did not immediately clear up the confusion. "Preacher, I've been calling you all day!"

"I know, Clack, and I'm sorry I couldn't get here sooner..."

"No, I don't care about that," Clack cut in, "I'm glad you're here. I need a favor."

Learning on the job, Matt didn't oblige him too quickly. "What do you need?"

"You've been feeding my dogs, right?"

"Yeah. They're doing fine," Matt assured him.

"I want you to take them home with you. Please go get them and take them to your house!"

"Clack, I've got two small kids at home."

"The dogs love kids, Preacher! Please say you'll keep 'em for me."

"For how long?" Matt was getting worried.

"I just need you to take them until I can get out of here and get things together again."

The pastor was actually beginning to cozy up to the idea because it seemed that he would be taking the dogs home instead of taking Clack, and he really wanted Clack to get some help before he was out on his own again. Still, he wondered what Abigail would say. They had talked about getting a dog before, but taking two home that were each as large as both of their children put together was not something they had considered. But like Clack said, it would only be for a short while. Halfway reluctantly and secretly excited, Matt agreed.

"Okay, dogs are taken care of, what about you?" Matt was ready to make a plan.

"I'm not ready to answer that yet, Preacher! But I have another day or so to think about it before they let me out of here."

Matt and Clack both knew that if he chose to leave, they would not stop him. It was a relief to Matt, though, that the man seemed content to stick around for the prescribed time period, although he did wonder what had transpired that gave him such resolve. Clack, as surprised as Matt to hear his own words, somehow felt peaceful there in the hospital. It was not that he enjoyed being there, but with the alcohol flushed out of his brain, he was enjoying the lack of pressure to do anything but sit and think. In his stroll through the past, he knew the demons would emerge again, but he wasn't that far along memory lane yet - so he was willing to continue the journey. And there might have been one more selfish motivation to stay put for now, but that would remain Clack's own little secret.

Matt really wanted to pray with Clack before he left. So, after a very short petition to the Lord for Clack to find wholeness again, the preacher volunteered to pick him up the next afternoon and take him *wherever*...

As he was exiting the room, Clack reminded him to go get the dogs right away. Nodding his head, he began to close the door when he suddenly remembered the supplies he had purchased. Stopping short, he pulled a brown paper bag from his back pocket, and threw it to Clack on the bed. Puzzled, Clack opened it expecting a Bible or a tract or something religious. Instead, he laughed as he pulled the contents from inside the sack - a pink pack of bubble gum and a minty-green pack of smokes with a camel on the box. "I couldn't pick between Kool or Newport, so I asked the clerk to give me the most popular brand." With that, he disappeared through the wide, heavy wood door.

Clack ran to the door and caught glimpse of the preacher just as the door was closing to the psych unit. Smiling, he yelled down the hall - "I don't really even like menthols, Preacher!" He would, however, smoke them all.

Matt cut through the main hospital to get to his car and was holding the doors to the elevator on the ground floor so an older man using a walker could make it in before they closed when a red head with a cell phone nearly knocked him and the old man down with the large purse hanging from her shoulder and resting on her hip. He simply smiled, said excuse me, and moved on as she continued her cell phone conversation. Thinking she, too, would pardon her clumsiness, Matt listened as she said to whomever she was calling, "John, that's what the information lady wrote, John! Well, John has really done it this time." Matt pitied poor John, whoever he was, and exited the hospital.

As he fidgeted in his pocket to locate his keys, he saw a familiar face. The pastor from South Mill United Methodist Church was making a visit at the hospital too. He and Matt often visited with one another, and when they met in the parking lot, they had to catch up on what was going on in each other's churches.

CHAPTER SEVEN

The redhead didn't knock or hesitate when she entered the room. Clack was sitting on the bed chewing gum when he looked up and saw his wife. She had a lot to say, but she stood there silently for what seemed like minutes until, finally, he spoke.

"Hey, Jenni." He knew she was coming. He'd been tipped off. An elderly man married to a not-as-elderly woman who lived next door had witnessed from a distance the exchange in Clack's yard the day before. Once, upon a short-lived attempt at some sort of reconciliation, Jenni had spent three days with Clack in his rented double-wide. She and the woman next door had exchanged cell numbers. Although Jenni stopped answering her calls a few weeks into the reports on Clack's drunken escapades, Jenni did, occasionally, listen to the messages. The one late last night said the dogs were home alone, and the nosy lady's husband called Clack to apologize for his wife's big mouth earlier in the day. Clack had been afraid all day that Jenni would get to the dogs before he could hide them.

"Clack, I need the keys to your house. I've come to get the dogs."

"First off, Jenni, my house is in Cardelville, and you have the keys to it because you live in it. Secondly, the dogs are not at the trailer here. A friend of mine is keeping them while I'm up here - and, besides..." As he seemed to be choosing his next words carefully, his left brow lowered and a stern coldness matched a now narrowed stare.

With a quiet deepening of his voice, his finished bluntly, "...you don't get the dogs."

Displaying no emotion and certain he was bluffing, she argued, "Clack, those dogs need a home. I was fine with you keeping them, but you can't even handle the responsibility of taking care of you."

"I know how you knew about the dogs, but how the hell'd you know where I was?"

"Next of kin, Clack. The hospital called." He didn't remember filling out any admission paperwork when he arrived, but then he didn't remember much. It was hospital policy to notify the next of kin when the patient was unable to make decisions regarding his or her own medical treatment. Since Clack was inebriated upon his arrival at the hospital, the admission clerk had called Jenni with a number she was given from the insurance company when verifying coverage. Clack was actually glad she knew.

"You see what you've done to me, Jenni?" He was, evidently, if only for the moment, over the notion that it was *his own damn fault*.

"Clack, I am not here to argue. Just tell me where Chop and Felix are, and let me take them home."

Clack had always thought those were stupid names for dogs. Chop was short for Chopin, named for Frederic Chopin, the genius Polish composer of the early 1800s. Felix, too, had a musician's name, after Felix Mendelssohn of the same period, known for being a child prodigy. The pair were favorites of Jenni's, from the Romantic era of music, but Clack failed to see the brilliance of such names. *Chop* didn't bother him so much since it sounded fairly tough and rugged. He had argued hard against naming a dog Felix, as both he and Jenni had grown up watching a cartoon cat by that name, and Clack felt that it could be embarrassing for a dog to have to run around with a cat's name. Early on in the naming debate, he and Jenni had agreed that she would name one and he would name the other, but both had to be named for musicians. Jenni withdrew the offer when Clack wanted to name his Angus. He believed it met the criteria, choosing the name from Angus Young, the Scottish-born, Australian founding member of the rock band AC/DC. He would have settled for Elvis or simply King. Jenni rejected the names, but she agreed to shorten Chopin to Chop. Clack was satisfied.

"Jenni, the dogs are not going to Cardelville. They're staying here, and my friend will take good care of them. He has two small kids, and the dogs will be happy and played with." She seemed consoled by the thought of the two canines rolling and tumbling through the yard with children if, in fact, Clack was telling the truth.

"Okay. You're not cooperating, so I guess I'll go." She started toward the door, "What's next, Clack?"

"I don't know." He felt the tears forming deep down. "I'll be alright."

"Call me when you get it together so we can sort out the dogs and the cars and whatever else the bill collectors don't take."

Clack nodded, tears trickling, and managed to speak, "I know I'm late, but Happy Anniversary. I guess this will be the last..."

"Don't!" Jenni cut him off and was out the door.

****

As Matt opened his truck door, he saw the rude redhead again. Hers had been a quick visit, and she returned to the parking lot crying. A sucker for hurting folks, a trait he really needed to work on, he walked her way. She was fumbling through the saddle bag she carried for her keys when he approached and asked if there was anything he could do. She ignored him briefly but then looked up at his kind, young face and smiled through her tears. "No, thank you. It's just been a hard day. Nothing a good cup of coffee can't help," she lied.

She found her keys, and Matt introduced himself. She returned the gesture, saying, "Nice to meet you. I'm Jennifer..." She stuttered. "...Grimes. Sorry, going through a divorce."

"Nice to meet you Miss..." Matt caught a big clue. "Did you say Jennifer? You wouldn't happen to be here to visit someone named Clack, would you?"

Her demeanor changed. "No...not to visit. Just to see how screwed up he is now."

Matt produced his business card and introduced himself again. "I'm Clack's pastor."

Jenni fought to keep her jaw from dropping too far too quickly – as shocked by that statement as any she'd ever heard. The idea that Clack even went to church was so foreign to the years she had spent with him that she didn't know how to respond.

"Clack goes to church?"

"Occasionally. Mostly on Wednesday nights with some of his coworkers." Jenni's glistening eyes were bouncing and rolling back and forth from the business card to Pastor Matt revealing the whirlwind going on behind them. Matt sensed the need to offer some clarity on Clack's newfound religion and added, "We have a big, home-cooked meal on Wednesday nights."

Still baffled, Jenni took Matt's card and looked at the name: *South Mill Baptist Church.* She wondered what would make this clergyman think there was anything redeemable about John Claxton Collins. She figured she would never know the answer to that. After a few pleasantries were exchanged, Matt offered his assistance to her in any way she might need. She graciously refused, indicating that her life was elsewhere and that's where she was going. As they were parting, however, a thought struck her.

"You wouldn't happen to know who might be keeping our dogs, would you?"

The urgency of Clack's phone calls and his insistence that Matt take the dogs suddenly made as much sense as did the abrupt entrance he had witnessed this woman making into the elevator a few minutes earlier. Since there were no children, at least none that Clack had spoken of, the dogs were leverage, and neither wanted the other to have them. Matt had to hunt for words quickly - words that would be neither a lie nor a betrayal of Clack's trust.

"What kind of dogs do you have?"

"Samoyed. They look a lot like polar bears. Big, white, and fuzzy," Jenni smiled. Silence followed but no tears.

"Mrs. Collins, I know we just met," Matt ventured in, uncertain his *superpower* would work on someone as worked up as Jenni seemed to be only moments ago. "And you may think this quite forward of me, and I know it is a couple of hours on the road back home, but would you possibly be willing to stick around a little while and join my family for an early dinner this evening? If you will, we might be able to locate those dogs of yours."

Sensing both intrusion into her private world and sincere warmth from Pastor Matt, she reluctantly agreed to come - a response that she, herself, seem surprised to hear, but if this man knew where her dogs were, she could walk away satisfied that she had won this round. Matt gave her directions, pointed her to a good cup of coffee, and told her to arrive around six. She smiled and said she would, thanked him, and then closed herself into her car. When he was out of sight, she thought she should cry some more but no longer found any tears. She would later describe her feeling after conversing with the pastor as one of the strangest she'd ever known...like the comfort and familiarity of an old, dear friend and the anxiousness of a new adventure. For now, however, she felt sure that this kind man had her dogs, or at least knew where Clack had lodged them, and that alone was enough to keep her in town until this ridiculously awkward dinner was over. Besides, she was certain she had some questions about Clack's interest in church, although she could not come up with any at that very moment. It just seemed weird.

Matt called Abigail, broke the news, and then thanked God for such a sweet, co-laborer in ministry to hurting people. Dinner would be ready promptly at six. Matt would go pick up the dogs, drop them off at the house, and return to the office to get in at least one last hour of work on Sunday's sermon. Abigail accepted her husband's plan. Lanie was leaving early, so the office would be quiet.

Matt did not have to wrestle the dogs into his car; they seemed eager to go for a ride. He dropped them off at home, introducing them quickly to Abigail and the children, both of whom were giddy with the idea of having pets. When he sensed that all were comfortable, he darted out the door, catching a glimpse of a big tongue licking M.J.'s face and hearing him cackle, "Mommy, he's giving me a bath!"

Matt drove straight back to the church, secluded himself in his office, keeping the outside doors locked so no one wandered in on him. He tried to protect his study time as best he could. He enjoyed studying and preaching to the people, and he was committed to delivering his messages biblically and accurately. Though his heart went out easily to folks in need - his time studying the scriptures and preparing for each week's worship service was focused and deliberate. He did not even mind ignoring the phone or occasional knocks on the door so that his time with the Lord and The Good Book were uninterrupted. Only someone with a key could disturb his solitude.

Stephen Heath had keys to the church. As Matt was saving his message notes to his flash drive, he heard the key turn the lock. Glad he was finished for the day, he quickly zipped up his backpack, flipped off the light, and headed for the door. As he exited the office, he met Brother Heath coming in.

"Hello, Stephen." Matt refused to call him by a title. "I was just headed out. What brings you by?"

"I've been calling all day. This is the third time I've come by."

"Out making hospital visits, you know. Didn't Lanie tell you I'd catch up with you tonight?"

"She did, but I needed..."

Whatever Brother Heath needed could certainly wait. It was 5:40, and Matt wanted to be there when Jenni arrived. Interrupting Stephen, the preacher graciously delayed the conversation.

"I hate to rush out on you, but we've got a dinner guest coming in just a few minutes, and I promised Abigail I'd be home. Can I call you this evening?"

Obviously flustered by being put off again, Brother Heath said that would be fine and walked back to the parking lot with Pastor Matt. Matt tried to engage him in small talk about the weather and a pothole forming in the parking lot that a committee needed to do something about. Neither of those items was on Heath's list of things to go over. Matt knew that and didn't hesitate to unlock and open the door to his pickup. As he did, the gust created by the opening door loosened several pieces of paper lightly tucked into the edge of the driver's side sun visor above the steering wheel. Matt fumbled in the air for them quickly, tossing them toward the passenger seat, and laughed out loud, looking over his shoulder at Brother Heath. Getting in the truck and starting the engine, Matt sang out over the engine's roar, "I'll call you this evening." He slammed the door unaware of the debris – a convenience store receipt – he missed as it wafted onto the pavement below. If he had seen it, he surely would have stopped to pick it up just in case littering was a sinful offense in Brother Heath's mind. He backed up, waved to the old man, shifted the little truck into drive before it had even quit rolling backward, and headed home. It was a short trip, not nearly long enough to listen to music or formulate another point for Sunday's sermon. He did, however, have enough time to raise one question – *I wonder what Clack is up to about now and what he would think about me inviting his wife to dinner?*

Clack was not thinking about the preacher. He sat with his face warming by the light of the setting sun as he sucked the last bit of life out of a Camel Crush® cigarette. He had behaved well enough, evidently, for the charge nurse on his unit to cave into his request to go outside. It was not the wide-open space Clack had hoped for when he made his demand, but it would do for now. The psych floor had a terrace, complete with a chain link fence on every side, connected to another that ran overhead. It allowed the patients to have a place to go smoke but prevented the angry patients from escaping and protected the truly sick ones from jumping to their death. Clack, at the moment, did not prefer to attempt either, so he reclined on a picnic table, feet on the bench, and breathed deeply the last minty vapor of smoke before lighting another one. Who knew a preacher would buy somebody some cigarettes? And, more importantly at the moment, why had he told him he liked menthol? Sometimes Clack was surprised by his own lies. Looking up through the little diamonds of his metal ceiling, Clack missed the big sky he used to gaze at in Texas. He had often, over the years, longed for those nights under an endless dome of stars on a blanket with his girl. He stared back down at the pack of cigarettes and shook his head in retrospect over the unfortunate chain of events that had led him from a young man in love under the big south Texas sky to a middle-aged man in shambles under the watchful eye of a psychiatric nurse. Though he knew he would be better served focusing on his present situation, he let his mind go where it yearned.

CHAPTER EIGHT

There were four weeks and two days between Thanksgiving Day and Christmas Day in 1971, and for twenty-five of those days, Clack was training halfway across the country from Jenni. But on the Thursday before Christmas, Clack flew back east. In the airport leaving Kansas, the public address speakers overhead faintly played the voice of Bing Crosby singing, "I'll Be Home for Christmas." Jenni picked him up, without the family, in Columbia, and surprised him with a hotel room for the night before sharing him with their families. Knowing that deployment was soon a certainty, Clack wanted to spend Christmas with his parents, and, reluctantly, Jameson Grimes acquiesced to the plan. The newlyweds did not have a preference as to which day was spent where, but Jameson expressed his partiality to Christmas Eve. Everyone knew that was only because of the public appearances that would be gained at the Christmas Eve service.

Christmas morning began early with a Waffle House breakfast en route to Wilmington. Clack's parents were giddy with excitement over the presence of their military son and his soon-to-be famous musician wife, at least that's what they told their friends. Clack's grandmother and aunt joined them for the mid-afternoon Christmas feast. Clack worried that Jenni would find the gathering boring in comparison to the circus that normally ensued around the Grimes' complex. Jenni found it peaceful and satisfying – she could sit on the couch and cozy up to her husband and just listen to the Collins women dote on Clack. She learned a lot about his childhood, his basketball accolades, and those embarrassing antics he pulled as a child that every parent likes to bring up when a new audience is present.

Neither of Clack's parents attended college. His dad spent a career as a heating and air condition service technician, and he had the knees to show for a lifetime of squatting down and kneeling in crawl spaces. He had retired when a mild heart attack interrupted what would be his last service call ever, and he had enjoyed his poor health ever since. His mother cleaned houses but never more than three a week. The job provided her grocery money and, from all outward appearances, little more. They loved their son, but he had outgrown their parenting early in his teens mostly because he was so athletic, and that kept him on a court or a field into the early evenings while his dad's lack of athleticism became a growing chasm between the two. Clack respected his dad, knew he was loved, and always hugged and kissed both of them after every high school game before running off with friends to eat pizza or roller skate or fish. On rare Sunday mornings, Johnny Collins would spend a few hours fishing with his son – but they found little to talk about, and by the time Clack was headed to college they had both accepted the fact that they just were not ever going to be very close. If Clack was close to either parent, it was his mom. She had been a faithful chauffer throughout his adolescent years, picking him up from practice and bringing him home for a home-cooked meal each and every night. On the car rides, she would inquire about practice, the school day, girls, and friends. Usually, after supper, she would sit with him at the kitchen table while he did homework and studied. Mostly his dad sat in a recliner watching television and falling asleep early. Clack and his mother understood because he started his days so early and worked so hard all day long. Neither parent ever missed a single game in which Clack played, and the Collins did their part as team parents – working in the concession stand, providing snacks for the team, and driving in the caravan of parents headed to away games.

Jenni adored Clack's mom and found her possibly even more nurturing than her own. Clack agreed that she was a great mom, and though affection was subtle in the Collins family, he did love her and his dad. Clack knew, though, that her mothering skills were practiced only within the confines of her home and that, once on their way back to Cardelville, she would do very little to bridge the long-distance gap between herself and her son and daughter-in-law. Maybe when they finally had children one day, his mom would make more of an effort at being a grandmother.

They traveled with a packed bag just in case, and, as it grew dark, Clack and Jenni decided to stay the night. They slept in Clack's bedroom where he spent every night while growing up. He joked with Jenni about how he was going to be in trouble when he got caught with a girl in his bed. The couple slept soundly and awoke to a mix of delightful aromas. The first to hit them was the fresh brewed coffee briskly cutting through the sleepy morning air. Next came the smoky whiff of bacon filling the house – introducing the eggs, grits, and homemade biscuits with which Clack had started each day for eighteen years of his life. He smiled at the smells he had not realized he missed. Suddenly, he was *really* hungry!

Jenni helped wash the breakfast dishes by hand and marveled at the amount of grease that now filled an empty coffee can underneath the kitchen sink. They made the bed, packed their bag, and said goodbye to Clack's parents and headed south to Cardelville. Clack remembered wishing they could stay one more day, just to be with his mom and dad once more before he was sent overseas. For the first time, it was hard to say goodbye, and he cried as he kissed them both. The tears continued as he backed the Pontiac out of the driveway.

Upon their arrival at Jenni's home, the congressman and Mary Ellen insisted that the two eat. Though they were still stuffed from a country breakfast, they snacked on the leftovers from the day before. Mary Ellen had a way of putting turkey and ham to good use following a holiday meal, and that day the recycled choice was turkey salad sandwiches. Though they lived fatter than Clack's parents did, Mary Ellen was still resourceful, and neither she nor Jameson liked to see anything go to waste.

The big surprise following the sandwiches was that there were a few slices of chocolate pie left from the Grimes' Christmas dinner. Clack couldn't believe it. He loved the dessert, and he knew that it was the handiwork of Aunt Janice. Thick meringue with peaks that looked like little ice cream cones drizzled with honey hid the rich chocolate filling. Clack didn't like meringue, though he thought it was pretty, so he always ate it off of the top first, saving the chocolate as his reward for digging through fluff. Jenni and her mother began to clear the kitchen table, and, as Clack watched their every move, he realized that he could not remember ever sitting at that table before. Every occasion with the Grimes family had been some sort of an *event*, and now it was just the four of them around a small round table in front of a bay window that overlooked a backyard dotted with pecan trees. It felt like home. His comfort was quickly disquieted, though, when the congressman spoke candidly, "They said anything about sending you to Nevada?"

Clack was caught off guard. Nevada? Why was the congressman asking him about Nevada?

"Why would they?"

"Don't worry, son," came the unsettling words of the former bureaucrat, "I hear things in Nevada are really very *quiet*."

If Clack looked puzzled, it was because he was trying very hard to appear that way. He knew what the congressman was talking about in Nevada. He would be spending two weeks there upon his return from the holidays. Jenni would go to Texas with him, and there he would break the news to her that he had to leave for two weeks. And somehow the old man was still connected to someone in high enough places to know what his son-in-law was training for. Jameson thought himself clever by talking in code at the kitchen table, but it irritated Clack. *Things in Nevada are really very quiet.* What was he trying to prove? Since it seemed he already knew, Clack played dumb just to match wits with a wily politician...or crazy old man - he wasn't sure which. He was, however, anything but ignorant of what was *quiet* in Nevada.

In 1968, a wealthy community outside of Los Angeles, California, had bought two helicopters from the aircraft division of Hughes Tool Company. The piston-powered Hughes 269 helicopters were used for police patrols over suburban L.A. The purchase, however, proved to be a waste of taxpayers' dollars when the noise from the helicopters was too much to bear. When the city told Hughes to either make them quieter or take them back and refund their money, an amazing result ensued. At the same time Hughes Tool was working to reduce the noise of the low-flying patrol birds, the CIA's Special Operations Division Air Branch was working with the Advance Research Projects Agency to cut the noise of military helicopters. The initial investment of $200,000 bought a new set of gears to slow the tail rotor, and the result was so impressive that the next check was a blank one. Rumor was that the CIA bought two before they were even assembled for use in the field. By 1970, test flights were being conducted at Culver City, California. Likewise, a quick training program for instructors was soon underway for pilots who would later train mission pilots from the Air Force at the secret base, Area 51, in Nevada. Clack would soon be training on the Hughes 500P light observation helicopter that emerged and had quickly come to be known simply as *The Quiet One.*

Obviously, the former congressman knew something, but how and what he knew were still in question. Clack made the safe assumption that his cunning father-in-law had heard through the channels that the government was developing a stealth helicopter and testing it at Area 51. It probably was an unconfirmed rumor, and the retiree was poking and prodding to find out more. Clack was a pilot-in-training, and a low ranking one at that. If the gossip Jameson was hearing had any connection to the training Clack was doing, the link would have to remain weak. Clack would not risk compromising any information to which he was now privy. The congressman would just have to wonder.

Jameson looked smug as he dabbed the corners of his mouth of any stray meringue. Whether he was pleased with Clack's silence about military secrets or with his own penetration of them was hard to tell. Regardless, the conversation had no dampening effect on family time at the Grimes' home. The girls finished the dishes, and they all walked together to the guest house to rifle through the lingering wedding gifts, some of which came in after the departure to Texas, and some of which were too gaudy to deserve the effort. They laughed at the worst ones. Others, that were just not the most tasteful of decor, were boxed up with the rejects for return to the stores where they were purchased. Clack and Jameson agreed that some of the pieces could go to Aunt Janice for display around the restaurant, but Mary Ellen quickly vetoed that idea with the sound reasoning that many of the wedding guests often ate at Dusty's, and they might recognize their wandering gifts. All in all, the afternoon proved to be a fun time of togetherness, one Clack would treasure for years to come.

____

An orderly carrying out the wishes of the charge nurse on Clack's pysch ward served to reunite Clack's mental faculties with his current physical confines. He glanced up one last time through the metal screen that separated him from the heavens, pulled one last toke on a cool smoke, and amiably returned to his hospital bed. He had landed on a happy memory, and he was peaceful enough to call it a night. He smiled as he remembered some of those hideous wedding gifts and caught himself wondering if some of them were still in a closet at the Grimes' guest house.

CHAPTER NINE

Matt pulled into the drive but then rethought the move and backed out to park along the street so that their guest could park closer to the house. He fully expected Jenni to have second thoughts about coming over for dinner, and, if she had to pull into the driveway, the chances of her backing out of both were lessened. He hustled inside, anticipating the last-minute preparations with which he would assist. M.J. and Maggie tried to greet their dad at the door, but two fuzzy animals wrestled their way to the front of the pack. Licks and hugs gave Matt a warm welcome home, and he quickly closed the door behind him to prevent any escape from this zoo.

Abigail was ready with a kiss, but the kids were too busy romping with the dogs to provide sound effects. It was a quick kiss anyway with Abigail's mind set on finishing up the dinner. Matt quickly offered a "What can I do?" and Abigail pointed to the fridge and said all that was left was to put ice in the glasses. Matt was impressed. With only a few hours notice, his amazing wife had whipped up a home-cooked meal, straightened the house, and set the table. He smiled one of those smiles that looked a little wily with only one side of his mouth and face rising, a smile that simply said *I've got a great wife!* He'd owe her for this feat – maybe out to dinner, perhaps even a movie. Either way, payback would be a pleasure.

The ice would have to wait long enough for Matt to hide the dogs in the upstairs bedroom and explain to Abigail and the kids why they were not to mention the dogs until and only if he did. And certainly not before dinner was over. Again, Matt was suspect that Jennifer Collins would take the first exit opportunity she was given, and, with dogs in tow, that could come sooner than Matt intended. He hid their water and food bowls, scooped up the rope toys in the living room, and shoved all evidence of them into the hiding spot with Chop and Felix. As though the canines were in on the secret they were all keeping, he made the *ssshhhhh* sound and laughed at their names as he closed the bedroom door. "Keep 'em quiet, Lord," he prayed as he headed back down to the kitchen.

At 6:05, Matt looked at his watch for the fourth time in the last two minutes. His concerns were becoming reality – Jenni had bailed. And why wouldn't she? This strange man, a preacher nonetheless, met her in a hospital parking lot three hours ago and invited her home to dinner. Matt knew that protocol was to spend more time building relationships with people before taking them home with you, but time was of the essence here, and he felt like he had to strike while he had the woman in town. Who knew if she'd ever come back within such a close proximity to her soon-to-be ex-husband...or possibly even to God? The bitterness toward both was apparent in her face, and Matt knew his ministry was one of reconciliation. If he couldn't get her to reboot with Clack, at least he might be able to help her find a little restorative faith. He was worried that chances of either taking place were gone. At 6:07, the doorbell rang. Matt breathed a quick *Thank you, Lord* – then went to the door.

Matt went to the door, trailed closely by Abigail. They would later laugh about the cat-like way Jenni entered their home, almost slinking in, nervous that this encounter could be a dangerous one. Jenni made a vain attempt to present herself boldly, strong and confident, yet pleasant – a sharp contrast, she believed, to the demeanor she displayed in the hospital parking lot just a few hours earlier. She was struck by how young the couple looked, especially Abigail, and she wondered, for a brief moment, if she had pulled into the wrong driveway by mistake. With the three of them trying desperately to somehow navigate around the awkward, Matt smiled and called Jenni by name. Abigail introduced herself, invited Jenni in, and steered the party to the prickly comfort of the living room furniture. Matt knew he had rushed this engagement, but he tried hard to make conversation – avoiding the obvious. But when the "obvious" is an angry man detoxing in a psych ward and a woman serving him divorce papers on their wedding anniversary and now sitting in your La-Z-Boy, how do you make small talk about the weather?

Maggie and M.J. were well-behaved children who had learned to wait until summoned before bursting into the room when guests were present. He knew well the reputation that pastors' kids have for being brats, and he and Abigail were working hard to make sure that these two broke with tradition. On this occasion, though, wishing the little ones would rescue them all from the clumsy drowning that was taking place, Matt finally thought out loud saying, "Where are those kids of ours?" Abby took the cue and called them to come down and meet their guest.

Matt sat back and marveled at the way his innocent children cut through the fog of tension in the room. Jenni was pleasant enough to ask about Maggie's school and what subjects she liked. Maggie told her she liked math and music, and that resonated with Jenni. She told Maggie that she liked music, too, and that was enough to launch M.J. right into a solo of "Jesus Loves Me." He went on to tell her that he was four, could count to one hundred all by himself, liked to finger paint with Mommy when Maggie was at school, liked peanut butter and jelly sandwiches without any peanut butter, had a Batman cape, and a 'mote control racecar... "wanna see?"

With that, Abigail calmed her son with a hand over his mouth and instructions to go wash his hands. "Oh yeah," he agreed, "I've been playing with the..." Matt anticipated it and, covering his mouth again, finished his sentence, "...neighbors." You've been playing with the neighbors. M.J. wanted to correct that - He had not been with the neighbors at all, but a strong hand kept his lips from moving until he was safely in the bathroom with a bar of soap in his hand and a whispered reminder not to mention the dogs in his ear. He whispered back not very quietly, "Oh yeah!"

Abigail invited Jenni to the table, and though Jenni would, under more usual circumstances, offer to help bring the food to the table or pour the drinks or something, she was more than willing to get out of the way, sit at the table, and hope this silly occasion would be over sooner rather than later.

At dinner, each of the Hardys alternated asking questions of Jenni, trying hard to avoid lulls in the exchange. Where are you from? Do you work? How long did it take to drive here from Cardelville? What are your hobbies? All trivial matters were open for discussion. Off limits, at least until after dinner, were Clack and the dogs. Fortunately, Matt was taking the last bite of the evening when M.J. crossed over by saying, "Where's your husband?" Matt almost choked, but Jenni fielded the question like a pro. "He's in the hospital. I was there visiting him today, and that's where I met your dad. He was kind enough to invite me to dinner at your house. Wasn't that nice?" M.J. nodded and smiled and affirmed his dad, "You're a really sweet daddy." Matt smiled and thanked him as he cut his eyes around at Abigail. Obviously, that was the signal to send the children back upstairs to play while the adults talked about grown up things. The children went without protest, but they had done their job of breaking the remaining ice between the pastor and Jenni, and for that, among many other blessings they manifested daily, Matt was glad he and Abigail had made them.

It felt comfortable to have the table between them, so no one made an effort to move the conversation back to the living room. Coffee was served, along with a slice of pecan pie, and the chit-chat began to take the inevitable turn to more serious topics. Jenni did not resist since she anticipated it, and, if she was honest, would admit that she wanted to talk about it with someone. Suddenly, this preacher she had known for a few hours, along with his wife, who had just served her a wonderfully home-cooked meal, seemed to be a safe audience on whom to unload some honest anger and real fears.

It was a roller coaster of emotion as the evening went on – first the joy of her first encounter with Clack on the quad at her college and the whirlwind of dating and engagement, when she felt like a man who oozed this wealth of potential had consolidated all of his time, energy, and affections on her. From behind this curtain of aging bitterness, a girl in love would occasionally peak. The ride continued to Texas where every day was like a honeymoon – followed by a slight dip when he was suddenly transferred to an "undisclosed" location. She even talked about Clack's deployment to Vietnam, and the sweet letters she would get every week while he was gone. Still, no mention of any drinking. It really sounded like Clack had almost always been a very noble man – a true southern gentleman.

Just as everyone was tightening their grip for the downward spiral of this coaster that they all knew was coming, a commotion upstairs shocked them all back to the present. "M.J., No!" came the shrill of Maggie's voice, and in a frenzied flash, two mounds of fur bounded down the steps. Their feet were still running when they hit the hardwood floors of the living room, but their toenails kept them from getting any traction right away. They looked like the cartoon characters that run off a cliff whose feet keep running while they are suspended in mid-air. But the flesh of their paws met the traction of the floor when they saw their long-lost Jenni!

She immediately leapt from the table and knelt in the doorway of the dining room to receive the licking and pawing that would go on for a long time – long enough for Abigail to move the dessert plates, coffee cups, and saucers from the table to the kitchen sink. While Jenni was lost in the fur, M.J. ran to his dad, tucked his face into this leg, and began to cry. "I'm sorry, daddy, I had to go pee-pee, and Maggie was in our bathroom and I had to go to yours and when I opened the door to your room I forgetted the dogs were in there and they ran out and almost knocked me down and...and..."

Matt smiled as everyone's attention, even Jenni's, turned toward M.J.'s explanation and the wetness of his little blue pajamas. "Well," Matt asked, "did you get to the bathroom in time?" M.J looked down, poked out his bottom lip even further, and said, "When the dogs stepped on me I think they squeezed it out of me." Everyone laughed, and, when M.J. realized no one was mad at him, he laughed, too, and then said, "Mommy, I need some dry pajamas." Abigail took her son by the hand and headed back upstairs. Maggie, ever the big sister, followed and began scolding M.J. for forgetting about the dogs hiding in the bedroom. Matt called behind them up the steps for Maggie to bring down the dogs' bowls so they could eat. Then, he turned and sheepishly faced the lawful owner of the stowaways.

"Let me explain," he began.

But Jenni cut him off, insisting that she had already assumed the dogs were there based on the silver metal trash can sitting beside the real trash can in their kitchen and the hint Clack had dropped when he said his friend who was keeping the dogs had two small kids. Matt hadn't thought about the trash can when he was hiding everything away, nor had he considered it when Jenni accompanied Abigail to the kitchen to pour coffee with dessert. They both laughed, and more than any other moment in the evening, the two felt a connection – and Matt knew he could build on that.

The slobbery reunion continued a little while longer, but Jenni was quickly abandoned when Matt took their food and water bowls to the kitchen. He filled them both and was relieved to see that Jenni had taken the break as an opportunity to return to the living room – this time looking more relaxed in the La-Z-Boy than when she first arrived. When Abigail returned, she announced that the kids were in bed, and Matt excused himself to go give goodnight kisses to each. By the time he returned, Abigail was already attempting to cruise with Jenni into the next phase of the Clack and Jenni Collins story. Jenni was just about to move from honeymoon to heartache when a blanket of guilt almost smothered her. She looked at the eyes of this young couple in love, the happiness of their tranquil home, and the genuine belief they had in some sort of hope for a bright tomorrow – and she choked. Like someone who had suddenly realized she had eaten an entire box of chocolates, Jenni grieved over her guilty pleasure. What had she been thinking? She didn't know these people. And here she sat in their perfect house with their perfect children reeling about a life that she no longer wanted to admit was her own. She paused, silent for longer than was comfortable, and then asked the Hardys to pardon her endless rambling, she had talked too much. Though Matt wanted to hear more, he knew better than to press their guest. Instead, he offered to go gather the dogs while Abigail fixed Jenni a coffee for the road. Jenni knew she had been weakened by the recollection when she heard herself say, "Don't wake the kids to get the dogs. Clack or I one will come back for them when it isn't so late." When Abigail hugged Jenni at the door, Jenni wished she knew this young lady better – she would love to hold on a little longer and just cry. Instead, she thanked them for dinner, left her cell phone number with them for anything the dogs might need, and headed home to Cardelville. Turning around on the front steps, though, she looked back at Clack's pastor and said, "Reverend, you're a good man! Maybe you'll do Clack some good, but you have your work cut out for you." Matt smiled but said nothing.

8:34 p.m. Surely it wasn't too late to call Brother Heath. Matt stepped into his tiny study, a sitting room really, and pressed the all-too-familiar numbers into the phone. It was no surprise when Dorothy answered the phone – Dorothy always answered the phone. Though she was his protector and promoter in all things South Mill, Dorothy Heath seemed very untrusting of any transactions her husband dealt without her knowledge. Everyone joked that Stephen wore the pants, but Dorothy told him which ones to put on every morning.

"Good evening, brother!" Matt greeted the old man! "Sorry it took me so long to get back to you."

Heath neither acknowledged nor accepted the apology but went right into the *list* of items that he had wanted to discuss on at least three previous occasions during the day. Matt took out a notepad to jot them down, although he ended up just doodling on the paper as the conversation drug on. It seemed that someone had left the water on in one of the children's restrooms on Sunday morning, and Brother Heath had found it earlier that morning still "just-a-tricklin'." Then, why had Lanie left the office before 2:30 today? And was that going to be deducted from her vacation or were they going to dock her for the hours? Matt would have wondered why Stephen had even been where there was water running, but he knew that this elder cleric found it necessary to fully inspect every square inch of the church building at least twice a week. He assured Stephen that he would speak to the children's workers about checking the water faucets every Sunday morning and Wednesday night after the last child was picked up by his or her parent. He also explained that Lanie had received all of the approval necessary for her to leave in time to attend her grandmother's ninety-eighth birthday party at the nursing home that afternoon. He knew that the elder minister probably thought that a personnel matter as big as leaving a few minutes early should have been cleared with at least two committees even though the structure of the church allowed for the pastor to manage the secretarial staff. This was what was so pressing? Really?

One last question before the phone call could end. "Who all were you visiting in the hospital today? I saw the Grogans and Miss Hughes, but you seemed to be up there a lot longer than I was. Every time I called Lanie said you were at the hospital. Is there someone in that I don't know about?" Matt wanted to laugh. Heath never shared with him who was in and out of the hospital, and now the old codger wanted his intel. Matt paused, calculated, and finally answered, "Grogan...Hughes....and a couple of families that have been visiting the church, some...*outsiders*." Matt couldn't resist.

Brother Heath was ready to end the conversation then and said, "Well, that's one way to spend the entire day out of the office." With that, he said goodnight and assured Matt he'd be by to see him sometime the next day. Had there been a day since he arrived in South Mill that Pastor Stephen had not said, "I'll be by to see you tomorrow?" A sickness welled up within the young preacher every time Heath made that promise. His visits were never good news.

CHAPTER TEN

Lanie Garrett had been hired at the church by Pastor Number Three, a fun-loving and kind middle-aged man, who sheltered her well from the politics of church. She was timid and quiet, a high-school graduate and a technical school dropout. Her life was simple with one eight-year-old daughter and the husband she had loved since ninth-grade, an auto mechanic who would eventually take over his father's repair shop where he had worked his whole life. She had pleasant phone skills, and she smiled politely at everyone who stopped by the church office. Her official duties were to answer incoming calls, prepare mailings, and publish the weekly church bulletins and monthly newsletters. Each pastor that arrived prior to Matt had revised her job description; some even gave her a new title. The one she disliked the most was *Confidential Assistant to the Senior Pastor*. Each time she saw it in print or had to type the words herself, she found it both cumbersome and anxiety-producing. The word *confidential* automatically suggested there were secrets, and, though there were things she saw and heard that were held in confidence, she felt like the title caused undue scrutiny, and she did not like the idea of eyebrows raising as people looked in her direction wondering what she might or might not know about them. It was a frivolous title anyway. The pastor who gave it to her shared almost nothing with her. She never knew his whereabouts, his schedule, or his sermon titles, which she needed each week to include in the up-coming Sunday's church bulletin. Inevitably, she would track him down late on Thursdays, ask for the title, and wait for another hour for him to produce one. Then, if the copy machine jammed, her end-of-the-week meant overtime, for which she would never be paid, while she waited for a repairman. Some weeks, she printed the Sunday bulletin with no title. It did not seem that people cared too much what the week's message was about. On the only occasion someone inquired about the plan for an upcoming sermon, she coyly smiled and quipped, "I'm sorry; that's confidential." It made her giggle, but it annoyed the matriarchal figure who asked. She apologized quickly and confessed that she did not know yet.

Though she shied away from any controversy that seemed to brew, Lanie had become well-versed at the true goings-on of a church office. If nothing else, the frequent interim periods gave her plenty of off-the-books experience. During these times of pastoral absenteeism, she found both the time and the energy to do things that would typically have fallen to the pastor... things like sending birthday cards to elderly members, calling and checking on the sick, and charting the attendance figures and offering stats. All of this was unofficial, as the church employed one of its own to be the *Financial Secretary* and do the sanctioned record-keeping. The position was filled by a long-time church member and retired school system bookkeeper, Mrs. Trudy Knight, and she very officially kept track of every dime given and every penny spent - answering directly to the annually-elected church treasurer, who, coincidentally, had been the same person, Mrs. Wanda Briner, for the last thirteen years. Trudy spoke often of retiring, and Wanda lamented the amount of time her volunteer position took away from her husband and family, but Lanie (and everyone else within earshot) knew it was all just idle chitchat, as both loved the power that comes when you hold the purse strings of the church. Any lofty idea that came from the pulpit on Sundays about it all being "God's money" was just misinformed spirituality. Jesus, himself, would have a hard time spending more than five dollars without a thorough inquisition and reluctant approval from one or both of these ladies and the finance committee that they either answered to or manipulated. There was a fine line. In truth, Lanie was glad that none of her ever-changing job descriptions included so much as emptying the quarters out of children's offering envelopes. Instead, she just watched the monthly, quarterly, and yearly financial reports, noting the dips in giving when the church was in-between preachers, and tracking the attendance patterns that coincided. She also keenly observed the rhythms and ways of the organization she served. Personality clashes. Grasps for power worked out in the committee life of the church. But there were also kind and gentle spirits, and lives were sometimes changed when those individuals led in what she thought was real ministry. She often wondered what would happen if that tenor became the norm around South Mill. Lanie was the shy, quiet type - and well-rehearsed at seeming naive, but she was, as Brother Heath once described her, wise. She knew when he said it that it was not a compliment.

When Matt Hardy arrived on the scene, he invited Lanie into his office for what he liked to call a *visit*. They talked casually for a few minutes before he asked her what she would like her title to be. They both agreed that *Pastoral Secretary* had a nice, ministerial sound to it, and it established a nice coziness between her and the pastor that *Confidential Assistant* aimed to do but missed.

Matt reveled in his people skills - his ability to gain the confidence and trust of his assistant, and he complimented her often, going forward, of her skill at being a good watchdog for him. She found deep satisfaction and comfort in knowing that her boss trusted her, and she vowed to herself to maintain that quality in their working relationship. So, when Pastor Matt called her on her personal cell phone early Wednesday morning, she was pleased with the implicitness of his confidence in her and professional in the guarding of such trust. She was, finally, the *confidential* secretary to the pastor.

"I'm going to be a little late coming to the office this morning," Matt began, after pleasantries of a good morning, of course. "I know that I will have a visitor this morning, and you know that I am handling a very tight-lipped matter. Remember my challenge from Monday afternoon?"

Lanie remembered being asked to pray for a suicide situation, and she immediately felt the guilt of forgetting to do so rush over her. "Yes," she replied. Lanie had also answered the phone every time Clack Collins had called on Tuesday, so, though she had never met the man, she knew exactly who Matt was trying to save. Playing it cool, she calmly asserted, "I know you are helping *whoever it is* through this tough time."

Matt knew that she knew. Lanie *was* wise, and he did mean it as a compliment.

"I need to see him first thing this morning, before I come into the office, so I need you to..." His mind stumbled with the thoughts.

Lanie rescued his words, "I can only assume you have a meeting at a medical facility of some kind. Most appointments at medical facilities are doctor's appointments, aren't they?"

"I...I can't ask you to..."

"Pastor, a lot of the people we work for jump to all kinds of crazy conclusions. Please allow me to jump to one or two now and then. I assume you have a medical appointment. Is there anything I need to know about your condition?"

Matt laughed. "No. I'm sure I'll be fine. He coughed twice, and they both laughed. "I should be in before noon, but I'll call if I am delayed."

"It *is* Wednesday, you know," Lanie reminded him. "Is there anything I can do to help you with your preparations for your Bible lesson tonight?"

The midweek service was held on Wednesdays, and, though much more informal than a Sunday sermon, Matt liked for his lessons to be well organized and rehearsed. He wished he was already prepared enough to let her help him, but he had thought little of it. "No, but thank you. Just keep my calendar clear for this afternoon so I can study."

Lanie gave assurance, and they ended the call. Matt silently prayed, giving thanks that the secretary he had inherited at this job was turning out to be an okay kind of lady. It took some of the weight of people like Brother Heath off of his shoulders.

He glanced at the digits on the screen of his phone, and he was already late. "Maggie! Grab your lunch! We gotta go!!" And with daughter in tow, Pastor Matt Hardy was out the door on his way to save one more little piece of South Mill, but not before creeping slowly through the morning carpool line.

Clack was up early. He took a shower, ate a bagel and a hard-boiled egg, and drank a cup of coffee that was more the color of pond water than the dark, rich brew he preferred. He brushed his hair and teeth, but he would have to wait until he got home to shave. In the psych unit, razors were off limits, as was any kind of silverware, real or plastic, thus the finger-food breakfast.

When Matt arrived, about ten minutes before 9:00, Clack had changed out of the hospital gown back into the clothes he was wearing on Monday when the whole saga began. In the pastor's hand was a brown paper sack, and in his other hand was one of those in-sulated, reusable grocery bags, the kind with a zipper on top and the foil lining inside. Abigail used these when she shopped, not because she was particularly environmentally-minded, but because they kept the cold things cold while she made her extra stops between the store and home. Clack hopped straight up from the chair in the corner of his hospital room as though a senior ranking officer was entering the room. Instead of a salute, Clack stuck out his hand to shake Matt's and offered a chipper *good morning*. Matt had to drop a bag on the bed to shake hands, and Clack looked it over. "I hope that's not a bag full of menthol cigarettes."

Unsure of the intended jab, Matt smiled and greeted Clack, then offered him the zipped bag. "It's not groceries, but it was the only bag I could find. I stopped by your house and grabbed you some clean clothes before I headed up this way. I hope I got stuff that fits."

"Preacher, you're alright!" Sorting through the bag, he thought out loud, "I don't guess you brought a razor so I can shave."

From the paper bag, Matt produced a rechargeable Norelco, one Clack had never seen before. "I got that as a gift a couple of Christmases ago, but I'm not an electric razor kind of guy and have never used it. They'll allow those in here, and if you like it, you can have it."

Clack sat down on the edge of the bed and the preacher sat beside him. Clack took the razor out, clicked the sliding button, and began massaging his face with the three round, rotating heads. He, too, preferred shaving cream and a blade, but this would do for now. Over the gentle hum of the razor, the two began to talk.

"How are the dogs?"

"They are loved and well-fed. Where do they sleep at your house?"

"They have crates, but to tell the truth, I usually fall asleep on the couch, and they seem to do fine on the floor."

"Well, they each had a bed to sleep in last night. I was going to put them in a bathroom upstairs, but before I could go wrangle them into it, the kids had each claimed one and were snuggled up with them in bed. Everyone is still alive and well this morning, so I guess the dogs didn't eat them during the night."

Both men laughed, and Clack confessed what Matt suspected, "Those dogs wouldn't hurt a flea. I'm sure they are enjoying their sleepover at your house. I'll pick them up this evening, if you're going to be home."

Matt was suddenly lost in those words. *This evening*. Clack was, obviously, planning on leaving today. His forty-eight hours were expiring, and he could leave at will since the hospital didn't strictly adhere to the clock. Right now Clack was peaceful...human...even charming. If Matt said the wrong thing, though, he knew that could change quickly. His own observations Monday, even though Clack was inebriated, were confirmed time and time again by Jenni's testimony last night. How was he going to talk Clack, a man who, at the moment, was in complete charge of himself, into submitting to going to get some real help before returning to life as he knew it? He had prayed for a peaceful process, but was this man going to listen to someone he barely even knew two days ago?

Clack continued to talk as the pastor wandered down one path and then another unable to find a way out of the maze his mind was creating. "I want to get my place cleaned up a little and then have you and your family over one night. I'll grill us some steaks!" Clack was planning ahead - and that, for a patient on suicide watch, was always a positive sign. "I hate to ask you for anything else, Preacher, but if you can give me a ride out to the site, I think if I show up for work today they'll let me stay on. Then I'll catch a ride back to the house after my shift, and I can call you and come and get the dogs."

He continued talking, which was fine with Matt because he could not think of anything productive to say at the moment. He felt weak letting Clack continue with his plans, but he had yet to land on a roadblock that he thought would stop the man. The more Clack talked, the more the preacher wanted to just go with Clack's agenda for the day. It would be easier to avoid any conflict. As Clack talked, he shifted from planning to telling about his work, how the hospital was going to be six wings, each three stories, with its own physical plant operations - a city within a city - completely functional even in a power outage or natural disaster. While he talked, he withdrew one item at a time from the grocery bag Matt had delivered and spread it out on the bed pressing out wrinkles vainly with his hands. First, the pants, a pair of work khakis. He grabbed them at the waistband, and flung them toward the windows, never letting go of his grip until they unfurled like a two-legged flag, snapping like a whip in the hand of a ringmaster. He folded them on the creases, and began smoothing them on the bed, though they were hardly wrinkled at all. He did the same with the shirt, holding it by the top seams where the sleeves met the shoulders, and he laid it across the back of the chair in the corner. He repeated the ritual with the undershirt Matt had packed, and even with the white athletic socks. The last piece of clothing out of the bag was a pair of blue plaid boxer shorts, which were snapped into shape much like the khakis had been, and with that, Clack began to undress, still spouting off details about the new Tri-County hospital and his work with Sawyer Industries.

Matt took a break from strategizing on getting Clack some therapy just so he could watch the spectacle of the clothing preparation. It was fascinating. Clearly the habits of a military man, never wanting to look rumpled, even walking out of a hospital after a couple of days of detox. After finishing his hand pressing of his entire ensemble, Clack finished removing his Monday clothing, taking the time to fold each piece as though he might be planning to wear them again before laundry day. Each button was fastened on the shirt, and then it was placed on the bed and folded. When he was finished, it looked like a new shirt being presented on a shelf or cubical in a department store. Matt thought, *why bother?* Clack did the same with the jeans he was wearing, and replaced the items in the green zippered bag. As he talked, he undressed, and as he undressed, he talked. Within just a few minutes, a mostly naked Clack stood between the bed and the corner chair, within arms' reach of the prepared clothing placed on both. Matt had been careful to maintain eye contact throughout the process, especially when Clack shimmied out of his underwear and stood there a few seconds talking even more before Matt abruptly said, "I guess I could give you some privacy."

"That's not something I'm accustomed to, Preacher!" That made sense. A man who spent most of his life in locker rooms and military barracks wouldn't be too hung up on modesty.

As Clack dressed, Matt was mesmerized again, but this time not with his own thoughts of trying to convince Clack to change his plans. Instead, Matt observed that this sixtyish-year-old was in perfect shape. His wingspan was supported by the mammoth breadth of his chest, which still displayed the fading markings of bench-pressed pecks. His mid-section revealed only the earliest signs of love handles developing, but there was no flab to hang over the waistband of his boxers at all. When Clack creased his left elbow and reached to put his right arm in his shirtsleeve, a most impressive bicep inflated. And as Clack buttoned the plaid flannel shirt, Matt felt a sudden need to go chop down some trees or at least buy a gym membership. A man twice his age was the most fit person he had ever seen. An impressive book cover, he thought, encasing pages of tragedy. Certainly not someone I'd ever want very angry at me.

Clack, completely dressed, sat down in the chair opposite the preacher, clothes all folded and placed in a bag for transport. "So, what do you think, Pastor?"

"About what?" conscious now of his preoccupation with other things.

"About a ride out to the job site? I don't have my wallet, but I can pay you back for the gas when I pick up the dogs."

Matt's chest heaved as he hunted for the right words. "Clack, what if you took a few more days off?"

Clack's eyebrows raised, his head tilted to almost begin to shake saying no, but Matt pressed on.

"There's this place I know, about an hour-and-a-half from here, where guys like you can... "

"Get some help?" Clack finished it with a condescending tone - personifying the insult of such a phrase.

"No. I don't think you need help. I think you need...healing."

Intrigued but defensive, Clack said, "What the hell do I need to be healed of? Alcoholism? Depression? Suicidalism?" Clack was sure he made up that last word, but it worked. "Which is it, Preacher? What's my diagnosis?"

"No, Clack. I don't think you are sick. I think you've maxed out your payload, and you just need a little maintenance. Can I explain?"

"Yeah! You need to." Was he mad? Even he wasn't sure.

"Well, first of all," Matt waded in with caution, "you have a lot of unfinished business. I wasn't even alive during Vietnam, but I know that my granddad had nightmares that cost him a marriage to my grandmother and two other women that came after her. I know that you miss your wife and that divorce papers are the worst anniversary gift ever given. I know that contract work is not what you meant to be doing when you turned sixty. And, if I can sound like a preacher for a minute, I know that God is not finished with his plans for you yet. I don't think you're suffering from alcoholism or depression or *suicidalism*. I think you just need to unpack a lot of crap that has derailed your life and find the motivation you need to hop back on a different track."

"You like trains, Preacher?"

"Huh?"

"Payload...derailed...different track..."

"Well, at least you followed me. Clack, I just want to see you happy. I want you to have joy in your life."

"What would make me happy would be a ride to work, you know!?!"

"Maybe it would...for the rest of your shift. Then what? You go home? To your rented place? What makes you happy then? The dogs? The alcohol? The papers on your kitchen table that someone thinks she wants you to sign?"

"Preacher, this is the worst pep talk I've ever heard. If you're going to keep going, I hope that's a bottle of whiskey in that brown paper sack, 'cause you and I are both going to need it."

"It's your lunch, Clack! My wife packed you a lunch. If I take you to work, you'll need a lunch."

"So, you didn't really think I'd go to this...this place!"

"I don't know, Clack. But I know it is up to you. I'm going to take you wherever you tell me to take you. I'll drive you to the work site, to the liquor store, wherever you want to go. I'll take you home, and even stop off and pick up Felix and Chop if you want. Whatever the future holds for Clack Collins on the other side of this hospital room is totally in your hands, and I'm here to be a good friend and help you go find it."

"What kind of dump are you wanting me to go to?"

"Oh, it isn't a dump! You've heard about these celebrities that go off to these five-star rehab facilities, right? Well, this one is four-star, at least. It is called *Respira de Nuevo*, and it means *Breathe Again*. They have massage therapists, kayaks, pontoon boats, snorkeling, a state-of-the-art gym, and indoor basketball, tennis, and racquetball courts. It's amazing. An old professor of mine works there as the administrator and one of the addiction counselors, but then, you don't need all that...right? And, the best part is that, because there are medical doctors on site, your insurance pays part of the cost, and you can qualify for medical leave at work, maybe. And, whatever insurance doesn't pay...well...we will figure out a way for you to not have to worry about it."

"This sounds like you want me to go on a vacation, but you're just not telling me about the group therapy sessions, the psycho-babble, and who knows what all else. I can't afford to be off work, Preacher. I'm sorry." Even as Clack said this, there was something in what Matt had said that jarred him momentarily, but he couldn't remember what. Whatever it was, what he said right after it made him feel just a slight sense of hope...a hint of peace.

"Clack, you took a day off work on Monday to kill yourself. Can't you take a few days off to live?"

What? The preacher's mouth was a Taser, and Clack was stunned. He replayed the words in his head. What would it matter if you took off from work to kill yourself? You wouldn't need a job when it was over. But, if you take off work to live, as the Preacher said, you wouldn't want to lose your job in the process. Or did that even matter at the moment? For a man who kept his wits about him these days, even when he was drunk, Clack was bewildered at the moment. Could a man take off from work to live? What would that even mean? Maybe I do need some healing? What would Jenni say? Who cares? She filed for divorce. It was too much to think about...too far ahead to consider. Today was wasting, and he needed to keep his job. That was the right choice.

"Preacher, let me call the nurse to discharge me, and I'll take you up on that ride...out to the work site."

Clack pushed the call button and assessed the room for left-over personal belongings, of which there were none. Everything was packed away in the insulated bag Matt had grabbed on his way out of the house that morning. With nothing else to assess, Clack looked at the young preacher. Suddenly, something about Matt captivated Clack. It was not his physique, although Matt had the body of an athlete – a much younger and smaller one than Clack. It was his eyes. The deep, almost navy-blue eyes surrounded by this boyish face were like a tranquil sea, not just calm but emanating peace, like a wise old man disguised in adolescence. Clack was suddenly intimidated by this man half his age and size. Matt stared at Clack, uncertain of his own next move, but looked away when Clack did not.

"What's the name of that place again?" Clack asked.

"Respira de Nuevo."

"Maybe I could put in for vacation time and go in a couple or three weeks."

"Maybe." Matt seemed to have lost hope or interest or something.

The young nurse was back, but this time Clack did not try to engage her in small talk. He wanted out almost as much as this nurse wanted him to leave. She gave him his paperwork, a phone number for the psychiatrist who had attended him there, with whom he was to follow up by making an appointment within twenty-four hours. She knew he would not do so, and she almost felt guilty for not caring. She offered a wheelchair, hospital policy, but Clack politely refused. "I appreciate the offer, ma'am, but I'd rather walk out with my friend here." The nurse fought against her sudden slack jaw, but her wide eyes could not hide her surprise at Clack's manners. "Thank you for all you did for me while I was here. If I ever come back, I'm going to request you as my nurse." He chuckled as she held the door open for them both. She was smiling the only smile Clack had seen from her. As the doors to the psychiatric unit flung open to allow a quick exit, Clack whispered loudly to Matt, "She's smiling because I'm leaving." Matt looked over his shoulder at the nurse. He wasn't so sure.

CHAPTER ELEVEN

In the parking lot, Matt unlocked the door of his S-10, jumped in, and reached across the passenger seat and pulled the door handle for Clack. Clack folded himself into the compact truck, adjusted the grocery bag he was holding, and tried to reach for the seatbelt before Matt took notice and offered, "You can move the seat back with the lever underneath it." Clack did, and reached for the side lever, too, to recline and get his head off of the ceiling.

"We need to find you a man's truck," he joked.

"It's not a tight fit for me," Matt laughed.

Still feeling deflated that his efforts had not worked, he prayed one last time that Clack might change his mind before they reached the site. He turned left out of the parking lot, looped around the hospital, and turned right onto Highway 89, for the twenty-two-mile drive to the construction site of the new Tri-County Regional Medical Center, a name that was humorously redundant. If it was for three counties, wasn't it automatically regional? As they sloped up the ramp onto the highway, a sign read "Mendelssohn Memorial Parkway." Clack saw it and thought how that must be just that portion of the road since it was just called Highway 89 on the parts he traveled to and from work each day. The name stuck in his head, though – *Mendelssohn*. Maybe a politician from the area or a doctor who established the hospital? A musician's name, though. One of Jenni's favorite composers. Felix Mendelssohn. A thought!

"How did you know the names of my dogs?" Clack burst forth with the question, turning his whole torso in the tiny seat to look the preacher in the face.

Busted? "You told me, didn't you?" Matt stammered and wished he could take back that last question. Why did he add the *didn't you*?

"Hmmph." Clack's only response.

Silence stretched the next mile into eternity, both minds reeling for what to say, but words would not come. Clack tried to replay the timetable from yesterday. What time did the preacher come? Leave? What time did Jenni show up? But days and hours in a hospital room run together. No way they met. And if they did, how would the dogs have come up in conversation?

"You promise my dogs are at your house?"

"Yes, Clack. Want to go check on them?"

Silence another mile.

Matt wanted to change the subject. The weather? Sports? He could think of no suitable topic to remove the discomfort of this car ride. Finally, a thought, "You need anything from the store? My treat?"

Clack wanted a pack of cigarettes, but he shook his head. He would just bum some off of someone at work. He was thinking. The same feeling he had while Matt was talking earlier had hit him as he saw that *Mendelssohn* sign. That had to have been when Matt mentioned the dogs by name - it triggered something in Clack. He hardly ever called the dogs by name, and he was certain he had not told Matt their names without offering an explanation that he would have definitely remembered. Matt had thrown him off the trail with his peaceful demeanor, but Clack knew what had grabbed his attention in the hospital room.

"She's one fine-ass white woman, ain't she?" A phrase Clack had borrowed from an African-American coworker.

Matt was offended, slightly, and completely floored by the comment. "What? Who?"

"That fiery red-head that you obviously met in the parking lot yesterday," he smiled.

Matt waited for Clack's mood to be clear. When he was sure Clack wasn't going to karate chop him in the throat, he breathed for what felt like the first time that day, inhaling through his nose, he was sure, every bit of oxygen available in the cab of the truck. His chest heaved and he blew out through his mouth as though he had been holding his breath the whole time.

"She is a very attractive lady, Clack. I enjoyed meeting her."

Clack wasn't mad. In fact, a wide grin rose on his face before he said, "You lyin' little dog-smuggling, cigarette buyin' preacher!"

Matt wanted to defend himself but just glanced quickly at Clack and then back at the road. "Give me some credit, Clack. I didn't let her take the dogs. That's what you wanted, right?"

"Good job! She'll get them eventually, I guess. How long did y'all talk?"

"The first time, or the second time?" Matt thought he might as well reveal it all now.

"You saw her twice?"

"Three times actually." Clack was shocked. "I ran into her on the elevator talking on her cell phone, going on about John Collins, and I, of course, didn't make the connection. Then, I ran into a friend in the parking lot as I was leaving, and I was just getting ready to go when she came out, fumbling for her keys, pretty upset."

"She was crying?"

"Yes, and I'm a sucker for a crying woman!"

"You're a sucker, I think, anyway. You're driving a drunk to work when he ought to be headed to rehab." Letting his own words sink in for a moment, he continued. "Okay, so that's two times. I'm scared to ask what the third time was."

"Well, first of all, I'm holding your dogs for ransom, so don't kill me."

"Spill it, Preacher!"

"I invited her to our house last night for dinner, and she actually showed up. I have no idea where she went between the hospital and my house, but she showed up almost right on time. My wife cooked, we ate, and she left about 8:30. We had a nice visit, talked mostly about you. I forgot to hide the trash can with the dogs' food in it, and she never let on that she knew the dogs were there until my son let them escape from the bathroom while we were having dessert." Sensing Clack wanted more, Matt added, "Clack, she was lovely."

"I know. She always was. And then I ruined it, ruined her... When is she coming back for the dogs?"

"We made no plans! She seemed happy with their temporary living arrangements. What do you mean you ruined her?"

"It's like I killed her, Matt." He called the minister by his first name! "I married up, man... I really did. She was the perfect Southern Belle. The only girl I've ever loved. I know that I wasn't the same after the war, but I'm still finding out every day how much it really did change me. Then, in '08, I lost everything with the economy. I tried to give her the life she deserved, and I failed her and everyone else in the process." Clack began wiping his eyes and fell silent again. Matt found silence the most prudent response for now. He silently prayed for Clack and Jenni.

Matt saw a McDonald's restaurant ahead, and signaled to pull in. "Let me buy you a cup of coffee." When they pulled into the drive-thru line, Clack said he liked his coffee black and excused himself to go inside the restaurant to the restroom. Matt ordered two cups of coffee, one with lots of cream and sugar, and one with nothing, two sausage, egg, and cheese biscuits, two orders of hash browns, and two apple pies. He paid then pulled into a parking place to wait on Clack.

Clack emerged, his eyes damp but refreshed, a garden after the morning dew. He packed himself into the cab of the truck, and looked at Matt square in the eyes. He took a huge sip of the scalding coffee, winced once, and spoke softly, "I need to breathe again."

Matt thought he knew what Clack meant, but he was assuming nothing right now. Clack repeated himself.

"I need to breathe again. How far away is this place?"

"An hour-and-a-half. Are you serious?" Matt was celebrating on the inside. He'd never been so quick at winning someone over, and, if he was being honest with himself, he didn't really think Clack would agree to go.

"Think they'll let me go to work in the daytime and come back at night?"

"No."

"Didn't think so! Can I use your phone to call Eric at work? I have no idea where mine is, and I need to tell them I'm going to be out a while."

Matt was giddy and almost threw the phone at Clack. He worked hard to keep a stoic expression on his face though.

Though Matt could only hear one end of the conversation, he knew Eric and was certain that he would run interference for Clack at work, buying him as much time off as was possible for contract labor on a temporary project. That thought did trouble Matt some, and he was sure it was on Clack's mind, too, but he let it fade knowing that God always opens a window...maybe.

Clack's voice almost broke as he was getting off the phone with Eric, but he held it together. "Eric's going to bring you some paperwork to church tonight, he says, and do you think you can get it to me at this Breathe Again place?"

"Of course. If you want, I can even take you to your house for the night, you can eat at church, and we can head there first thing in the morning. It'd give you time to get things packed and in order."

"Preacher, things haven't been in order for me in two-and-a-half years. One night would be a drop in a very big bucket. If I'm going to this place, I'd better go now before I realize what kind of craziness you have cursed me with. Maybe you can send me some of my clothes and all. My wallet is in my top, right-hand dresser drawer."

Matt turned left out of McDonalds, headed back in the direction they had come. He looked at the clock, and it was 9:35. That would put them at Respira de Nuevo by 11:00ish, an hour or so to get Clack checked in, and he would be back at the office by 1:30 or 2:00 at the latest. He needed to call Lanie. Clack ate a biscuit while Matt explained to Lanie that his appointment was going to go long. She told him everything was fine at the office, that *no one* had even been by to check in, and that she was pulling together some notes for him from the next chapter of I Corinthians, the book from the Bible he was teaching through on Wednesday nights. Matt was liking this secretary more and more every day.

At 11:03 a.m., Matt turned off the highway onto Esperanza Way, in Altaville, right up to the front steps of a grand Antebellum mansion. White columns made the two stories stretch toward heaven and made Clack rethink this manipulated situation in which he now found himself.

They were greeted by a sweet lady named Vera, who immediately called for Matt's old professor. Dr. Charles Norman, who everyone called Chuck, hugged Matt, shook Clack's hand, and immediately began a tour of their facilities. Clack noticed right away that there were only men there and questioned it. Chuck jokingly said, "We only specialize in helping guys breathe. *Dating Again* is two miles down the road." Sensing more was needed, he explained, "*Respira* is a men's recovery facility. Guys only! Here we work toward recovering from whatever has sidetracked the life that God intended for us. We wouldn't want to get involved in a dating or marriage relationship without being back on track first, so we keep it guys only. Of course, your significant other is welcomed to visit on Sunday afternoons between 2:00 and 6:00 p.m."

Clack looked surprised - a new expression for Matt to observe from this giant of a man. Grinning then with just the left corner of his mouth, he offered a sidebar to the preacher, "You realize that you're the most significant *other* I have right now."

Matt retorted, "Then I hope you realize he's not talking about conjugal visits."

All three laughed out loud. Clack wondered how long it had been since he laughed like that. Was he already breathing again? Chuck said, "Matt can come anytime...not just on Sundays."

Matt added, "I'll see you at least once a week, and I'll bring you menthols when I come."

Surprised again, "Please don't! I hate those things. Just plain, filtered cigarettes, Marlboro, please!" Laughter again!

After a thorough inspection of the lake, the boats, the gyms, the gathering places (group therapy! Clack knew it!), the dining room, the spa, rocking chairs, hammocks, library, chapel, and driving range, they stopped off in a private studio apartment, complete with a refrigerator, microwave oven, coffee pot, and mini-bar, stocked up with bottled water, soft drinks, popcorn, candy bars, and fruit. There, at a desk, Chuck logged into his laptop computer and handled Clack's entire registration, accepting the fact without question that his wallet and insurance information would be forthcoming whenever Matt could get it there. Within minutes, Clack was welcomed, invited to lunch, and seated with his own personal concierge, as they called him, but Clack knew he was a therapist in disguise. His name was Blake, and he was...okay!

Matt explained that he needed to get back to the office soon, and the concierge excused himself to get another helping of something off of the buffet. While alone, the peaceful eyes again met the steel of Clack's own and Matt offered his encouragement.

"You'll love this place. They'll love you. I know that you don't know me well, but I am a friend. I promise that you can count on me to pray for you every single day you are here. I will watch over your dogs like they are my own. I will check on your place. And I will not tell anyone where you are or what you are doing. I can't thank you enough for trusting me on this place, and I'm so glad you decided to come. Please don't quit until you are able to breathe easy."

"Thank you!" A hard but heartfelt gratitude as he grabbed Matt's arm, "And, if you think that Jenni needs to know where I am at any point in all of this... when you think the time is right...you can tell her...if you think you should... I just don't—"

"—I'll see you in a couple of days," Matt interrupted the anguish. "I'll bring your wallet, your paperwork, and your clothes. Let Blake know what else you need. He has my number."

"Matt!" Clack called across the dining room. "You're right. I hardly know you, but for the last three days, you've been exactly where I needed you to be at the precise moment I needed you to be there. I don't know how to explain that, but thanks!"

12

CHAPTER TWELVE

Matt was already dialing Abigail on his cell phone when he hopped in the truck and threw it in reverse. He'd have to wait twenty minutes, though, because there was no cell phone reception in the hills of Altaville, which, he guessed, helped make it the peaceful haven that it was. When he finally did have a signal, he called his wife with the exciting news of Clack's agreement to the therapy. Matt was a kid telling about his exciting day at school, and Abigail fought tears as they reflected on how it seemed that God had orchestrated every step, how Clack was probably a really good man, and how Jenni looked so tired last night - an odd conclusion for people who had never seen her looking any other way. "Thank you, Lord, for taking care of today," Abigail vocalized a short prayer. She complimented her husband on his incessant love for people and commented that he had already put in a full day of ministry. He agreed but said it would be motivation for him as he went into the office to prepare for his midweek message. He knew Lanie would be glad for him to be back so she could stop covering for him. He said goodbye to Abigail, and she told him she needed to go grab groceries, pick up Maggie at school, and then head home to get ready for Wednesday night church. "We'll see you at supper," she said. "Love you!"

"I love you!"

As he drove, he thought about Lanie and how awkward it must be to be bulldogging for him. He thought it was silliness that he even had to cover up where he was and what he was doing. It wasn't like he was a rebel playing hooky from high school - he was serving God by helping people overcome life's difficulties, and wasn't that ministry? Why do I have to justify my whereabouts to anyone, anyway? He was confident in his training and in his people skills. Even his teaching and preaching was something for which he received ample compliments. He had worked part-time in churches while he was attending seminary, the graduate school for those studying theology. Never, though, in class or in his church work had he been prepared for those who would seek to monitor his office hours, his personal life, and his daily interactions within the community. Stephen Heath was one of those people who really believed he was in charge of the church. Though he was retired and not serving in any official capacity at the time, he maintained a key to everything, including the church's post office box, filing cabinets, desk drawers, storage buildings, and offices. For all Matt knew, the man had keys to the house the church furnished for their pastors to live in, too. He shuddered at the thought.

Just under the 90 minutes he anticipated, he pulled into his parking space in the back parking lot at South Mill Baptist Church. The cooks were already there for Wednesday's meal, and he was always excited to smell their creations. Those ladies could cook! The smell of cakes or confections of some kind greeted him in the parking lot, and, though he had two breakfasts today, his stomach was suddenly gnawing at him. He grabbed an apple from the lunch bag he had planned to give to Clack. Maybe it would tie him over until he could eat some of that good-smelling food.

Lanie smiled as he entered the church office suite, handed him a stack of mail and two phone messages. One was from a copier salesman who called quite often to inquire about the church's future needs for copy equipment. He tossed that one in the trash can beside Lanie's desk. He didn't need to look at the other one to know it was from Stephen Heath. What did the old man want? Though he didn't even speak the question out loud, Lanie was following him into his private office with the answer.

"He wanted you to go with him to a lunch meeting of local pastors. He said that you should have it on your calendar that comes from the district office."

"I've been to those meetings. No one my age attends, just retired people or preachers at little bitty churches that have always been attended by and run by the same families. I don't want to spend my lunchtime listening to grumpy old men complain about their salaries, their deacons, and their wives. I don't think that is good stewardship of my time and energy? Do you?" He wasn't really expecting an answer from Lanie, and he didn't get one. "I hope he didn't pester you too much."

"I am so used to him by now that I just go on working around him when he's in the office."

Lanie followed Matt to his desk and pointed out the notes she had printed from a variety of commentaries and online sources for him to dive into in the few hours he had before the place became overrun with people coming in early for choirs, missions groups, and supper. He thanked her profusely for her above-and-beyond work today and asked if he could repay her the favor.

"I'd love a sermon title for Sunday by tomorrow morning, if possible," she said apprehensively.

"You'll have it in an email from me by the end of the day today. How's that?"

"Above and beyond!"

Chocolate sauce cake. The sweetness swirling through the air in the parking lot when Matt arrived back from Altaville was chocolate sauce cake. It wafted from the exhaust fan vents in the church kitchen and danced its way into the nostrils of everyone who was attending church that evening. It was preceded by country fried steak, soaked in egg and battered with flour before it was fried. Gravy was on the side and could top the steak or the rice that accompanied it. Green beans were on the plate, too, as they were almost every week, and they were southern green beans, meaning they were cooked with butter, apple cider vinegar, salt and pepper, and a dash of sugar to "sweeten them up a tad," one of the cooks liked to say about almost every vegetable she cooked. Broccoli salad with raisins, red onions, cheese, mayonnaise, and chopped pecans was also on the menu, and the line was long to get a plate filled with the decadence the kitchen crew had put together. Matt grew up on southern cuisine, and he now considered Abigail a great cook, too, but he thought the cooks at the church were the best he'd ever known.

Senior adults usually arrived first to sit around the tables drinking decaf coffee while they waited for the "blessing" that would open the line for business. Every week, Pastor Matt was summoned from his office to come down and bless the food. He wasn't always at a stopping point right at 5:00, but he knew that appetites grew impatient if he didn't make his appearance and offer up the prayer. He was right on time tonight, and he was not planning to return to the office for any last-minute preparations. Lanie had done a good job pulling resources for him, and he could mingle, sip on sweet tea, and gab with the kitchen crew while he waited on Abigail and the kids to arrive. They never showed up before 5:30, since waiting in line with two little ones was something akin to wrangling small cattle. If they sat down at a table by 5:40, there was just enough time to eat, wipe hands and faces, and usher the children off to their children's ministry programs they would attend while the adults had Prayer Meeting. *Prayer Meeting* was a relic of a name that seemed to be stuck on the 6:00 midweek service hour in southern churches. In reality, it would be an hour in which there would be announcements, Bible study, and lots and lots of prayer concerns mentioned, followed by a very brief prayer, if there was still time.

The line for supper would grow until about 5:20, at which time most of the people who were eating would already be in place. Those who got off from work right around 5:00 would arrive in time to get in line somewhere near the choir room, from where they would wind to the left down the hallway, prop along the doors of a mechanical room, step away politely from the women's and men's restroom doors, and finally emerge through the double wooden doors propped open by triangle wedges cut off of two-by-fours and jammed underneath. There, they would be greeted by the smiling, or maybe not, face of Trudy Knight, the church bookkeeper and her friend and church treasurer Wanda Briner, who would tell you how much you owed for your meal. Often men would arrive to find that their families had already gone through the line and left a balance for them to take care of. The jovial ones would make comments like, "What? All that for one plate? I'm just paying for myself." Wanda and company would sometimes joke back, depending on their relationship with the patron, but they always got the money out of them. A few select individuals were sometimes allowed to charge their meals if they had forgotten their checkbook or wallet, but the next week would be the extent of the terms of credit. Wanda had been known to actually invoice folks who had to charge their supper and then didn't come back to Wednesday night church for more than two weeks. Neither T-ball practice nor the flu was a sufficient reason to miss paying your Wednesday night meal balance. Pastor Matt had heard rumors of people who had actually left the church for good after paying one of Sister Wanda's *friendly reminders*. He made sure he paid for his family's meals each week in advance.

About 5:30, Matt wandered to the rear of the line to wait on Abigail, M.J., and Maggie. As he passed by Ms. McIntire, she asked him if he was feeling alright. He assured her that he was great and asked how about her current state of being. She nodded and said, "Well, I'm just fine, but I don't want anything to be wrong with my pastor." Matt thought that was a strange thing to say. When he rounded the corner of the line, past the mechanical room, Wanda Briner's husband Hugh looked him up and down with his left eye squinting like he was eyeing home plate about to throw a curve ball. Matt reached out a hand to shake, but Hugh kept both of his in his jacket pockets and said, "Glad you could make it." Another uncommon greeting, not that Hugh was ever very friendly. He was, after all, Pastor Stephen's best friend. No one had ever said that about him, but Matt was a keen observer of people.

Abigail came down the hall from the other direction, handing a whiny M.J. to his dad and kissing her husband quickly on the cheek just to avoid any impropriety in the eyes of any prudish beholders. "Did you get everything done?" she asked.

"Yes, with a lot of help from Lanie," Matt replied.

"Why doesn't she ever stay for supper?"

"Probably because she doesn't have to."

"Good point."

Neither Abigail nor Matt dreaded Wednesday night suppers, though they did understand Lanie's avoidance of them. Inevitably, if the secretary was on the premises, someone would need something copied, mailed, stamped, folded, found, or filed. The pastor who had hired her had been adamant about her sticking strictly to her office hours, insisting that if church members needed something from her, they could contact her during the hours for which they were paying her. She had found that to be good advice, and though sometimes choosing to stay for a special performance, concert, children's musical, or celebration of some kind, Lanie left the office most Wednesdays by 4:30 just to establish the fact that she was off the clock. She had never attended one of Pastor Matt's sermons either, but she always took home a CD of the week's services for herself before sending them out to the "shut-ins" on Mondays.

As the Hardy family was almost to the fellowship hall, the door to the ladies' room flung open, interrupting the line. Out walked Ms. Mabel, of the rutabaga fame. She immediately took M.J. out of Matt's arms, kissed Abigail and Maggie on the cheek, and put her free arm around the pastor and pulled him in close. "Oh, my pastor! I'm running so late tonight, and I was afraid I would miss out on this scrumptious dinner. Turns out, I'm right on time to eat with your beautiful family."

Matt adored Ms. Mabel. He knew he wasn't supposed to have favorite church members, but she was an exception. She was well connected with the "old guard," as he liked to call it, but she had none of the disposition and rudeness that was inherent among those who had so long ruled the roost at South Mill. She was in her eighties, but only on paper. She followed Major League Baseball religiously, a diehard Braves fan. She swam laps every morning at the Y. And she never missed a chance to hide Easter eggs, serve hotdogs to the community children at Halloween, or rake leaves on Saturday workdays at the church. She was a charter member of the South Mill Garden Club, and she was the President Emeritus of the local library board. A dandy lady, in Matt's mind, with more energy than a woman half her age.

"How were the rutabagas?" Ms. Mabel asked.

Not wanting to lie, Matt smiled and said, "They were literally gobbled up within minutes."

Clasping her hands together at her chest, Ms. Mabel celebrated her preacher's love for her dish. Matt felt guilty for not feeling guilty. He smiled, and Abigail choked back a giggle.

When the pastor and his family, including Ms. Mabel, reached the cashier's table, Matt pulled out his wallet and handed Wanda Briner a five-dollar bill and said, "I'd like to pay for Ms. Mabel's meal tonight." Wanda stared blankly at the pastor, looked to her left at Mable, then back to Matt. "Keep it up, Preacher. People are already wonderin' if we're paying you too much."

The comment caught Abigail off guard, and it showed on her pretty, young face. Without hesitation, she quipped, "I'm actually the one paying for Ms. Mabel's meal tonight. No need for budget revisions."

Matt's eyes widened. "Nice one!" he said under his breath. Abigail cut her eyes around at him without smiling.

As Matt bent down to help Maggie place the napkin and silverware on her tray, a loud *DING* reminded Matt he needed to silence his cell phone. As he did, he saw the text message from Lanie: *Just remember you had a long doctor's appointment this morning and that's why you were out of the office.* Now the comments about his health from Hugh Briner and Ms. McIntire made sense. The grapevine had grown rapidly today!

Matt, Abigail, Maggie, M.J., and Mabel sat with Eric Pressley and his two teenage daughters, who doted over Maggie and M.J., and even offered to take them down the hall to their missions classes while Abigail finished her chocolate sauce cake leisurely. With great discretion, Eric offered an apology for adding so much to Matt's plate with his phone call Monday. Matt leaned across the table toward Eric to avoid eavesdroppers and said, "you saved a man's life this week Eric. Don't even think about apologizing. That's what ministry is all about, and I am flattered that you thought to call me." Eric smiled humbly and said, "I have some paperwork I am supposed to give you," as he slid a manila envelope across the table. Eric quickly handed it to Abigail, who stuck it in her purse beside her chair at the table.

Pastor Matt stood up promptly at 6:30 and announced that it was time to begin Prayer Meeting. Those who were still finishing their meals or dessert could continue to do so, "but we're going to go ahead and get started." He began by reading the announcements that were printed in the midweek bulletin, a ritual that he had been unable to escape since coming to the church as its pastor. There were committee meetings and Vacation Bible School volunteers needed and an extra choir practice coming up this Saturday morning. The list was shorter this week than normal, but that simply allowed for more time for unprinted announcements to be made from the church members around the room. One that caught Matt by surprise was that the quarterly church Business Meeting was in two weeks on Wednesday night in place of Prayer Meeting, and they would need a quorum just in case there was some business on which the church needed to vote. And in a Baptist church, someone thinks everything that comes up requires a vote of the people.

Though this provided a night off from teaching, the thought of these conferences always made Matt wince. They had historically been fraught with conflict, a very visible display of the carnality of God's people. They often argued about money, though the church seemed to be doing just fine financially. They argued about staff members - sometimes vacation time, sometimes salaries, sometimes job performance...all matters Matt felt should be discussed behind closed doors by the Personnel Committee, or, better yet, by Matt and the staff member alone. But fighting the traditional system of a democratically run Baptist church was a mountain on which Matt was not yet ready to die. So, he cringed and prayed that no visitors would show up on a Business Meeting Wednesday night.

The menu would be fried chicken! That almost always ensured a quorum. The church bylaws required at least sixty church members present to vote on any business transactions of the church, so the menu was set and publicized to help reach that goal. If numbers were short on any given Business Meeting night, the teenagers who had already been baptized and joined the church would be fetched from the youth group meeting to attend. Maybe this would be a peaceful meeting without the need for arguing, teenagers, or visitors in the midst. Ordinarily, Matt welcomed visitors, but he had been to some of these meetings that would turn him away from the church if he was just checking out the place and the people. He had heard stories about one Business Meeting several years before his arrival to which the police had been called just to escort people to their cars to avoid a physical fight. The issue at hand had been quite divisive, and wounds were still being licked by some of those involved. The squabble had been over multiple issues involving weddings held in the church building. One was for a mixed-race couple, a union loudly opposed by some of the deacons at the time. The other had to do with a church member who was marrying a man who had been divorced, whose wife was still living in the community. Scripture had been used and misused on every side of the debate, and people left feeling betrayed, defeated, and angry. Both couples were eventually married in the South Mill facilities, but neither couple attended there anymore.

Matt finally got through the announcements and began his teaching time. He waxed eloquently about St. Paul's letter to the Christians at Corinth and how there could be some definite parallels between the culture in ancient Corinth and the one in South Mill. Though the teens and children were elsewhere in the building, their parents were in Prayer Meeting, and they, along with Ms. Mabel, Ms. McIntire, Old Gene Gable, and a few more took notes, nodded their heads in agreement, and demonstrated contemplative visage with each of Pastor Matt's points. Hands would go up, questions would be raised, discussion would commence, and God's people would leave later having truly studied a passage in the Good Book. Near the back, however, others, mostly older church members and their less-old offspring would sit without Bible in sight, their arms folded across their chests. Some would doze and others would whisper loudly around the tables – maybe about the Bible lesson and maybe about something totally nonrelated to church or Jesus or the Bible at all.

When the lesson was concluded, Matt asked if there were any prayer concerns to add to the list printed in the midweek bulletin. Inevitably, some mentioned the very same ones already in writing. Others added relatives, coworkers, and friends to an already endless list. Matt was convinced that the only way to get off of South Mill's prayer list was to die. And even that night there were several names removed by that very method. The young pastor grew weary as the concerns continued for this aunt's toe that might have to be removed and this cousin's coworker's son who was battling depression. Certainly those things were important, but was anyone in his congregation really going to pray for these distant relatives' concerns? Probably not. Finally, Brother Heath spoke up without raising his hand or being called upon to say, "Let's keep our pastor in prayer. He had a rather lengthy doctor's appointment today, I'm told, and I'm sure there are concerns on his mind this evening." Matt panicked momentarily but covered by smiling cordially, thanked the elder pastor, and concluded by saying, "Well, I'm just fine, but I always welcome your prayers for me and my family. Let's pray!" He found himself growing angry at such an absurd prayer concern as he spoke to God about all of the others.

With that, the evening came to an end and the children emerged from their classes and choirs. Everyone was out of the building within a few minutes except for the adult choir members, who would stay for an extra hour to rehearse. Sometimes Matt would get stopped on his way out to talk about lessons or people or building maintenance issues, but tonight he managed a clean getaway and was home in time to tuck both children into bed, read a quick story to Maggie, and watch the early edition news cuddled up with Abigail on the couch before calling it a night himself. Together, at the foot of their bed, Abigail and Matt prayed for their children, their marriage, their home, their church, and their ministry. They thanked God for what he was doing in Clack Collins' life, and they prayed for him to have a restful night. It had truly been a good day!

CHAPTER THIRTEEN

At the suggestion of Clack's personal concierge, Blake, Matt did not visit Respira de Nuevo the rest of the week. He did, however, with help from Abigail, put together a care package that included the clothing Clack had requested, the paperwork from Sawyer Industries Eric had delivered, and a batch of homemade cookies - teacakes Abigail called them. Inside, Matt packed a simple note encouraging Clack to stay the course at the "resort" and to pray for the Lord's strength to get him through. After work on Thursday, Matt took the contents to the Ship-It-Store to package and overnight to Clack. He filled a box from the store shelf and walked toward the young girl behind the counter. Without making eye contact, she began typing into the shipping computer without saying a single word to her customer. The game was on.

Matt often took on a little challenge, or maybe it was a social experiment, with young clerks like this who could seemingly manage an entire transaction without speaking a word to the person on the other side of the cash register. He mostly did this at the big Wal-Mart, where he typically left as the victor in the matchup. Sometimes he would talk incessantly, asking trivial, sometimes silly questions just to force the young employees to talk against their will. Today, though, he would simply try to maintain the most minimal exchange and still get his parcel shipped successfully. He thought it was funny, though probably tragic on some deeper level, how some teenage and young twenty-somethings avoided any kind of engagement with adults.

Matt placed the package on the scales and pointed at the shipping label. The girl, who Matt guessed to be around seventeen, typed the information from the label into the computer and, much to Matt's delight, turned the monitor toward him and pointed at the screen for him to verify that she had entered it correctly. She had. After printing a barcode and sticky label, she adhered both to the box and then pointed back to her monitor for Matt to see how much the deal would cost. He reached for his wallet, removed his debit card, swiped it through the card reader, typed in his pin number, and received his receipt. He smiled at the clerk. She did not smile back. He returned his card to his wallet and tucked away the receipt as he turned around toward the door. The silent shipping girl took the box, added it to a stack behind her, and stopped Matt in his tracks when she said, "The tracking code is on the receipt if you want to know when it gets there." He couldn't keep up his mute exchange now. He turned quickly, flashed his dimply grin, and said, "Thank you!" She still did not return the smile, but she did say, "I've been to your church."

Matt tried to shed his guilt as he shook his head back and forth quickly and then stopped himself before looking too shocked. He had to respond now. "Really? When?"

"I dunno. Sometime last summer with my grandma."

"Who is your grandma?"

"Ethel Hughes."

Matt caught her off guard, then, when he said, "I think you were there on the first Sunday in July. We had lunch that day, right?"

"Yeah!" She was impressed; Matt could tell.

The truth, though, that only Matt knew, is that the first Sunday in July was the last time they had a covered-dish dinner at church after the morning service. If she had come to church with Ethel Hughes, then it had to have been on a day when they were eating. He wondered if she actually attended the service, or did she just show up afterwards to eat? He had to dig further.

"Did you enjoy it?"

"Not really."

"Oh? Why not?"

"I just didn't like the music," she said.

At least she didn't say she hated the sermon. Matt was relieved. He read her nametag now, and finished the encounter with a friendly salutation. "Well, Jasmine, it was nice to meet you, and I hope to see you again sometime...either in here or at church. Tell your grandmother I said hi."

For the first time, Jasmine looked like she might smile...but it was a fleeting look. Matt waited it out until she finally turned around and went back to work. He would not count this one as a win in his secret little game.

Weekends were golden for the pastor and his young family. Friday evenings in the fall, Matt often took Maggie and M.J. to the South Mill High School football game while Abigail got some time to herself. After the unusually eventful week, Abigail had big plans to do *nothing!* She picked up a Sippy Cup from the hearth in the living room, removed a half-eaten bowl of applesauce from the kitchen table, rinsed both, threw them into the dishwasher, and turned on the machine. Remembering that she had a hot bubble bath in store, she quickly released the locking latch on the dishwasher so that it was opened just enough to not run yet. If the hot water supply would not satisfy both of them, it was definitely the Maytag that was going to come up short. As she climbed the stairs toward the master suite, she knew she was being followed, and before she reached the top step, she was overtaken by eight fuzzy white feet on their way to wherever she was going. She sighed and allowed Chop and Felix to lead the way to the bedroom and their own little part of her private escape. One dog leapt onto the rocking chair in the corner of the bedroom, while the other positioned himself halfway through the doorway to the bathroom before flopping to the floor. Abigail laughed a little at the inconvenience but stepped over the pet to enter her solitude. She sang softly, a habit she had picked up while running bath water for babies, as she filled the tub, undressed, lit three aroma therapy candles, and tested the temperature of the water with her hand. Satisfied that it was warmed to her liking, she turned off the overhead lights, stepped in, sat down, and finally sank to her neck and closed her eyes. It didn't bother her that Chop or Felix, whichever one it was, was there with her. He relaxed, too, exhaling a low groaning growl, like a deep snore, as he let his chin sink deeper into the tiled bathroom floor. Both drifted off to a light evening nap.

The ballgame was one of the most exciting of the season for South Mill. It was even more exciting for Matt. M.J. took his shoes off and accidentally dropped them down underneath the bleachers. In retrieving them, Matt ran into a middle school boy and his girl-friend who had found their way down there for a heavy make-out session. "If they know who I am," Matt chuckled, "they are doubly embarrassed. Nothing like getting caught by the preacher." Maggie's teacher from school was there watching her teenage son play wide receiver, and Maggie headed up the bleachers to say hi. On her way there, she tripped and hit her nose, causing it to gush blood for most of the second quarter. At half-time, Matt, feeling badly about the busted nose, agreed to pink cotton candy at the concession stand, Maggie's first ever that he could recall. It would also be her last since they discovered right then that the red dye made her wild with energy and splotchy with hives. A doctor sitting next to the Hardy crew suggested Benadryl on the way home, the clear liquid, to both knock her out and remedy the patches of red skin the candy had triggered. Matt questioned himself, "Did I know this about Maggie?" But he refused to interrupt Abigail's evening to question or alert her about the situation. In the end, South Mill tromped their opponent, M.J. got his shoes back, and Maggie, whose skin quickly returned to its usual pale white after the drugstore stop, fell asleep on the way home in the car and would be carried to bed by her gallant father.

A light rapping sound startled Abigail out of her respite. She couldn't be sure she actually heard it, as she was pretty certain she was dreaming about someone knocking on a door. Chop or Felix, or whichever dog that was, didn't seem to notice, so she assured herself it was all in her head. Moments later, though, his ears pointed straight up and he turned his head in the direction of another sound, which was enough for Abigail to bring her therapy bath to an end. She stood up, turned on the warm shower, and began rinsing off the bubble bath before going down to welcome her troop home. As she put the whole of her body under the running shower, the water suddenly splashed cold before regulating again to a slightly less warm temperature than before. She turned down the cold handle just a bit to warm it back up and thought that Matt must have closed the dishwasher when he came in and started it running. After just a few seconds of the hot shower, Abigail stepped out of the shower, toweled off, and wrapped up in her terrycloth robe to go downstairs and resume her mom duties. Chop, the one who had been in the bathroom with her, was already gone and was standing at the front door wagging his tail as she reached the bottom of the steps. "Matt!" she called, but no one was home. She wandered into the kitchen to find that the dishwasher had, in fact, closed and started its cycle.

Maybe the dog bumped it she reasoned. It was easy to do. She had accidentally started the dishwasher multiple times by leaning back against the countertop above it reading a recipe or something that had just arrived in the mail. Maybe she had even forgotten to unlatch it before she went upstairs. While in the kitchen, she poured a glass of milk, grabbed a cookie from the pantry, and found her way to the sofa in the living room. She clicked the remote and pulled the big throw pillows close to watch the rest of a home renovation show. Both dogs, now downstairs again, got cozy on the couch beside her. She was enjoying, she decided, the comfort of big dogs to protect her little home and family. Of course she knew they were not there to stay, but perhaps it was time to get one of their own.

M.J. entered first. "Mommy! I dropped my shoes, Daddy got them back, a boy and girl were kissing, Maggie hurt her nose, but Daddy gave her medicine, and now she's asleep." Processing all she had just been told, Abigail rose to meet her husband carrying his sleeping beauty through the door. She went ahead of him to the bedroom and turned down Maggie's covers. Matt tucked the tired little girl in, they both kissed her on the cheek, and Felix took his position at the foot of her bed.

"Well, congratulations," Abigail announced. "You wore one of them out good!" Matt had to admit that he had some help from the allergy medicine and suggested they go tackle *Shoeless Joe* downstairs.

M.J. was standing at the front door when they got back downstairs. He was watching something on the street, a car. "Whatcha doin', Buddy?" Matt asked.

"Just waving at the man from church."

Abigail looked at Matt? "Did someone go to the game with y'all?"

He was quick with "No!"

"What man from church, M.J.?"

"I dunno...the old one."

M.J. was not good with names at church. He typically went skipping, running, and humming past everyone there. He knew Miss Pat, his Sunday School teacher, and Mr. Jimmy, her husband, who often attended the class just to have an excuse to miss out on his own senior adult men's group. M.J. could name the twelve disciples, every one of the neighbor's eight cats, and an assortment of tigers, kittens, owls, and princes from his favorite television show, but the church people were just not that interesting to him, so he just brushed past them on his way here and there when he was at church. He once reasoned to his parents, "everyone here knows my name, so I don't have to know theirs."

Matt closed the door and locked it, but not before looking up and down the street for signs of tail lights. He saw none. Leading Chop to his place in M.J.'s room, Abigail and Matt put the little one to bed, too. He quickly changed, brushed his teeth, jumped on Chop, who was already in the bed, in a full embrace, and kissed his parents goodnight. "Sweet dreams, M.J." Abigail said.

Matt did not go to his study but returned to the home remodeling show with Abigail. When he asked how her night off had gone, she simply said, "This house makes noises." Then she smiled at her husband and asked, "So how long do we get to keep the dogs?" He never thought he would hear his wife ask that question.

"I don't know! I guess I need to call Jenni."

Sometime around midnight, Matt and Abigail woke up on the couch, turned off the television, and climbed the stairs to their bedroom. They were both exhausted from a long, good week filled with blessings.

CHAPTER FOURTEEN

Discharged on Wednesday! That's what the charge nurse told Jenni after she went through an entire routine to verify her identity over the phone. No further information was available. Jenni was ticked but not shocked. She knew he did not have it in him to get the help he needed. She absolutely knew that deep inside that hard tank of a man there was a kinder, gentler one, but she was convinced that he was lost forever...to her and to himself...and to the world. Yet, he was going to church. That was the prickly part for her thoughts about Clack that week. Why hadn't he told her? Then again, they weren't exactly on speaking terms. He only called when he was really, really drunk, so she simply declined any call from him that had come in over the last several months. But he was going to church?

Jenni's plan kept changing, but it loosely revolved around a trip to South Mill on Saturday, go by the hospital and offer a peaceful solution about the dogs to Clack, one that involved sharing custody of them, and finally swinging by the pastor's home to retrieve Felix and Chop. But with Clack loose and on the move, those plans were now pointless.

The last three years had been horribly rough, especially after the economy collapsed in '08. The one blessing, Jenni kept telling herself, was that Clack had not killed himself. There were times when she would not have blamed him if he did. Other times, she felt guilty for thinking it would be a relief. Truthfully, though, she had expected it so frequently that she stayed angry at him in anticipation of it, pretending it would make it easier to accept when it did happen. He had been handed the world on a platter in so many ways as a youth, but the last decade had witnessed the crumbling of the mountain she had married. That's when the drinking really started, though she knew it was just the outworking of a much deeper pain and problem. When he came home from Vietnam in the '70s, he had gone through lots of counseling to get over whatever it was he endured there. He drank a lot then, but after about a year, he quit. He finished out his ten-year pilot's commitment, and the couple moved back to Cardelville, where he got busy building houses on some startup money that Jenni's dad had invested with him, finally launching his own business in the early nineties. They had enjoyed success together, investing their lives and small fortunes into Collins Homebuilders, Inc., and it was profitable, so much so that in 2001, Clack asked his college roommate, Jed, to become his partner. They had studied together in the engineering classes, and they had stayed in touch over the years. Jed was working as a civil engineer with a consulting firm out of Columbia back then, but he readily left the corporate world behind to help Clack manage the development side of a business that had the prospect of dotting the Palmetto with houses and subdivisions in a wide range of price points. Clack was riding the magic carpet of his talent and vision, and though they were working long and hard hours, Jed and Clack were having the time of their lives.

The sound of a mail truck jostled Jenni back to the present. She enjoyed drinking her morning coffee on her patio. She never called it *her* patio though. It was, after all, her parents' patio, her parents' house, and her parents' everything. Both had passed away, Jameson nearly nine years ago and Mary Ellen just five years later. As their only child, Jenni – and Clack – got everything, and she was thankful that it was free and clear of any mortgages since they had managed to lose everything else. And though it was *their* home, Jenni's name alone was on the deed and tax assessor's bills in the hopes that it could not be tied up in one of the many lawsuits in which Clack was named. Mail still arrived addressed to the late congressman and his wife sometimes, though it was arriving with less and less frequency. Jenni enjoyed seeing it come, as it made her feel like they were still there with her in some way. She wished her parents had been with her through the entire ordeal with Clack, but in other ways she was glad they never saw the disaster that he later became. Jameson, especially, passed on quite proud of his successful son-in-law, and, for that, Jenni was grateful.

Jenni strolled to the mailbox, thinking to herself that it had come a little early this morning, but then on Saturdays, she guessed, the mail carriers wanted to get done quickly and actually have a weekend. She flipped past a power bill, an advertisement from a local car dealership, and a coupon for pizza and wings at a local spot. She stopped cold, though, when she saw her name on the address line of a plain white envelope. She recognized the handwriting and suddenly became more interested in saving some money on pizza and wings. Returning to the patio, she sat and looked the envelope over. What could he possibly want to write about? There was no return address, so his whereabouts remained a mystery. She finished a cup of coffee, went inside to pour another one, threw a load of towels into the washer, and finally returned to the wicker glider outside. With a cocktail of hurt and curiosity, she slid a fingernail under the flap and sliced open the envelope. She did not want to read anything from Clack, and thankfully this was short.

Dear Jenni,

I got out of the hospital on Wednesday. I know you probably don't care. I want you to know that I know I need help - I have for a long, long time. I'm not sure how I came to arrive at the place I am staying, and though I've only been here a day, I know it is a place that can help me. You probably hoped this letter included the signed divorce papers, but I do not have them here with me. I will see what I can do about getting them delivered to me. I don't want you to think I am ignoring them. I will contact you soon, within a couple of weeks.

Love,

Clack

Jenni strangely felt nothing as she folded the letter back into the envelope. She wiped a tear that came more from her memory than her heart and resolved to contact the preacher and make plans to pick up the dogs. It was still early, though, and she knew not to call a house with small children that early on a Saturday morning. One thought lingered, though, as she began her morning routine, "If he's not in the hospital...where is he?" She was certain it was somewhere he had no business being. But it no longer was her concern.

Matt was cleaning up the breakfast dishes when the phone rang. Saturdays usually featured pancakes or waffles, and Matt was the cook! He was the first one up on most Saturdays, as he enjoyed some time to pray long before the house began to teem with the life of two children and now two pups. Recognizing the number, he gave a cheery "Good mornin'!" It was Evan Daricott, the music director at the church. Evan had absolutely no musical ability, other than a smooth, silky voice that sounded a lot like Elvis in his early days. Somehow, that and his love for music was enough to qualify him to be the music director for the church. He didn't lead the choir; the choir led him. The church loved him anyway! And Matt enjoyed his whimsical attitude and impeccable commitment. The two exchanged Saturday morning pleasantries, then Evan got down to business.

"I need some help, Preacher! The piano player is sick with the flu, and her husband just called to say she won't be at church tomorrow. What do we do?"

This was not a new problem, as Sister Sue Gibbs sometimes had to be out. No one liked the idea because she was about as good a pianist as there was in South Mill, and she could, as the church folks often said, "make that piano jump up and down." She was classically trained, but she also had a knack for Southern Gospel, and she could literally play anything written or just by ear. Rumor was she was once a pianist at a big night club in Atlanta, often leaving the piano and singing with the band, but she would neither confirm nor deny that rumor, and, since she was at church most every Sunday, most people dismissed it as false.

"Well, Evan, who can we call?"

"We usually call Doc Figgins, you know, the pharmacist... "

Matt knew him well. With two kids under the age of eight, you got to know the local pharmacist quickly. "Give him a call," Matt interjected.

"Can't! He got his finger caught in that combine harvester they use out there on his daddy's farm, and it took the end of it clean off. Says he may not ever play piano with both hands again."

Matt lamented the trials of pastoring in such a rural community. Though South Mill was, in fact, city-sized according to the census records, it was still a farming town, and there were plenty of complications that came with that distinction. If they needed a bluegrass band or a fiddle player, there would be several handfuls to choose from. Trained pianists, though, that could keep the music moving in the Sunday service of *the* Baptist church in town were rare. Doc Figgins, though he attended the Presbyterian church in the next town over, was always glad to fill in when called upon. Plenty of rumors circulated around him, too, but since he was only a substitute pianist, no one asked too many questions about why a man his age had never married, dressed better than anyone in South Mill, had a real flair for decorating, had so many friends who were women, and had so many buddies with whom he went out of town to the big city often. None of that mattered much at the Presbyterian church Doc attended, and, right now, it didn't matter at the Baptist church either since Doc had removed part of a finger. The funny part in all of that was that he was farming when he did it, something Matt couldn't imagine Doc doing.

"Evan, who are our other options?" Matt questioned.

"I've been through the list, and I ain't comin' up with nobody. Sally Ann is on a trip with marching band this weekend, Herbert can't play nothin' but chords, and Ole Vivian Nix is pushing a hundred, can't hear, and can't keep up with us singin'! I just don't know what to do, Preacher!"

"Well, you'd better learn to play the piano before tomorrow," Matt jabbed.

"Yeah, well, I'm gonna start calling around looking for someone...anyone who can play and play good. I was sort of hoping you knew some folks, too."

Matt was at a loss for a single name to come to mind. He had been in town only six months, and it was not likely that he was going to know anyone Evan hadn't thought to call. He encouraged the young director, told him to keep making calls...that someone was out there that could and would do it, and promised to search his brain for anyone he could think of. He immediately considered calling the local funeral homes; often they had musicians on standby... maybe one was free for church tomorrow.

Matt sat down at the kitchen table and thought about the music at church. He remembered the service back in July, the same service Ethel Hughes' granddaughter, Jasmine from the Ship-It-Place, had attended. She had not liked the music, and Matt remembered that he did not like it that day either. With the Fourth of July holiday so close by, Sister Sue had taken off for the beach with her husband, and Vivian Nix had filled in. No matter how fast Evan and the choir tried to take the music, Vivian had her own tempo. Slow. He remembered how they had sung "Victory in Jesus," and though the congregation had finished the song, Vivian kept playing until she, too, reached the end of the verse. With so many new visitors coming, the last thing Matt wanted was a service in which the music was subpar. In his way of thinking, bad preaching can be excused, but bad music leaves a lasting impression on people. Something had to be done to make sure tomorrow was a good day. For now, though, all he knew to do was pray that God would provide them a really good pianist.

With the kitchen clean now from the syrupy feast, the family headed out to enjoy a beautiful fall afternoon in South Mill, a jaunt to the local farmers market where Matt picked up some boiled peanuts, and a leisurely stroll down the trails along the river. M.J. threw rocks in the water. Maggie ventured out onto some larger ones to throw bread to some geese. Chop and Felix came along for the fun too. It was a banner day, and the Hardy family loved wasting a Saturday together. Abigail and the kids were more than enough for Matt to completely miss the fact that he left his cell phone at the house. On the drive back home, he looked in the usual places he might lay it in the car, and that is when he remembered his phone call with Evan and knew he had left it on the kitchen table. No worries, though. It was, after all, Saturday, and that was his day off!

They stopped by the grocery store for some ground beef and hamburger buns. Hamburgers on the grill were a favorite Saturday night dinner. Abigail immediately began pattying out the meat, while Matt looked at the three calls he had missed while absent from his phone. All three were from the same person, Jennifer Collins. "Uh oh!" Matt thought. "The dogs!"

He dismissed himself to his study to return the call, and Jennifer picked up after just one ring. She sounded chipper, friendly. Matt was glad. She shared with him how much she had enjoyed their time together Tuesday, and she hoped that they could get together again soon. She suggested that, since Clack was absent from the picture for a while, it might be best for her to come soon and retrieve the dogs and relieve his and Abigail's burden. Matt was at a loss as to what he could say to assuage her. They were her dogs, weren't they?

Matt had to ask her if she had heard from Clack, and she told him about the letter. She asked Matt if he knew where Clack was, and Matt's hesitation and stammering answered for him. He immediately wished he had not brought Clack up at all. Jenni lightened the mood, laughingly accusing him of not being very accomplished at hiding large, fuzzy dogs or large, alcoholic men. He admitted he was lousy at both. Oddly, Jenni did not inquire further about Clack's whereabouts. She seemed satisfied just knowing that Matt knew where he was.

Jenni went forward with her plans, suggesting to Matt that she drive to South Mill tomorrow, on Sunday, to pick up the dogs. She explained that she had called earlier in the day so that Matt and Abigail could break it to the kids early to avoid too much antici-pated separation anxiety at bedtime. Matt agreed to the plan, on one condition. "Come tomorrow morning for church, and let us treat you to lunch afterwards." Jenni nearly choked. Church? She had not anticipated that invitation. But perhaps it would be eye-opening to see what Clack had found intriguing enough to start attending.

"What time would I need to arrive?" Jenni took the bait.

"Worship begins at 11:00. Abigail can meet you out front, and you can sit with her and the kids."

It was what Jenni said next that almost brought Matt to tears and to his knees.

"It'll be odd sitting anywhere in church other than the piano bench. I've played almost every Sunday somewhere since I was thirteen."

Matt swallowed hard. He couldn't ask her. He just couldn't.

"Well, since you brought it up, I will go ahead and tell you that, unless something has changed since breakfast today, that seat is open tomorrow."

Jenni paused..., offered up a quick "Oh!" Then saved the day for Pastor Matt!

"Matt, I play..., you know that. I said I would come tomorrow and I will, but if you need someone to play, I would feel much less conspicuous sitting there as your guest pianist than as some *friend of the family* or, potentially, Clack Collins' estranged wife."

Matt breathed a heavy sigh into the phone and said, "you just got an upgrade on the restaurant we will take you to for lunch!"

After a few more minutes of nothing but church business, Matt arranged for Jenni to arrive by 9:00, take a few practice rounds on the ivories, meet the music director, whom she would surely need to educate a little before the service, and go over the choir selection for the morning. Though Jenni would fetch $200 easily from most of the larger churches for an hour of her service, she told Matt that lunch would be a sufficient repayment this one time. He would, he assured her, arrange for more than just lunch, and she seemed satisfied at the suggestion of a check. Knowing what he knew about the financial situation Clack and Jenni had faced, he would feel like a cheat letting her play for no compensation.

As the conversation ended, even the prospect of telling the children that their doggies would have to go home tomorrow was brightened by the holy sensation that divine intervention was taking place with Jenni and Clack, and God was letting Matt be a little part of the plan. And, besides, the music would not be terrible at church tomorrow! If Clack could be believed, Jenni might even play better than Sister Sue.

Abigail was thrilled when Matt shared the conversation with her, and she started thinking of the best place to take Jenni for lunch, somewhere upscale but affordable on a pastor's salary. Abigail always kept a close eye on the money, although they seldom ran short. She kept them on a budget and balanced the checkbook to the penny each month. She was meticulous about a lot of things, and their family finances were among those things. That reminded her of something. "Where's the bank statement? I saw it on your desk earlier in the week, but I couldn't find it this morning."

Matt looked around on his desk in his study, but he couldn't find it. He opened a side drawer and pulled it out. Seeing that it was already opened, he said, "you've already seen it."

"I didn't open it; you did."

Matt just shrugged and said, "I don't remember that, but okay." It had been a hectic week.

Matt left the study and headed out back to light the grill. Hamburgers were a good way to end a Saturday! For the first time in the day, Matt thought about Clack. *I wonder what he is having for dinner tonight?*

CHAPTER FIFTEEN

Jenni arrived promptly late at 9:07 a.m., which was earlier than Matt actually expected her. He was used to musicians running on their own time, and if Jenni was as good as Clack's stories made her out to be, she did not need to be in a hurry. Matt was waiting in the parking lot, a place he typically avoided on Sunday mornings, but it was still too early for most South Millers to arrive at church. It was a unique church, he assumed, in how the parking lot could be totally empty at 9:40 a.m., when Sunday School began at 9:45, yet by 9:50 the place was packed. These church people had a keen way of arriving right on time and not a minute too soon. The exceptions were leaders and teachers like Miss Pat, who taught M.J.'s class, who would surely be on campus by 9:15 to make sure that her crafts, lesson, and snacks were all readied for her little class of three-and-four-year-olds, as though they were the most important people in the church. And, to Miss Pat they were.

Jenni looked rested and, as Clack had described her, beautiful, more beautiful today than Matt remembered from Tuesday. She was dressed in her Sunday best. A deep green suit, with a beige ruffled-front blouse and a broach that looked antique in the place of the top button. In such fine fashion, Jenni's red hair looked luminous, and her brown eyes were smoky quartz glistening in the morning sun. She was twice his age; it was okay to look. He was staring, of course, and quickly forced himself to look away. "Welcome to South Mill Baptist Church!"

"It's lovely. Looks just like the Baptist church in Cardelville...just larger."

"Well," Matt admitted, "if you've seen one traditional Baptist church in The South, you've seen them all. Architects don't have to be very creative to please a bunch of Baptists. Just red bricks and white columns out front, with a steeple taller than any of the other churches in town..."

Together they walked through the office door, turned left and left again, making their way down a long, sloped hallway to the sanctuary. Jenni commented on how all churches have the same smell, and Matt agreed, although after some time he had stopped noticing it. As they entered the darkened sanctuary, Matt gestured toward the piano, saying, "your seat of honor, Madame!"

Just then, the lights began to flick on, one row of golden brassy chandeliers at a time, until all three rows, left, right, and center, were illuminating the burgundy-carpeted aisles and the matching pew cushions. *Traditional* was the word, and the entire building was exactly as Jenni had expected, so the only thought that came to mind was, again, *and Clack goes to this church?!* Matt, on the other hand, was startled by the sudden illumination of the room. It was Brother Heath, who had entered from the front doors of the church, as he did each week, and began turning on the lights and unlocking the doors. He was startled as Matt greeted him with a hearty "Good morning', Brother!" Heath, who was seldom at a loss for words, even if they were meaningless ramblings, stammered to return the greeting, darting his head back and forth from Pastor Matt to the emerald standing next to him. Matt, sensing his confusion, introduced the two.

"Reverend Heath, this is Jennifer Grimes. Ms. Grimes, this is the Reverend Stephen Heath, the founding pastor of the church. Ms. Grimes will be playing for our service today."

Heath, seeming ignorant for asking, questioned, "Playing what?"

"Piano."

"What? Where's Sister Sue?"

"She has the flu."

"When did you find that out?"

"Just yesterday. She was too sick to come to church today, and her husband called Evan."

Realizing quickly that this was information Heath thought he should have already been aware of, Matt continued to reveal details of the current situation. "And, did you know that Doc Figgins had lost part of his finger in a combine accident? Tragic...someone as talented as he is. Well, nevertheless, Ms. Grimes is in town visiting and agreed to play for us this morning. I'm sure you'll enjoy it."

"Yes, well, nice to have you here, Ms. Grimes. Thank you for coming." The greeting was rushed and did not sound sincere. With very little else said, Brother Stephen returned to unlocking doors and turning on lights. Every interaction with him was awkward, but the introduction that morning produced some of the strangest behavior he had witnessed from the old man.

Others entered as Jenni was adjusting the piano bench to her comfort. Many stopped and said a polite hello to both her and the pastor as they placed Bible and sweaters and the like on various pews to mark their spots and ensure that no one sat in their place before they returned from the Sunday School hour for the worship service. One woman even came in with a seat cushion, placed it on the second row on the piano side of the church and then eyeballed Jenni from a distance and then up close. Finally, Evan arrived, and Matt left Jenni in his incapable hands to prepare for the morning services.

An hour-and-a-half later, the congregation of South Mill sat mesmerized by the incomparable talent of Jennifer Grimes. No one had ever sat quietly during the preludes played by Sister Sue. Yet, even the gossip came to a halt as the old ladies entered the sanctuary to the stirrings of "Jesus What a Friend for Sinners" infused with "Two Part Invention #8 in F," by Bach. A mix of familiar with classical seemed to mystically transform the churchgoers at South Mill that day into worshippers. Then, with more flair than Sister Sue had ever mustered, Jenni transformed into a one-man-band style playing the congregational hymns and choruses. As people commented leaving the church that day, they said things like, "Wasn't she wonderful?" and "The music has never sounded so good." No one commented on how good the sermon was, though, but Pastor Matt was just as pleased as if they had.

After shaking hands at the front foyer of the church of almost everyone in attendance, Pastor Matt greeted his wife, children, and Jenni. Piling into the minivan, they rode together to lunch at Lena's, an upscale restaurant on the town square. Matt and Abigail seldom splurged like that, and they weren't used to being in the company of doctors, lawyers, and other members of the upper crust. Jenni, however, seemed right at home in such company, and complimented them on their lunchtime dining choice. They thought it was the best choice considering all they had asked of Jenni and all she had agreed to in light of the fact that, until Tuesday of the previous week, she did not know these people existed.

Matt and Abigail gushed over how beautiful the music was in the church service. Jenni received the compliments with the same grace Clack had described when detailing their first encounter, and though she did not need the plaudits of the Hardy family, it felt very comforting for someone to shower her with praise. No one but her parents and Clack had done much of that in the last thirty years, and more recently, no one had. So, she soaked it up like rain on parched ground. Lunch was adjourned for the sake of getting M.J. home for a nap, and, since Jenni's car was still at the church, she was urged to come by the house – not just to pick up the dogs – but also for a slice of pecan pie and some coffee, neither of which she could refuse. At the house, Jenni removed her jacket and broach and, surprisingly, stretched out on the oversized, comfy sofa to eat her pie, drink her coffee, and once again become lost in the tale of love gone terribly wrong.

She told Matt and Abigail about the magical weeks in San Antonio and about the heartache of uncertainty while Clack was in Nevada, although she had not known that at the time. She told about his deployment to Vietnam, and how, even in the letters home, his personality was changing. She told how, in the first year after returning, he would shake at the sound of airplanes flying too low over their house. She stared off blankly in the distance as she talked about his purchase of a pistol that he insisted stay beneath his pillow when they slept. She talked about how, after the second year home, he began to get back to being Clack again and seemed to enjoy teaching on base, but her delivery was less convincing and, though she was not meaning to, she felt as though she were somehow lying to Matt and Abigail. But she wasn't, at least not really. Clack had gone back to normal in most ways, but Jenni always felt like he closed and locked a room in his heart or his mind or something to be that way…like there was always this *something* there torturing him, but he grew skilled at keeping it at bay.

"What changed?" Abigail ventured in.

"I don't know. When his time was up, we moved back home to start a family. But we couldn't have kids; we lost two in the first trimester, and then we stopped trying. Clack always blamed Vietnam…Agent Orange, I guess. We wanted kids, but I just wanted to be happy, and honestly, Clack was enough to keep me that way. I think he felt pressure to give my parents a grandchild, and that would have been nice, but it wasn't in the cards."

"Then, we hit it big!" Jenni continued. "The economy was booming, we were building houses, and we were getting rich...at least in our opinion. His best friend went in business with him, and they started building houses all the way to the coast. I stopped keeping the books because it became too much. We had eighty or so employees at one time, and Clack and Jed were in big business. He was in the office or he was on the road every day, inspecting his job sites, and things were good I thought. They had borrowed a very large amount of money and had six subdivisions developing all at once. The payoff would be huge."

Jenni thought hard for a moment before pressing on. "Then, 2008! The market crashed. I rode with him to the bank the day he dumped an entire box of house keys onto the bank president's desk and told him that they were all his...that he was closing up and had no way to repay the debt."

Matt wanted to ask, "Is that when your marriage began to fall apart?" Abigail put it in much tamer terms and asked, "Did you take care of each other through that difficult time?"

"We lost everything...but we had my parents' house, so we didn't lose that, and it became home. Clack lost more, though! There was one house that they had held onto. It was a large one, half-a-million-dollar home, and it was under contract. When the market started tanking, they put it all in Jed's name, not in the company's portfolio, and they would have split the profit. Jed got the call that the contract had fallen through, that the buyer's financing was not going to be approved." Jenni's voice cracked and tears welled up. "Clack found Jed hanging from the deck of that house later that afternoon."

Matt and Abigail cried with Jenni. Clack had never told that story. No wonder he was so messed up. He really did need some healing.

Matt asked, "Jenni, not to major on the minors here, but what happened to that house?"

"Jed's family got it. His wife, Beth, sold it shortly after that for about a quarter of what it was worth just to be able to support herself and pay off their debts. Last I talked to her, she was moving in with her daughter, Collins – named after, well . . . you know." The tears flowed again.

"That's when he started to drink a lot," Matt finished the story.

"Yes. The only person he ever drank with when he was younger was Jed. Jed always had a bad influence on Clack, but, somehow, I always felt like it made Clack more human to be around Jed. And the two of them in business together was as perfect as a business partnership could be. They never disagreed much, and, at the end of every week, we were all still friends – no, family!"

"Clack blames himself! He didn't want Jed to take that house on in his name, but it was the only way to keep from losing it when the business was going to fail. He drank, at first, to "toast" Jed. Then he drank to numb the pain. Then I think he drank to try to forget, but the more he drank the more he remembered. Whatever darkness he locked away after Vietnam, the frustration of his distant relationship with his dad, the inability to make a family of our own, and then the loss of the only person besides me that he really, truly loved was all just too much."

"He's angry, and I can't blame him, but I can't live with him either!" Jenni began to sob as she commented on the failed union that had withstood even the crumbling of their empire.

Matt couldn't help himself; he had fallen in love with these people. He began to weep. Abigail put her coffee down on the end table and slid across the fluffy, cloud shaped pillows to Jenni. Like a mother holding her own daughter, Abigail took the older lady in her arms and held her as they both cried. Matt passed a box of tissue and retreated to his study to compose himself. He thought he heard the front door open and close and assumed Jenni had needed some fresh air. When he returned, though, he found both ladies still in an embrace, exhausted and asleep on the couch. He covered them gently with a blanket and went out the back door to pray on the porch.

"We've taken on a mountain here, God! I'm not sure we have the tools to help these people heal." Even as he prayed, he was amazed that their marriage had lasted this long and that Clack hadn't followed through with his threat last Monday. "God, they've had enough! Too much! I don't know how, but help them." And, even as he prayed, Matt couldn't help but wonder if there was any hope for either of them now. If anyone ever needed to breathe again, it was Clack Collins.

When Matt reentered the house, the sound coming from the living room was startling. Abigail was gone, and where the dignified concert pianist had been sitting was a creature clad in green, mouth wide open, sucking the paint off the ceiling as it snored. Matt's face retracted as Abigail appeared from the bathroom after cleaning up her tear-streaked mascara. Upon seeing Matt's face, Abigail had to dive back in the bathroom to stifle laughter so as not wake Jenni.

"What do we do now?" Matt asked his wife.

"I'm going upstairs to finish my nap. You try sleeping with that going on in your ear."

Matt joined his wife upstairs for a quick nap, but he set the alarm on his phone to wake him in just thirty minutes. He didn't want Jenni to be alone too long. Much to his surprise, Jenni slept those thirty minutes and then three hours more. Poor thing, he thought. She must be completely spent.

Jenni awoke to the smell of the grill, and although she blushed with embarrassment over her long nap, she felt comfortable enough with her new friends to accept their invitation to stay for dinner. Afterwards, Matt drove Jenni to her car at the church parking lot. She apologized for going on about her nightmare of a life, and Matt assured her that he and Abigail were there for her, and for Clack, to listen or talk or cook or whatever. Jenni gave Matt a quick hug and pressed the button on her remote to unlock her car. As she backed out, Matt called after her. "Wait!" I have a check to give you." She rolled down her window and thanked him for the check and for a lovely day. Matt jumped in his truck, buckled up, and threw it in gear to follow her, but Jenni didn't make the right turn off of the highway to go to Matt's house. Instead, she held her hand up out of the sunroof, waved, and continued north toward Cardelville. When Matt turned into his own driveway, he looked at his phone and saw a text message from Jenni that simply said, "Great day! See y'all soon!" He texted back, "Dogs?" His phone lit up with "Another week won't hurt!" Matt laughed and thanked God that they would have at least one more chance to talk with Jenni.

CHAPTER SIXTEEN

An inspiring Sunday church service followed by a meaningful afternoon sharing family time with their new friend gave Matt the opportunity to meet Monday morning with a new enthusiasm. He would work in the office until about 1:30 or 2:00 and then head north to pay a visit at Respira de Nuevo. He found himself both nervous and excited about seeing the condition and possible progress Clack had made.

Monday mornings in the church office were reserved for administrative tasks. He would review Sunday's attendance numbers, be informed of the receipts total from the weekly offering, and sign letters to any visitors that filled out an information card while attending on Sunday. Matt enjoyed signing them even though they were form letters that were simply filled in with different names and addresses. And, if he had met them personally during their visit, he would jot down a quick, hand-written note at the bottom of the letter – just to add that personal touch. Before he arrived in South Mill, the church had practiced what they called Monday Night Visitation, at which church members would, under the pastor's direction, gather, pray, and fan out across South Mill to visit the homes of anyone who had filled out the information cards the day before. The practice was outdated, in Matt's opinion, and quite intrusive in the opinions of many of the recipients of the infamous visits. Though Matt had tried to conduct the weekly canvassing effort his first three weeks as the pastor, he threw caution to the wind and cancelled it after week number three. The decision came when a faithful churchgoer named Judy Putnam, a woman in her late-sixties, had shown up with her husband, Grover, to join the effort at *reaching out* to Sunday's visitors. When Matt handed her their assignment, he made the mistake of describing the visitors to the Putnams. He did so in hopes they had interacted with them on Sunday. But when he mentioned that the husband was the man with "tattoos up and down both arms," Judy's body language betrayed her otherwise charitable facial expression. Matt watched from a window as she tore the tattooed man's visitor's card into pieces before getting in the car to begin their visits. No one seemed to mind forgoing the nerve-racking event, and Matt found it much less frustrating to do it himself than to watch the attitudes displayed toward the *outsiders*. So Matt signed letters, wrote personal notes, and found opportunities to interact with guests in more natural settings like baseball games, hospital waiting rooms, and PTO meetings. And, for the first time in years, church services on Sundays were beginning to feel well-attended...or crowded, depending on who you asked.

After signing letters, fielding questions from the secretaries, and answering a couple of phone calls from some kind church members complimenting the Sunday service, he pulled his Bible from his backpack and began flipping to I Corinthians to reacquaint himself with Wednesday's lesson material. He did not close his door or ask Lanie to run interference on Monday mornings because he knew people left church on Sunday saying things like, "Oh, I need to run by the church office tomorrow morning and..." He wanted to be available to anyone who thought on Sunday that they might need him for something on Monday. On that Monday morning, though, there was only one church member who needed him. Stephen Heath!

Lanie was on the phone when he walked in, but she smiled her most cordial greeting receiving no reply from the wrinkled face of Brother Heath. She had tried during one of his interim tenures to talk him into grinning more with his teeth, explaining to him that he had one of those upside-down smiles that made him look sad or mad even when he wasn't. So, she made sure she smiled a toothy grin at him each time he walked past her without making an attempt himself. Covering the receiver of the phone, she called out to him as he forged right past her desk, "Your smile's upside down again!" He did not react.

Matt used to jump to attention when Stephen entered the room, but these days he just sat back and greeted the elder churchman with a "Good morning, Brother!"

Sparing any greeting himself, Stephen barked, "Did we hire a new piano player?"

No leaky faucets? No coffee spilled on the carpet? Matt was visibly caught off guard by this morning's topic.

"Not that I know of," was the unrehearsed response. Immediately, Matt wanted to retract the words. Of course they had not hired a new church pianist, and if they had, he would most definitely know of it.

"Well, who was the redhead? She seemed awfully friendly...with that piano."

Matt immediately recounted to Stephen the conversation from yesterday morning when he had introduced the two of them.

"I think she's a little highfalutin for a church like ours, don't you?"

Matt's confusion over Brother Heath's concern in this matter was competing for space in his brain with the anger his attitude was invoking. He sat quietly for a moment, choosing his response or lack of one carefully before reclining in his chair and choosing to display casual rather than callous. Heath had yet to sit down, but he took Matt's tilt backwards as an invitation to do so. This would not be a quick fix.

"Sister Sue has the flu. Doc Figgins lost a finger. So, we needed someone."

As though he had not heard a word the pastor said, the elder preacher began his summary of the situation. "People talk to me about stuff. I don't know why they talk to me, but they do."

Matt's mind provided commentary – *they talk to you because you are always stirring them up.*

"I'm hearing that Sister Sue's feelings are really hurt that you would go looking outside somewhere for a better piano player. She was only planning to be out one Sunday, but now there's *this* gal. Don't get me wrong, the music was good, real good, and I think that's what people are telling Sue, and she's got upset over this, and there wasn't any need to upset someone who has given so much of her time to the church over the years..."

Matt recoiled, "I would never disregard Sue's contribution to this ministry."

"Well, you have! I'm sure she's insulted and embarrassed that this fancy playing gal showed her up on Sunday."

"How would she even know?" Matt had to ask.

"Well, Preacher, you know people talk!"

Matt tried to sound professional. "I can't imagine anyone talking about anything from yesterday that would have upset Sister Sue. Besides, she is sick and shouldn't be taking a bunch of phone calls. We had to have someone who could fill in, who would keep our music at a level of excellence that our people have come to expect as part of our corporate worship of God. Sue has set that standard, and, unfortunately, she couldn't be with us yesterday."

Heath seemed to be distracted by something under his fingernail and was using one on the other hand to clean it out.

Matt, though he knew he shouldn't provide evidence that he cared, finished his statement with a question, "And, who are *these people* that talk to you?"

"Now that would be a betrayal of their confidence, Preacher!" Matt could see the piety dripping from his lips.

"Let's just say," Heath continued, "that a lot of folks feel like Vivian would have done just fine. She's filled in before, and she's good enough for church, Preacher. This ain't Carnegie Hall."

There it was. Good enough for church. The attitude that had kept South Mill the way it was for years now – a small-minded gathering, like a family-run business, with survival as its main objective but little interest for impacting the community around it, much less the world, with its message of hope, joy, and love. It was the attitude shared by many of the older members of the church, many of whom were related to one another either by blood or by marriage, and most of whom kept the phone lines hot across the county on Sunday afternoons and, Matt was sure, on Monday mornings, too.

Matt, feeling like the mission was under attack, decided to defend the church that he believed South Mill could be. "Do you remember the first Sunday in July, Brother Heath?"

"Not off the top of my head, no."

"Well, a young lady I ran into last week did. She had visited the church that day. Let's just say that our music was not very good. I remember it too. But that young lady has not been back since then. Maybe if Sue had been here that day, it would have been different. Maybe if the lady who played yesterday had filled in then, the music might have been better. I'm not saying that church is all about music, but I am saying that we need to give the best we can give to those who come in here each week...so they'll keep coming back...so they'll open themselves up to the experience…so they'll listen when we tell them about Jesus. I know that's what Evan wanted when he called me Saturday for help finding someone to play on Sunday. Don't you want that, Brother Heath?"

"I've spent my whole life telling people about Jesus!" Heath fired back, indignantly.

But have they listened? Matt wanted to ask but knew better than to do so.

With that, the old man stood up to leave but not before one last innocuous question, "We did pay her, didn't we?"

Unsure of the right answer or tone Heath was hoping for from him, "Of course, we did," Matt said as matter-of-factly as he could.

As Brother Heath turned to leave the pastor's office, he offered one last quip. "Vivian would have done it for free, but I guess you get what you pay for, huh Pastor? You enjoy your day now!"

Matt could not even bring himself to say goodbye or offer the old man a blessed day. He just sat at his desk staring at the door to the outer office where Lanie was busy sealing and stamping the envelopes to mail to yesterday's visitors. He stood up, walked out to her desk, picked up the last two and licked and stamped them himself. Without saying a word, he turned and carried the entire stack of eight with heavy hands to the mailbox at the street, placed them inside, raised the flag, and closed the door on the box. As he trudged back to the office with no lighter of a load, he prayed out loud, "Lord, what's the old man up to?" He neither expected nor heard an answer.

Once back in the office, Matt tried to focus on his lesson plan and sermon preparation. He found neither enough to distract him from the morning's encounter. It gnawed at him, and, though it was against his better judgment, he finally picked up the phone and dialed Sister Sue's number. She answered after three rings, and he thought she sounded awfully weak. He intended to do most of the talking.

"I hope you're feeling better."

"Some better, I guess."

"Well, I don't want to keep you, but I did want to check in on you. We sure did miss you in church yesterday. It just isn't the same without you here. Turns out pianists like you are hard to come by."

"Well, I don't know about that," she feigned humility.

"I had to go all the way to Cardelville to find someone to fill in that could even compare to your ability." In truth, Jenni was much better than Sue, but Matt was trying to be diplomatic. "And it cost me a lunch at Lena's just to get her to come." Again, not exactly the verbatim definition of truth.

"Well, Pastor, I'm sorry to be out, I really am. I'm hopin' I'm on the mend and can be back next Sunday...if you'll have me."

"Well, why wouldn't we? You're the best!"

"You're sweet! South Mill is blessed that you're our minister."

Cautious but curious, Matt waded in deeper. "I hope you're not upset that we hired someone to fill in yesterday. That's all it was...filling in."

Sue, mustering some pep for the moment, decided to set the record straight. "Pastor, musicians, as you probably know, are sensitive folks. We are prideful and usually flamboyant. Just look at Doc Figgins! I've played the piano in church and I've played in...well, other places...but that's another story. I'm getting older, and with age has come some humbling. What I do in church each Sunday is my service to y'all and to God."

Matt prepared for a scolding, but Sister Sue had a surprise for him.

"I play because you need me, Matt! You're good for this church and this community. But you and I both know that good preachin' isn't worth much without good music, and I hope that I am able to add something to the services. So, let me clear something up for you, 'cause I have a pretty good idea of why you're calling, not that you aren't truly concerned about my health."

Matt braced himself. "Okay."

"My feelings are NOT hurt! I do NOT think you are trying to replace me, and, if you are, that's fine, too! Like I said, I only want to be there if I can fill a need. I got a phone call from a meddlesome woman yesterday afternoon asking if I knew what you were up to with this new woman playing the piano. I said I had not heard from you, which was true, but she insisted on telling me how fancy the woman was dressed, how professional she looked, and how lively the music seemed with her playing. I told her how I wished I could have been there to hear her play, which was true...I love to hear other musicians, and then I told her that our conversation was making me feel worse and I that I was going to have to go. The minute you called me, I knew that she had put her own wicked spin on those words of mine, and shame on her! But I love our church and I love you, Pastor, so don't you think for a minute that I'm upset with you at all. In fact, I would love to have that woman's number so I can call her myself from time to time and ask her to fill in. That would take the burden off of you and Evan, and it would allow me to travel more with my husband and grandkids. Plus, I hear she's quite a looker, and, while I'm not telling you who called me yesterday, I'll tell you that I'm betting there's an old preacher that got in trouble for looking a little too long toward the piano bench yesterday morning."

Sue continued, "So, you just rest easy. I am not upset at all. I do, however, have the flu, and I would like to go lie down now. But I will let you know earlier this week if I can't be there next Sunday. Okay?"

Matt chuckled. "Okay, Sister Sue! Thank you! And, I am so glad you told me what you did. Get better soon! We really did miss you yesterday."

"One last thing," Sue interjected, "If you really want to hurt my feelings...just ask Ole Vivian to fill in! She is not a big fan of mine, and if that's all it takes to cover for me when I'm out, then I really do overestimate my contribution!"

They both laughed, Matt assured her he would not, and they said a peaceful, friendly goodbye. As he hung up the phone, Matt wondered again what the old man was up to. Surely this was more than just Dorothy being upset that Stephen noticed a beautiful woman playing the piano. Then again, Dorothy was a force.

That phone call alone freed Matt's spirit to work on what mattered, his sermon. He dug in and spent the better part of three hours studying scripture, commentaries, and what he could find online about St. Paul's epistle to the Corinthians. When he realized it was a quarter 'til two, he went out of isolation to chat with Lanie. There were no phone calls to return, no one clamoring for a face-to-face with him. Weekly clerical work was going well, and the waters were smooth sailing it seemed. Matt was pleased and said he was going out to make some visits and would be gone the rest of the day. Lanie pleasantly smiled and said she would see him in the morning and that she would call him if there were any urgent needs while he was out. He thanked her, returned to his desk, packed his laptop and Bible, and left for the day.

In the truck, he dialed Abigail and reminded her he'd be home late for dinner. She remembered and had just checked out at the store and was packing the groceries into the trunk of the car before going to pick up Maggie from school. She told him to tell Clack that she said hello. Though she had never met him, she felt particularly familiar with and fond of him. Matt assured her that she would meet the man soon enough, one way or another. Before getting off the phone, Matt did share with his wife that he'd had quite an unpleasant morning with Brother Heath. Abigail then shared with Matt that she had passed Dorothy Heath in the grocery store and that the old woman brushed right past her without even speaking to her or to M.J.

"Well, what did you do?" Matt had to know.

"Nothing! I didn't care. Besides, M.J. handled it."

Matt cringed! "Ohhhh noooo! What did he do?"

Abigail laughed her way through the explanation. "He wanted a bag of gummy worms, so I let him open them to have just two while we were in the store. I don't know what got into him, but he wanted to share with people, and he was passing them out to people left and right. People thought it was cute, so I didn't say anything to stop him, but when Dorothy passed by without so much as a hello, he threw one at her." Abigail began to snicker.

"What did she do?"

"I don't know! I don't think she ever even felt it." Abigail snorted as she finished, "When we left the aisle we met her on, the poor gummy worm was still hanging onto her butt! I guess gummy worms cling to cheap polyester."

Matt laughed hysterically, even though he felt guilty for doing so. But it was funny, and Dorothy Heath's backside would definitely have provided quite a landing pad for an airborne worm. They ended the conversation with chuckling *I love yous* and *goodbyes* and each went on about the business of the rest of their day. Matt smiled all the way to the county line...a little humor helped ease the pain of the morning.

CHAPTER SEVENTEEN

Matt arrived at Respira de Nuevo at 3:30. Walking through the large front French doors into the reception area, Matt was immediately greeted by a smile from Vera, the receptionist, who was looking over some paperwork with Matt's professor, Dr. Norman. Chuck turned around on the cue of Vera's smile and said, rather loudly, "Matt, thank God you're here! Maybe you can help talk Clack down off the roof!"

Matt gasped and choked on the air. Vera laughed politely and somewhat ashamedly as Chuck continued. "Yeah, he's been up there all day fixing gutters and resealing dormer windows!" Matt caught his breath and pointed a finger, bit his bottom lip, and shook his head at Chuck!

"You can't make jokes like that in a place like this!" Matt said as he began to smile. "And, Vera, I thought you were so sweet. I guess I misjudged you." Vera's smile broadened as she turned around to her computer and got back to work.

After exchanging pleasantries with Matt, Chuck led Matt toward the building where Clack had busied himself. "You should send us more skilled contractors as clients, Matt. We'd have this place looking like new in no time."

Matt looked around trying hard to observe anything that needed repair. But, when your buildings are mostly original nineteenth century architecture, there probably would be a lot of upkeep he thought. "How's he doing? I mean, other than on the construction projects, how's he doing?"

Chuck smiled the smile of someone who was not going to reveal much, and Matt appreciated that. "He's peaceful. He may have a lot to tell you...or he may not. I don't think he regrets coming here. I do think he'll be extremely glad to see you."

Without announcing his arrival, Chuck motioned in the direction of an extension ladder leaning up against a converted carriage house. "This is our chapel, and Clack seems particularly fond of it for some reason. Unfortunately, it is also the building in the most need of repair."

"That could be why he likes it so much," Matt said as he placed his left foot onto the bottom rung of the ladder.

At the top, Matt pondered whether he should just surprise Clack or announce his arrival. After all, he'd hate to startle a man on a roof who thought he was up there alone. So, stepping off onto the roof, he called to Clack, "Need any help?"

Without even looking his way, Clack accepted an offer that was given in jest and said, "Here, Matt, hold this glass while I caulk around it." Matt had to lie down on the roof to do what was asked of him, placing one hand underneath the window and reaching inside the dormer. He held one hand on the inside of the pane of glass and another on the outside while Clack worked and talked. On the roof, both men worked at keeping the conversation light, discussing things like brands of tools, the best gutters to use on an old roof, and how South Carolina had beaten Tennessee on the road last weekend in football. Clack said he had watched the game in the rec building with a Tennessee fan who took the loss way too personally. The staff here made tailgating food and, by the time the game was over, Clack and the Tennessee fan were the only ones still watching and eating. "And I thought I could take off a few pounds here," Clack joked.

When the last window was sealed, Clack invited the preacher down off of the roof with him to get ready for dinner. "They serve us really early, 5:00, kinda like an old folks' home. But there is a snack bar open late, and they bring room service when you ask for it, which, by the way, I haven't done, since I'm not sure how this is all getting paid for." Matt had every intention of staying for dinner, and he would simply snack on whatever Abigail had fixed when he got home later.

"Order the room service, whatever you want, Clack. I don't think they'll be sending you a bill."

Clack opened the door to his studio apartment and invited Matt in to sit while he got ready. Matt found his way to the only seat in the room other than two chairs at the breakfast table and a swivel-back, rolling chair tucked underneath a desk. It was a leather recliner made for a body much larger than his, but he enjoyed the way he became swallowed up by it. He pulled out his phone and tried to check for messages before remembering that there was no cell service way up there. Clack emerged after about five minutes, all showered and appearing as a cleaner version of himself. He whipped the desk chair around and sat in it, leaning backwards as it seemed to naturally find its way to a reclining position. Matt had to sit up and give up his reclining position to be able to see Clack as they talked. Once Clack was adjusted and comfortable in the desk chair, Matt asked the simplest of questions he could. "How's it going?"

The question, though cliché, sounded sincere coming from Matt, and Clack was looking forward to spending time with him. The conversation began barely deeper than the rooftop chat. Clack asked about the dogs. Matt told him how they were still there with his family – that Jenni had not taken them yet. Clack asked about work, and though Matt had no real update, he told him that Eric had shared with him Sunday that everyone at work just wants Clack to be well and get back soon. Clack interpreted the news as still having a job when he got out of rehab. But, as time passed, both men found their way into deeper water, each continually monitoring the other's face to determine the depth and consequential peril of continuing on that course. Matt asked Clack about the *program*, and Clack admitted that it only felt like rehab here and there, that most of the time it felt like he was in some kind of summer camp for grown people.

"I sat on the porch drinking my coffee this morning, looking out over the water, and I kept trying to convince myself that I wasn't just wasting time. I've always been busy – had a job. Here, I just...I don't know...I just feel. And I don't think I like that, so I find little things to do to keep me busy. Like fix the gutters and windows. If I don't get out of here soon, I may remodel the entire place. But I think that I think better...or feel things better when I am doing something with my hands. I can't just sit around thinking."

"I understand," Matt chimed in. "Your career and my career are so different. Just listening to you, I realize that I think and feel for a living. At the end of the day, I don't have a project that I can look at and say *that's what I accomplished today.*"

Then, smiling, he continued, "It would be rewarding, I think, if every day I could look up at a dormer window and say, 'Well, today I held that pane of glass right there in place.'"

Both men laughed. Clack became the counselor for a moment, offering some encouragement to the preacher. "You took on a pretty big project last week. And, even if it isn't done yet, you got a stubborn ass to get the help that he needed. I think that's something you should be able to look at and say *I did that.*"

"I know. I just think that if I built a house or landscaped a yard or performed open-heart surgery, it would be sort of satisfying to be able to look at the finished product."

Without meaning to say the next part out loud, Matt concluded, "But, I'm sure some church member would come along and tell me everything that was wrong with whatever I thought I had accomplished."

"Well, when I get out of here, you and I will find us a project, and we won't even tell anyone about it. We'll just do it, and when it is done, we'll sit back and look at it and congratulate each other. Even if it isn't perfect."

Matt liked the idea and gave a contemplative nod of his head at the prospect of it. "Sounds good!"

In this tranquil sea, Clack ventured onward. "You heard from Jenni? I wrote her a letter."

Matt nodded, this time with definitiveness. "I did."

"Did you tell her where I was?"

"To be honest, she didn't ask. She seemed satisfied that I knew where you were. In fact, I'm pretty sure that's what she said."

"So, she doesn't give damn?"

"I wouldn't say that. I would not say that at all. I think she very much does care, but she seems to be satisfied not knowing exactly where you are. Maybe she is trying to stay positive."

"Or safe," Clack decided. "If she doesn't communicate with me...see me, I can't hurt her. Maybe that's what she thinks."

"I think you're giving her too much credit for thinking this through," Matt said. "I think she is, very much like you, just feeling her way along right now. Maybe she's just tired of having to feel for herself and for you too."

Clack almost winced. That stung. But it made good sense. Clack thought that would be something to process on the porch later in the darkness, alone. Right now, it was time to eat.

Clack and Matt walked together to the dining room where most of the other residents were gathered, some sitting alone and others grouped up around larger tables. A small buffet was steaming to their left, and each decorated a plain white plate with mashed potatoes, a medley of steamed zucchini and yellow squash, and a homemade yeast roll (Matt took two), before ending up at a carving station where the chef offered London Broil or roasted turkey breast. It was too close to Thanksgiving for either to choose turkey. "Looks delicious," Matt said to the chef, who took the compliment with a huge smile.

"You should have been here Saturday," Clack joined. "This guy fixed the best ribeye steak I've ever sank my teeth into."

Through a toothy grin, the chef advertised his product. "Just wait 'til you taste the shrimp and grits this Friday!"

"I may never leave!"

Sitting down with two other residents at the luxurious facility, Clack introduced each man to Matt. But it was Clack's introduction of Matt that touched the young pastor's heart. Everywhere he went, he was introduced as *my pastor* or *our minister* or *Reverend* or some other respectful but ascetic title. When Clack presented Matt to the guys that night, he said, without hesitation, "Fellas, this is my *friend* Matt." And because Clack was always himself, never looking to impress anyone, Matt knew that he did not choose the word *friend* because he was embarrassed to be affiliated with a *man of the cloth*, but because that was the predominant relationship in which Clack found himself with Matt. A true friendship.

Clack walked Matt to the French doors, doors that were not locked, not guarded. Clack could leave anytime he wished, and no one would chase him, strap him down, or force him to return to his room. He could just as easily continue to the parking lot with Matt and collapse himself into the little S-10 truck and go back home. But the thought never crossed his mind. He was actually anxious to get back to the porch overlooking the river so he could think about his feelings and process his thoughts from his formal sessions earlier in the day and his friendly one with Matt that evening. They agreed that Matt would come again next Monday, if not before. Friday's shrimp and grits were tempting.

As Matt took the first step off of the porch, he whirled around and hollered toward the closing door, "Oh, I forgot! Abigail said to tell you hi!"

Clack jerked the door back open and smiled, "I can't wait to meet her."

On the drive home, before hitting good cell reception, Matt had time to think about the weird connection he was forging with this alcoholic. They were friends. That meant so much to Matt, and he had to process why that distinction felt so good. Why did it mean more than being his pastor? And why didn't Clack introduce him as such? Matt remembered the first time he donned a clerical robe, black with satin panels extending from around the neck to the floor with a white stole adorned with gold-stitched crosses near his knees. He felt so important, so "holy." Now, though he was still young and inexperienced, he had gained enough wisdom to accept the fact that *Pastor* was just a job title. And don't even get me started on *Brother*, he thought. Could anything sound more self-righteously fake? He felt certain that somewhere the title was used in sincerity where people really thought of one another like that. He thought he remembered somewhere in the Bible, maybe in the Gospel of Matthew, that Jesus had told his disciples not to use titles like "Rabbi," because they were all just brothers. Friendship, in Matt's opinion, was beyond the vocation. And though he must stay faithful to his sacred duty to God in Clack's life, the intimacy was...holy, wasn't it? Whatever it was, Matt concluded, it was more real than any he had with the members of South Mill Church, with the exception of, perhaps, Miss Mabel.

CHAPTER EIGHTEEN

Clack returned to the table to sip coffee and swap stories with the doctor and professor. All three were married, and all three marriages were on the rocks. The doctor blamed long hours and late-night drinks that led him into the arms of a lonely nurse for his marriage troubles. The professor used a failed attempt at publishing last year as his excuse for his latest bout with the bottle, but it sounded as if his marriage crashed long before his book deal. Three otherwise successful men sat victim to one common enemy, and each was there because he was tired of losing the battle. Clack marveled at how each, resourceful and intelligent, productive and living a financially comfortable life at some point in the past, had fallen prey to a chemical that removed all dignity associated with their own successes. At the same time, he found some solace in the fact that he was in the company of others who had failed. Then, as though waking from a dream, Clack was keenly aware of the truth – he was not like these two. They had never gone through the hell that he had. If he had lived either of their lives, he would not be sitting there right then. How could they even understand why he drank? He didn't even understand, but he understood he was done with these two for the night. Waiting for a pause in the conversation, Clack politely excused himself and thanked them for sharing the table. No matter what was troubling Clack, he had learned the art of a cordial exit. After all, he was married to a congressman's daughter. He scoffed at the thought, realizing that his relationship with Jenni was the one departure that he had not managed with any degree of gracefulness at all.

That thought carried him to the resident building where his suite and the one next to it, which was unoccupied at the time, shared a beautiful back porch overlooking a narrow river fork that Clack assumed must be a tributary of the Catawba River. He lit a cigarette and retired to the comfortable motion of a rocking chair underneath a ceiling fan humming a broken rhythm on low speed. There was no need for the fan, really, as it was quite cool for a November night in the Palmetto region. Pine trees towered above him, but with most of the leaves now off of the Dogwoods underneath, he had a clear view of the moonlight flickering on the water as it danced across small rocks and cascaded on toward the lake below. Something about the air...the breeze...the water reminded him of Wilmington. He seldom thought of home, but for a moment he reminisced about how this time of year, in another lifetime of course, ushered in basketball season and how, once upon a time and in a land far away, he'd be leaving a gym about now, walking and talking with his buddies. They'd prop up on the trunk of a car, hang out in the parking lot talking about a couple of cheerleaders or a teacher they all despised until, finally, the coach, wanting to get home himself, would yell for them to leave. He'd drive home just in time for dinner with the family before starting his homework so he could keep his grades up and get into a good school where he could continue to play the game. He questioned his decision to leave basketball behind that freshman year at college. Maybe life would have been better. Maybe he wouldn't be an alcoholic now. Maybe he wouldn't be sitting in a rehab facility smoking a cigarette alone on a back porch. Maybe he wouldn't be in the middle of a divorce that he hated. Maybe he would have never married Jenni. The thought struck a nerve. *I would have never even met Jenni.* No, the military decision was a wise choice; it was just every decision since then that seemed to be wrong. The last thought he had before dozing in the rocker was that Jenni's life would have been better if he had stuck with basketball.

Matt could not get home without driving past the home of the Reverend Stephen Heath, a house not visible from the road, as it sat nestled in a thicket of pine trees flanked by overgrown azaleas. The landscape played host to the church's annual Easter Egg hunt, a tradition the older children endured while they waited for their own colossal game of hide-n-seek. In addition to the overgrown azaleas, there were shrubs and magnolia trees whose arms drooped low to the ground, fortress after fortress of secluded spots in which to take cover while waiting for the one counting to commence the search. It was a nice piece of land, which Stephen and Dorothy had acquired cheaply thirty years ago, the asking price reduced because of how close it sat to a loud, though seldom used train track. The only thing that separated it from the Heaths' home was about 200 yards of city green space behind a row of thick cedar trees that Stephen had planted to serve as a buffer. The old man told Matt on his first visit there that since planting those trees they hardly even noticed or heard the train when it did pass by. Matt was sure that was just pride talking.

It was almost 8:00 when Matt cruised into South Mill, and he did not look toward the Heaths' house as he rushed home to see his children before they were tucked in for the night. He was still angry at both Dorothy and Stephen for their morning escapades, and he'd not dignify them with even an interested glance in their direction. He slammed on brakes hard, though, when Hugh Briner pulled out of the Heaths' driveway without even looking to see what was coming from either direction. The silhouette of Wanda's head bobbed to one side and then the other as they bounded onto the road and straightened out into one lane just ahead of Matt. The Briners could not reach their home without passing by the parsonage, and Matt ran right up on their bumper when they slowed to a snail's pace and swiveled their heads around to take in anything that might be of interest at his place. He turned on his blinker, coasted into the driveway, and marveled at how fast Hugh accelerated to get out of sight. Nosy old farts, Matt thought to himself.

M.J. heard the car outside and met his dad at the door in a towel. Bath time was over, and he was about to put on his pajamas and go to sleep. He seldom had a day when he did not see Matt at all, and he was giddy to greet him with a huge hug and kiss at the door. Just as quickly, he ran back up the steps, grabbed the neck of one of the beasts that had taken up residence in his house, and finished getting ready for bed. In the mind of a four-year-old, the world was safe with Daddy home. Maggie was tucked in already, but she was still awake for a goodnight kiss and prayers with her parents. Matt kept it brief so as not to disrupt the orderly schedule that Abigail kept during the week. He tucked Maggie back in, kissed her once more, and then, because she insisted, he kissed Chop. But not on the mouth. He did not believe that a dog's mouth is cleaner than a human's, and he was not putting his lips anywhere near that long black snout. A similar routine in M.J.'s room, and he was headed downstairs to unwind. A dinner plate was still warm in the oven, and he nibbled on it while turning on the television and waiting on Abigail to join him for a debriefing of the day.

Clack awoke to a nightmare on the back porch. A scream? Was it real, someone in trouble? Did he dream it? Maybe it was a peacock he had seen on the farm that neighbored Respira. He had heard them scream before, and they sounded eerily human sometimes. Or was it him screaming? A nightmare he could not remember? He looked at his watch. It was still early, just ten after nine; he had not slept long. So, he composed himself and, quite deliberately, thought about what Matt had said about Jenni being tired of feeling for both her and for him. That was why he had ventured out onto the porch in the first place, to process that thought. He would create a new nightmare, but he was wide awake for it now.

Clack lost himself in endless questions and rambling thoughts for more than an hour all centered on the theme of Jenni's feelings. How did Jenni feel? *Well, she feels mad at me. And, I guess she's sad that she's getting a divorce – or maybe not. She was sad when her dad died. And she was even sadder when her mom died. That's how she felt. Why would she need to feel mine? Dig deeper, Clack!*

The truth was, and Clack knew it, that he did not want to delve into the tragedies of their lives. If anything could push him right back over the edge, those things could. He had to be careful. He thought out loud, "This place is pretty safe." And with that, Clack gave himself permission to wander into what, in many ways for him, had been the unknown.

First, he thought about what Jenni must have felt when he would rather caress a pistol than to touch her in their bed. *She wasn't there. She doesn't know. I wasn't crazy; I was scared. I had not slept a peaceful night in two years, and I certainly had not slept without a weapon. Vietnam may have been over, but do those of us who were there ever get over Vietnam?* That was enough on that line of recollection. It did not require him to relive his days deployed to deal with his adjustment to life back in the States. Two different worlds. That was how he had categorized it back then, and that was how he would leave it. Jenni had nothing to do with that other world, and he was out here on a porch to think about her world.

He knew how she felt when the business was booming – elated! *We had friends over for dinner. We went out every weekend with this couple or that client. Saturdays were spent on the boat. Sundays were spent in bed. ALONE! A new thought. Jenni was at church...playing the piano. I was alone in bed on Sundays. Jenni was alone! We didn't need that extra money then. Why was she going to church to play piano? Did it mean something more to her?*

The idea of Jenni alone generated another painful episode. Jenni had been alone when she lost the babies. On both occasions, Clack was delayed. The first time she began spotting while he was at a builder's convention in Atlanta. He drove back as fast as he could, but she was already crippled by the news. The second time, he got stuck in construction traffic in Florence, where he had gone to check on a development they were building. He had left in plenty of time to meet her at the doctor. It was just a regular checkup, but there was no heartbeat. He got there to see her doubled over the steering wheel in the station wagon they had bought when they got pregnant the first time...a wagon built to haul a family around. He held her. He put her in his truck. He took her to her parents' house. He watched over her. She cried. He clinched his jaws tightly and wrestled the knot in his gut into submission. She went to sleep, and he slipped out quietly to a bar.

Clack continued to jog his memory. He remembered the company Christmas party he could not miss, the one he had forbidden Jenni from missing. He was so angry that she was not there. He had wanted her there to celebrate what they had built, what the company had become, but she insisted she be in Edisto, at the beach house, where her dad had asked to be taken when he could hardly catch a breath anymore. Clack was sleeping off the hangover from the Christmas party when Jenni called to tell him her father had died that morning. He said, quite simply, "Well, you made the right choice to go be with him last night."

He remembered that he *was* there when Mary Ellen passed away. She had a massive heart attack on the Fourth of July, just before they took the boat out on the lake for the holiday. Clack did CPR while Jenni called the paramedics, and they were all with her in the cardiac care unit room when she died. And he was there at the Grimes' home for three days following. He greeted guests, received dishes prepared by ladies from the garden club and the Methodist church, and entertained the men who tagged along with their wives to pay respects to a truly great lady. But as hard as Clack tried, he could not picture Jennifer in any of those memories surrounding her mother's passing. He knew she was there, and he knew he was there. But had he been with her?

Then, the market crash. Clack remembered losing tens of thousands of dollars a day. He also remembered Jenni having a home-cooked meal ready every night and the table set. And he thought of all of the times he would walk past that set table, fix a plate of food, and disappear into his office to crunch numbers and try to figure out how to make it when all indicators clearly proclaimed it was over. When the math made him angry, he would knock back whatever liquor he had on hand, and then head to bed long after Jenni fell asleep each night, foolishly thinking he was sheltering her from the storm they were living. Even now, Clack knew that Jenni felt the avalanche, and those dinners were her way of trying to cushion the blows. She had sunk most of her inheritance into the company, yet Clack had acted like the struggle was his alone.

The next stop on this remembrance road was not one Clack wanted to make, and he would not linger long. Jed had been there at their first college date. As inappropriate (and funny even now) as it may have been, Jed had toasted their marriage. And Jed had named his own daughters after the two people that would love them as much as he and Beth did – two people who would have none of their own. The oldest girl was Collins, and her younger sister was named Jennifer.

The tsunami of emotion engulfed Clack, and he fought to breathe the truth of the revelation. *A crazy man came home from Nam in the place of the man she married, and she had to pretend everything was normal. She didn't go to church every Sunday just to play the piano. She went to pray for me. The babies Jenni lost were my babies, too, and she had to cry enough tears for two parents. The best daddy I've ever known wanted us by his side when he left this world, and Jenni had to face it without me. The grandest lady to grace the state left her one daughter without much warning, and she grieved alone while I played party host. Jenni watched her investment in both a company and a marriage get tanked, one by the economy and the other by hard liquor. And when my friend died, Jenni didn't just lose Jed, she lost most of me, too.* And what had been more of a passing thought when Matt spoke the words became the key to the vault of Clack's heart. *Of course Jenni is tired of trying to feel for her and for me, too. I've shared none of that with her the way I should have. Even at the hospital room last week, I made light of our anniversary, like I was the victim. And now it's all too late.*

The reality of the last thought and the certainty that it was his own damn fault infuriated Clack. He leapt to his feet, grasped the railing of the back porch, looked up through the pines at a cloud veiled moon and almost screamed at God for making him so stupid that he could not have seen any of this earlier. Instead, he just screamed into the darkness and whirled around and grabbed the arms of the rocking chair and hurled it off the porch into the darkness of the wooded river bank below. Clack fell onto the pine boards beneath his feet and lay there sobbing for what seemed like an eternity. Then, recognizing his own need for rest, less the emotions take him beyond his threshold completely, he dragged himself to the door that led inside to his apartment. He stripped to his boxers and let his clothes crumple into a pile at his feet. Then he sank into the sheets of his bed and clutched a pillow and, once the tears permitted, he slept.

By six the next morning, Clack was awake and looking in a mirror. He showed the signs of a rough night but felt none of the headache and nausea that rough nights usually used to tell him *good morning*. His mind was clear, but some things from last night were not. He remembered having a nightmare. *Was the whole thing a nightmare?* He pulled back the curtain hoping to see a rocking chair, and he did. He pulled a t-shirt over his head and staggered out onto the porch still in his boxer shorts. He held the rail to steady himself, more out of habit than need, as he faced a new situation to which he was unsure how to react. He was studying it hard when Blake, his "concierge" came from a side corridor and sidled up beside him. Clack looked at him with the wide eyes of pure confusion.

Blake spoke first, slowly, pausing between words. "Not to try to tell you how to remodel or anything, but that's an odd place for a rocking chair, don't you think?"

Clack looked out toward the trees again but still did not speak.

Blake forged on, seemingly unbothered by what he saw but speaking in breathy, hushed tones like he was admiring a work of art. "It's just sort of hanging there, like a great big Christmas ornament."

Clack smiled then exhaled one breath of surprise in the form of a laugh. "I don't know what to say…"

In Clack's fit from the night before, he had not thrown the rocking chair to a splintery destruction but had somehow flung it so that the top crest rail had lodged on a protruding branch of a pine tree. Like a peg on a coat rack, what was left of a tree limb had been wedged right between two of the back center slats, and there it hung.

"…I owe you a rocking chair."

"Why?" Blake offered sarcastically. "There's nothing wrong with that one. It looks quite nice hanging up there on display. Like a front porch at a Cracker Barrel!"

"I'll get it down," Clack insisted, "but I'm not sure how at the moment."

Both men smiled, and Blake dismissed Clack saying, "I'll see you at breakfast."

Clack nodded and stepped toward the door to his place but stopped Blake with his words just before he disappeared through the access door. "I think I had a breakthrough last night."

The omniscience of Blake's smile was reassuring. "I assumed you broke something. Let's talk after breakfast."

Clack retreated to his room, gathered his crumpled clothes from the floor beside his bed, placed them gently in the hamper, and began his morning routine of shaving, showering, and preparing himself for a productive day. His plan had been to paint his project from yesterday. That would take a backseat to a little tree climbing expedition. He hiked up the wooded path to the mansion and entered the dining room door. The coffee was hot, and Clack needed his morning jolt.

CHAPTER NINETEEN

Tuesday morning was quiet and without interruption in the church office. Matt heard the door open several times, assuming with each instance that it was Brother Heath coming in for one of his morning meetings about something Matt had done wrong. Not everyone who came and went from the church office during the week did so to see the pastor, but curiosity and a growing bit of paranoia made Matt venture out to ask Lanie who all had come and gone. Without reacting to his nosiness, Lanie noticed, shrugged, and said, "Maybe he said all he needed to say when he came in yesterday." Matt smiled back at her, but, since there had seldom been a day without a call or visit from Brother Heath, he had to wonder what the old man was up to.

Matt packed his Bible in his waistband and left the office an hour early for lunch. He had one hospital visit to make, and then he was meeting Abigail and M.J. for lunch. David Adams, a quiet and faithful church member, was having a kidney stone blasted and removed, and Matt had assured him Sunday that he would come by and check on him. The whole ordeal had been revealed to Matt in somewhat of a humorous way. On Sunday morning, David, who often said no more than *good morning* to anyone at church each week but never missed a day of Sunday School, worship, or Wednesday night prayer meeting, exited the church service through the front doors of the church (which he never did) amidst the typical crowd of hand shakers and chatty churchgoers. He lingered in the foyer, awkwardly, like a shy kid at the school dance, keeping his head and eyes downward, sometimes leaning on a wall or furniture until it was just Matt left behind after thanking the last flatterer for his compliments on the service. David, after looking in every direction to make sure they were alone, began his confession to his pastor. "Preacher, your wife was at the grocery store the other day when I was there, and... " his nerves stalling his speech, "I'm normally a teetotaler, but these kidney stones have about killed me, and..." Matt tightened his grip on David's hand and placed the other on his shoulder. David elaborated, "...the doctor told me to drink beer to try to flush it out. I knew I should have shopped at the grocery store across town, but I just never dreamed I run into anyone I knew that early in the day. I'm a good Baptist, Preacher, and I'm so sorry your wife and boy had to see me with that beer in my shopping cart."

Matt stifled laughter, and consoled the penitent parishioner. "David, I'll explain all of this to Abigail as soon as I get home today. I'm sure she didn't think anything of it." And that was true. Abigail probably did not even know who David was, and, if she had seen him with beer, she would have never have even questioned his motives. Though Southern Baptists were known for their strong stance against imbibery, most, if not all, that Matt and Abigail knew were known to drink occasionally at least socially. Poor David, though, was not one to do so, and, though his conscience was hurting, his kidneys were hurting worse. "Neither I nor my wife nor God are going to judge you on this one, David!" Matt assured him. David nodded quickly and quietly and began to leave as awkwardly as he had arrived. "But," Matt called behind him, "I gotta know. Did it work?"

"I passed one," David bragged. "But they're gonna blast the other one at the hospital Tuesday morning. I may be in there a day or two. Don't know yet."

Matt assured him he would be checking in on him and that, though he might end up on the prayer concerns list for his procedure, his other secret would be safe within the walls of the Hardy home. David smiled and let the door close behind him.

On Matt's short drive to the hospital, he looked at his cell phone twice, each time expecting there to be a text message or a voicemail from Lanie that he had missed a visitor. As much as he hated having to "visit" with Brother Stephen every day, the fact that the old man did not show up that morning was even more unnerving. In one sense, it prolonged the dread and multiplied it as the day went on. At the same time, it caused Matt to question what Heath might be out doing to further complicate the work of pastoring the South Mill Baptist Church in the wake of the old mainstay. Oh, well, Matt reasoned with himself. No news is good news. Right?

All three parking spots marked "CLERGY" were vacant as Matt cut the engine and cruised into the closest one. It would not be uncommon to see Stephen Heath's car parked in one of them too. However, Heath had made it a point more recently to park elsewhere since he was not officially a vocational clergyman anymore. Of course, if a particularly busy day at the hospital filled the parking lots leaving only spaces in the satellite lots available, Heath came out of retirement and pulled his clergy sticker out of the glove compartment, flung it up on the dash of his car, and parked right alongside the working ministers. He had, after all, served churches around South Mill longer than most of the other ministers there now had been alive, and, "in my own opinion," he often said, "I've earned the right."

As Matt adjusted his belt to secure his Bible, he caught a glimpse of a familiar head of coifed white hair emerging from a side building of the hospital from a door Matt had never noticed or used. Dorothy had accompanied Stephen on the morning trip to the hospital, which Matt thought was an odd change of pace. "He always beats me here," Matt sighed. And after wrestling a few seconds over whether to speak to the Heaths, Dorothy accidentally acknowledged Matt's presence by whispering rather loudly to Stephen, "Oh Lord! What's he doing here?" At that, Matt threw up his arm and waved his hand briskly, "Good morning!" Both forced a quick wave back in his direction but continued to their car without any further exchange.

Matt checked in at the chaplain's office for a room number for David, took the elevator to the third floor, and found David resting after his successful procedure and still feeling quite loopy from the drugs. Just in case they prevented David from remembering Matt came to see him, he pulled a business card from his wallet, jotted a quick note down on the back of it, and left it on the food tray so David would be sure to notice it when he came down from his pain meds. He did not bother reading scripture or praying when a patient was in a lot of pain or medicated heavily to alleviate it. He celebrated a very quick visit and, once outside, began dialing Abigail on his way down the front steps.

Abigail and M.J. met Matt in the parking lot outside of Moss' Pharmacy for lunch. The local prescription shop had been in business since 1908 and in the Moss family until just twelve years earlier when Perry, the only son of its founder, finally grew tired of filling prescriptions and retired at the age of eighty-one. He was still in remarkably good health, and, after selling the Pharmacy, moved with his wife to Florida to be near their daughter. Doc Figgins, a pharmacist who had worked there since graduating pharmacy school back in the early eighties, bought the place from Perry Moss. Doc had changed a few things around, including adding a drive-thru window and remodeling the retail area, but mostly the store still resembled its one-hundred-and-something-year-old self. That included the lunch counter. Moss' had the best sandwiches in town, and, it drew a hefty crowd each day between the hours of 10:30 and 1:30. It was located in the medical district just a few blocks away from the hospital and was surrounded by doctors' offices. It was successful as a pharmacy because it was so convenient for folks coming out of appointments with prescriptions to stop by and get them filled. The lunch counter was successful because neither the Moss family nor Doc Figgins was very fast about filling those prescriptions. Rather than go home and return later for the medicine, people would either shop in the retail section for birthday cards or gifts, or they would wander into the restaurant area and enjoy a really delicious meal while they waited. Corey Kaiser had been hired as a server in the 1970s, and when Doc bought the pharmacy, the Mosses insisted on selling the lunch counter as a separate entity to Corey, and he continued to manage and do most of the cooking still. Doc didn't mind sharing the business with Corey. They had gotten along pretty well since Doc joined the pharmacy staff – so well, in fact, that they bought a house together and still remained *roommates* to this very day. "It worked out well," old folks around the community would often say, "since neither of those boys ever got married." Matt and Abigail laughed in spite of themselves every time someone relayed that piece of information to them. They were pretty sure that most people knew the truth but avoided it by pretending otherwise.

Corey knew the Hardys and, anytime they came for lunch, came out from behind the counter to personally take their order and dote on M.J. and Maggie. He was, Matt believed, the nicest man in South Mill, and his family enjoyed eating there as often as they could.

Corey knew what M.J. wanted, but double checked with the young patron just to make sure before serving up a hotdog with no bun, French fries with a puddle of ketchup on the side, and a small vanilla milkshake with no cherry and no whipped cream. Abigail had a grilled chicken sandwich, and Matt ordered the specialty, a *Spoon Burger*, which was nothing more than hamburger meat scrambled in ketchup and mustard and served on a bun with a pickle secured with a toothpick on top, but there was something about the way Moss' lunch staff fixed the little burger that made it a delicacy according to Matt's taste buds. This little drugstore with its quirky staff and quaint lunch counter was a small-town tradition that Matt loved.

Normally, as they finished up lunch and paid their tab, Doc Figgins would come from the pharmacy side of the store and sit down at their table to say hello. Today, though, Doc was absent, and Matt assumed it was due to this farm accident that had maimed his finger. He asked Corey, quite discreetly, "Doc still nursing that finger?"

Corey shook his head in a pitying way and said, "He's so sorry he couldn't play for y'all on Sunday. There's still a good bit of pain, and, to be honest, I don't know if he'll be able to play at all like that ever again." Everyone knew Doc could play piano better with one hand than most musicians could play with two, and, if he still had nine fingers that were normal length, Doc would find a way to play it again. He loved music, and, Matt guessed, would have pursued a career in the arts if family had not pressured him to study the sciences.

"Tell him we asked about him," Abigail joined in.

As Matt reached for his wallet, he noticed a devilish look in his wife's eyes. "What are you scheming on?" he asked.

"Nothing. I was just thinking I should cook dinner for them, and you and I could take it to their house."

"You're just being nosy now!" Matt joked. "But I think it would a very nice gesture."

"Oh, Corey!" Abigail sang across the lunch counter, "I'm cooking dinner for you and Doc Thursday night. Can I drop it by about 6:00?"

Corey, with both gratitude and reluctance, agreed, and Abigail secretly patted herself on the back for the idea. *Matt's not the only one who can do nice things for people.*

Matt returned to the church office. He had a premarital counseling session set up that afternoon for a young couple who had become engaged over the summer. Scheduled for Valentine's Day, theirs would be the first wedding Matt performed at South Mill. Matt had only been at the church a couple of months when they asked him to perform their ceremony. Matt knew, though they had never discussed it, that Brother Heath had fully expected to be asked, but they chose the younger minister over him, and Matt was humbled and flattered by the request.

After discussing the biblical definition of love and learning more about their individual lives and backgrounds – what attracted them to one another, what they hoped to emulate from their own parents' marriages and what they hoped to do differently, Matt set up the next session with them for December, and then one more for early January, so they'd be done with their three counseling sessions well in advance of all of the last-minute wedding details. He prayed with them and for their marriage and wrapped things up within an hour so they could get back to work. He knew that premarital counseling was a bother to most couples. They just wanted someone to officiate the ceremony and sign the marriage license, but the counseling sessions gave Matt time to get to know them so he could make the wedding more personable, and it did give the brides-and-grooms-to-be an opportunity to open up about ideas and ideals they might not think to talk about together until they argued about them for the first time after they were married.

After the young couple left, Matt returned two phone calls to some church members, one who had been studying her Bible and had a question about a passage in the book of Hebrews, and one who wanted to know if he could borrow a couple of tables and some chairs from the church for his family's Thanksgiving meal coming up in a few weeks. Matt did not really think that he was the person who had to approve the borrowing of church property, but he had found the best practice was to simply say okay and then pass the call back to Lanie to make notes and place them in a file...just in case something borrowed did not find its way back to the church before it was needed, or before Stephen Heath noticed it was missing and put it on his list of things to discuss in the next *visit*.

At 3:00 p.m., the weekly church staff meeting convened on Tuesdays. It was an odd time of day to have a staff meeting, and mornings would have been preferred, but both the children's pastor and the music director were part-time, so they held other jobs during the day. Tuesday of each week was a convenient time for the full-time youth pastor, Lanie, Trudy, Matt, and the part-time staff to get together. It was, for everyone, an inconvenience that they had each grown to enjoy on some level. South Mill was blessed to have part-time staff who loved the church and were as effective in their ministry jobs as they were in their actual careers. The team would discuss outreach events, summer camps, Vacation Bible School for the upcoming year, and whatever else might be on the minds or agendas of the fine ensemble paid to keep things going day-by-day within the life of the church. With the holidays just around the corner, meetings like these seemed a little more exciting and a little longer. Choir presentations, children's parties, youth group caroling, and the list went on. Finally, only Matt and Evan remained, and they spent the last half-hour or more discussing worship service plans – things like what songs went best with Matt's planned sermons, which staff member would offer the opening prayer each week, how the service had gone the week before. Both had nothing but praise for the music last Sunday, but Matt did share the details of the conversation he had had with Brother Stephen, as well as the follow-up phone call to Sister Sue. Evan was surprised by neither but offered to field any of those complaints from folks like Heath going forward. "As far as he knows, I hired that woman to play," Evan offered an out.

Matt agreed, and added, "But you aren't the one he vents to every day."

Together, the men prayed, gathered their notes from the meeting, and walked out of the office to the parking lot. Matt noticed the pothole was getting larger, and he made a mental note to bring it up in Sunday's deacons' meeting. *Another monthly roasting to look forward to.* But, as he considered the banter of the regular deacons' meeting, it occurred to him that it had been since Monday morning that he had seen or heard from Stephen Heath. He didn't know whether to simply be relieved or to anticipate the worst. It was certainly peculiar to not hear from him. Matt assumed the wave across the parking lot at the hospital that morning must count as their daily interaction, and he was very satisfied with one like that.

Wednesday went as smoothly as Tuesday had and, as expected, by mid-afternoon, the sweet aromas of the Wednesday night menu were filling the corridors of the church building. Matt's nose chose yeast rolls as its focus that afternoon. And, when Matt thought they had probably had time to finish baking, he took an early trip down to the kitchen to butter one up and sample it well ahead of time. The cooks had come to expect him to pop in, and though they fussed about him getting in their way and putting both his nose and his fingers in their food, it was all fun teasing, and Matt enjoyed the repartee as much as he did the snacking.

Matt was mingling up and down the line that was forming for dinner well before the time to say the prayer over the food. He tickled the toes of a baby, magically pulled a quarter from the ear of a five-year-old, fawned over family photos a new grandmother had just picked up from the photo lab, and politely declined an invitation to cut the line and get ahead of all those people who would show up later. A decent crowd had formed, and the line was about to curve down the hallway toward the children's classrooms when Matt happened up on the Wellers, the couple he had visited in the hospital, and both boys were with them. Ball practice was over for the season, and they had heard about the good food and the fun kids' programs and wanted to check them out. But before Matt could explain how glad he was to see them, he heard a familiar growl come from down the corridor. It was Brother Heath and Hugh Briner together. Whatever the opposite of a "dynamic duo" would be, this combination was it. Matt would not have to strain to hear what the growl was about, and neither would the Wellers or anyone else nearby.

"Preacher, get down here!" Hugh Briner bellowed.

Matt trotted in their direction to, hopefully, lessen the distance between them so they would lower their voices, but proximity would make no difference.

"This water fountain's been leakin' all over this carpet, and you haven't done a thing about it, have you?"

He was about to explain that he had not been down that hallway this week and had no knowledge of a leaking water fountain, when Stephen added to the situation by yelling at an uncomfortable volume.

"And why in Heaven's name is there a helium tank sitting in the hall outside of the kids' music room? Do you know what that would do if it fell over on one of these little children?"

Matt knew the answer to both of those questions. The second one was obvious, but the first one was that the church had been loaned a full tank of helium for balloons at the fall festival they hosted, and it was in the hallway because the nice man from Global Air, whose name Matt could not remember at the moment, was supposed to have stopped by and picked it up earlier that week.

Before Matt could adequately explain any of that, both men launched into him about the problem with his generation, poor work ethic, not waiting on the man to come pick it up but to return what you borrowed from people, and how someone was going to get hurt under his careless watch.

Matt's utter embarrassment over the undeserved scolding manifested itself in his own angry outburst. "Enough! There are people around. Can we continue this in one of these classrooms?"

"No!" Heath snapped.

"There's nothing else to discuss, Preacher Matt!" Hugh Briner added. "Just do your job!"

Matt immediately took notice of how out-of-breath Stephen Heath had become in just that short encounter. Could he really be that angry over something so trivial? He was left alone to sort that out as the two men disappeared up the hallway, talking quietly now as they went. Both made their way to the front of the serving line, cutting in front of everyone else who had been waiting, offering no apologies for either display of rudeness.

Matt cared deeply for people, and, as he had learned over the years, that passion often was accompanied by fierce emotion. He was angry and embarrassed. He felt like crying, but he also felt like punching both of them. Instead of either, he knelt down in the puddle and turned the water off to the leaky fountain. He then gathered the helium tank like a tackling dummy on a football field and carried it out the back door of the church building and around to the office door. It would have been a shorter walk to go back up the hall, but he refused to haul the thing back past anyone who had witnessed the ugly exchange because of two things he believed at that moment: neither of those issues was part of his job as the pastor of that church and those two old men had no right to talk to him like that. He stored the helium tank in his office just in case the man from the gas company came early tomorrow to retrieve it, and, if he didn't, Matt would put it in his truck and return what *someone* had borrowed. As much as he wanted to hide out in his office, he would not be defeated that easily. So, he returned to the dinner line just as the last few folks in line were serving their plates. He joined Abigail and the kids at the table with Ms. Mabel and, of all people, the Wellers. He was proud that Abigail had sought them out to sit with his family and that the only other person at their table was the sweetest lady in the church. He smiled his best smile, said hello to the family again, and sat down to make new friends. He was careful not to let the thought racing across his mind come out of his mouth. *Screw the old men!*

When dinner was over and the children were off to their activities and classes, Matt stood up to take prayer requests, pray, and teach on "following the way of love," from I Corinthians, Chapter fourteen. When Stephen Heath fell asleep during his lesson, Matt wanted to throw his Bible onto the table to startle the codger awake, and when Hugh Briner stood up to go do whatever it was that he always had to go do on Wednesday nights, Matt wanted to yell, "you might need to hear this one, Hugh!" Again, he stuck to the lesson plan and spoke with authority, wisdom, and kindness, and several, including the Wellers expressed how much they enjoyed the evening before leaving that night. Abigail knew how to read her husband well, and she would wait anxiously for him to arrive at home to find out what had transpired that threw him so off balance.

He could not recap the event without becoming angry all over again. Abigail did not try to calm him. She simply relived it with him as he bellowed like Hugh and yelled and breathed heavily like Stephen. When Matt finally settled and plunked down in his chair, Abigail stood from hers and went to him, placing her arms around him from behind and her lips gently against his cheek. "I don't know what to say," she spoke. "There really is nothing *to* say. This is why there have been seven before you, I guess."

Matt looked up as she released her embrace. "Well, those old men have no idea that *eight* is their unlucky number." He and Abigail both laughed, as Matt was not much of a threat to anyone. There was nothing menacing in his character. She watched as his beautiful blue eyes glistened. Regardless of his efforts to hide any emotion, those eyes were billboards of what was going on in his heart. She was sure that, if the old men had looked him in the eyes at all, they knew how angry they had made him.

Sleeping did nothing to remove the sting of the Wednesday night attack, and Matt secretly hoped for and dreaded a visit from the old man just so he could refuse to meet with him on Thursday morning in the office. There was no one to visit in the hospital, and Clack was too far away for another trip in the same week. So the young pastor sequestered himself in his study and told Lanie emphatically that he would take no calls and would see no visitors, "not even Brother..."

Lanie cut him off, "He's already called this morning and said to remind you to call a plumber."

Matt steamed, pursed his lips, and then looked at Lanie for sympathy. She delivered it by saying, "I've already called, and there will be one here today before noon."

Matt smiled, thanked her, and closed his door to the world and picked up the telephone. The girl who answered at Global Air assured him they remembered the helium tank and would "just pick it up when we have our next delivery out that way." Not knowing where their place was anyway, Matt thought that sounded perfect. He laid it over on its side because he agreed that a helium tank could be quite dangerous.

CHAPTER TWENTY

South Mill High School was playing football on the road Friday night, which was fine with Matt. He had no plans to take his crew to another game that night no matter how much "me time" Abigail needed. So, he loaded the little ones up and headed off to an evening of fun at Adventure Road, a small town, kid-friendly amusement park. A round of mini-golf ended with Maggie as the winner, but M.J. got the prize for losing the most balls along the course. They ate hotdogs and French fries covered in ketchup and washed it down with a Coke Icee®. Matt was slurping the last bit of icy liquid, moving his straw around and around the bottom of his cup like a vacuum, when M. J., leapt from his chair and squealed with delight, "MOMMY!" M.J. ran to Abigail and hugged her at the knees, but Maggie just said, "Hi, Mom!" and continued slurping her own remaining drink. Matt, though, greeted her with a look of concern and suspicion. "What happened to alone time?"

"I'll tell you later," she spoke quietly to Matt. Then louder to the children, "I just didn't want to miss the fun. Anyone want to ride go-karts?"

With two parents to drive and two children to ride, that was now a possibility. Earlier, Matt had to break the sad news that they could not ride because neither of the children were allowed to drive the carts themselves, and with room for only two, he could not leave one of them standing outside of the track while the other rode with him. When the boys lost to the girls, the children were ready to play some quarter-craving games like Skee-Ball®, and Whac-A-Mole®, and that gave Abigail a chance to explain her presence to Matt while watching the children closely but out of earshot.

"So," Matt whispered, "Why'd you come?

"I got scared. I think ..." she hesitated, thinking it through before articulating it.

"...someone was in the house. In fact, I think someone was in the house last Friday night, too."

Matt voiced perturbed concern. "What do you mean? Why didn't you say anything then?"

"I heard something. The dishwasher turned on, and I thought you were home. Then, you and the kids were later coming in. I thought I was just imagining things."

"What happened tonight?"

"I lighted my aroma therapy candles and turned on the hot water. I went into the bedroom to undress, and as I sat down on the bed, I swear a beam from a flashlight shined up the stairs. I mean, maybe it was car lights or something, but Chop and Felix heard something, too, and both of them went tearing down the stairs barking like I've never heard them before. You would have thought they were trained attack dogs the way they were acting." She began to tremble and her voice broke into an airy whisper, almost crying. "I heard a door close. The dogs were on their hind legs at the front door still barking like crazy. I grabbed my shoes and car keys and ran out the side door and got in the car. I saw the flashlight beam again in the backyard as I backed the car out of the drive. I tried calling you, but you didn't answer."

Matt reached for his phone and panicked, "I must have left it at home." Matt placed his arm around his wife's waist and pulled her close. "Okay! Okay! You take the kids for ice cream or a drive or something and I'll go check it out. I'll call you when everything checks out."

"I'm being a baby," Abigail apologized. "I'm sorry, Hon!"

"Don't be ridiculous. Let me go see what's up."

He drove slowly past the house three times before pulling into the drive. He left the car lights on and approached the front steps cautiously. He rattled his keys before placing one in the lock of the front door, and he jumped when one of the dogs let out one quick "woof!" Once they saw it was Matt, they nudged their bodies up against his and stayed in stride as he walked through the downstairs rooms and into his small office. The lamp on his desk was on, which is how he remembered leaving it, and, keeping his eyes narrowed and aimed at the window to the side yard, he slid his hand to the corner of his desk where his charger was plugged into his cell phone. His hand slid smoothly without touching anything. His focus shifted to his desk, and his cell phone was not there. "I could have sworn I charged it this afternoon," he thought aloud.

Everything seemed in order downstairs, but just to be sure, Matt checked the side door and the door to the back deck. Both were locked. He grabbed Chop by the collar and let him lead the way up the steps, being careful not to let the wood creak while he climbed. Then, he second guessed that effort and wondered if he really did want to sneak up on someone that might be up to no good on the second floor. He opened the linen closet door, checked M.J.'s and Maggie's bedrooms, opened their closets, and ran his hands through the hanging clothes until he touched the wall behind them. He looked under the beds. He checked the kids' bathroom, and held his breath when, with one strong yank, he flung the shower curtain open. Then, he entered the master bedroom and repeated the process all over again. In his and Abigail's bathroom, he could still smell the faint scent of the Amber and Vanilla Blossom candles that had been lit to relax his beautiful wife before something rattled her so. Everything seemed in order, so Matt returned to the kitchen and picked up the landline to call Abigail. Instead, he dialed his own phone, and, though the sound was faint, he could hear it ring. He wandered around the downstairs listening to the faint tone. When it stopped ringing completely, he returned to the kitchen and dialed it again. He opened the front door, and the tone was stronger. Matt walked toward the car and saw the light from his phone's screen underneath. He looked around cautiously, not wanting to be clubbed on the head while he knelt down to retrieve it. He then reached his hand underneath the car and drug the phone through the gravel until it was in plain sight right at the edge of his driver's side door. "I guess I dropped it getting the kids in the car tonight," he reasoned.

Using the cell, he dialed Abigail and assured her it was safe for her and the children to come home. Everything seemed to be in place. No one was there. While he waited for them to arrive, he turned on the television for some noise to make him feel at ease and to mask any unsettling sounds the house might make. He turned on all of the floodlights and opened the door to the back deck and walked onto it with a flashlight in hand to illuminate and scour the wood line. Everything seemed quite normal, peaceful even. Had Abigail's imagination gotten the best of her?

He heard the minivan pull into the driveway behind his car, and he walked down to meet them there. He hoisted up and carried a sleeping M.J. to the house, placing him on the couch. He and Abigail spoke in coded language so as not to alarm Maggie, but when Matt ran down the condition in which he found everything, Abigail gasped and said, "I turned your desk lamp off before I went up to take my bath."

"Are you sure?

"Absolutely!" Abigail was emphatic, and Matt knew not to question her again. "And," she added, "I left without blowing out the candles in the bathroom."

Matt rechecked all the locks on the doors, cradled M.J. up to his chest again, and said, "Come on, Maggie! We're going to have a slumber party in our room tonight." Maggie was thrilled, and the four of them piled into the king-sized bed with Chop and Felix positioned on blankets inside a locked and barricaded bedroom door. Matt did not own a gun, and he had not played golf since college, but he slept that night with a nine-iron propped between the night stand and the headboard. He reached for it each time he woke during the night to both make sure it was still there and to be certain he could reach it without fumbling were he to need it.

Saturday morning came early, and Matt was up with the sun. By 8:00, he was making a phone call. Matt's parents lived in Texas, and Abigail's were in St. Louis. The closest family members to them, in proximity – certainly not in terms of any meaningful relationship – were Matt's uncle and aunt, Bill and Vickie, who lived in Clinton, where Bill was a retired insurance agent and Vickie was a retired professor at Presbyterian College. Matt got Uncle Bill on the first ring, and he seemed chipper enough that Matt felt like he hadn't awakened him. After a few minutes of small talk, Matt took charge of the call and got to the point. After explaining their recent concerns over possible intruders, Bill agreed that he and Vickie would drive to Columbia and babysit the kids while Matt and Abigail took care of some business. M.J. might not remember his great uncle, but Maggie would. Though they were not close, when Matt and Abigail moved to South Carolina, Bill had promised his sister, Matt's mom, that he would check in on them often. This would be the second time they had seen one another.

Saturday morning pancakes would be eaten at McDonald's, and the kids were ecstatic. Just after 10:00 a.m., they arrived in Columbia, at the Riverbanks Zoo, for a "surprise adventure." Again, the kids' excitement was uncontainable. At a picnic table on the lawns near the gates, Uncle Bill and Aunt Vickie were waiting. Bill and Vickie hugged the whole family and Matt reacquainted M.J. with the relatives. Abigail assured both of the children that they lived close enough that they would visit the zoo often, but today she and Daddy had some business they had to take care of. With one kid on each hand, Vickie led the way to the gate while Bill reached out to shake hands with his nephew. Matt felt something weird in his uncle's palm, and when they let go of their grip on one another, three one-hundred-dollar bills were left behind in Matt's grasp hand. Matt tried to refuse them, but his uncle said, "Take it. That's the least I can do."

Matt felt the need to thank him more appropriately and went in for a full front-on hug.

Uncle Bill, always the comedian, hugged back and said, "Now, cut this out. Makes me feel like I just hired a prostitute or something." Matt laughed and then explained the money and the joke to Abigail, and then she joined in on the hug and laughter.

Bill, Vickie, Maggie, and M.J. were off to visit the animals in the zoo, and Abigail and Matt were on their way to the Palmetto State Armory, a firearms store and shooting range. For the thirty-minute drive there, Matt and Abigail discussed the pros and cons again of having a gun in their home. She was insistent that they keep it under lock and key, and Matt was in agreement, as long as it was an easy access lock, one the kids could not open but that he could trip in a matter of seconds. Abigail surprised Matt when she said that she wanted to know how to shoot it. It was settled. They would purchase a gun and then spend a few hours on the range with someone who could train them in how to properly use it in the unfortunate event that they ever had to. After an hour of browsing the merchandise, comparing prices, and holding a variety of pieces in their hands, Matt selected a Smith & Wesson M&P SHIELD Nine Millimeter. It was less expensive than a Glock, and it would accomplish just as much and, according to Abigail, seemed easier to use. Matt's background check came back clear, and the bill of sale said the gun was his. He even had some change left over from what his uncle had given him.

Reservations were not needed at the range that day since most shooters that might otherwise be there were probably in the woods enjoying deer season. Once they were trained on the gun, about forty-five minutes were spent with the two of them competing in target practice. When Abigail hit the target, a silhouette of a man, square between the eyes, Matt looked somewhat shaken and said, half-jokingly, "Remind me never to sneak up on you." And, since they used Uncle Bill's money for the gun, they were able to use their own to purchase a biometric gun vault that would recognize their fingerprints and open for fast retrieval of the firearm when and if they needed it. Since neither Matt nor Abigail had a conceal carry permit in South Carolina, or any other state - or the need for one - the gun was unloaded and placed in the biometric vault, which was packed to travel home in the back cargo area of the minivan. The Hardys were now packing heat, and they felt safer and more terrified than they ever had in their married life.

They stopped by a shopping mall where they found designer men's suits on sale. Matt needed a new one, and they would not find that quality at a nicer price, so they bought one. Matt felt like the whole goose and gander proverb was apropos, so Abigail got a new dress, as well as a new pair of shoes, both of which were also on clearance. They also spent a little time and more money than they meant

dnesday night was a church Business Meeting – the quarterly
turous event Matt despised. And the very last announcement
s that the regularly scheduled deacons' meeting would be held
night at 6:00 in the conference room. Matt did not necessarily dis-
e deacons' meetings. It was just that he didn't count some of the
cons among his favorite church members. Stephen Heath and
gh Briner both happened to be on that list.

With the administration of the church out of the way, the open-
prayer was prayed, and the congregation stood to sing the first
nn of the morning under Evan's direction. From the perch of the
pit, Matt could make eye contact with everyone in attendance,
d he often smiled in one direction or another at someone special.
the voices filled the room, the doors at the back opened for a few
comers. When Abigail looked up at her dapper husband in his
w suit of clothes, she was surprised to see such a boyish grin across
face. She had to wonder what had caught his attention and made
so happy all of a sudden. She knew better than to think that
was just the joy of the Lord that had him beaming. Whatever it
s, his eyes followed it from the back of the room right down the
aisle to the row where Abigail and Maggie were seated. It was
nifer Grimes, back at church, and no one had even asked her to
y the piano. Abigail leaned over Maggie and hugged Jenni, and
ni leaned down and hugged Maggie. "I didn't know you were
ning," Abigail spoke into Jenni's ear over the music.

Jenni looked up at Matt, smiled, and then leaned to Abigail's ear,
either did he! He always tries to be so sneaky with me. I thought
be the one with the surprises today."

Both ladies laughed and then sang with the rest of the parishion-
a glorious hymn of joy. After the service, Jenni waited until the
sic was finished and then introduced herself to Sister Sue. She

to on some Christmas presents for the kids. After all, what were the
chances that they would be out shopping without them any time in
the near future? Gun on the bottom of the stack, flanked by toys,
and the clothing was draped across the entire loot to keep it well
hidden from the children on the ride back to South Mill. They met
Bill and Vickie at a restaurant called California Dreaming, a place of
their choosing, and the grownups ate their weight as the little ones
went on and on about how much fun they had at the zoo, occasionally nibbling on a shared portion of chicken tenders and fries.

The families vowed to spend more time together, and Uncle Bill
asked discreetly, "Did you get everything taken care of?" Matt said
they did and offered again to repay his uncle to no avail. They had
eaten early in an effort to be home long before dark, so goodbyes
were short, and they hit the road. If anyone spoke of being hungry
later that night, a bowl of cereal or a ham sandwich would be the
short order. Matt could not imagine being hungry again for a week
though.

They made it back to South Mill by 5:30, and it was not quite
dark yet. Everything at home was undisturbed, it seemed, so anx-
ieties were low. Matt would unload the Christmas presents and hide
them in his closet once the kids were asleep, but one purchase did
not need to be left in the driveway long. Reaching underneath the
heavy pile of kids' toys, Matt grasped the steel box and clutched it
close to his body and covered it with the garment bag that held his
suit. Abigail's dress and shoes were added for extra layers of disguise,
and all were safely delivered to the master bedroom closets. Matt's
plan was to keep the gun safe in the closet under piles of clothes and
to bring it out nightly, open it, place a loaded magazine in the gun,
replace the gun into the safe box, and then store the box overnight in
the close reach of the top drawer of his nightstand. If he stuck to that

routine, he was sure the kids would never know that their parents even owned a gun, and that was important to Abigail and Matt.

As evening came to a close, Matt wanted to look over his sermon notes one last time before Sunday morning's service. He tucked everyone in, including Abigail, who seemed exceptionally tired, and retreated to his little office to study. When a noise outside his window startled him, he convinced himself it was only a tree limb scratching at the siding of the house in the breeze. He did, though, email the sermon notes from his laptop to his iPad and continue studying upstairs in his bed. Chop was with M.J., Felix was with Maggie, and he and his new purchase were with Abigail. He was convinced they were safer than ever before.

CHAPTER TWENTY-ONE

At church on Sunday, Matt made sure to stay [in his] office until just before the service so that he did[n't] any disgruntled old men. He was seated in the pulpi[t] prayerfully to Sister Sue's prelude music by the time [...] came from the back of the auditorium and stopped [...] row to shake hands, hug a neck, or speak to someone [...] age to the third row, where he would be seen by any[one] have missed his entrance or come in even later tha[n] looked his way far too long before realizing that his [...] betraying him. He was smiling at Brother Heath, bu[t] a menacing one. He turned quickly to look at Abiga[il] side of the aisle, and she was shaking her head at hi[m] too, saw the revealing look in his eyes. Quickly and s[...] told his face to cut it out, and his face obliged.

When Sister Sue concluded, the youth pastor stoo[d] the podium, and said, "Good morning, Church!" A[...] congregation followed in response, and the service [...] The youth pastor read down the list of announcem[ents] printed in the bulletin that each worshiper had be[en] they walked in. Matt's face had to be corrected again[...] the last two announcements were ones about whi[ch] gotten, perhaps not so accidentally. The second to t[he]

complimented her playing, the two pianists hugged, and Matt saw them exchanging phone numbers. This was a good sign.

When he had shaken the last hand after the service was over, Matt closed the front doors of the church and trotted to the parking lot. Jenni smiled as Matt hugged her and said, "Well, this is a pleasant surprise!"

Jenni said she had enjoyed last Sunday so much she just had to come again and that she insisted on taking them to lunch today. Matt knew that Jenni was keenly aware of her own financial situation, and that, if she was inviting them to lunch, the most insulting thing he could do was insist on paying. He would offer, but if she refused, he would back off quickly and thank her profusely. Regardless, the whole family was excited to spend another Sunday lunch with Jennifer Grimes Collins, and Matt had something he needed to ask her when they were alone.

The K&M Cafeteria was the choice for lunch that Sunday. Abigail warned her children before going through the cafeteria line to not let their eyes be bigger than their bellies. Neither knew what she meant so she explained that there would be salads and fruit and desserts and more long before they got to the important things like vegetables and meat and not to be so excited to see all of that beautiful, colorful food that they got more than they really were hungry for. Matt took M.J. through the line to monitor his choices and veto when necessary. Abigail did the same with Maggie. No one oversaw Jenni, though, and she admittedly got more than she meant to and was slightly embarrassed at the size of her meal when the server who carried her tray to the table spread the contents of it out in front of her.

The conversation was light and much shorter than the one from the previous Sunday. When lunch was over, Abigail invited Jenni back to the house for some coffee or...a nap. Jenni laughed and thanked her but refused saying she had only come for church because she enjoyed it so much the week before. She said she might even surprise them and return again next week. Matt said that he thought that would be a great idea, and Maggie agreed with her dad.

As they walked together to the cashier, Matt was about to make his offer to pay for lunch when a hand reached out of a booth and grabbed his wrist. He and his whole crew stopped to see who had taken hold of him. It was Stephen Heath. Matt had not noticed his car out front, nor had he seen them until that moment in the restaurant. Who knew which family arrived first? Stephen and Dorothy sat on one side of the table and faced the Briners on the other. Matt smiled and was polite, "Well, hello folks! Good to see y'all!"

No niceties were returned, other than a wicked smile from Dorothy directed toward M.J. Abigail noticed and forced one right back at her. Stephen, letting go of Matt's wrist, pulled his napkin to his mouth to wipe the corners clean and spoke first. "Sermon was a little long this morning, wasn't it?"

Matt looked at his watch nervously and said, "Not any longer than usual – I don't think."

Wanda Briner took up the cause from there. "Then maybe they all need to be shorter. We don't have time for the music."

Matt had no idea how to respond to that. They sang all the music they had planned to sing, so what was Wanda talking about? He could only speak the truth back to her and did by saying, "We have not had to cut out any music because of the length of my sermons."

Hugh joined the conversation then and said, "Well, people don't want to get out of church so late. You gotta start wrapping things up sooner. We are just now sitting down to lunch."

Matt felt Abigail and Jenni backing away from the table, and he knew this might not end well if he allowed himself to feel rather than to think. "I'll keep that in mind, folks! Thank you for stopping me to say hello. Good to see you all!" None of what he said was true, though. He would not keep it in mind other than as a frustrating thought...certainly not to consider changing something. They did not stop him to say hello, and he knew that for a certainty. And, it was not good, if he were being honest, to see any of them. They were rude and out of line, and as he made his way to the door, he became enraged and thought how dare they stop me and criticize me in a public restaurant when we have a guest with us.

By the time Matt regained his composure, Jenni had already paid. He just thanked her and then apologized for the rudeness of his church members. Jenni smiled and encouraged him saying, "I don't think your sermon was too long, and I don't think it is any of those people's business how long you preach. You're a great minister. I drove all the way from Cardelville to hear you, you know?"

Matt thanked her again for coming and for lunch. He remembered what he needed to ask her. It was about the dogs. Without telling her why, he asked if he might keep them just a little longer. He did not want to explain that they were a burglar alarm for his family at the moment and that their presence made him and Abigail feel safer and that they might have chased off an intruder two nights earlier. Jenni simply said she had not come for the dogs...only for church. She promised to talk to them later in the week and then pulled an envelope from her purse. "I promise this isn't the reason I came today," she explained, "but, if you see Clack or have a way of getting this to him, please do."

Matt looked at the envelope. It was sealed, and he immediately wanted to know what the contents said to Clack. "I'll get it to him."

Jenni saw his eyes. "He can read it to you if he wants to." With that, she walked to her car.

Abigail had the kids strapped in and ready to go when Matt reached the van. Matt sensed her anger, and she proved him correct when she said, "It's a good thing we don't have our purchase from yesterday with us, or your wife might be in the back of a cop car by now." Matt did not react, and they rode home in heated silence.

The children took naps, but Abigail was too mad to sleep, and she loved her Sunday afternoon siestas. Matt, who was getting used to being blindsided could sleep and did for about an hour on the couch. He snored while his wife fumed, and when he rumbled himself awake, Abigail was quick with the questions. "Who do they think they are? They think they run the church and our lives, don't they? Who in their right mind burns a preacher in effigy at the Sunday dinner table with him standing right beside them? Is this what they did to the other preachers before you?"

Matt wiggled himself upright on the cushy sofa and, because he was still groggy and because he simply did not know, he just shook his head and left the questions to float about in the air. Abigail had another one, though she was hesitant to ask it because of all it might imply. But, she and Matt talked about everything.

"You don't think a church person was..." she let it linger.

"...coming in the house?" Matt finished it for her. Matt let that thought ruminate and produce the worst outcome in his mind. *What if it was the old man or one of his cronies? And what if they come snooping around again and I'm home? What if I were to shoot one of them? How would I ever explain that to the church?* Suddenly, he regretted buying the pistol. *But what if it isn't one of them? Who could it be?* The regret passed.

At 5:00, Matt showered and put back on the clothes he had worn to church that morning, minus the coat and tie. "I have to go to a deacons' meeting," he explained to his family. Abigail confessed that she was nervous for him going there and for her and the kids staying home. Matt tried to lighten things up a bit by saying, "Well, if it is one of them, they'll be with me – so y'all should be safe." Abigail did not smile at the quip.

"Keep the doors locked, and I'll keep my phone on vibrate the whole time. I'll step out of the meeting if you need me." With that, he kissed the little family and headed to the church building.

Deacons' meetings at South Mill were predictable. The older men would gather early, stand in the parking lot making small talk and wait on enough to show up to start the meeting. The younger ones would arrive, speak to the older men, and gradually ease their way out of the parking lot conversations and into the church building, talking about work or their kids or some other meaningful topic. Matt never lingered outside. He came in, retrieved the meeting agenda from Lanie's desk, laid it out on the table in the meeting room, and sat down and waited for the rest to join him. Matt knew where to sit, and it was important that he get his seat. Though the meetings were somewhat informal, nothing like a city council meeting where everyone had assigned seats and name plates that designated them, everyone *always* sat in the exact same seat. Matt chose to sit at the opposite end of the room from one particular deacon, Jim Pethel, who found it within his rights to chew his tobacco throughout the meeting and spit into a Diet Mountain Dew bottle that he would empty on the ride to the church. Sometimes there would be a sip or two left as he sat down in the meeting, but he would quickly drain them and use the empty bottle from that point on as his spittoon. Matt found the practice disrespectful and disgusting. Jim would often miss the opening of the bottle and a bead of brown spit would run down its side until it found the table or the floor where Jim was sitting. Matt smelled that wintergreen scent whenever he had reason to go into the conference room during the work week long after Jim had been there. The church was supposed to be a tobacco-free campus; he had read that in the church bylaws when he was hired. Obviously, it was only a smoke-free campus, but he knew that was not true either since he often saw cigarette butts in the shrubbery beside the front doors of the church every time certain ushers were on duty for a particular month. It explained clearly why they lingered so long outside after collecting the morning offering.

When all of the deacons assembled, the chairman, Casey Briner, Hugh and Wanda's son, called the meeting to order and opened with a word of prayer. He looked over the agenda and declared to the group, "We don't have much on the list for tonight, so we shouldn't take too long." Each deacon was assigned to a committee in the church, and if he had anything to report, he would bring an update to the "board of deacons," a phrase Matt hated. *Where in the Bible does it ever mention church ministry leaders sitting on something called a board?* He knew that, if pressed, Baptist deacons would be willing to call themselves a board of directors as though they oversaw the assets and operations of a Fortune 500 company. "The word *deacon*," Matt and every preacher before him often said, "means servant or minister." Deacons would nod in affirmation of that definition, but the prideful terminology continued. Even Stephen Heath, who had sat on the other side for so long as a pastor enjoyed the distinction of being named to the board and, not-so-jokingly, often poked fun at himself and others by saying, "I used to work for the church, but now I run it," indicating how much power the deacons assumed they held.

Reports began with a kind old deacon who served on the benevolence committee, a team responsible for addressing needs of impoverished people in the church and its community. Dalton Tyler spoke briefly, reporting that the church had, through its "word-and-deed" offerings, provided fourteen families with food assistance in the last month and that they were organizing the donation and distribution of twenty Thanksgiving meals for some families in need that they knew of in the community.

Hugh Briner chimed in, "Well, it seems that the welfare system is working well in the church." he chuckled, proud of his little joke.

Casey, his son, corrected him by speaking one word, "Dad!"

The finance committee deacon shared the good news that the church had spent less than it took in all year long and that, with year-end giving just around the corner, it looked like the church would finish strong for the year. The children and youth ministry team report included the fun that was had at the Halloween season fall festival and how they had seen a record number of new faces in attendance at church the two Sundays following the event. Without meaning to, the children and youth team deacon reopened a wound when he reported the donations they had received for the festival, including a large tank of helium for balloons donated by Global Air. Both Hugh and Stephen looked at Pastor Matt with narrowed eyes. The properties committee rep shared that there had been a few leaking fixtures in the church building, including a water fountain that nearly ruined a patch of carpet in the children's hall. He then thanked Brother Heath for taking care of that issue and saving the church an unnecessary expense. Brother Heath humbly accepted the thanks with pride, and Matt marveled at his audacity. *Way to save the day, Brother Heath!* The decorating committee was making plans to meet the Sunday after Thanksgiving to deck the church halls for Christmas. Few others had reports to share primarily because their committees did very little. And so, it was turned over to the pastor to share his report with the deacons.

Matt glanced at his notes and provided a report on the number of visitors that the church had seen in its services over the last month, a record number. He provided statistics on how many were first time visitors and how many were repeat "customers," and some of the deacons laughed with him at the terminology. He spoke of the good relationships that the church staff was building within the community and the respect that the community was developing for what he called this "significant ministry." He shared his sermon plans for the month of December and the upcoming New Year, and he thanked the deacons for their diligence in the work of their various ministry teams and committees. He concluded by challenging them that what they were about was bigger than any one of them, and that they must "not grow weary in well-doing," a reference to the sixth chapter of Galatians in the Bible. He made good eye contact around the room as he spoke, at least with those who would look back at him. Others, mostly from *the old guard* looked down or fidgeted or doodled on their agendas while he spoke. Finally, when he was through, he asked if anyone had any questions for him. One last thought popped into his brain and then out of his mouth as he closed up his notes from his report. "As a matter of prayer concern, David Adams had kidney stones removed this past week, but he is home and seems to be feeling better."

Stephen Heath looked up from his fingernails on receiving that news. He almost barked a question right at the pastor. "Did you bother telling anyone else that Brother David was in the hospital?"

Matt responded calmly, "He preferred to keep his condition private until it was all over." Then, he looked hard at Brother Heath and continued. "But you knew he was there and went to visit him. I saw you at the hospital when I went on Tuesday morning."

Hugh Briner looked sharply to his left at Brother Heath as Heath glared at Pastor Matt. He finally raised his chin and nodded, indicating that he did remember making that visit, but Matt was suddenly not convinced. *Was Stephen not aware that David was in the hospital? Did I know something he didn't know? If he didn't visit David, then who was he visiting Tuesday morning, and why hadn't he shared that information with anyone?* Brother Heath loved to keep secrets.

With the end of the pastor's report, the floor was opened up to any new business. Jim Pethel raised his Mountain Dew bottle and said he had a question for the personnel committee representative. Matt shook his head back and forth like dog flinging off bath water. That was a surprise. Eric Pressley was the personnel committee's deacon representative, and he was kind and a fan of Pastor Matt. Thank goodness for that, Matt thought when Pethel posed his inquiry. "Does the personnel committee keep up closely with the hours our church staff puts in each week, particularly the pastor's secretary?"

Eric responded without delay. "The pastor oversees his own office staff members, so, no, we do not actively keep up with secretarial hours."

Matt knew who put Jim up to that question. But, when Pethel had a retort, Matt had to wonder what he had done to upset Jim. "Then, who keeps up with the pastor's hours?"

Matt had taken the advice of the pastor he worked for in his church staff position during seminary to keep a written log of the hours he put in each week and how those hours were spent. He did not verbalize that information in his deacon reports, but it was in the written notes that he submitted to be entered with the minutes of the meeting. He carefully slid a copy out of his portfolio to Eric, who slid it to Jim and said, "*We* do, Jim! Every month. And Pastor Matt's hours are down from a month ago. He's only averaging about sixty-four a week right now. But if you're wanting to suggest a review of his pay to better compensate him for what he does and the hours he puts in, I can get with the committee and make a recommendation to the finance committee."

Jim was defeated. "No. That's not necessary," he said as he spit into his bottle.

Immediately, Hugh Briner spoke up and said, "He makes enough to treat old ladies to dinners and buy things he doesn't need. I certainly don't think we need to be talking about any kind of increase."

No one had a response to such an unsolicited interjection. Matt felt the need, though, to defend himself and offered. "I can speak to that. I bought Ms. Mabel's dinner a couple of Wednesdays ago because of all the kindness she has shown to my family. It was seven dollars, but I don't really think that is anyone's business."

Another deacon spoke up and agreed that it was not any concern to them how the preacher spent his money. But Stephen Heath felt the need to correct the misunderstanding. "No one is talking about the seven dollars for Mabel's dinner. But Sunday lunches at Lena's are expensive, and then you took the same woman out to the cafeteria today. Who is this mystery woman, Pastor Matt?"

Matt was now on full alert. He was under attack, and this was just the tip of the iceberg. "Last Sunday, she was our guest pianist while Sister Sue was absent." As soon as he said that, he was sorry because he knew that could open up another line of questioning that would be just as asinine. "And today," he continued, "she was simply a visitor that enjoyed herself last week and wanted to come again."

"Or is she your pick to replace Sister Sue?" Casey Briner, the chairman, joined in the inquisition.

Matt wasn't sure which direction to look now for support. Casey had never been anything but professional and kind as the chairman. It was assumed that he was not of the same twisted mindset that his mother and especially his father were known for. Was he now joining ranks with the old guard?

"No!" Matt was insistent. "Sister Sue's job is safe. She was sick, and we needed a substitute."

"So, you just happened to have an extra girl lying around that could play the piano?" The words were out there before Hugh could wrangle them back into his mouth. Even he was taken aback by the suggestive tone of what he said. The room was frozen; shock sat on the faces of everyone. Even Jim Pethel let his slack jaw dribble brown goo down without his bottle underneath to catch it.

What the hell? Matt never cursed out loud. It was not becoming of a young preacher. But he thought it just the same. He was almost yelling when he finally gave his answer. "This lady who played the piano...who my family treated to lunch last Sunday...and who returned the favor by buying our lunch today...was a visitor in our church. She is a classically trained pianist, who, out of the goodness of her heart, filled in here last Sunday for pennies compared to what her going rate would be anywhere else. And, as far as me having her...what did you say? Lying around? I'll have you know that I did not even know this woman until a couple of weeks ago..." He had to think quickly so as not to lie. "...the same week she filled in for us."

Matt was not done. His blue eyes were steel sabers and he was aiming them right at Hugh, Stephen, Jim, and maybe even Casey, darting back and forth from one to another as though deciding which one to pierce through. "I don't know what has provoked this line of questioning, but if I'm being accused of abusing my position or not doing my job or...something else...I want it in writing." He then stood, excused himself from the room, and politely asked Chairman Casey Briner to meet with him privately after the meeting concluded. He wanted to kick his chair backward out of his way as he rose, but he would not provide more ammunition to his adversaries.

When Matt left the room, a sly smile crept across the blue-gray lips of Reverend Heath. He assumed command of the vessel and quoted scripture, "Fools give full vent to their rage, but the wise bring calm in the end."

When no one responded, Stephen trudged on through a spiritual coated soliloquy. "Our pastor is young and is still learning the ways of this high office. Let's table these discussions for now, and let me provide him some helpful wisdom that I have gained in my fifty plus years of shepherding God's flock and see if that proves fruitful."

The silence of the room grew deafening when Eric Pressley, the youngest deacon in the group spoke up and addressed the old man. "Seems you've shared your wisdom with several of our previous pastors, Brother, and you're always generous with your offer to do so. Let me ask one question of you and maybe of some of our other brothers gathered this evening. Should we go ahead and appoint a committee to start searching for Pastor Number Nine, or should we hold off on that until you completely run Pastor Number Eight in the ground?"

"That's out of order," Casey ruled. "And I think it's time we adjourn!"

Heath insisted on the last word and offered the Bible again, this time directed straight at Eric, "Do not touch my anointed ones; do my prophets no harm."

Eric wanted no more of the sermonizing and did not wait for the prayer that would close the meeting. He, too, stood and left, not as concerned as Pastor Matt about what to do with his chair as he exited.

Matt was pacing behind his desk when Casey complied with the request for a private debriefing. He assured Matt that everything was okay. He admitted his own misstep in suggesting that Matt had a replacement for Sister Sue, explaining that he had just heard the rumors floating around. He babbled on about how his dad and Brother Heath were just used to things being done a certain way, and, while he was not aware of everything they had on their minds for the meeting, he was sure that both, since they were good, godly men, would share their concerns in a more biblical and personal way with both him and Matt soon enough. "And then we can all sit down and talk this out like Christians." Just then, Casey's cell phone rang, and he answered it promptly. "Okay, dad, I'm coming!" He reached to shake Matt's hand, and Matt returned the gesture, and Casey excused himself explaining that his dad had said, "Pastor Heath needed some help in the parking lot." Matt did not care what Pastor Heath needed.

With the building empty, he sat alone at his desk in silence. He was angry, and this was a new emotion for him. He was saddened that anyone was thinking less of him because of what a few old, cranky sinners had suggested about him. And he was scared that, if they would lie about him in a deacons meeting, they might do worse to him outside of the church building. He needed to get home to his family!

He cried as he recounted the episode to Abigail in bed that evening, but, for the first time in their marriage and ministry, he withheld some information from his bride. She did not need to know some of the harsh comments that had been hurled his way by the church leaders. All she really needed to know was that they were gunning for him and his job. But they had not called him there; God had! Nonetheless, his feelings were hurt, and he was emotionally drained. His only prayer that night was, "Why God?" And then he slept.

22

CHAPTER TWENTY-TWO

On Monday, Maggie was on time to school, and, while Matt waited for the crossing guard to release the parents, he typed a quick text message to Lanie letting her know he would not be in until close to lunchtime. He admitted to himself that he was conflicted over going to see Clack so early on a Monday. He even considered the move might be self-indulgent since he enjoyed his time with Clack so much. His presence in the office was probably more prudent just so he could try to put out whatever fires were still smoldering from the night before. But more than anything, he wanted to do something that mattered, that made a difference. Since no one that he knew of was in the hospital, and since there were no crises through which to help church folks navigate, he was thankful he had Clack to distract him. And, though it felt childish when he put it into words, Matt needed a friend on Monday morning, and Clack was the closest thing to a friend he had at the moment. Besides, he promised he would be back on Monday, and it was definitely Monday.

On the drive to Altaville, he replayed the video in his mind of Sunday night's meeting. He was baffled by how things had spun so quickly out of control. And, though he felt certain he had not, Matt was forced to recount his steps and actions over the last five-and-a-half months at South Mill and question whether he had acted in a manner unbecoming of a minister. The recap did not take long. Yes, there were some regrets. *Aren't there always?* But he was committed to the conclusion that he had loved the people well and had been a godly leader and example. The church was growing for the first time in a long, long time. Young newcomers to the area, the Wellers being the latest, were finding their way in the door and, once they connected with another group of young families, joining the church membership. He wrestled behind the wheel with questions that he would not, were he in anyone else's presence, speak out loud. It became a conversation with himself that shortened the hour-and-a-half drive and made him wish he had longer in the car.

It began with questions like, "Did I misunderstand God's calling to this little town?" followed by answers like, "No! All the signs were there. I am exactly where I am supposed to be." As he drove, his rambling monologue took him to reminders of the warnings he had heard in seminary about small town churches where pastors were a dime a dozen and where everyone's favorite Sunday lunch was roasted preacher. He certainly had been the dish for the old man and his crew at lunch many times, especially yesterday. He thought about how to fight back, maybe accuse the old man of breaking into the house – let the church know what a terrorist he was becoming. He contemplated quitting his job and just disappearing during the night with his little family without warning from the Podunk town. Let them wonder what became of him. But, since he did not want to leave, he mulled over the idea of a terrible accident befalling Stephen and Hugh, but guilt took over and he found himself quoting the scriptures, "'Vengeance is mine,' says the Lord." Then, he half-prayed and half-wished out loud, "I wouldn't mind, though, if you went ahead and settled the score, God." He raised his eyebrow and rumpled his chin at the idea but immediately felt conviction again for letting hatred begin to grow in his heart, so he confessed and asked for the Lord's forgiveness.

His mind wandered back to the pictures he had seen of so many of his predecessors. With seven men before him in the role he now filled, not one of them had called, emailed, or written to wish him well or offer advice or prayer when he became the new kid. He found it odd but assumed it was, perhaps, a professional courtesy not to call and talk about "the way things were when I was there." But there was that one odd relic he had found tucked deep into the back of his top desk drawer when he was unpacking into his office that had intrigued him. It was a postcard that had the word *WELCOME!* in big letters across the front, and the church's address was on the back with a place to write a note. The card was from the stacks of similar ones that the now defunct visitation team used on Monday nights when they went in search of guests from the Sunday before. Matt originally thought the one left in his desk drawer was one a teenager had written ugly words on and had been confiscated by a preacher before him and stuffed it in his desk drawer and forgotten. He had looked at it for days before filing it away in a folder where he placed everything passed on to him in the first weeks on the job that he might or might not need down the road. Today, though, Matt thought of it, and particularly the words penned on it, and wondered if, perhaps, it had been left for him as some cryptic message. In the space where a kind, inviting note to a church visitor would be handwritten, an angry hand had written the message, "When the shit really starts to stink, funeral flowers can be quite fragrant." Still unsure of its full meaning, Matt reckoned that things definitely reeked for him right now, and maybe – just maybe, the message was affirmation that others who had gone before him had entertained the same ill-will he had prayerfully pondered in the truck that morning.

He snapped back to reality quickly with the ping of gravel on the undercarriage of his truck bed. Unconsciously, he tapped the brakes and felt the small truck fishtail slightly letting him know he had reached the end of the paved road and was quite close to Respira de Nuevo. He tried to shake the glum from his brain and focus on Clack. Perhaps the visit would be sufficient to reconnect him with the joy he typically felt when he went about the work he had committed his life to pursue. And if it didn't, Clack was usually good for a laugh or two, and that would be a welcomed consolation prize today.

The grounds were quiet when Matt silenced his engine and stepped out of his Chevy. More cars were in the parking lot than he had noticed before, and that made sense. It was the dayshift, and mornings were spent in sessions with therapists, life coaches, and recreational facilitators who did not live there and drove in and parked for work each day. He knew that any time with Clack would be short during the morning hours, and that was okay. He had come because he had promised, but he knew that he should not spend his whole day away from whatever trouble was brewing back at the church.

Vera was typing away at a computer but stopped everything and smiled her warmest when she saw Matt walk in. She did not ask if he wanted coffee; she just walked across the room and poured him a cup. He took it, sat down on a sofa in the great hall that was now the reception office and thanked her as she returned to her desk. She was there long enough to pick up her phone, press a button, and say into the receiver, "Blake, Pastor Matt is in the mansion." She then left her work behind and sat down in a chair adjacent to him and began talking about this and that. Matt asked good questions, and Vera matched him with each one. She was a delightful host, and Matt enjoyed the conversation so much that he did not even notice the thirty minutes that passed before he heard a door open and saw Blake coming in. He stood, as did Vera, shook hands with Blake, and told Vera how much he enjoyed his visit with her. He would later reflect on how whatever work was pressing at the moment at her desk was so easily abandoned to sit and talk. She was either very good at her job and could spare the time or so incredibly competent at her job that Matt didn't realize she was doing it while she sat and shared a cup of coffee with him.

Blake welcomed Matt by offering him another cup of coffee. Looking down at the cold remnants of the last one, Matt accepted. Vera quickly jumped up and supplied both men with a hot cup. There seemed to be no rush to move from the great hall in the mansion to a conference room or to wherever Clack was being kept at the moment, and the two of them sat and talked for a few minutes about football, family, and upcoming holiday plans. The casualness of the conversation did not lessen as Blake turned the conversation to Clack's progress at the facility. He spoke of his positive attitude, his willingness to work through his past and his future, ignoring his present residential status because, after all, he was simply taking a breath between what was and what would later be. Matt nodded, taking it all in, gaining an understanding of the approach to rehabilitation that made Respira have such a high rate of success and their clients have such a low rate of relapse. Blake explained that many of their residents returned and sometimes stayed much longer than their initial intake period, but, "we don't call those relapses...they simply need to catch their breath, if that makes sense," he divulged.

Wanting to know more about Clack, Matt asked, "So, how is Clack's breathing?"

Blake smiled and nodded. "He's had a good week since he saw you last. He's finishing up a group meeting in just a few minutes. Why don't we walk that way, and I can show you some of his handiwork while we go? I don't know that we're going to want to see him leave us. He has this place looking pretty spiffy."

As they left the mansion, Blake pointed out the newly sanded and repainted doors on the back porch. The paved stone pathway was new, too, and Blake gave credit to Clack and some of his dinner buddies for knocking that out. "He can go all day without taking a break, Matt. He works circles around the rest of us. He skips most of the recreation activities to do projects around the place. So thanks for sending him here." Both men laughed.

Clack was the first one out of the meeting room and lit up when he saw Matt. When he reached him, he consumed the small preacher in his arms with the hug of a gentle bear. Matt placed his arms around Clack's back and the two embraced like they had been friends for a lifetime and apart for half of one.

"Did Blake tell you about my breakthrough?"

Matt looked to his left to where the kind concierge was standing, smiling.

"That's your news to tell, Clack. Not mine."

Clack looked at a clock on the wall in the hallway. It was time for his morning meeting with Blake, so he asked, "Blake, can Matt join us today?"

Blake's head began to shake back and forth as though he was going to refuse, but, instead, he said, "I'm going to yield my time to Pastor Matt today. Y'all have a lot to talk about, and I think it will be helpful for you to share your progress with him. I'll meet you at lunch and can talk then if you need to."

With that news, Clack put a massive hand on the preacher's shoulder and almost carried him like a paper bag out the door. They walked to the residential building, and Clack continued pointing out projects he had completed, as well as those he had on his list to do. "Probably won't get 'em all done before I leave this place, but I'll come back and work when I'm free."

Matt got an ominous feeling that Clack swiftly validated. "And *you* can come help me!"

Matt smiled out of one side of his mouth already feeling tired at the prospect of it and breathed a heavy, "Uh huh."

It was a warm November morning in the south, and the fall colors were still partially decorating the landscape, so they bypassed Clack's apartment and exited a hallway door onto the back porch overlooking the river. Three rocking chairs were positioned to their left, and, as Matt went to sit in one, Clack yanked it away and said, "Better sit in one of these over here! That one's seen better days."

Each seemed to inhale the landscape for a moment before resuming their talk. A breath of cool air floated past, and the trees shivered as the morning sun set the vibrant valley ablaze. Their limbs waved and fanned the red and yellow and orange flames of autumn. The dread of day melted in the warmth of that moment, and Matt was glad he had come so early to this beautiful place.

Rekindling the conversation, Matt spoke first, "They seem to be enjoying your skilled labor around here. They'll probably want you to stay a while."

"Actually," Clack took over, "I probably will be out by the end of the month."

"Really?"

"Yeah, that's what I wanted to tell you. I had a pretty big breakthrough about a week ago right here on this porch. Something you said that day about Jenni and feelings and I don't remember the rest. But it triggered some stuff in me. It was like I was being lured to this very spot, and the lights just began to come on in my brain. And, without going too deep into it, I'll tell you that I've been pretty self-absorbed the last few years...well, the last few decades."

Matt nodded but said nothing, inviting Clack to continue.

"I've seen a lot of F'd up shit in my day, pardon my language..." Matt laughed at how Clack cleaned up one word but left the other one out there and how, for the first time, he seemed to notice.

"...some of it, I've been the victim to. All of it, I've tried to play the victim in. But, coming here has helped me see that the vast majority of it, I have actually caused."

Matt wanted to say something trite like *don't be so hard on your-self*, but he knew that Clack had come to this epiphany through lots of prayerful and professional counsel. He would not dare inter-ject his banality into the process. Clack chewed on his next words carefully.

"Did you know they have a military counselor here?"

Matt shook his head. He did not know.

"He's older than me." Clack's sentences were slow and choppy. Matt was careful not to interrupt. "He was in Chu Lai and Da Nang." Matt knew enough to know those were in Vietnam.

"Ever heard of Hanoi?" Clack asked.

Matt had heard the name but knew nothing of its significance. "Yes, of course!"

"Know anything from history about Operation Linebacker II or the Christmas Bombings?"

Matt did not remember either of those terms from his history classes, but he would not disrespect his friend's service by admitting ignorance of what, obviously, were significant missions for Clack or for this military counselor. He knew how tight-lipped most Vietnam veterans were about what they saw and experienced over there, and he scooted to the edge of the rocking chair as one set of those lips loosened up a bit. But Clack did not divulge any details. He simply said, with a strange look of satisfaction in eyes that were calmer than Matt had seen them, "If hell has a basement, we were in it."

Matt took the lengthy pause as a chance to make an assumption. "So, the military counselor here has helped you make peace with what all you experienced in Vietnam?"

Clack laughed at the question. "No!" But then he explained, "You've heard that war is hell – well, it is. And, you're a theologian, so you know that hell is filled with all evil all the time. What I've come to know is that I'll never make peace with what we did...what I did...what we saw...what we lived through over there, but I'm at peace knowing that I won't. And that's probably the best any of us can hope for."

Matt could see that Clack was really okay with that revelation, and he patted himself on the back for having the wherewithal to get Clack to come to a place like this where he could, in fact, breathe again. He smiled, reached out, and patted Clack on the knee and said, "Thank you for telling me this."

Clack grabbed Matt's hand and almost jerked his arm out of socket as he jumped up excitedly and said, "That's not all I have to say!" Clack drug the preacher, not letting go of his hand, which Matt found both intimidating and sweet, to the railing of the porch overlooking the sloping woods to the creek. Letting go of Matt so he could place both hands on the railing, Clack continued his story.

Matt heard all about the drinking, the collapse of both a marriage and a booming business, about the love Clack had for Jameson and Mary Ellen, about the investment they had made in his company, and about the failure he both experienced and became. He learned that Clack drove to South Mill one day about a year ago to see an addiction counselor that a friend from Cardelville knew, and how, after seeing a sign for Sawyer Industries and the new hospital construction, he stopped, applied, and was hired on the spot. He never even called to cancel his appointment with the therapist. Clack thrived on working hard and putting in long hours, but he confessed to Matt that all of that was so he could avoid the pain life had dealt him. He continued his disclosure by admitting that when his hands and mind weren't busy with work, he had to silence the echoes of his past with something, so he drank. Clack's eyes began to moisten as they merged with the babbling stream below on which they were now fixed.

"I used to drink with this friend of mine. Just sometimes. And it was fun and innocent really, just boys being boys. Three years ago, he died, and I drank a lot more after that. I think I felt like it kept his memory alive, but it did just the opposite." Clack had plunged into the depths of his soul now, and his heart's thoughts bubbled to the surface. "I only drank with *him*, and he's gone now. And, unless, or should I say *until*, I see him again, I have no reason to drink." Then, he stood in silence...smiling.

Matt was overcome with the realization that this was a holy moment – that Clack had, quite possibly, experienced healing from the pain of much of his past. His eyes, too, glistened as the morning air propelled the day onward.

Matt finally found words. "You've made a lot of progress in a short amount of time."

"I think another week here, and I'll be a completely new man."

"Then, you're welcome!" Matt broke the weight of the last hour with jokes.

"Thank you!" Clack conceded.

When it seemed that Clack has said all he wanted to say, Matt explained that he needed to be getting back to the office, though he wished more than Clack knew that he could, in fact, stay. The peace of Respira de Nuevo was a lifetime away from the chaos to which he had to return. Clack walked him back to his truck in the main parking lot. As they walked, Clack said, "I was surprised to see you so early today, and I was actually going to have Blake call you and ask you to wait until Wednesday to come this week."

"Why Wednesday?" Matt asked.

"They said I have earned a night out. Sort of like R&R or leave in the military. But, I was hoping you'd come and take me home for the night."

Matt's eyes were a display of dread that he could not hide.

Clack read them and reassured him. "I'm fine, Matt! I only want to go home and get some clothes and some tools. I need to replace a set of steps and cut a new window for the boathouse, and I don't have what I need. Plus, I have this rocking chair at home that I want to bring to my back porch. Gotta replace that rickety one you tried to sit in. I promise I'll come back first thing Thursday morning. I actually love it here, and I am not trying to escape."

Matt smiled, agreed, and hugged his friend goodbye. "I'll be up shortly after lunch on Wednesday," he spoke over his shoulder as he slid into the driver's seat. Hearing the crinkling sound of paper underneath him, he reached and grabbed an envelope he had sat on. "Clack!" he called out. "Someone asked me to give this you; I almost forgot."

Clack recognized the almost calligraphied handwriting on the envelope and smiled, seeming genuinely glad to get something from Jenni. "You almost forgot?"

Matt shrugged innocently. "I wasn't sure you'd want it; I don't know what's in it."

"You are a terrible carrier pigeon. See you Wednesday."

Matt sat there staring at the letter in Clack's hand. He wanted to say, "read it to me," but he knew that would be invasive. Clack kept waiting on the truck to move and then caught a clue and said, "You wanna know what's in here, don't you?"

Matt's eyes were as wide as a kid's on Christmas morning, but he hated to admit his nosiness.

Clack laughed as he ripped the envelope opened. He quickly scanned the contents of Jenni's note and gave Matt a very generic report that it was nothing bad, just some encouragement. "She still hasn't asked where I am?"

"Nope! But I think she knows you are someplace important."

"Well, tell her I'm at Disney World!"

Matt laughed as he thrust the truck in reverse.

Clack called to him as he eased out of the parking space, "Seriously...tell her I'm getting better."

CHAPTER TWENTY-THREE

Matt hit the office door at full speed, realizing he was much later getting back than he had indicated in his text to Lanie. She smiled and said good morning even though it was pushing one o'clock. She handed him the weekly stack of letters to sign as he brushed past her desk to his office door, which was closed and locked. Matt looked around for a place to lay the stack he was handed so he could fumble for his keys, but Lanie quickly produced her own key and unlocked the door for him. Lanie always had the door to Matt's office opened when she arrived before him, but the oddity of it being closed and locked that late in the day did not strike him until she followed him in and closed the door behind her. Matt immediately became worried and asked what was up.

"Brother Heath was here," Lanie apologetically said.

"Oh, okay. What did he need?"

"That's the thing." Lanie relayed her own worry, "I don't know."

Matt looked puzzled.

"He called about 8:30, asking to speak to you. I told him you were not in, and he grunted and said he'd be by later. I assumed that meant when you got back. He showed up about twenty minutes later, and..." Lanie paused, "...I'm sorry, but he came in your office. He slipped in while I was in Trudy's office, and I am not even sure how long he was in here before I noticed him. I walked in to place a phone message on your desk, and when I turned around, he was sitting on the couch."

"Doing what?"

"I don't know. One of his sons was with him – the youngest one – I never remember his name. They were just sitting. I said good morning. Brother Heath said they'd just be a minute. And his son didn't say anything. I told him you were out for most of the morning, and he said he did not need to see you – that they were just out shopping."

"That's weird."

"I know, and that's really all he said."

Matt knew about this youngest son of the Heaths. Once, when Matt was having a morning coffee visit at Miss Mabel's house, she had talked too much and let the Heath's secret out. There was a son, much younger than any of his siblings – in his late twenties, about Matt's own age, who had gotten involved in drugs when he was in high school. Then, in his early twenties, he had been cooking meth with his girlfriend, who later became his wife and then his ex-wife. When he was caught and arrested, she escaped without charges and left the state. He was supposedly clean now and out of jail, and he was moving back to the area to open a sign business or print shop or something. Stephen and Dorothy had never mentioned these plans, as this would be the third or fourth venture the boy had begun since he had been released. Not one had succeeded. No one knew why the boy kept trying to start his own businesses, but it was assumed that it was because no one would hire him with his drug and criminal record. Matt had, at one time, thought he might like to meet this son – that he might be able to somehow help turn his life around. That was when Miss Mabel warned him off saying, "Some people never change, and he's been a loser his whole life." That's when she covered her mouth, lightly slapped herself on her wrinkled jaw, and scolded herself saying, "Mabel, your big mouth has done it again." She then apologized to the preacher and offered him another cup of coffee.

"Where are they now?" Matt asked Lanie

"He left about fifteen minutes after that. I'm not sure if he was mad at his son or what. He did not seem agitated, but he seemed winded and looked pale."

"Vampires always look pale," Matt said, and his face immediately showed that those words were supposed to have stayed in his head. He apologized.

Lanie did not respond, though she did not mind that he said it. "I looked around, and I don't think they touched anything of yours or snooped through your stuff." Matt smiled kindly at her and assured her that he was not upset at her. He did feel violated, but that was not a new feeling. At least a dozen times in his short tenure he had come into his office to find Heath making himself at home, always waiting on Matt to arrive. And, with someone possibly doing the same these days at the house, Matt was growing accustomed to the feeling that nothing in his life was private anymore. He thanked Lanie, opened his office door, always a gentleman, and closed it behind her when she left the room.

Bringing someone with him was a new move for the old man, and Matt was thrown off by it. Surely he did not bring his son, who already had negative feelings toward the church, with him to pick up where he and his gang had left off the night before. What did the old man want? And did Lanie know more than she was telling? Matt was paranoid now, and he was questioning his own ability to distinguish allies from adversaries. He was glad she was not in the room now to read his face. He had to snap out of it, shake some light back into his head where darkness was creeping in. He did, literally and rapidly, shake his head and throw backwards against the soft cushion of his leather desk chair reclining all the way back with the momentum. Just then, his office door flung open, and he lunged forward to an upright position. It was Lanie again, and she hadn't knocked. He now read the worry on her face.

Without excusing her intrusion, she blurted her statement at him. "I just have one more thing I need to say. I...I would have never let him in here without your permission. And, I don't know if it was within my rights to do it, but I kicked him out. I don't know what he was up to, but it felt creepy, and I told him he had to leave." She was talking fast. "I told him that this was your private office, and, without an invitation from you, he had no business being in here. I don't know why I did it, but I did. I didn't see them doing anything wrong, but it just didn't feel right." Then, with a curled lip and batting eyes, she chose her next words carefully and added, "Brother Heath can be a very difficult man, Pastor."

"I'm finding that out for myself!"

"Well, I'm sure he's very angry at me," she worried aloud.

Lanie needed camaraderie, and Matt smiled as he said, "Welcome to the club!"

Before closing the door behind her and returning to her Monday tasks, she offered one last gesture just in case Matt, too, was upset with her. "That's why your door was locked, and I won't open your office before you arrive anymore."

This is Lanie, he thought, the pastor's confidential assistant. He did trust her...implicitly. She was an ally. Matt knew this to be true, but he realized that the recent attacks on his ministry and his character were causing him to be the one acting outside of his typical nature. He looked at her with kind eyes and said, "No need to change your routine, Lanie. It really won't make a difference anyway; I'm sure he has a key."

Lanie formed a worried smile and returned to her office, closing the door to the pastor's study as she went. Matt's mind raced but produced no definitive thought as a prize. Finally, he resumed full tilt in his chair and stared at the ceiling for at least five minutes before giving up on figuring anything out. He reached for his pen, separated the letters, and began looking over the names of the newcomers from Sunday. He had forgotten in the fog of the deacons' meeting that there had been so many new faces in the morning service. He paused a moment to prayerfully consider the facts. The church was growing under his leadership. People in the community liked him and his little family. If he could strip all of his latest troubles away, South Mill was a pretty decent little town. He concluded the process with a peaceful resolution – *I am exactly where you want me to be, God*. And, at least for the moment, he believed it.

Jotting notes to the visitors he remembered meeting, Matt was somewhat joyful as he conducted his pastoral duties. When all were signed and sealed, he stood to deliver the stack to Lanie for mailing. When he did, he glanced down at the helium tank still lying on its side against the wall beside his credenza. So far, no one had come to retrieve it, and he chuckled at the thought of Stephen Heath seeing it there during his unsolicited morning visit and enjoyed a little guilty pleasure at the prospect of it firing the old man up again. For now, it, too, was exactly where it needed to be. He smiled and went out to talk to Lanie.

Handing off the stack of mail, Matt suggested he get busy producing a title to his Wednesday night lesson. Lanie reminded him that it was a Business Meeting night, and he would not need a lesson. He would have been relieved that he did not have to scramble to be ready to teach, especially since he had another road trip to make on Wednesday, but the anxiety a church Business Meeting produced for him far outweighed any such liberation. "That's right," he said without feeling. "I'll get to work on Sunday's sermon." Lanie just smiled and said, "No rush on that title."

He spent the rest of the afternoon reading the Bible, searching through commentaries, and Googling and reading sermons preached on the same passage by other ministers he followed. Seldom was a man good at preaching and pastoring; he either favored the studying or preferred the personal interaction with people. Matt was talented at both. He enjoyed his afternoon jotting down notes and imagining how he would put them all together in an eloquent delivery on Sunday. Without the task of teaching midweek, he knew he would be even more engaging this week than most. He found it fun to read the ancient words and make them relevant to a modern audience. He was enjoying reading a sermon preached by a scholarly pastor he admired when he scrolled too far down the page and was accosted by the next sermon title in the man's series, *"Praying for Your Enemies."*

For the next half hour, Matt had no choice but to wrestle with his own present reality. He hated to think of Brother Heath as an enemy, but, as far as Matt could see, that's exactly what he was. Heath's efforts at discrediting Matt to the church leadership were apparent in last night's meeting, but what might the old man be saying to the church members out in public on a daily basis? His criticisms of Matt's methods and decisions were broadcast in the presence of church visitors in a crowded restaurant. The possibility that Heath or his minions were snooping through Matt's personal effects were becoming more likely. All of it combined led Matt to the scary conclusion that he did, indeed, have an enemy. An old, wise...no crafty, and evil enemy.

Coming to that conclusion was easy. It was what followed that Matt was having a hard time accepting. As he pondered the predicament, he remembered the story a famous preacher with a successful television ministry had told when he came and spoke for several days in chapel services at Matt's seminary. The renowned evangelist told how animosity had grown between one of his church members and himself when he was a young minister. After fighting did nothing to resolve the issues, he resolved to simply pray for the man daily. After several months of doing so, the man did something (Matt couldn't remember what) to make a public spectacle of himself and lost all credibility within the church and ended up leaving. Matt didn't know why he had not thought of that story sooner. He knew now that he, too, had to *pray* for his enemy. And, not wanting to simply speak a few words about the man in any inclusive prayer he might otherwise pray, and unwilling to do it in the presence of his wife and children, he began to scheme over ways to pray for Heath in a bold, up close, and personal way.

Finally, Matt concluded that close proximity would be most effective vantage point from which to see if his petitions were making a difference in the old man's life. He mulled over a variety of scenarios. He could embark on a lengthy prayer each time Heath entered the office, but that might tip the old man off to what he was doing. Then he envisioned marching right up to the front door of Dorothy and Stephen's house and declaring that he had come to pray the evil out of them. As entertaining and enjoyable their response to that would be, he knew that was not prudent. At last, he settled on the idea that he would stop just shy of the front door to their house. In the thicket of azaleas and pine trees, Matt could shroud himself and focus his eyes and heart on the home where the enemy resided. He waffled momentarily when he pictured himself being caught hiding in the bushes outside of the old couple's home. But certain he could explain how Heath was behind the break-ins at the parsonage, he felt like his creepiness would seem mild by comparison.

He mapped out a route through the county's green space by which he would remain in the shadows of shrubs and trees the entire time. It would not be too far out of his way on his nightly jog – the one he had stopped taking three months ago and the one he would convince Abigail he must resume immediately. He did not want to trouble her with his crazy idea of praying so close by to the Heath's home. There were elements of this whole ordeal that he felt he must keep to himself so as not to overburden his sweet wife. She had already experienced more of its brunt than she should have. In his commitment to always be truthful with his wife, though, he promised himself that if she questioned him at all he would disclose the fullness of his plan. She would not worry about him being gone for a short time in the evening, especially with both cars parked in the driveway. He would go early enough after tucking the kids in that he would return in plenty of time for the two of them to watch television, snuggle, talk, and pray together just like they did every night. He kicked back in his chair again, reclining fully and, this time, propped his feet up on his desk, crossing his right one over the left – a good posture for someone who felt so good about his plan.

As Matt tossed his backpack into the truck to head home for the day, he remembered that he had wanted to look again at that card that had been so mysteriously left behind by someone before his arrival. He shrugged and dismissed the need to read the words again, certain it would bring him no more clarity than before. As he pulled out of the parking lot, he did, however, recite the words of it once more, this time cleaning it up a bit, "when the *crap* really starts to stink, funeral flowers can be quite fragrant." He was pleased that his dark day had not left him as dejected as whoever had sat at his desk and penned those haunting words.

Over dinner, Matt told Abigail about his good visit with Clack, about how he hoped to be finished with the program by the end of the month, about how he was using his construction skills to remodel the place, and about how he had seemed so at peace over everything, even the letter from Jenni. Abigail was intrigued and curious. "What did she say in it?"

"I wish I knew. He didn't say, and I couldn't bring myself to ask. But he didn't get angry when he read it."

"I guess that's a good sign," Abigail concluded.

As they cleared the dishes, the children hurried to get their last little bit of playtime in before baths. Matt made it a point to tell his wife about his unwelcomed guest who camped out in his office that morning. While he did want to shelter her from some of the ugliness Heath was dishing out, he was calculated in telling her about the intrusion just in case he ever needed to defend his plan of action, which was the next thing he chose to tell. "I'm going to go out for a jog tonight. Okay?"

"Okay?" Though supportive, Abigail's voice lifted toward the end revealing her surprise.

"I got out of the habit at the end of the summer, and I need to be exercising. It'll help blow off some steam," Matt explained himself. "Besides," he sought to lighten things ups, "I know you married me for my body, and I'd hate to disappoint you."

"Whatever!" Abigail smiled and kissed Matt on the lips then announced, "Bath time!"

Both kids scurried up the steps, Maggie to the master bathroom, and M.J. to the Jack and Jill between his room and Maggie's. While they bathed, Matt dug out a pair of black jogging pants and a black compression shirt. He dressed quickly, put on his running shoes, and prepared for bedtime stories and prayers.

"Daddy's dressed like a bad guy," M.J. said as he dove headfirst across Chop into the bed. "You going to rob a bank?"

Abigail looked at him and raised an eyebrow. "Why are you wearing all black? You may get run over by a car."

"I have a reflector vest." Matt shrugged as he defended his wardrobe selection.

Together, the Hardys tucked in their children, said bedtime prayers, gave their babies goodnight kisses, and turned off the lights. Maggie interrupted the darkness with, "Hey, you didn't kiss Felix!" Both returned and put their lips as close to the dog's head as they could stand and close enough to satisfy their daughter. She laughed and said goodnight before wrapping her arms around her canine friend.

Abigail grabbed a magazine she had picked up earlier that day. Matt flipped on the porch light and exited through the front door, locking it with his key from the outside. He stretched for a moment on the front steps then trotted off toward the park with the light of the streetlamps bouncing off of the neon green and metallic silver stripes of his vest. To ease his guilty conscience, he decided to actually jog for twenty minutes before beginning his clandestine mission.

Only slightly out of breath after a brisk run, he ducked behind the dugout at the youth league fields, tucked his reflective vest in his pocket, and walked it off through the woods on his way to the side yard of the Heaths' place. He met no one along the way and even kept cool when he heard a dog barking somewhere on the other side of the wood line. South Mill had leash laws, and he had never seen a stray in the six months he had lived there. Surely that one barking was fenced in the backyard somewhere far enough away from his destination to pose no threat. When he reached what he thought must be the property line, he made sure to stay low to the ground and close to the woods so as not to set off any motion lights on the property.

The woods were mostly pine trees, but a few straggling leaves from a variety of other trees let out a crunch every few steps Matt took. He was relieved to reach the grass of the Heath's lawn that only whispered under his feet. To get to the thicket where he desired to pray, he would need to muster a quick sprint across a wide-open part of the front yard. Again, he was concerned about motion lights. Counting down from three, he darted from the shadows, a quick blip on an otherwise motionless lawn. There were, evidently, no motion lights. Within seconds, he was tucked behind a badly over-grown azalea that was flanked on all sides by others that were just as dense. The adventure of sneaking around in the dark almost made him forget why he was there, but as he looked up at the tall pines that canopied him and knelt on the soft blanket of straw they had shed, his position on the ground felt enough like a prayerful one to remind him of his purpose. He focused his eyes on the front porch, unable to see any motion inside the lighted windows of the house, and he began to pray for his enemy. He fell backwards in surprise, though, when the garage door began to flip upward and Dorothy's blue Buick began backing out. As she finished her backward maneu-ver and shifted into drive, the headlights swung full beam right at his hiding place. She never slowed down but tossed tiny pieces of gravel backwards at Matt as she left the house. Matt pulled up his long black sleeve to see what time it was. 7:26. He spoke out loud, "Now where is that old bat headed?" Immediately, he felt conviction for calling her that and corrected himself saying, again out loud, "That's not how you should talk about the people you are supposed to be praying for."

Wanting to be faithful to his task, Matt spent the next ten min-utes praying. He asked God to give him a love for Brother Heath and

Sister Dorothy. He prayed for their marriage, for their family, and even for the son who had come home to start a sign business. He prayed that he would stay sober and clean. He prayed that Stephen would welcome him home without judgment. Then, he began to pray for the current state of affairs between himself and the Heaths. He prayed that God would thwart any efforts the old man was making to be divisive, to damage Matt's character, to spread rumors, and to place himself in better light by smearing the reputation of others, specifically Matt's. He concluded by saying simply, "God, help me and Stephen to come to a peaceful relationship," stopping short of asking God to make the two of them become friends, which seemed to Matt like asking for too much of a miracle. And he did not pray that Heath would make a public spectacle of himself and have to leave the church in shame, but if God chose to answer the prayer that way, Matt was perfectly willing to accept that outcome.

With his mission accomplished, he made a mad dash back across the front lawn into the shadows of the wood line, and emerged from the baseball field into the light of the South Mill Park. He unfurled his vest from his pocket, placed it around his back as he picked up his jogging pace and headed home. The plan had worked, and Matt felt accomplished in carrying it out. He took the front steps two at a time, unlocked the front door, and quietly, so as not to wake the kids, rejoined his wife for their nightly alone time. As he sat down beside her, Abigail lowered her magazine, pinched her nose, and said, "You smell like a sweaty boy. Go take a shower!"

Feeling invigorated from his escapade, he batted his eyebrows at her and said, "Wanna join me?"

The smack of her magazine on his head gave him her answer. He showered alone and soon returned to cozy up with her on the couch. They talked about her day, about Maggie's schoolwork, and other pleasant topics. After the first ten minutes of the eleven o'clock news, they knew no more than they had before turning it on, so they went to bed and slept peacefully through the night with their new home security system securely located in the top drawer of Matt's nightstand.

CHAPTER TWENTY-FOUR

Abigail's cell phone punctuated her last moments of good sleep before Tuesday became even busier than expected. It was not that uncommon for the landline to ring in the wee hours with the news that some church member had fallen ill during the night and might need the pastor to pray by his or her side in the emergency room. A cell phone ringing earlier than the Hardy family typically woke up was, perhaps, something more personal and jarred Abigail from a drool-puddled pillow. She spoke quietly to keep from waking the kids, but, as the conversation continued, she spoke in more normal tones realizing that the subject matter of the call meant everyone needed to be awake and out of the bed. Matt, who was always up and ready first, was just stepping out of the shower when he heard the phone ringing. A puddle had formed on the floor where he stood wrapped in a towel trying to discern who had called at such an hour, and Abigail frowned and flicked her hand at him to get back onto the bathroom tile floor. "I don't think it will be a problem," she said to the person on the other end of the conversation. "Let me just check with Matt real quick. Can you hold on?" She groggily searched for the mute button, pressed it and spoke to her soggy husband. "It's Maggie's teacher. She says that one of the moms who was supposed to chaperone the field trip today is sick and wants to know if I can go in her place."

"Fine with me," Matt said as he shrugged, relieved that the phone call was not some bad news. When Abigail just looked at him with a cocked head and pursed lips, he thought maybe he had given the wrong answer. "Oh, wait!" he retracted his quick approval assuming he was supposed to. "Don't you have that thing today?"

"What are you talking about? What thing?" Matt had confused the both of them.

"I don't know!" Matt threw his hands up in frustrated inquiry and laughed at his wife. "Why are you looking at me that way? I thought you wanted me to say you couldn't go today or something. Maybe you don't want to spend your day with six-year-olds on a cattle farm."

"Of course, I want to spend the day with my daughter and her class, and it is a dairy...not a cattle farm. But, what about M.J.?"

"Take him with you? And where do you think the milk in the dairy comes from? Cows!"

"I can't. There's not room on the bus. And when I think of *cattle*, I think of meat, not milk."

"Then, he can come to the church with me..." Matt's words sounded more like a question than a plan, and his raised shoulders and twisted face expressed the uncertainty of his offer.

"Do you think that's a good idea?" Abigail cautioned him.

Matt thought for a quick second and said, "It'll be fine. Go! Have fun!"

Abigail unmuted her phone and spoke as she headed to Maggie's room to wake her. "I'm glad to do it. Thanks for calling!" She ended the call and sat down next to Maggie on her bed and said, "Guess who is going with you on your field trip today?"

Maggie yawned a big "Who?" as she sat up in the bed.

"Mommy!"

Suddenly wide awake, Maggie squealed, "Yay! Mommy!"

The family added some unusual pep to their morning routine to get everyone out of the house on time.

Matt and M.J. arrived first for the workday, and, before Matt could even unlock his own office door, he wiped fingerprints off of the copy machine glass and closed that lid back, wrestled M.J. from Lanie's swivel chair and hit "escape" on her computer keyboard to hopefully undo whatever M.J. had pressed on the keys, and saved the electric pencil sharpener from a blue ink pen embossed with the church's name and logo, another relic from the visitation days. He now understood why Abigail had looked at him twice when he said, "fine with me." Finally in his own space, Matt situated M.J. at the large desk, shoved a piece of copy paper in front of him and told him to draw something. "And don't move," Matt instructed as he retraced their steps to make sure nothing else was amiss in the wake of their morning entrance. He was not certain that Windex could be used on the glass of a copy machine, but he took a chance anyway. Lanie's computer seemed to be back in hibernation mode, and Matt saw no other concerns. After peeking back in at M.J., who was scribbling away on the paper, Matt ran to a classroom in the children's wing and hoisted up a small, pint-sized wooden table and a red plastic chair that seemed to fit perfectly underneath it. When he returned to his office, he placed them both in the corner behind his own desk, and M.J. turned in the big swivel chair to investigate. Matt smiled at his tiny protégé, "Look! Here's your desk for today. You can work at it while I work at mine." He grabbed the bag Matt had packed full of his favorite things from home, scooted his legs under the table, and busied himself with a coloring page, crayon in one hand and a Spiderman action figure in the other. For now, the boy seemed content and occupied, and Matt began to organize his own desk for a day of studying since M.J.'s presence would limit his other routines like counseling and visits within the community.

Matt heard Lanie come in and soon smelled fresh coffee brewing. Lanie faithfully brought a cup of hot coffee to her boss every morning – not because he expected her to but because she drank it throughout the day, and it made her feel less like an addict when she could serve it up to someone else in the office. Soon, Lanie came into the room carrying two coffee mugs. Matt looked up when she said, "Good morning, Pastor!" and M.J. bolted from his chair and hugged Lanie around the knees just as she awkwardly bent at the middle to lean far and sit both cups on Matt's desk. She reached down, picked M.J. up, pulled him in close, and smooched all over his little face. M.J. dodged one of the kisses to rear back and look her in the face and say, "I get to come to work with you today, Lanie!"

"I heard!" Lanie responded in a sing-song voice before she gave him one last kiss, put him back down on the ground, and handed him his very own coffee mug filled with chocolate milk. Matt looked puzzled until she cleared things up by saying, "Abigail texted me a few minutes ago."

"Warning you?"

"Preparing me for our special guest," Lanie corrected him. From the first day Matt and his family had met Lanie, there was a special bond between her and his son. He appreciated more than she knew how she went out of her way to make him feel important. She was not a church member, so she did not know M.J. as the pastor's kid. She saw him for the sweet, smart, small for his age, cute kid that he was. And the feeling M.J. had for Lanie was mutual. Like a little grown man, M.J. returned to his *desk* and drank from his mug while Lanie and Matt discussed the day's administrative needs. Hearing the voice of someone much younger than the typical church office guest, Trudy and the youth pastor came in search of the source. Trudy, though much more reserved than Lanie, welcomed M.J. and asked if he would be willing to help her with some counting later in the morning. The youth pastor reached over Matt's desk to give a high-five to the tyke and called him "Homeslice." Matt looked at the party forming in his office and simply said, "This is nice, everyone gathered together in my office having fun. Maybe I should bring a guest every day." The staff laughed, visited a few more minutes, and then all returned to their work for the day.

After a few phone calls came in, Lanie knocked on the pastor's closed door and entered when he waved her in with his hand. She spoke to M.J. first and said, "Hey, little man, how'd you like to come work in my office for a while? I have some envelopes that need to be licked and stamped and some pencils that need to be sharpened. Then, we can walk together to the post office." She continued talking to M.J., but provided information Matt needed. "Your daddy needs to run to the hospital to make a few visits, but we can have some fun and get some work done while he's gone." She placed a sticky note down on Matt's desk on which she had written two names of church members, both of whom were admitted to the hospital sometime the day before. Two informed church members had called, one after the other, to let the church office know of the hospitalizations. Matt squinted at Lanie and asked, "Are you sure?"

"Yes, I'm sure that I want M.J. to help me out for a while, and I'm sure that his dad needs to go make some visits. So, have fun!" Matt appreciated the way Lanie was handling him. M.J. gathered the coloring page he was working on and a box of crayons and scampered off behind Lanie. Matt was reluctant to leave the boy with a babysitter that was being paid to do church work, but Lanie seemed to have the situation under her own capable control.

When Matt reached the hospital, he circled the parking lot several times looking for Stephen Heath's car. Though he did not see it, he braced himself for the encounter he would surely face in one of the hospital rooms. The first visit was to a lady in her late sixties who had undergone knee replacement surgery the day before, and, when Matt realized that he was the only visitor in the room, he flashed a dimply grin at her and greeted her by saying, "Good morning! I'm here for your 9:00 dance lesson." Though still in pain, she was elated to see her pastor and enjoyed the jokes and easy conversation he was so gifted at making. The second visit was to the cardiac floor where a man of forty-three years was being prepped for a heart catheterization after some severe chest pains after dinner the night before. The gravity of that situation minimized the laughs and called for serious prayer and encouragement. If things went well, he would be released on medication, but if there were blockages, he would not emerge from those ominous push-button-activated doors without, at minimum, a stent or two, and in the worst-case scenario, without bypass surgery. Matt observed that the man's aging parents were by his side, along with his wife and two teenage sons, so he asked them all to gather around the bed where they all held hands as Matt prayed a compassionate and kind prayer. Everyone shared how they were sure this was all going to be okay, how these procedures were quite routine these days, and how he had the best doctor in the region performing the surgery were it to be necessary. Optimism was the mood in the room, and the patient himself told his oldest son that the pastor had been at his football game a couple of weeks ago. The conversation shifted to the oldest son's success on the field and college hopes and to the youngest's interest in theatre and the auditions they were having this week for the winter musical at the school. No one was thinking about the worst possible outcomes but planning for getting this procedure out of the way and resuming life.

A knock at the door seemed to surprise the gathering, even though nurses had been coming and going regularly throughout the morning. Without waiting for a "come in," the knocker opened the door to a crack-width and stuck just his head in and asked,

"Can you squeeze another visitor in?" When Matt saw the roadmap wrinkles on the large nose of Stephen Heath protrude around the opening door, he almost answered the question with a loud *no*. But it was too late. The old man had entered, and with him came the solemnity that was characteristic of a pious old preacher. He eyed Matt momentarily but chose to ignore his presence completely. He crossed the gray tiles of the sterile room with the grace of a funeral director, looking down and shaking his head from side to side as he approached the family. Matt made note of how closely his skin color matched the pale floor and how antiseptic his demeanor was too.

"So sad that you all are here for such an occasion," came the long, drawn-out words of the old preacher. "I know this really puts a damper on Thanksgiving next week," he continued – his speech becoming slower with each syllable he spoke. And Matt thought the holiday might actually arrive before the old man finished speaking. After introducing himself around the room as the retired pastor at South Mill, though everyone knew who Brother Heath was, he asked if he could pray with the family. The wife spoke first and said, "We appreciate that, but Brother Matt just finished praying." Again, Heath eyeballed Matt. When the awkward silence reached a pinnacle, the old man smiled and grabbed hold of the hospital bed and said, "Well, more prayers never hurt anyone," and launched off into a lengthy and bemoaning prayer for the life and death situation this family was facing. When *Amen* was finally spoken, dread filled the faces of the family and the youngest boy was nursing puddles forming at the bottom of his eyelids. Brother Stephen looked around at the sad faces and seemed to shift his own expression to one of satisfaction. Permanence began to attach itself to Heath's presence as he reached for the arm of a chair in which to sit, but the father of the patient abruptly grabbed the reaching hand and manipulated it into a handshake and began leading the old man to the door as he said, "Thank you so much for coming. Let me walk you to the elevator." Matt choked back laughter, but his eyes smiled brightly, and he, along with both teens and their mom and their grandmother silently shared a joyful moment. The grandmother spoke first and said quite simply, "I'm sure he means well." They all nodded in apparent agreement.

When the nurse asked everyone to step out while she finished prepping for the procedure, Matt took it as his cue to leave, too, although no one in the family seemed in a hurry for him to depart. He promised to be praying and wrote his cell phone number on the back of his business card for them to call if they needed anything and couldn't reach him at the church number. They thanked him, and he hurried to the elevator certain that Brother Heath was long gone.

Matt and M.J. had a picnic lunch on the church playground with the burgers Matt picked up in the McDonald's drive-thru on his way back from the hospital visits. Both enjoyed a few minutes of the warm fall sunshine as M.J. played on the swings and slide and Matt read from a scholarly commentary on Sunday's scripture lesson. A car door closing snapped Matt out of his book, and he groaned as he saw Stephen Heath shuffling across the parking lot toward the church office door. "Come on, M.J.," he said heavily. "Daddy's got a visitor."

As the Hardy boys came in from their time in the sun, Lanie's eyes met Matt's and mirrored the same questioning look of what to do with M.J. Without hesitation, Lanie reached for the boy's hand and said, "I have some folding you can help me with while your dad meets with his guest." Lunch and a playground had primed him for his afternoon nap, but M.J. was silently content to go with Lanie. She disappeared with him into the office work room, and Matt was left alone in Lanie's office with the elder preacher, who was staring at M.J. and Lanie as they went disappeared the doorway.

"Come in," Matt invited, and the old man followed him into his office without speaking. Once inside, Matt closed the door behind them and waited until the old man sat down to head to his own chair behind his desk. Stephen did not sit right away but instead examined an apple slice and a grape that were lying on the corner of Matt's desk. Matt had not noticed that M.J. had deposited the last few bites of his morning snack there on his way out with Lanie the first time she had rescued him. Matt chuckled an embarrassed laugh, and grabbed up the fruit and wiped the residue with a paper towel he produced from a bottom drawer. Though it was all gone within seconds, Brother Heath used the tiny mess as his intro and launched into a tirade. "This is what I'm talking about with you!" Matt was ready for a fight; He'd been rehearsing since Monday morning, but when Heath was triggered by M.J.'s snack, the young pastor was caught off guard.

"I beg your pardon!"

"No! I beg yours, Pastor Matt! This furniture is not yours, but you just leave food all over it like it's a picnic table." Becoming angrier by the minute, the old man began to spin around as though taking a panoramic tour of the room he had seen hundreds of times. In the center of the room with his arms elevating as he turned, he continued his lecture. "In fact, none of this is *yours!* Don't you know that everything any of us have is on loan from God? You're not being a good steward. This isn't your desk! This isn't your office! That house you live in isn't yours either. Lanie isn't your secretary, and she sure as heck ain't your babysitter. In fact, this isn't a day-care...it's a church office! And it is all on loan to the pastor while he's here. But when you can't handle the things you've been allowed to use, they get taken away from you. How 'bout that?"

Matt was shocked by the berating, but he was infuriated by the fact that it was seemingly without cause. M.J. was here for a day, and he left a couple of pieces of fruit behind. As his face turned red, Heath's turned blue, but Matt barely noticed as he turned to find his chair and hopefully, like he had practiced, hide his anger, at least temporarily, from the old man. As he turned to sit, he noticed a spilled cup of juice, and though Heath would not see it from his vantage point, Matt kicked the cup under his own desk as he spun to once again face Stephen, who was no longer standing nor spinning. He was sitting, gasping for air. It was beyond Matt's comprehension that someone - anyone - could be so angry at him that he would become breathlessly enraged. Matt had planned to remain calm, and the fact that his nemesis was so visibly irate gave Matt even more reason to keep things from escalating. He would simply hear the man out and, when he finally calmed down, gently and professionally tell the geezer off.

Heath sat silently for a few more moments staring down at the ground. When his breathing slowed and his color returned, he, too, seemed prepared for a more peaceful presentation of himself. "I came here today to discuss with you some of the concerns that the deacons and I have about you, but the list just keeps on growing, doesn't it?"

"What list? What are these concerns?" Matt was calm, his words slow and calculated.

Heath did not raise his voice though it seethed with animosity toward the young preacher – another new level beyond what Matt had anticipated. "I tried to defend you to the deacons," he lied. "I told them that perhaps your youthfulness was causing you to make some poor judgments. But, perhaps the biggest misstep was ministry in the first place." He let the words sink in and then raised the question. "Is it possible, Brother Matt, that you misunderstood your calling?"

Silence. A long silence.

Finally, Brother Heath continued. "I am compiling the list of areas in which you could improve were you to choose to. I'll have it ready tomorrow. You see, you could learn a lot from a seasoned veteran of the pastorate like me...but you think you already know it all, don't you? You have abused your position, you have misused your resources and those of the church, and you have engaged in...well, let's just say impropriety." The old man braced himself on the arms of the wingback chair and, using more arm strength than legs, shakily rose to a standing position. Again, he seemed quite winded from the exercise. Turning to Matt, he offered his counsel. "If you are called to be a pastor, the pastor at South Mill, you should get your own house in order. And, don't forget what I said about being a steward of all that has been loaned to you. It could easily be taken away."

Matt could smell the betrayal, and though he cringed at what the answer might be, he found it necessary to ask the question anyway. "Will I be provided this list, or are you just going to accuse me of these misdeeds publicly?"

Through his bluing lips, the Reverend Stephen Heath flashed a condescending yellow grin. "Now, you know I will give you every opportunity to right the wrongs. I'll provide you a written copy, like you asked for, well ahead of and in every effort to avoid a public revealing of anyone's sins." As he clasped the doorknob to turn it and leave, he pontificated for his own amusement, "I mean, isn't that what the Bible says we Christians should do?"

Matt sat alone, his own breath now shallow and rapid. What had he done? What did they think he had done? He tried to frame his own version of their list, but all he could think of was that he preached too long, he invited a really good pianist to fill in, and he bought Miss Mabel's dinner. What else could be on the list? Anything they had on him had to be fabricated. Would this old man and his allies actually lie about him just to get him to leave? Or did whoever broke into their house...oh, wait, it wasn't *their* house...did whoever broke into the church's house where Matt's family lived find something there that gave the impression of impropriety? Matt would not know, and Brother Heath would not divulge anything before the appointed time.

Matt resolved that the old man was something far from holy. A wolf in sheep's clothing. His thoughts ran circles in his brain. He's bringing false accusations against a man of God...a good man...a good husband, father, preacher, and pastor to the people of this little town. How dare he question my calling? I know I'm supposed to be here. He's the one that needs to go. He felt guilty for that last one, but he admitted to himself that it was a real sentiment. He stood robotically and stepped out of his office into Lanie's and then into a hallway where he could see Stephen's car out the window. Slowly, the old man put the car in gear and headed out of the parking lot. Matt questioned why he was even watching him leave. Then, as the old man began to pull out onto the road, Matt winced as a box truck with the name of a landscape company on the side crested the knoll of the road in front of the church, blew an alarming horn, and slammed on brakes to avoid hitting Pastor Heath's sedan. Heath continued to ease into the lane headed toward his house without seeming to notice or be surprised by the commotion behind him. Matt turned and spoke a thought out loud that surprised him. "There was your chance, Lord!" And Matt's lack of guilt about saying it allowed him to finish his audible contemplation. "Funeral flowers really could be quite fragrant."

He returned to his office taking note of the fact that he heard no sound of M.J. in the workroom with Lanie. A vibration in his pocket alerted him to a text from Abigail that the field trip was over, that they were back at the school, and she was headed that way to pick up their son and rescue Matt before the weekly church staff meeting. Matt peeked inside the workroom and found Lanie sitting with a sleeping M.J. on her shoulder. He whispered and smiled a sad-eyed thank you to her and took the boy to his own chest. He felt like napping, too, exhausted from an emotional afternoon. He carried his sleeping son to his own office, closed the door behind him, and sat down in his oversized leather desk chair and began to rock. As he did, he prayed that God would protect his little family from the evils that were lurking in their midst. As he prayed, his tears began to flow. Tears of sadness? Tears of fright? Tears of anger? Tears of exhaustion? He did not know which, and he did not care. For a moment, he just felt like crying, and it felt good to do so. He held M.J. closer, pulled his soft blue blanket from his backpack, and rocked his little boy peacefully while daring the universe to try and mess with his wife and children. And, in a moment of defiance, Matt leaned back and propped his feet up on the desk that was *loaned* to him. He could have, just as easily, lay M.J. on the couch, but Matt needed to hold him tightly for a few more minutes.

Abigail was surprised when she came in and found both her son and her husband asleep, but the moment had to be captured, so she shushed Maggie, dug her phone out of her purse, and snapped a photo of her two men both sleeping like babies. She hated to wake them, but she knew Matt had a staff meeting. She kissed her husband on the cheek, and though it startled him, he sat up slowly and smoothly carried M.J. to the car and strapped him in his car seat. Outside the car, he asked Maggie about the field trip, told Abigail that she smelled like a barn, and then kissed her on the lips and said he'd be home early...that it had been a very bad day. She was immediately concerned and curious, but it would have to wait.

The rest of the afternoon crawled by. At 3:20, the staff had finally all arrived, and Matt went through the motions of a staff meeting. There was talk of holiday gatherings for children and teens, as well as discussion of beautiful music that was being prepared for the start of the Christmas season. Matt smiled for the first time in the meeting when the youth pastor bemoaned the annual plans for a New Year's Eve all night "lock-in." When the conversation waned, Matt suggested they close the meeting in prayer. He had paid very little attention to most of what was said, and he was hopeful that Lanie's notes would inform him of anything he might have missed that he actually needed to know. He was seldom this disinterested, but his plate was stacked higher than he could digest at the moment.

At home, he chose not to share much with Abigail – just that Stephen had come by to gripe some more and that, perhaps, the church Business Meeting tomorrow night could be a nightmare. Abigail held her husband's hand and gently raised it to her lips to kiss. "You're making a difference in this town. That's why the devil is working so hard to shut you down." Her words were cliché, but both she and Matt believed them to be true. Then she stood, walked to the front door and picked up Matt's running shoes off the floor. "And don't let them distract you from your other goals, too." Matt had forgotten all about his late-night prayer run to the Heaths' house. And, as unmotivated as he was, he knew tonight was more important than ever if he was going to trust God to handle the situation.

By 7:15, Matt was hidden in the shadowy shrubs and on his knees to pray, this time making sure his head was low enough to not be seen if car lights should shine in his direction. Sure enough, at 7:20, Dorothy backed out and kicked up dust on her way to wherever she went. Stephen was alone in the house, and Matt began to pray specifically for the old man. His thoughts from earlier in the day and his questions about this illusive list kept interrupting his communication with God, so he stayed much longer than he had the night before just to finish his prayers. At 8:10, the headlights lit up the house as Dorothy returned from somewhere, and Matt breathed a whispered *Amen*. When the garage door closed completely, Matt dashed from his hiding place and trotted back through the park to the sidewalk that led home. He felt better...still mad...but better.

When it was time for bed, Matt opened the closet door to retrieve the encased pistol they had bought, but it was not in its place. Panic spun him around to face Abigail, and she returned the look of dread over the discovery. His mind raced as did his feet right to his nightstand, and when he yanked open the top drawer, he exhaled loud relief to find it still there from the night before. In the rush of an unusual morning and in the newness of the hide-the-weapon routine, Matt simply had not returned it to the shelf in the closet. Abigail wanted to fuss, but she was too relieved to do so.

Matt slept close to the middle of the bed and held his wife until they both fell asleep. Abigail was wise enough to know that her husband was troubled, and, though her faith in God and their calling to minister to the mostly kind people of South Mill was strong, she felt inadequate at the moment to strengthen her husband's faith in those things. So, for now, she was just glad to be his comfort object. She ran a hand across his chest, impressed that it was still somewhat chiseled, though he never worked out anymore. She let it rest there and felt his breathing begin to slow. In the moonlight, she could see his long dark lashes glisten with tears that had been squeezed out by tightly shut eyelids. Silently, she prayed for a peaceful sleep for Matt until he was lightly snoring against her shoulder. "Sleep tight,

my handsome prince," she whispered, and then silently prayed Matt
would win this wicked contest.

CHAPTER TWENTY-FIVE

Clack sat at breakfast alone and remained at the table analyzing Jenni's letter for somewhere around the twentieth time and sipping coffee that was quickly approaching room temperature. Finally, taking matters into his own hands, he rambled through a couple of drawers and cabinets until he found the large, pre-packaged coffee filters used in the big, restaurant-style coffee makers and brewed himself a fresh pot. When a heavy-set black lady on the kitchen staff came out to empty the last trash can from the morning meal, she looked confused – then perturbed that a previously emptied pot was now steaming and three quarters full. She looked at Clack and batted her eyes, but he just glanced her way, flashed a cool smile, and said, "Go ahead and have a cup. I just made a fresh pot." She wasn't rude, but she was not bubbling with hospitality when she responded by telling him that breakfast was over. Her hair was graying, and she had an accent, but Clack could not distinguish which Caribbean island might be her native home. Fearing she would dump the hot coffee down the drain, Clack stood and approached her as he said, "Good! Then you have time to drink a cup with me." He took the coffee pot in hand, grabbed a foam cup from the stack and poured as he asked, "How do you like yours?" She batted one eye at him again as though she was looking down the barrel of a gun and getting him in her sights. She began to turn her back to him and then reconsidered. Instead, she smiled accusingly and said, "You're quite the charmer, aren't you?" Clack winked and handed her the cup of coffee with one hand and with the other slid a container of creamer packets toward her on the counter. "You won't need any sugar, will you, since it will sweeten by just being held in your hand?" She looked at him and pursed her lips like she might call him an ugly word, but the lips quickly spread out into a full-faced smile as she let out a deep, rich belly laugh that caused Clack to do the same. She took the cup and added cream until it reached the rim and, without spilling one drop, raised the cup to her lips and sipped it down.

With her head she pointed toward his table. "Go get your cup! You get one more, and then I'm washing the pot." Clack thanked her, did as she had instructed, and offered to help her with the trash. She politely refused his help and went right back to her morning tasks of preparing the dining room for lunch, but she ignored Clack's table for the time being.

Alone again, he reread the letter and tried to come up with a fitting response. He would give whatever he ended up writing to Matt when he picked him up later in the day and ask him to deliver it to Jenni. He thought it would be easy to write back if she had said that she loved him, that she missed him, that they should work things out, or that they should move on with the divorce pronto. The truth, though, was that the letter Jenni wrote said very little about him, her, their marriage, or their future – together or apart. Instead, she said things like *I'm glad you're getting help* and *I'm praying for you.* Jenni had not said that to him out loud or in a letter in many years, and Clack was certain of that. He remembered the last time he read it was in the final letter he received from her back when he was in combat almost forty years ago. To him, and he was trying not to put words in her mouth, saying that she was praying for him meant that he was in her heart, that she cared. And that was news to him…good news! The rest of the letter was about Pastor Matt, which Clack thought was annoyingly weird and strangely meaningful at the same time. She talked about how she had, at first, disliked him because he was hiding the dogs and, worse, had befriended her drunk of a husband. She went on to confess that she found him and his family to be genuine Christians who really cared about him and her. She reminded Clack of how guarded he was with his heart but how, when he let that guard down, he loved deeply. So she expressed her hope that Clack would continue that friendship with Matt and try to make others like it. She said that she planned to do so herself. That they both needed loving people in their lives and that they should work at and protect those types of relationships. She included a couple of tidbits about the dogs, how they were fine and well cared for and how she was in no hurry to take them back to Cardelville. She signed the letter, "*Love*, Jenni!" It brought Clack a peaceful feeling, but he was well aware that she did not use the word in a sentence, as in *I love you, Clack!* He emerged from the depths of his analysis by laughing at the idea that at least she still knew how to spell it.

If Clack was honest with himself, he was actually a little nervous about leaving Altaville for the night. He had not stepped foot back into his trailer since being ratted out by his coworker and hauled to the hospital weeks earlier. He was sure that the place had been searched by someone at work or by the neighbors or by Jenni, and he hoped that whoever it was had removed the bottles of booze when they removed the pistol that he said, up until a week or so ago, was to blame for this whole mess. There was nothing about the trailer that felt like home. Clack realized that, when he and his counselor had talked about him going home for a night, some part of his brain thought Cardelville and Jenni, though he never entertained that notion consciously. His anxiousness over the night ahead of him was more of a distraction than he thought possible, and it made it more difficult to write a letter back to Jenni. When none of the attempts satisfied him, Clack packed up his pen and paper, threw six crumpled sheets in the trash, and made his way to his morning group session.

In group, he confessed his anxiety about going home but called it a necessary first step in moving on. Some others in the room who had faced the challenge before offered words of advice and encouragement. They suggested that Clack go out to dinner, take a long walk, visit with a neighbor, and a bunch of other activities to keep him out of the house until he was sufficiently tired and ready to go to bed and sleep. Clack listened but made no definitive plan for the night. His main purpose was to organize and pack some tools to bring back with him.

The thought of tools reminded him that he needed to measure a wooden beam on the front porch of the residence building. It would be his first task when he returned to sure up a roof over that porch before it sagged more and started pulling away from the building and possibly causing some leaks when it rained. When the morning session concluded, Blake, his concierge counselor walked with him to the residence building and held one end of the tape measure while Clack extended it from its square metal casing, pulled a pencil from the top of his ear and jotted down the length, width, and height in a little notebook he kept in his back pocket. He then drew a quick sketch on the tiny page, looked up at Blake and smiled, then flipped the little book closed and returned it to his pocket. He engaged Blake to examine the rest of the porch to assess any other features that needed repair, and, satisfied that the support of the roof was sufficient to remedy the pending problems, he nodded and said, "Well, I'll get started on it tomorrow. Remember, I won't be here for afternoon sessions today."

Blake nodded then spoke with a solemn tone. "Clack, tonight is a real test, okay? Not so much to see if you can go a night without falling back into your habits, but a test of how committed you are to your own goals. I've seen a lot of men leave on one of these one-night-out agreements and never return."

Clack took it all in, looking as serious as Blake about the message he was receiving. So Blake continued. "The most impressive thing about you, Clack, is your way of seeing a situation, coming up with a solution, and handling it. You have done that with your addiction these last few weeks and with these unsolicited construction projects you've taken on and so many other things around here. Please do that with your life...handle it...look for solutions."

Clack had begun a continual up and down nodding motion with his head throughout Blake's commendation of him. Now, he had a question for his counselor. "You didn't say anything in session today, so what would your advice be about my night back in my place?"

"Make a checklist of all you hope to accomplish while you're there. Make it realistic – don't plan more than you can accomplish in the short amount of time. Then, when you've accomplished your goals, take a walk, watch something on television, and go to sleep, satisfied that you've *done your job*. And then, come back here! *Please* come back here!"

Clack let out a thoughtful laugh and reached to his back pocket for his little notebook again. Holding it up for Blake to see, he said, "This is all I'm taking with me, Blake! I'll be back – if for nothing else to get my clothes and personal items. But I'm coming back for more than that. I'm healing here. I know that. I think more clearly here than anywhere I've been in a long time, so I'm coming back. Besides, like you said, when there is a problem, I fix it. And, this roof we're standing under right now is a problem. And then there's the staircase. You wanna see my whole list?"

Blake smiled, pounded Clack on the back, and said, "Let me pray for you before you go."

After a very short prayer, Blake told Clack he'd see him tomorrow and headed toward his own office. Clack hustled inside and began tidying up his studio apartment, making sure there was nothing else besides his little notepad he needed to take with him. He thought about his wallet and decided he should take it too, just in case he needed his I.D. or the twelve dollars cash he had somehow been able to hold on to the whole time he'd been at Respira de Nuevo. As he tucked the leather trifold into his back pocket, he pondered his inexpensive stay at the place. "I wonder who's paying for all of this?" Then, he wandered to the dining room to grab an early lunch and wait on his ride.

Matt Hardy wondered the same thing about the financing of Clack's recovery and, for that reason, arrived unannounced to Clack and met with his old professor turned rehab administrator before hitting the buffet line and sliding into a chair across the table from Clack. He had already finished his lunch, so he did most of the talking while Matt wolfed down his. Conscious of the time, of his own obligations at the church that afternoon, and of Clack's need to be home well before the sun began setting so he could gather his tools and take care of any business he needed to while places like banks and post offices were open, Matt wasted no time on second helpings. Clack had no need to go to a bank or post office, but he did want to get a head start on the sunset only because he knew how difficult the nighttime could be for a lonely alcoholic. He explained his difficulty writing a letter to Jenni that seemed appropriate. He verbalized how he knew that writing anything was a far cry from what all needed to be said, but he also knew that a face-to-face with Jenni was probably not the most prudent plan of action yet. He was a passionate man, and she was a redhead. The combination of the two, if ill-prepared, could be deadly. So he wanted to say sweet and nice things in a letter – but previous attempts on his part at being "sweet and nice" had served to make her pretty mad. So, he was struggling. "I can finish it tonight," he resolved. "I'm going to need something to do!"

On the drive back to South Mill, Matt brought up the Jenni letter again. "Hey, have that letter you're writing finished by 7:45, because Abigail is baking an apple pie, and you're having dessert at our house."

"You really don't have to do that."

"Well, we wanted to have you over for dinner, but tonight is Wednesday, and we have church services, and..."

Matt tried to think of a polite way to discourage Clack from coming to church that night. He didn't want it to seem like he was not welcomed, but it was church conference, and, with all that was going on at the moment, he was afraid Clack would leave with a really bad taste of Christians. If that could be avoided, it would be the best thing. Unresolved over the rudeness of the statement, Matt continued, "...there's nothing really interesting happening tonight except a Business Meeting where the church people vote on a bunch of stuff that no one really cares about."

Clack took the bait. "I'll have plenty to do until you get done. I'll come over at 7:45. I'll need the address."

"I can come and get you."

"Matt, I need to drive...you know, I need to *know* that I *have* to drive."

"Gotcha!" Matt nodded and gave him the address, which Clack wrote down in the back of his little book.

From there, Clack took the wheel of the conversation and asked Matt point-blank who was paying for his stay at the facility. Matt looked sharply to his right at Clack and said, "Funny you should ask." Matt began to explain his entire conversation with Chuck.

"Respira is very careful to make sure that most of their services can be covered by a client's insurance, which you do have, so about sixty percent of your costs are going to fall under that category."

"What about the other forty?"

"Well, it gets a little trickier from there. There's this network of churches that provide money to Respira in their missions budgets, and they use that money to cover a portion of what patients are left with after insurance. Our church actually donates to them, albeit a very small dollar amount every month. It's figured in with a percentage of our missions giving."

Clack had no idea what that meant, and Matt didn't care to try to explain it, so they both let it be whatever it was. Clack knew there was still more.

"And who pays for everything beyond that portion?

"Well, typically, the client would set up a payment plan when he exits the program, and before you get all worked up, let me finish."

"I'm not worked up...I'm just broke!"

"Chuck has been getting estimates for a lot of the work that needed to be done around the place. They had not decided on any contractors to do the work when you came along." Matt smiled and almost cried (he actually had cried in Chuck's office when he first learned the news). "So far, you've saved them twice what you would owe them, so you owe them nothing, and they are indebted to you...so you can stay quite a while or even come back someday if you need to." Matt realized how that last part sounded and quickly recovered it by saying, "But I hope you never need to!"

Clack reached around Matt and hugged him, a very easy accomplishment with such a small truck and such a long-armed man. Matt laughed and said, "I doubt they'll pay for my truck when you cause a wreck, man!" Clack released his grip on his chauffeur and both men laughed. Then, a haunting thought crossed Clack's mind.

The rest of the ride back was filled with friendly chitchat, stories about growing up, and a few momentary dives into the painful and no-so-distant events of Clack's past, but neither wanted to dwell there very long. Clack was trying to come up for air from the dark waters of his alcohol use and personal demons that drug him down there to start with, and Matt was as nervous as he could be about what might lie ahead for him in Business Meeting with a reckless list of offenses being compiled by Stephen Heath. So, they laughed a lot...even when the stories were not particularly funny.

Just after 2:30 p.m., Matt pulled his little Chevy up to the gate in front of the rented double-wide, shifted the transmission into park, and handed Clack a key to the padlock that Matt had purchased and placed on the gate when he picked up the dogs. "Want me to come in with you?" Matt offered.

"Naaa...I'm good I think."

Though neither was convinced, Matt made the decision to let Clack face his place alone. After all, he couldn't hold his hand forever. "Then, I'll see you at 7:45. Okay?"

"I'll be there!" Clack confidently assured the pastor. "Thanks for this! I guess we'll make the trip again tomorrow?"

"Yessir! You just let me know what time we need to leave."

Clack thanked him again and turned to unlock the gate. Letting the gate swing wide open, Clack walked the short, sandy driveway to the steps that led to the back deck. As he did, he passed by the metal canopied carport that held some of tools he would need, along with a world of junk that neither he nor anyone he could imagine knowing needed. He stopped and lamented the useless accumulation of a mostly stuporous stay in the low-rent dwelling. Gripping the handrail of the back deck, he was even more enlightened to his previous condition by how loose the railing was from the steps. He'd repaired everything he could at Respira in the short time he'd been there, yet things were falling apart at home, and he had not even taken a hammer and nail in hand to steady the railing.

Clack continued to discover the ugliness of his most recent binges when he unlocked the back door to find that, contrary to his assumptions, no one had come in and cleaned the place. The booze bottles were still there, but they would not be a stumbling block for him since none held a single drop. He staggered soberly to the bedroom where his sheets were in a twisted pile in the center of a bare mattress – the remains of a wrestling match with them in search of a good night's sleep. He wondered how long he had left them that way because he honestly could not recall the last time he slept anywhere but on the couch in that house. From the smell coming from the bathroom, he could assume that he had not flushed before he had ventured outside to find the pastor on his front lawn that fateful day. He reached for the handle and gave it a push, but the swirling water only stirred up and intensified the smell of old urine. Amazed and privately humiliated at his living conditions, he fell to a seated position on the corner of the tussled bed and reached for his steno pad in his back pocket. Above his ear, he still held the pencil and grabbed it with his other hand. Flipping to the little list Blake had encouraged him to make, he added one more little box that would need a checkmark before nightfall and wrote out beside it, "CLEAN THE NASTY HOUSE!" He took another look around before getting busy on his task list and laughed out loud, "If they think I'd rather stay here than come back there, they're crazy!"

Clack was amazed at how much a determined man with a plan could accomplish in a short amount of time. By 6:00, he had checked all of the chores off the list. His tools were packed, and his house was clean, very clean. It even smelled clean, and Clack noticed. Looking around for something else to do, he concluded that anything else could wait until he was back again in a few weeks. He was hungry, and he was sure his pickup truck was feeling deprived. He fired up the engine and headed into town to find a pack of cigarettes and something for dinner, both of which would need to be bought with the twelve dollars he had in his wallet.

CHAPTER TWENTY-SIX

By 4:30, Matt had prayed twice and looked out every window for Stephen Heath's car. Without hearing from him, Matt allowed himself to assume the night might go by without a fight...perhaps the last two nights of his hidden prayer vigil had worked. He sat down at his desk to look over his brief "state of the church" report he would present at the evening Business Meeting. Lanie had emailed the agenda out earlier in the day to everyone who would be presenting that night. Looming near the bottom, just above "New Business," was the dreaded bullet point: "Deacons Report." Matt planned his report to be even shorter than usual this time partly because he did not know how long that last report would take and partly because he wanted to get the whole event over. He would not have to worry about another one for three months. Perhaps by then the turmoil that Heath was creating would be over.

He almost dozed off reading the bland words of a meeting agenda when the church office door startled him out of his chair. He stood, looked out the privacy window into Lanie's office, and saw the old man grinning with pride as he announced to Lanie, "Pastor Matt is expecting us." The *us* referred to Stephen Heath, who Matt had been expecting all afternoon, and Hugh Briner, who Matt had not expected at all. He glanced back at the bottom corner of his computer screen to see what time it was. 4:51 p.m. Thirty-nine short minutes before the evening meal began. Matt swallowed hard, but the lump in his throat was still there. He would have almost no time to craft any kind of sensible response to whatever nonsense was on this list that was about to be thrown at him. He walked to the door, opened it, faked a polite smile, and said, "Come in, gentlemen." He had forgotten to produce some enthusiasm before speaking.

They were very enthusiastic and strangely polite. Each man reached out to shake Matt's hand, called him Pastor Matt, and invited him to sit near them on furniture in his own office. Hugh Briner told him he hoped he'd had a good day, but Matt just nodded as he took in the whole charade being played out in front of him. Stephen began the conversation, making sure he smiled as he spoke as if, perhaps, his cheap grin would ease the tension in the room. Then, Matt considered the possibility that he was not faking a smile after all but was actually happier than he had been in months over the prospect of lowering the boom on his young replacement. He stammered through an obviously unrehearsed monologue remaining true to form by coating everything with spiritual terminology. Matt had promised himself that he would simply remain silent like Jesus did before his accusers. An annoying little voice in his head gently reminded him, though, that those accusers also nailed their victim to a cross.

"We're not here on a witch hunt, Brother!" Stephen Heath began. "As you know, the deacons have charged me with seeking some resolution to our current dilemma."

What dilemma? Matt was unaware of a dilemma. He was keenly aware of a nightmarish problem, one that he felt sure predated his tenure at this church. There was an old man who felt like he owned the church, and not even God, were he to apply for the position, would be a suitable pastor in the opinion of this retiree who idolized himself and highly overestimated his own skills in the vocation.

"I have, with input from others, compiled the list I told you about yesterday."

Matt knew that by *others*, Brother Heath meant Hugh Briner, maybe Jim Pethel, and their little band of liars. And, quite possibly, their wives.

"But before we look over the list, let me offer this nugget of wisdom. Many young Christians fancy themselves as being called into the ministry, but, as you might have learned by now, ministry is no playground, and it isn't summer camp. There are expectations of the pastor that, according to God's Word, must be met. And when they aren't met, there have to be consequences. Wouldn't you agree?"

Uh oh! Matt had to say something. "Go on," he said, neither agreeing nor arguing with the old man.

"All I'm saying is that sometimes we find out too late that we should have chosen a different career. Not saying that's necessarily true of you, but let's leave that to you and the Lord to decide after you consider the list."

And there it was! The goal of the entire farce. Heath would be satisfied only when Matt reasoned that his best course of action was to resign and look elsewhere for employment. Matt was resolute, though, that Stephen Heath would not be the voice of God in his life. He was well-liked by most. His kids were happy there. Abigail was enjoying life in the small but growing town. Unless they flat out fired him, Matt was in it for the long haul.

Hugh Briner, who never wasted words on trying to be tactful or polite, chimed in. "What he's sayin' is that we think the preacher ought to act like a preacher." Matt's eyes widened at the directness of such a statement. "And, we think his wife ought to act like a preacher's wife." Hugh's voice had become more of a gravelly, low growl as he finished his short speech. "It's in the Bible, that stuff is!"

Matt fought the urge to react when Abigail was implicated, but he won the fight and sat silently staring directly into Hugh's shifty eyes. When the silence became good and awkward, Hugh looked down at the sheet of paper in his hands and told Stephen to continue.

Both men seemed to be growing agitated over the fact that they could not seem to get a rise out of the pastor no matter how hard they poked at him. Matt just transferred his gaze to Brother Heath's pale green eyes and raised his eyebrows to indicate he was open to whatever else the old man had to say. "So," Stephen fumbled for words, "Let's just run this down. Shall we?"

He handed Matt a copy of the document he and Hugh each held in his hands, and he began to read the bullet points without including any of the details and explanations, which was understandable since, in Matt's mind, there could be no reasonable explanation for any of it. The list read:

Ineffective church staff management.
Poor stewardship of church resources.
Unavailability to church membership.
Lack of leadership qualities.
Poor time management skills.
Misuse of church property (parsonage).
Spiritual immaturity.
Habits unbecoming of a minister.
Personal house out of order.
Misrepresentation of the Kingdom of God in our community.
Ethical/Moral failure.
Anger management issues.
Appearance of Impropriety.

Matt read each point as Brother Heath spoke it aloud, and with each entry on the list, Matt felt the stab of evil daggers through his chest, his back, and his head, each one penetrating into his very soul.

What really got his dander up was that each point was accompanied by a reference to a scripture passage, and, without having each Bible verse from the list memorized, Matt cringed at how out-of-context each citation had to be. Never mind the fact, the cold hard fact, that nothing on the list was true. He felt the color of red filling his cheeks, and he knew the heat would turn his deep blue eyes to geysers within moments. He looked down, checked his emotions, ran his tongue up and down the inside of his cheek, then clinched his teeth so tightly that he thought they might splinter. When he knew he had dialed all systems back under control, he looked at one man, then the other, back and forth, back and forth. His mind raced. He would read the list again, along with the scripture verses, but he would not do so with the devil and his imp sitting in the very room.

Having seen and heard enough, the young pastor stood to his feet, nodded to his unwelcomed guests, walked the short steps to his office door, turned the knob, and opened it swiftly. The old men looked at one another clearly confused and suspecting that Matt was walking out of their meeting. Their confusion gave way to insult when Matt turned and looked in their direction and said, "Gentleman, you've done what you came to do. Thank you for sharing this *informative* list with me. I'll give it the consideration it deserves, but you two should probably go get in line for dinner."

Stephen looked sharply at Hugh and quipped, "See, there's that youthful arrogance."

"Hmmmph," Hugh grunted.

Briner was the first to exit, and as Heath crossed the threshold of the office door, he rattled off more Christianese in an effort to dominate Matt and to impress Hugh and anyone else within earshot, "Pride goeth before the fall!"

The insult pushed farther than Matt meant to allow it, and he refused to let scripture be misused on him and fired back viciously,

"Good, Brother Heath! You know Proverbs sixteen, verse eighteen. Turn one more page in that Bible of yours, and read Proverbs seventeen, verse seven!" And though he did not slam the door behind them, he closed it with purpose. He stood frozen for a moment, panicking over his own use of the Bible in his retaliation because he had shot from the hip without verifying that his weapon was properly loaded. Now, after the insult, he darted to his desk, grabbed his own Bible and flipped to Proverbs 17:7, where he found what he hoped Brother Heath would also find, "Eloquent lips are unsuited to a godless fool – how much worse lying lips to a ruler!" And with as much humility as he could muster, he whispered a victorious "Yes!" to himself.

Coming down from his tipping point, Pastor Matt fell into his chair and placed his copy of the list on the desk in front of him and, holding his head in his hands, began to read it over again. A knock on his door startled him, and he was shocked to see Trudy, the financial secretary's face in the window. He motioned for her to come in, and she opened the door and said quietly, "Pastor, I'm sorry to disturb you." And then, in what was seemingly an explanation of her unusual presence at his door since she was not his secretary, she said, "Lanie's already gone for the day."

Matt smiled and said, "Okay...," still wondering what she wanted.

"There's a church member here who needs to talk to you if you have a minute. She's pretty upset."

Matt was upset, too, but if a church member needed him, then he would put his own turmoil aside. "Oh, of course! Thank you, Trudy. Send her on in." A young lady named Becky, who Matt knew fairly well, came in, said hello, apologized for just showing up, and then began to cry. Matt looked at Trudy, who was still in the doorway obviously wondering if she had done the right thing. Not knowing what the current crisis was, Matt took precautions and held up his palm toward Trudy as if to ask her to stay put for a minute or two. To his guest, he inquired, "Do you mind if Trudy stays?" Becky said it was fine, that it was not something personal or confidential. So for the next fifteen minutes, Matt listened and passed tissues as Becky told him (and Trudy) of how her mother back home in Birmingham had just called to let her know that her dad had been diagnosed with cancer. With an ability that could only be a true gift from God, Matt shut off his concern for his own problems and was as present with her as any pastor could be. He even cried a few tears with her. When Becky had no more to say, he took her hand, prayed for her, for her mom, and finally for her dad – for healing, for good doctors, for the right treatments, and for important and sweet family times in the midst of what, at the moment, seemed like the beginning of some very worrisome days. When he said Amen, he passed another tissue to Becky and then one to Trudy, who was demonstrating a real need to blot her eyes. Becky smiled, said she felt better just having talked to him, thanked him for his prayers, and promised to keep him posted on her dad's condition. Trudy reached and grabbed her hand for a moment and promised her prayers too. As Becky left, Trudy looked back at Matt and said, "I'm sorry!"

"Why? This is what I do!" Matt smiled at Trudy.

Trudy returned the smile with one that looked like sincerity mixed with shame, but Matt either did not notice or chose not to ask questions. It was time to go say the blessing over the Wednesday night meal, and he was determined to be the one to do it this week. He looked at his desk, grabbed the unstudied list, folded it and placed it in his pocket. He was filled with anxiety over what the old man was going to do next with it, but, for now, Matt didn't give a damn about that freakin' list.

After the blessing, Matt wandered through the crowd gathered and talked freely as he did regularly with the church folks. He looped around through the back door of the kitchen where the dishwashing had commenced since the food was already on the serving line. The old cook, the one Matt was playfully flirtatious with most weeks, saw him and hollered over the whirling exhaust fans and humming dishwasher, "Oh, good! Look who came to wash the dishes!" Matt smiled and said he would but he was late for an important dinner. As he backed out of the door, she walked his way and said, "There's trouble in those blue eyes! What's wrong, preacher baby?" Matt assured her he was fine, that it must be the smoke in the kitchen bothering them. His dimples deepened as he grinned at her and continued the joke by telling her that she needed to quit burning the food. She threw a dish towel at him and grinned right back.

The fried chicken that drew a multitude on Business Meeting nights was as tender and delicious as ever, yet Matt only nibbled at his. The Pressleys sat with the Hardys again, and, though Matt wanted to question Eric over what the deacons had really asked Brother Heath to accomplish, if anything, he held off because Ms. McIntire, too, was in the mix at the pastor's table. He was glad, too, because when Miss Mable, who was noticeably absent tonight, sat with them, she wanted to hear all about what was going on in his world. But with Ms. McIntire present, no one else needed to talk. She carried the conversation, and everyone else mostly listened. Matt was not in the mood to talk, and even zoned out for most of what Ms. McIntire had to say.

With the children dismissed and the tables mostly cleared, Casey Briner stood up to the podium and called the church Business Meeting to order. The usual reports were given, including the minutes from three months ago by the church clerk, the treasurer's report, and briefings from any committees who had something to share. A few committee leaders stood and shared basically the same report they gave the last quarter, which, in Matt's estimation, meant they were not accomplishing much. The only thing the agenda required the church to vote on so far was the request from a church in Tennessee to have a family's membership transferred there – something Baptist churches did between themselves. Matt thought the same thing he always did when the motion was made to grant the request. Why was this something that needed a vote? The people moved two states away. Was there really the chance that a church was going to refuse to allow their names to be removed from the membership roster?

Finally, the finance committee presented its report, and that was always the report that required the most voting. The youth wing needed a new water heater, so the church was asked for their approval to spend the money on it. Approved! The church would soon be receiving their annual Christmas missions offering, and the committee sought permission to send the money on to the designated recipient organization. Approved! Postage had gone up slightly, and rather than overspend the "Mailing" budget, the committee wanted church approval to just pay for stamps from the "Office Supplies" budget, which still had ample funds available through the end of the year. A few grumblings about the USPS' frequent rate increases were followed by approval! And committee reports were over.

When it came time for the Ministry Report, Matt stood and made his way between the tables to the podium. He hated Business Meetings, and by the time he rose to give his presentation, his nerves were almost unbearable. When he slid two metal folding chairs out of his way in one of the aisles, they were, in his head, clarions announcing the arrival of the soon-to-be ousted king.

He looked down at his notes as he said, "Good evening!" He looked up when many of the church members responded, "Good evening, Pastor!" He did like that about a southern church. One lady called out, "How are you tonight?" Smiling at the impromptu spirit, he answered her with, "Well, I'm doing just fine...and you?" The two-person conversation could have continued for all he cared, but there was business to conduct, so he glanced again at his page and began a professional presentation of his facts and figures. He spoke about his sermon plans for the holidays and the New Year, as well as about outreach events that were planned by the youth ministry and children's ministry leadership. He beamed with pride as he shared the number of new families who had found a church home at South Mill and had pledged their membership with the church. Many nodded and said "Amen!" He always practiced ahead of time, which enabled him to make good eye contact with the parishioners while he spoke, but his eyes stuck on one table as he shared his report this time. There, in the back of the room, right between two of the old men who either talked over him or slept on most Wednesday nights when he was teaching sat Miss Mabel. She was swaying back and forth smiling big as though she were listening to some beautiful concert music. Who knew what was really going on in that mind of hers? But beside her sat an unusually tall man, thin and striking, gnawing on a chicken leg without a care in the world or a concern in the room – the only person still eating in the whole place. When Clack realized the preacher had spotted him, he smiled a greasy grin and waved the chicken leg at Matt to say hello. Matt didn't want Clack there, but he had to smile when he saw him, and somehow his presence made Matt feel more at ease. He continued his report, asked if anyone had any questions, and, when no one did, he returned to his seat to weather the oncoming storm.

"Let's now have our deacon's report." Casey looked around as though he was waiting for someone to take the floor and finally said, "Oh, I guess I'm supposed to give that." His report was short and uneventful, simply sharing with the church that the deacons had met, had heard from committees' representatives, and had received the pastor's ministry and personnel reports. When he was done, he asked if there was any old business to discuss, and there was not. He then asked if there was any new business to come before the church, and, when silence prevailed for a good five or six seconds, Matt almost breathed a sigh of relief. But then the shuffling of a chair turned the attention to table in the middle of the room where Stephen Heath was standing up to speak.

When all eyes were on him, the old man needed to catch his breath before he began his delivery. Obviously, it was breathtaking to roast a fellow clergyman. Finally, his blue lips began to speak. "For those of you who might not know me, although I am pretty sure everyone does, I am the retired and founding pastor of the South Mill Church, Reverend Stephen Heath. He stopped with each phrase, seemed to draw a deeper breath than the last, and pushed through with a dramatic tone. "Unfortunately, there's nothing new about the business we must discuss within our church tonight."

Heath had the attention of everyone in the room. Even Clack had stopped eating and was looking in his direction. Matt could not believe this was happening. He had underestimated the man and was now about to witness how evil and powerful he supposed Stephen Heath to be. His little team was about to, in the presence of most of the congregation, make broad accusations that would surely end in terminating the pastor before the meeting adjourned. He heard it happening with his own ears, but it felt like a twilight dream, like he was not really there. Flabbergasted, he swallowed hard and grabbed Abigail's hand and whispered, "He's about to lie through his yellow teeth to this whole church." She squeezed hard and held on tight.

"From time to time," Stephen continued, "our deacons hear rumors and various talk from amongst the church members and community outsiders about things that ultimately affect our church's reputation and influence in the area." Matt wished he would quit beating around the bush and just say what he had to say.

"As you know, our new pastor is very young and, as young folks often are, inexperienced. Well, it has come to our attention that there are some areas of his life and ministry that might need to be addressed for him to be what we have hired him and asked him to be for South Mill Church."

Gasps interrupted the silence that followed that last statement, and murmuring began at every table. Finally, a young man at the back corner table spoke up and said, "I don't know what you're talking about, but don't you think this needs to be discussed with the pastor in private before you do this in front of all of us?"

"A delegation has attempted to meet with our pastor in a one-on-one dialogue, but as I'll point out momentarily, he kicked us out and demanded we leave his office."

Casey Briner, sensing that things were about to progress beyond his ability to reign them back in, spoke into the microphone and said, "Brother Heath, I'm not sure the deacons were anticipating you bringing a report to the church on...well...anything."

"That's okay," Heath pompously replied. "I'll make it brief."

Casey looked at Matt apologetically. The room was quiet, and Matt was amazed that the church would allow Heath, as though he were a ringmaster, to conduct a circus show with full charge of all that would be said and done. If they were willing to let him talk, were they also willing to believe the lies that he was about to tell?

Heath continued. "It has come to our attention that our pastor has been conducting some aspects of his personal life, as well as his duties as our pastor, with some impropriety. There is speculation of misuse of church staff and church resources, poor oversight of the secretarial staff, frequent absences from the church office during office hours, misuse of the church's parsonage, unhealthy habits, temper issues, overspending in some areas of his budget, and questionable ethics. And to go just one step further, the Bible says that a man of God must have his own house in order, and, well, we're just not sure that is the case for Pastor Matt. So, our deacons have charged me, or at least I understood them to do so, to both investigate these concerns and to help our young pastor navigate through these to a better understanding of what his office requires of him. But, as I said, Pastor Matt was not very willing to take godly counsel on, well . . . anything."

Casey Briner was now staring at Brother Heath with his mouth gaping open, unable to formulate any sort of response to what had just been unloaded. Finally, someone whispered to him, "Is there a motion?" Casey snapped to and repeated the question to Stephen Heath, "Do you have a motion?"

Heath smiled coyly and almost laughed off the question as absurd. "Noooo. We have no intention of bringing any kind of motion for action to the church *tonight*. We simply want to pass along the information and ask the church members to come to us with any particular concerns you might have while our investigation proceeds. Perhaps there is nothing to these accusations or perhaps there is more than we know. But we're all part of God's wonderful family, and we need to be lovingly honest with one another even when honesty is unpopular."

Paling in color, Brother Heath suddenly sat down as though he had nothing else to say. Someone else voiced their thoughts about how the Bible calls for church discipline and how it was very difficult to bring up such things and just leave them out there for the church members to wonder about. Another spoke up and said that someone needed to be disciplined, but it wasn't Pastor Matt who needed it. All of this was spoken in hushed tones and "off the record," but in a shock-filled room, even hushed tones were audible.

An elderly man who was somewhat hearing impaired and probably missed most of what had been said asked if the pastor had been given an opportunity to speak to the church about anything included in Brother Heath's statement.

Casey looked at Matt and said, "Pastor?"

Matt stood, looked across the crowd with puddled eyes, from one side of the room to the other, making contact with everyone there before allowing his cracking voice to say, "Brothers and Sisters, you know me. I love Jesus, and I love all of you, and I am as shocked as you are at what I am hearing tonight, although I must confess, I had some warning. About an hour-and-a-half before this meeting tonight, I was given a list that Brother Heath and Hugh Briner, although he has remained quiet throughout this meeting, thought encompassed their grievances with me. I do not know the specifics of any of these accusations, as the details were not included in my list, but I'm pretty sure I would know if I had committed any of the sins or unethical actions about which they speak. I did not kick anyone out of my office, but I did dismiss the meeting so that I could look over it and compose a list of questions myself. However, a church member in crisis came in, and I was occupied ministering to her needs right up until time for dinner to begin. So I have not had a chance to really even study the list. I will. And if I am guilty of any of these types of mistakes, I will be the first to say I am unfit to serve as your pastor. But as I said at the beginning, you know me! My life is an open book, and you see me live it each day right in front of you at the ball field, at the grocery store, at the hospital, at the pharmacy..." He paused, looked at Abigail, who was crying, and concluded by saying, "I guess that's all I can say to the matter at this point in time."

Stephen Heath began to slide his chair backward as if to be preparing to stand again when Miss Mabel jumped out of her seat in the back and started walking toward the front of the fellowship hall. As she shuffled along, she raised her voice quite loudly and said, "I move we adjourn! Who wants to second it?"

Ms. McIntire, as though she'd been suddenly stung by a bee, threw her hand high in the air high and shouted, "I second it!"

Miss Mabel, when she reached the pastor, wrapped her arms around him, kissed him on the cheek with everyone watching, and whispered, "Don't you worry!" Then, she looked at Casey Briner and said, "Didn't you hear the motion? What are you just standing there for?"

Casey, who looked as he had been under water for the past hour, shook himself back into the moment and said, "Yes, there's a motion to adjourn and a second. All in favor please stand."

Since everyone was already standing, there was no way to deny the unanimous vote. Miss Mabel, who was close enough now for the microphone to pick up her voice said in a demanding voice, "Good! We're adjourned. Now y'all go home!"

As Matt scanned the dissolving crowd for friends and foes, he suddenly missed Clack. He was not there anymore, and he wondered at what point he had exited the room. He hoped it had been sooner than later, but hopefully he'd know for sure over a piece of apple pie in a few minutes. He turned to kiss Abigail goodbye, told her to get the kids, to shake it off, and to head home to meet Clack. She looked at him like he was crazy to still want a guest over after the beating he just endured. He assured her that they needed to stick to the plan...for Clack's sake. She reluctantly agreed and made a quick exit.

When Matt could break through the murmuring crowd, he passed through to his office, gathered his backpack and Bible, locked his office, and left through the back door. He made it to the truck without having to talk to anyone, and he drove home in silence.

He was too mad to cry, but he was hopeful he could suppress the anger until Clack left. He would never forgive himself if the events at church sent Clack back into a binge. And if that did happen, how would he explain it to Chuck at Respira?

CHAPTER TWENTY-SEVEN

When Matt turned onto his street, he saw Clack's truck parked on the curb in front of the house. His headlights illuminated the front porch when he turned into the driveway, and he was surprised to see Clack sitting on the top step surrounded by the two huge white dogs and two playful children in the front yard. Clack was tossing a rubber ball to M.J., but each time he did so, one of the pups would bound off of the porch to catch it first or retrieve it after M.J. missed it in the dark. Out of the truck and trying to mask his own forlorn face, he smiled at Clack and said, "Honey, I'm home!"

Clack laughed and tossed his head backwards to point in the direction of the front door. "I've got the kids. Go check on your wife." Matt nodded and pulled his tired body up one step at a time and crossed the front porch into the living room. Abigail was in the kitchen, grabbing plates from the cabinet and pretending to be okay. When she saw Matt, though, her face hid nothing. "What the heck, Matt?"

"I don't know!"

"Is this what he does? Ruins people's lives?"

"Maybe."

"What now?"

"We wait! On what, I do not know. But Heath isn't done. There will be rumors and meetings and who knows what all else, but it'll be okay."

"How can you say that? Half of that group tonight now thinks that their pastor is some immoral, unethical, despicable human being and is singing the praises of a lying son-of-a-bitch (she covered her mouth, shocked at her own choice of words) who is going to, once again, save their precious little church!"

She began to cry, and Matt took her in his arms and held her close. "Listen to me, Abigail! God is still in control!"

"Stephen Heath thinks he *is* God!"

"Maybe he does. But we know different, right? And the God we serve brought a recovering alcoholic to our house for apple pie tonight. Didn't he?"

Abigail lifted her face from the folds of Matt's shirt and looked toward the front door. "You're right. Let me wash my face, and let's eat. But I'm still worried...worried and scared. I knew something was wrong the way you were sleeping last night, but I never dreamed..." Her voice dropped with her face.

"I know. We'll make a plan!"

Abigail went to wash up, and Matt threw open the porch door to welcome his guest. He clasped his hands together, faked a chipper attitude, and asked, "Who wants pie?" Chop and Felix responded first, as though they understood the question, and bounded into the house. Maggie and M.J. both squealed, "I do!" and scrambled under their dad's outstretched arms and through the front door. Clack stood slowly from the stoop and looked Matt up and down before asking if he was alright.

"I'm fine," Matt lied, "I knew it was coming – just not like that. I didn't expect you there tonight."

"I got hungry, went looking for food, and smelled something good. Figured it couldn't hurt. I may have been wrong. The old lady that sat with me was nice though."

"Let's talk about this later," he suggested. "Right now, let's eat some warm apple pie."

Clack made a circle on his belly with his palm and licked his lips. "I've been waiting all afternoon for this."

For the next half-hour, the troubles plaguing the Hardy family were almost forgotten. They listened and laughed as they got to know Clack Collins, and Abigail knew exactly what Jenni had seen in this charming man so many years ago. Both became lost in the moment and found themselves entrenched in what they believed was real ministry. At 8:30, Abigail stood and removed plates from M.J. and Maggie, who were showing signs of wild tiredness. Putting one hand on the back of each little head, she said, "Let's get you two bathed and in bed before you get a second wind and stay up all night." They moved on command, kissed their dad, and said good-night to Clack. M.J. shook his hand, and Maggie hugged him.

"Cute kids!" Clack declared.

"Thank you! They are the joy of my life."

With a tone more serious than Matt was accustomed to from Clack, he said, "Then you've gotta protect them."

"I know," Matt sighed. "Thankfully they're not old enough to understand anything that happened tonight."

"What did happen?" Clack had to ask.

Matt slid his pie plate to the center of the table, leaned on his elbows and began to try to summarize his current nightmare. "Stephen Heath, the man who spoke, was the first pastor of the church when it formed by splitting off of another church in town almost twenty-five years ago. No doubt now that he was in the middle of the controversy that caused the split. Anyway, he's a retired minister that likes to keep his fangs in the blood of the church, and he has successfully outlasted seven pastors before me, although I suspect he was behind their departures." Matt sat for a moment and then thoughtfully continued. "The church is growing now, mostly with young families coming, and he's losing his stronghold. I guess he's not going down without a fight."

"Are you ready for that fight?"

"I'm not much of a fighter, honestly!"

"So he's already won?"

Matt thought for a moment then asked Clack, "Are you up for a walk?"

"I got nothing else to do. Where are we walking?"

"I go on a run every night, and that's where I do my fighting. Can I show you?"

"Well, now I'm intrigued. Let's go! But you said walk, not run, correct?"

Matt hopped up the steps to where Abigail was getting the children ready for bed. "Clack and I are going on a short walk," he called to her.

"I'll wait up," Abigail answered from M.J.'s bathroom.

When Matt returned, he handed Clack a black sweatshirt and a black stocking cap. "Put these on. Okay?"

"We going to rob somebody?"

"Hopefully we're going to rob someone of their win in this battle."

The two walked down the street with their head uncovered at Matt's insistence. He said, "I want anyone who sees us to assume we're just out for an evening stroll."

"Aren't we?"

"No! You'll see."

At the park, Matt led Clack past the swings and around the dugout into the wooded pines. Clack put on the beanie and pulled it low. "I can't go back to rehab if I'm in jail, Matt!"

"You're not going to jail. Just come on."

At the edge of the wood line, Matt said, "Now stay low and move fast." The two shadowy figures raced across the leaf-strewn yard in front of a well-lit house and ducked into the cover of the azaleas just thirty feet from a large bay window. "Are you okay?" Matt asked his veteran friend.

"You trying to give me flashbacks? What the hell are we doing here?"

Matt whispered his explanation. "This is Stephen Heath's house. A few nights ago, I began sneaking over here and hiding in these shrubs to pray for the old man and his family. That's my weapon, Clack. Prayer. I'm asking God to do what I don't know how to do."

"From what I heard tonight, God has a different idea in mind."

Matt looked at his friend in contemplation and simply responded, "Maybe."

Matt noticed that Clack seemed totally relaxed. Absent were any signs of nervousness or fear of being caught. Matt, on the other hand, was shaking a little, something he had not noticed on either of his other trips to the thicket. He whispered to Clack, "Usually, I have to lay lower than this because his wife leaves every night about 7:20 or 7:30, and her headlights cross right over my head."

"Where does she go?"

"I don't know, but she's back within about thirty minutes."

After staring at the house for a moment, Matt looked at Clack and asked, "You ready to go?"

"We just got here, and you haven't prayed for him yet."

"It may not seem like it, but I'm pretty mad at him right now. If I pray for him tonight, I'm going to pray for God to kill him."

"Why don't we just go knock on the door and do it ourselves?" Clack joked.

"Are you crazy?"

Wobbling his head around like a bobble-head doll, Clack shrugged and said, "Maybe. I am crouched down in someone's front yard spying on them with their pastor."

"Good point! Although, I doubt they'd call me their pastor. Let's go!"

With agility and grace, the two danced their way back across the moonlit yard and into the woods. Emerging around the baseball field, they removed their head covers and Clack shed the much-too-small sweatshirt. "This is nuts," Clack said, laughing. "But it *was* fun! Can't wait to tell this when they ask me about my one-night-out in group therapy tomorrow." Matt, too, laughed at the thought of Clack telling this wild story.

Back home, the two sat on the front steps and talked for a few more minutes. Matt explained his strategy of not fighting evil with evil. He was committed to staying at it for a few more days, at least, until the heat got turned up to the point that he had to take some other approach. Clack admitted how impressed he was with Matt's patience and peaceful plan. He said he hoped it worked but warned Matt to be careful. If he were ever caught in that yard, there would really be no way of explaining his way out of it. "You'd have to kill him then," Clack said. Matt took it as a joke, but he was not convinced Clack meant it that way. The duo then decided to call it a night.

"You gonna be okay out at your place tonight?" Matt asked.

"I'm fine. I was already tired, but this little adventure has me ready for bed."

"I'll see you bright and early? I'd like to go and come before nine or ten o'clock."

"I'll be ready at 6:00! Is that early enough?"

"Yes! I'll see you then."

Clack opened the driver side door to this pickup and said, "Tell your wife thanks for the pie. I know she wasn't in the mood for company tonight."

Matt smiled and then had a frightful thought. "Clack, you don't believe any of that stuff the old man said about me tonight, do you?"

Without hesitating, Clack answered, "Not a chance! If any of it was true, you'd be doing more to defend yourself. Take it from someone who knows guilt...it makes you fight." And he closed the door, started the engine, and pulled away from the curb slowly. Matt had not considered the truth of Clack's statement before, but he was impressed by the wisdom Clack demonstrated in saying it. And he was suddenly impressed with himself for the way he was embodying it.

Before going to bed, Matt decided it was time to let Abigail in on his little secret adventure with Clack and his nightly runs. She was supportive, but she was not yet ready to commit herself to praying for these people that she, at the moment, hated. She, unlike Clack, did not even care if Matt someday got caught sneaking around. After all, someone had been sneaking around their house, and, if he got caught, then maybe the truth would come out. If not, how could it possibly make it any worse than things already were?

Matt felt the need to stay awake and contemplate what the next move might be from Heath and his crew, but it had been a busy and emotional day, and the thought of sleep won the argument. He looked in on his sleeping babies then retrieved the locked box from the closet and placed it beside him in the nightstand. He practiced placing his fingers on the recognition pad a few times just to make sure he could open the case in the event he needed the gun in a hurry at some point. Each time, the lock snapped open, and he lifted the lid just to look at his investment. Matt prayed himself to sleep thanking God for loving him and for giving him a beautiful wife, two incredibly smart and talented kids, and a really good friend. Then he prayed for Clack to have a peaceful night. After that, he sort-of drifted off into dreamland and slept soundly.

CHAPTER TWENTY-EIGHT

Clack stood on the back porch of his trailer and smoked a cigarette before going inside. When he went in, his intention was to crawl in bed, but he could not bring himself to dirty and rumple the fresh, clean bed sheets. So he grabbed a blanket and a pillow and located himself on the couch for the night. He flipped and turned, flopped and tossed for much longer than he cared to, but still too hyped to sleep, he sat up. He had not expected his visit back to South Mill to come with such exhilaration. He had only expected to run from temptation – not through the woods. He felt badly for his friend, and he tried to consider the best possible outcomes letting each scenario play out in his mind. First, he decided that Matt should hire a kickass lawyer and sue the old man for defamation of character. He was pretty sure that was a thing. Then, he entertained the prospect of Matt putting together a delegation of his own to go and threaten bodily harm if the old man didn't back off with his accusations. Clack was willing, if needed, to lead that delegation. It crossed his mind that perhaps the old man would be run over by a train and the whole problem would just go away, but there was no train that ran through South Mill on a regular basis, so the chances were slim. Finally, he realized that the best solution for Matt and his sweet family, and the more likely one to happen, was to run away from trouble. But that did not please Clack at all. So, he prayed. He talked, yelled, cussed, and begged. It was the longest prayer Clack had ever prayed, but the essence of his prayer was mostly repetitive rambling. He told God that he liked Matt. That, though he wasn't sure exactly how or why, he needed Matt. That Jenni needed Matt and Abigail in her life. That he needed Jenni. Then he said that Jenni needed to forgive him. Then, he pleaded with God not to take another friend from him, maybe the only friend he had. Then, he told God that Matt needed to convince Jenni to take him back. Then he told God to disregard that one – that this was about Matt, not him. It went on like that for a long time.

In the end, Clack was convinced that the answer was for Matt to stay at South Mill Baptist Church, that he simply could not cave under the pressure nor could he be asked to leave because of the motives and slander of the old preacher who just couldn't let go. When he finally said, "Okay, God, that's all I've got. Amen, I guess," he sat and stared at the wall for another minute. He then reached to pick up Jenni's letter and read it again but decided it would have to wait. He was suddenly exhausted and thought he could sleep. He folded one pillow in half and placed it underneath his head and tucked another between his knees and curled up in somewhat of a fetal position because his body, when fully extended, overstretched both ends of the couch. He unfurled a woven cotton blanket across most of him and was unaware of the world around him again until the first shimmers of the morning sun came glittering though the front window.

When Matt arrived to pick him up just before 6:00 a.m., Clack had the gate unlocked and wide open. Clack's truck was loaded with the tools he needed, along with a fishing rod, a tackle box, a rocking chair, and a few more clothes. Matt parked, jumped out, and looked at the ensemble and asked, "Want me to start unloading this into my truck?"

Clack said, "Nope! We're taking mine. I'm afraid yours would buckle under the weight." Clack tossed Matt the keys, and added to the fun insult, "You think you can drive a man's truck?"

Matt tossed them back and said, "You drive up! It's your truck. I'll bring it back and park it right here." So Clack backed out, and Matt closed and locked the gate behind him. On the way out of town, Matt looked at every car that passed and every man or woman entering a store or restaurant at such an early hour. He couldn't help but wonder if they had heard the news about his moral turpitude, and he really questioned whether, perhaps, one of them could possibly explain it to him because he certainly didn't know.

"Whatcha thinking, Matt?" Clack interrupted the silence.

"I'm wondering if there are people who think worse of me today than they did yesterday."

"Probably."

"Thanks for the encouragement, Clack!" Then he asked, "Do you?"

"Matt, do you remember who you're talking to? Nothing you have done, hell, nothing on that list last night, would qualify you to be a reprobate in my book. The things I've done would scare the hell outta you. So even if the things being said were true, and I don't believe any of them are, I would still call you my friend."

Matt just nodded. Then Clack added one more quip. "I'm alive today because of you, Matt! Maybe I ought to tell your church people that."

After that, Clack wanted to talk about Jenni. Matt admitted that he didn't know much to say, but under the circumstances, she was the most pleasant subject the two of them could discuss. Clack asked if she was happy. Matt gave him an emphatic no. Clack was surprised at Matt's quick response but knew that it was the truth. Clack's next question was tougher. "Do you think I've ruined her life?"

After letting the question ruminate, Matt finally said, "Yes. If you do nothing else than what you have done so far, you have ruined her life."

"What do you mean?"

"She's filed for divorce from a man she loves because he has become a man she does not know. She married a military hero – a man who knows what it means to strategize against an enemy and then attack. Last night I told you I wasn't much of a fighter. But you are, Clack! You've fought against a communist regime. You've fought against the demons of your past. You've fought against an addiction. And, from all appearances, you won every fight. So, fight for her!"

Clack wiped a tear and after a few minutes of silence said, "You say she loves me?"

"I see it in her eyes and hear it in her voice when she talks about the life y'all made together. The chokeholds you're being freed from up there at Respira are about to be ancient history. You'll still have some of the scars, sure, but you won't be the man you were when you went into rehab. You'll be you again. In fact, I think you probably already are. So without the fear, without the hurt, without the sadness...without the bottle...do you want to be the man who let his marriage crumble? You're looking for redemption, full restoration. To me, that means recovering that love affair with Jennifer Grimes! Right?"

Clack said nothing. He blew his nose in an old napkin from the dashboard and then reached for another to wipe the tears from his cheeks. He bit his bottom lip and held the steering wheel tightly. For more than fifteen miles, he wrestled with his own emotions, and when he finally felt like they were in check, he asked one more question. "She'll take me back?"

"I can't say that for sure," Matt counseled him, "but if I'm betting, my money's on yes. At least that's what Abigail and I are praying."

"You sneaking around in the bushes outside of Jenni's house, too?" Clack couldn't resist.

Matt laughed, "No, Abigail does that one."

Clack asked advice on how to say what he needed to say in his letter. Matt suggested that he simply address each of the points she included in her letter, almost like they were carrying on a conversation so that, if read together, it would sound like a dialogue. Clack thought that was a good idea and promised to try it first chance he got later on in the day. Clack then made Matt promise that, if he was going to fight for his marriage, Matt would fight for his job and his reputation back in South Mill. By the time they reached the gravel road of Altaville, they'd made a year's worth of conversation and a lifetime's worth of commitments.

Clack had made arrangements to store his tools in a garage, which they found unlocked and empty upon their arrival back at the facility. Matt helped unload the truck and promised to drive safely on his way home. Before leaving, he prodded Clack not to work so hard on fixing the broken features of Respira de Nuevo at the cost of failing to fix his anything that still needed to be fixed in his own life. Clack agreed to keep his remodeling of the place on the low end of the priority list, and Matt seemed pleased.

Clack had one more pressing question that he'd failed to ask because he feared the answer, but it was now or never, so he said, "Hey, Matt!" Matt stopped walking around the front of the truck and stepped back toward Clack. "I meant to ask you last night, but with everything that was going on... They said I can invite my family to Thanksgiving dinner here on Thursday. Would you and the family want to come?"

"Crap!" Matt mumbled and looked at the ground. His response surprised Clack. "We can't, Clack! We're having Thanksgiving at our house."

That was the answer Clack had been afraid of hearing, and he dreaded spending a holiday alone, even if he was surrounded by the other residents.

Matt smiled slyly as he continued, "Yeah, it's going to be a busy morning, I'm sure, keeping the kids out of the way and helping Abigail in the kitchen and setting up tables and chairs and all that."

Clack did not appreciate hearing about the festive plans, but he listened politely until Matt finished his spiel by saying, "So, I'm going to need to pick you up really early that morning so you can help with all of that."

"What?" His mind was trying to catch up.

"Yeah, man, I'm sorry. I was supposed to have invited you last night and I forgot. We were all a little distracted. But, yeah! You're coming to our house. I won't take no for an answer. Miss Mabel is coming too. Her kids can't make it this year. You can sit by her again if you want."

Clack was overjoyed and speechless. Matt finished the conversation for them both by saying, "I'll come early on Thursday morning, let's say around 7:00. Be ready!"

Without a warning of any kind, the long expanse of Clack Collins' arms reached around the preacher who was half his size and pulled him in close. For a much longer time than Matt expected, Clack hugged him. When Matt comprehended the sincerity of the embrace, his emotions swept over him and he began to weep. Clack, too, gave up on holding back the tears, and the two simply held on to one another as though all the trouble of their private worlds was frozen in time as long as they didn't let go. And in some spiritual way, they each believed that it was.

Finally, Clack thanked Matt and let him go. Matt climbed into the driver's seat of Clack's Ford F-250, and Clack chuckled at the sight of Matt in a *real* truck. He gunned the engine and peeled out of the parking lot just to make Clack nervous, then slowed down considerably and stuck his arm out of the window to wave goodbye. As he bounced down the gravel road and searched within himself for why he was so emotional, he realized that his sadness was mostly over leaving Clack behind. He had become his true friend, and it hurt to go home without him. Then, as realization gave way to revelation, he cried more at the thought of the other people that he had fallen in love with in South Mill. These were the people that God had sent him to love, and he was *not* going to leave them behind. He sat up straight like he thought a man driving such a big truck should, wiped away his tears, and said in his best impression of a western gunslinger, "You'd better hold on tight, Stephen Heath, 'cause I'm mad as hell, and I ain't going nowhere!" He felt silly as soon as he said it, but the sentiment was authentic. He would weather the storm, and, if necessary, fight for a job that he really did love.

With Matt gone and the staff still unaware of his presence, Clack pulled the rolling metal garage door about two-thirds of the way down to hide himself inside and took out Jenni's letter to work on the assignment Matt gave him. He answered Jenni word for word, phrase for phrase, as though they were having a conversation. He imagined her beautiful freckled face speaking directly to him the words she had penned. He wondered how her hair was fixed as she wrote and where had she been sitting as she composed what was certainly a difficult letter for her.

Where she said, "I'm glad you're getting help," Clack wrote, "I'm finding so much of the help that I've needed for so long at this place Matt recommended." When she said, "I'm praying for you," Clack responded with, "I feel your prayers, and God is becoming more and more real and personal to me every day that I'm here." Because the words reminded him of what she would write to him in Vietnam, he added, "I didn't survive Vietnam without your prayers, and I appreciate them so much...then and now."

Where Jenni's letter shifted the focus to Pastor Matt Hardy and his family, Clack wrote, "You're right about the Hardy family. They are the real thing. If there's ever been anyone like Jesus, I think Matt is him." He told her how glad he was that she was okay with letting the dogs stay with them, that he had witnessed firsthand how much the children and the animals enjoyed each other. Of course, he understood if she was lonely and felt the need to take one or both of them home for some companionship. He would not be upset or angry if she did.

Then he reread her warning about how guarded he was when it came to letting people into his heart. He confessed that her advice was accepted but late. He explained that, though he wasn't sure how, this *kid*, Matt Hardy, had become his best friend. One minute Matt was rescuing him, and the next they were joking and cutting up together like he used to with old pals. He didn't mention any by name, but the thought was there.

Then, in his final read-through, he saw the words that he had skimmed over in every other viewing of her letter. She told him that he needed to protect that kind of relationship. And he wrote fast in response to that suggestion. "Yes," he wrote, "Matt's is a friendship that needs protecting. He's not so popular right now with some of his church members, although I'm not completely certain why. But because you asked me to, and because I believe it is my God-given responsibility, I am committing myself to protecting him...because you and I both need him and his family around for a long, long time."

He took his cue from his wife on how to close the letter and signed it simply, "Love, Clack." It was subtle, but it was there. And perhaps that was exactly what she thought when she ended her letter that same way. He stuffed it in an envelope, addressed it, and pulled a stamp from his wallet and stuck it on. He grabbed the metal handle of his garage unit door and flung it upward letting the autumn sun kiss his face. He felt good! Really good! Faced with a sunny day and a bluing morning sky, he looked toward the heavens and made a declaration. "I'm going to fight for you, Jenni, because I promised Matt I would. And I'm going to protect you, Matt, because I promised Jenni that I would. Now, I gotta go to therapy so I can get outta this place!"

He walked with assertiveness through the front door of the administration building and dropped his letter off onto Vera's desk. It startled her, and she looked way up at the radiant blue eyes on the handsome face at the top of the long body in front of her. He smiled his best smile and asked, "Would you mind dropping that letter in the mail? It's to my wife!" Vera recognized the change in a resident often before they realized it for themselves. She said, "It would be my pleasure, Mr. Collins," and silently thanked God that he was breathing again as she watched him stroll down the hall to the dining room where hot coffee was waiting.

CHAPTER TWENTY-NINE

By 9:00 a.m., Lanie had begun to panic and placed a call to Matt's cell phone. After the second ring, she heard the pastor's voice say, "Hey, Lanie!"

Lanie tried not to sound frantic when she asked, "Where are you? Are you coming in today?"

Matt apologized for not letting her know he was going to be late and assured her that he was only twenty minutes out and would have a sermon title for her shortly thereafter.

"I'm not calling for a sermon title. I just need to know if you're willing to take appointments today because lots of people are calling and wanting one."

"When you say *lots*, how many are we talking?"

"Pastor, I have twenty-six calls to return to people who want to know what time they can come by."

Matt was speechless. He didn't have private meetings with twenty-six people in most months. He knew it wasn't because of his popularity or some crisis that required pastoral counsel. It was, instead, because they all felt the need to question him about whatever rumor they had heard. As much as he wanted to deny anyone a one-on-one with him, he knew he would learn more in those appointments than he could anywhere else, and right or wrong, he felt he needed to know what was being said. So, reluctantly, he told

Lanie, "Schedule the first one at 10:00, and give them each twenty minutes. Let me have a twenty-minute break to eat lunch about 12:40. Okay?"

"Are you sure?" Lanie was overwhelmed.

"Yes, but you are my 9:40 appointment. I need to brief you on what all is going on."

He heard her voice crack on the other end of the phone, and he was sure she had jumped to her own. When she hung up, the heaviness of the last evening once again weighed on his heart, and he, too, began to compile a list of his *other* options. Perhaps his tough-guy declaration as he left Altaville was premature.

No sooner than she had said goodbye to Matt, Lanie's phone buzzed with an intercom call from Trudy. Lanie heard the urgency in her voice as she said, "Lanie, can you come to my office for a minute?"

Trudy Knight, the financial secretary, spent her Thursdays filing through the paperwork that passed before members of the finance committee and the church treasurer, Wanda Briner, on the Wednesday night before. Expense requests were usually approved and checks were signed, and it was Trudy's job to distribute the forms and disburse the funds according to their instructions. As Trudy sorted, she created stacks for staff members, mostly, who had asked permission to spend money from within their expense accounts or their ministry budgets. A reimbursement request from the youth pastor for pizza he bought at a youth workers' planning meeting. APPROVED! A check the children's minister needed to pay an early deposit for summer camp the church kids would attend next year. PREVIOUSLY APPROVED/CHECK SIGNED! An expense request from Evan, the music director, for a bulk order of guitar strings. APPROVED! A reimbursement request from Pastor Matt's professional expense account. DENIED!

Trudy stopped breathing for a moment. In the years she had been at her job, she had never seen an expense request from any of the eight pastors denied. It was her job to collect all of the receipts and other necessary documentation and make sure that, when it got to the hands of one of the finance members, everything was in order. And she was very thorough with that job. Her first thought was that she had messed something up, but with a closer look, she knew she had never touched that report before. Yet, there it was, in black and white and big red letters: DENIED. Pastor Matt's request for a reimbursement for an expense apparently made two weeks before for...Camel cigarettes. The receipt was attached showing he had used his personal debit card to make the purchase. She reached and pushed the intercom button on her phone. Lanie was close, in a professional sense, with Matt, and she would have some insight. When Lanie arrived, Trudy's bewildered expression was the first thing she noticed.

"What's wrong, Trudy?"

"I'm not sure," Trudy stammered. "Does Pastor Matt smoke?"

"Not that I'm aware of. Why?"

Against church policy, although there was nothing of the sort in writing, Trudy showed the expense request to Lanie. Lanie scrutinized over it, flipped the receipt over and scoured the backside of it as though something might be written there indicating some kind of joke. When Trudy didn't break, Lanie began to disparage her for not intercepting it before it got to the committee. "You could have told him that he would get in trouble for submitting something like this, Trudy!"

"Lanie!" Trudy was almost in tears. "I've never seen this before. And I don't think he has either. I mean, he obviously bought them – it's his debit card receipt, but he would not ask for a reimbursement on something like this."

Lanie examined the request again and threw it back onto Trudy's desk and said emphatically, "That's not his handwriting."

Trudy reached into a file where previous requests were kept and pulled out an old request from Matt to compare the penmanship. Lanie was correct. "Something's not right, Lanie."

Lanie straightened from crouching over Trudy's desk and looked at Trudy accusingly. "You're right, Trudy!" Lanie had never gotten involved in the church politics, and she knew how close Trudy had always been with Wanda Briner. She knew that both ladies, especially Wanda, had, at times, thrown power punches because they held the purse strings of the church. Likewise, Lanie knew that the most dangerous place for her to be was between these two and whoever they were railing against at the moment. But this time she didn't stop short of saying what was on her mind. "Trudy, how could you? He's been so sweet to you!"

"Stop right there," Trudy snapped back. "I'm not part of this. I cried myself to sleep last night over what they're saying about him. After you left yesterday, a church member came by to see Matt right after learning that her dad was dying of cancer. You should have seen the sweetness of that man as he listened to her, held her hand, and prayed the most beautiful prayer."

Lanie stood staring at her, anger and sadness pouring from her eyes. "You promise you didn't know?"

"Lanie, if my friends are part of this, and I suspect they are, then I have been taken for a fool. I give you my word that I am not one of *them*."

Lanie considered Trudy's avowal for a moment before saying, "I believe you. But you have to show it to him as soon as he gets here. Okay?"

"Okay!"

Lanie was in the middle of scheduling twenty-six appointments when Pastor Matt arrived five minutes before he had said he would. She paused between calls to buzz Trudy to let her know. Trudy was clearly rattled as she crossed by Lanie's desk and knocked on the door to the pastor's office, which he had closed just to hold off any surprise guests until he was ready to face the masses. She began by complimenting him on everything she had relayed to Lanie about his compassion for Becky the night before. He thanked her and said he appreciated her sitting in with them when she was probably needed elsewhere during all of that. Unsure of how to broach the subject of the reimbursement request, she led with one statement she knew to be true. "I'm afraid I have some bad news to share."

Matt could not have been less surprised by that. All the news he was getting these days was bad, so he just said, "Bring it on!"

Without delaying the inevitable, Trudy said, "Your reimbursement request was not approved."

"Reimbursement request?" Matt was confused. "Reimbursement for what?"

Unwilling to say it aloud, Trudy passed it to him and said, "I'll just let you look at it."

Matt took the paper from Trudy's trembling hand and studied it. Trudy became more nervous as Matt's face cycled through several shades of red before he looked up at her. With a calm that defied his blistery cheeks, he asked, "Where did this come from?"

"It was in my stacks this morning. I swear I had nothing..."

Matt cut her off. "I know you didn't."

His mind raced. He knew what he usually did with debit card receipts – stuck them in his sun visor in the truck until a sunny day when he would pull it down and get showered with them. It must have blown out, and someone with an axe to grind found it. He looked at Trudy who had not budged from where she was standing. "I should explain," he said.

"There's no need," she assured him.

"Yes, there is. I bought them. There's no denying that." His voice was cool and steady. "They were for a friend...a friend who was breaking a lot worse habits than smoking, and he...needed them."

Trudy smiled and wiped a tear. "I'm sure you did the right thing."

"Habits unbecoming of a minister." Matt said in a low tone, no longer talking to Trudy.

"I beg your pardon," Trudy said.

Turing his head upward and looking her in the face, Matt explained, "That's one of the complaints against me....habits unbecoming of a minister. Jim Pethel can dip and spit all through a deacons' meeting, but nobody wants a pastor who smokes cigarettes. It's unbecoming."

"I'm sorry, Pastor!" Trudy said most sympathetically.

"Me, too! Can I keep this?"

"Of course!" she replied and started to leave. At the door, she froze, obviously thinking of her next move since she was naturally aligned with any and all of the people making Matt's life so difficult at the moment. Matt watched her slowly turn back around and face him and listened intently as she said through tears, "Don't leave this church! I like you and your family a lot, and after last night, I know what a decent man you are. The way you helped that girl last night when her heart was breaking..., we haven't had many ministers that could do that, and, well, when my heart breaks one day, I'm going to need someone like you." Without giving Matt a chance to respond, she turned and exited quickly, closing the door behind her. She did not stop at Lanie's desk but choked off the words over her shoulder as she hurried by, "They weren't his. He's being set up."

Matt pulled out the crinkled-up list he had shoved in his pocket the night before, flattened out its wrinkles on his desk with his hand, scrolled with his index finger down to "Habits unbecoming of a minister," and drew a line through one bullet point. He wondered how many more he would cross off as the day progressed.

Troubled, Lanie took her cue to enter. Matt filled her in on all he could and asked her to be extra guarded with any information she passed along to anyone over the next few days. Lanie nodded a lot, said little, and wiped tears over the hurt that someone was causing to the best pastor she had ever worked for. "Thank you," Matt said, and told her she could open the floodgates but to interrupt him every twenty minutes so that he didn't hold up whoever was next in line. It promised to be a very busy and emotional day.

There would be no lawyers, no defamation lawsuits. Matt was facing a smarter enemy than that. The only direct accusations that would be made about him or his family had been done so in THE LIST. Outside of that, shadows of doubt had been cast broadly across the church and community. If specifics had been identified, the young pastor could, more than likely, prove the allegations false. In the event he found it impossible to present convincing evidence to the contrary, though, he might stand before the church and repent of his sin and somehow be restored with forgiveness and brotherly love. Whether the old guard that was working so hard against him had or had not ever considered the latter, they knew better than to make themselves liable or place their reign in jeopardy by committing slander. Reverend Stephen Heath was almost a professional when it came to defending himself against rumored transgressions. Even when they were true, what could not be proven had a way of finding its source silenced. And, so, very craftily and carefully, a handful of South Mill's finest ambassadors embarked on a seed-planting mission, working tirelessly to preserve the church's purity that might be tainted by sinners, otherwise known as outsiders, if the church continued to expand its ministry and membership. And those seeds had already begun to sprout – even before Matt had seen the list on Wednesday afternoon.

The team had worked very quickly to sow seeds of deception throughout the community. Seemingly overnight, although Matt knew it had long been in the works, almost every item on the checklist had been carelessly thrown out there into the wind. Little tidbits of truth planted in the fertile soil of wicked imagination, intentionally cast with wide parameters making evil presumption the natural fruit of the labor. And now, the good people of South Mill were left to harvest whatever conclusions they chose.

At some point earlier in the week, a local gathering of old men with nothing better to do than sit and drink coffee and eat biscuits each morning and bitch about the government and the minorities listened with animosity as Hugh Briner complained about the mess going on at his little church. His coffee club crew loved gossip as much as they enjoyed fussing about how much their wives thrived on it. So, it was to be expected that they would spread a variety of tales when Hugh suggested to them that this young pastor that the church had hastily hired thought it appropriate to use church staff members to babysit his kid during office hours. By the time the tale cycled back to an oblivious and previously uninterested member of South Mill Church, Matt was making the secretaries, youth pastor, and even the custodian take a day each week to babysit while they were still "on the clock," while the young pastor went gallivanting all over creation with his wife, who, evidently, didn't see the need to work and help support their family. Matt listened politely when the 10:20 appointment told him, "These people aren't paid to be your personal servants. That's not their job!" *Ineffective church staff management.*

Jim Pethel built on the "gallivanting" thread and told the guys and gals at work, many of whom had relatives that attended South Mill, how his pastor was never in his office when church people had a crisis. "There's this one man," referring to Brother Heath, "who tries almost every day to get in to see him. Most of the time, his secretary says he's out making visits or busy studying and doesn't have time to see anyone." By the time that kernel popped, multiple versions had Matt sleeping until noon each day and only coming into the office to check phone messages and drink coffee. Someone decided to add in that the church pays his cell phone bill, "but he won't give anybody the number." The 11:00 guest shook an old, crooked finger in Matt's face and said, "Whoever heard of having to go through a secretary and make an appointment to see my preacher. You ain't no CEO, ya know!" *Unavailability to church membership.*

Wanda made sure that she shared with the girls at the beauty shop how horribly Sister Sue, the pianist at the church, had been treated by the kid pastor. "She had to be out ONE Sunday because she had the flu, and he replaced her with some high-falutin redhead. She even showed back up the next Sunday thinking she was gonna play her godawful music in that church again, but Sister Sue was already at the piano." Old Vivian Nix's son, a retired insurance salesman was the 12:00 noon appointment, and he spent fifteen of his twenty minutes explaining to Matt the downfalls of being a micromanager. "Evan's the music director; let him do his job, and you stick to the preaching!" *Lack of leadership qualities.*

Ethel Hughes, the "shut-in," came by at 12:20, and Matt learned a lot from the tongue lashing, in which she said, "You should be ashamed for how you've treated poor Dorothy Heath, Mr. Hardy!" Confusion gave way to enlightenment about her complaint with him, but more importantly, where Dorothy went every night at 7:20ish. "That woman's a saint! A real angel. Why, every single weeknight at 7:30, she brings me a plate of dinner." So that's where she goes, Matt thought. Ethel continued her rant, "And for your wife to just laugh when that kid of yours assaulted her right there in the grocery store with handfuls of candy... Near 'bout knocked her down!" She continued to sing Dorothy's praises and finally did so at the expense of Abigail when she said, "Us old folks couldn't live without Dorothy Heath. I don't see any other preachers' wives out delivering food to us homebound members." Matt wanted to defend Abigail and say, "Actually, she's at home today cooking dinner to take tonight to a nice homosexual couple we know," but Matt knew by the political stickers with which she had adorned her walking cane where she stood on that subject. She finished him off by saying, "Your wife and kids are a reflection of you." *Personal house out of order.*

Lanie's timing could not have been better when she interrupted his 12:20 appointment right at 12:40. The church member in with him was telling how her roast beef had burned a few Sundays before because he "didn't let us out of church 'til quarter of one." He took her counsel with grace when she said over her shoulder, "You need to say what you need to say in your sermons and be done with it. No use saying the same thing over and over again," as Lanie practically drug her out of Matt's office. *Poor time management skills.*

As best as Matt could guess from his 1:00 appointment, Wanda Briner had started her campaign Monday morning when she was making the church's bank deposit and chatted up the branch manager, whose whole family attended South Mill, although quite irregularly. "I hope our offerings keep coming in," she told the manager, "because that pastor doesn't worry about what anything costs. I mean, he's got a helium tank in his office that he ordered from Global Air back in October, and he's in no hurry to get it back to them." Without saying that the church was paying for it, which would have been a lie since it had been donated, Wanda stirred the pot just as well by saying, "I don't even know what the daily rental charge is on a large tank of helium." Fortunately for Matt, a bank teller, who happened to be a very pleasant church member and served on the children's ministry committee, came by to fill him in. Her exact words were, "I know they donated that tank, but not everyone else does." She even volunteered to return it for him, adding, "It just doesn't look good to still have it here." Matt thanked her and said that would not be necessary. He did, however, roll it underneath the couch before letting Lanie show the next appointment in. *Poor stewardship of church resources.*

"You know this office used to be his," a last-minute add-on told Matt at a 2:15, when Lanie let him in for a "quick word with the pastor...five minutes, tops!" He had come from the Thursday lunchtime Rotary Club meeting, where he sat beside Stephen Heath. "Try putting yourself in Brother Heath's shoes and think about how it would feel to be yelled at and basically tossed out of the office that used to be yours." That one got Matt's blood boiling, and his face betrayed him again. "Ah," the man said, "You do have a temper. Heard you even stormed out of the deacons' meeting Sunday night. Best get that under control." At that, Matt informed him that he wasn't on his schedule, and he had other people waiting to see him. As the Rotarian left, he took his hand and brushed it across Matt's desk and then did the same with the couch. He then said, "You know, I remember when Brother Heath furnished this office right out of his own pocket." No one had ever told Matt that little fact, but he really didn't care at the moment and even doubted the veracity of the statement. He stood with an open expression waiting for the guest to finish the thought, but, evidently, that was all he had to say. As he left, he jabbed one more time by saying, "I know you're good at showing people the door, but I can find my own way out. Good day, Pastor!" *Anger management issues.*

Church member after church member came and went from the pastor's office all day with one story after the other. There was the sprinkling of kind-hearted saints among them who just wanted to pledge their love and support for the pastor, but they were hardly a breath of fresh air in the midst of a toxic afternoon.

At some point during the parade, Lanie paused the traffic for Matt to take a call from a disgruntled Abigail. "Did you know they were coming to steam clean the carpet today?"

"No!"

"The man said someone from the church had booked the appointment."

"Did you let him in?"

"I didn't think I had a choice. But just so you know, when he got finished, he made several comments about the dogs – how he was surprised that the church let us have them on those nice wood floors and expensive carpets. He took pictures, Matt. I didn't know what to say."

"No need to have said anything," Matt stated flatly. "The dogs haven't made any messes."

"I didn't say he took pictures of any messes." Abigail was irritated. "He just took pictures of the dogs."

Matt reflected on that for a moment and knew he had been correct in his assumptions about the instigators of the whole upheaval covering their tracks. One of them, whichever one was breaking in on a regular basis, already knew the dogs were there. The carpet cleaners were sent just so they *discover* the dogs without having already known. He had to give it to Brother Heath and Hugh Briner and Jim Pethel and the entire mutinous bunch – they had thought of everything. What a sin it must be to have a dog in the holy, church-owned parsonage. *Misuse of church property (parsonage).*

By the time he and Lanie closed up shop at 5:15, Matt had lived his dream of spending his entire day with church people, but it had turned out to be a nightmare. One by one, the parade of sheep from his flock had helped cross off almost every bullet point on Brother Heath's list. Because *Spiritual Immaturity* and *Misrepresentation of the Kingdom of God in our community* were somewhat generic and may have just been umbrella terms under which everything else fell, Matt crossed those off the list before he packed up to go home. That left only the two biggest ones, *Ethical/Moral Failure* and *Appearance of Impropriety.* He was certain that those webs were being spun somewhere, but the appointment slate had been cleared for the day, and he wasn't answering the home phone that night. He would just have to wait to know fully what was coming next.

CHAPTER THIRTY

Matt arrived home to hugs and kisses from his two most perfect creations, and he cursed himself for not defending his family when they had been part of the collateral damage in his office at times throughout the day. Abigail was oddly pleasant considering the unwelcomed solicitation from earlier in the day. Matt looked around and said, "Wow, these carpets do look cleaner. Do I need to take my shoes off?"

"I don't care if you go play in the mud and then walk in on them," Abigail reverted back to her afternoon attitude.

"Well, at least they'll look nice for our Thanksgiving dinner."

The thought of a holiday feast was the furthest thing from Abigail's mind at the moment. There was not much from the past twenty-four hours over which she felt compelled to give thanks. What *was* on her mind was the dinner that was hot, packed, and ready to deliver to Doc and Corey. "We said we'd have it there by 6:00, so everybody go get in the van."

Doc and Corey lived in the next county over, but the drive was still only twenty minutes. Nevertheless, the children pressed play on the DVD player and became engrossed in a Disney movie they had seen hundreds of times. When Matt knew they were not paying attention, he whispered to Abigail that he was thinking of adding some new bullet points to Brother Heath's list. "I'm going to need your help, though, with a Bible verse against 'Going Inside a Homosexual's Home.'"

Abigail didn't find his humor to be very entertaining at the moment, although she had not considered that they might get to go inside. Now she was hoping that they would. Word around town was that the decorating was quite extravagant. She had never been inside the home of a gay couple. This would be her first, and she was secretly excited about it. But as far as Matt's list was concerned, she was sure he was safe – not because there weren't some ignorant church folks who would tie Matt to the railroad tracks just for going inside their home, but because Doc and Corey were apparently off limits. Even Brother Heath had regularly tried to hire Doc to play the piano at the church before Sue came along, and the pharmacy and lunch counter were favorites of most everyone in the church and the town.

If Doc and Corey had heard any of the rumors ushering in Matt's demise, they played dumb. Their hospitality was incomparable to any the Hardys had experienced. Corey gave a tour of the beautifully refurbished farmhouse that had been in Doc's family for over 150 years. It bordered on being a mansion, but Corey explained that the Figgins had just kept adding on every time someone had another baby or got married. Doc took M.J. and Maggie out back to see a couple of "babies" - calves that had just been born that week. Immediately, M.J. wanted to take one home as a pet. After a few minutes of casual chitchat, Abigail, not wanting to overstay their welcome, told their hosts to stop being so polite and send her and her family home so that the two of them could eat while the food was still hot. Both Corey and Doc hugged the whole family and promised to invite them back over for a barbeque when the weather warmed up. Matt waved out the car window and yelled, "I'm holding you to that!"

As they pulled out onto the state highway that would lead them back to South Mill, Abigail looked in the rearview mirror and commented, "They're so nice. Why can't our church people be that sweet?"

"Some of them are," Matt reminded her.

"You're right," she said.

Abigail had doubled everything when cooking for Corey and Doc, and she served it up to Matt, Maggie, and M.J. when they returned home. Dishes were washed, dogs were fed, baths were taken, television was watched, and prayers were spoken. Matt convinced Abigail that he had to live up to his commitment and take his "nightly jog." He didn't kneel long in the pine straw that night, but he did witness the departure and return of Dorothy at her regularly scheduled times, and he was proud of himself that he had learned the truth about where she went. He would not, though, grant her sainthood for delivering food to Ethel Hughes. He chuckled at that thought as he watched Dorothy's tail lights fade behind him. He found it strange that, though he positioned himself nightly in front of the largest window on the house, he never saw any movement inside while Dorothy was gone. He thought how perhaps Stephen just sat and watched *Jeopardy* or something while she was out. But he could not embolden himself enough to creep closer to the house and have a look.

Back home, he held his wife close, and they dozed on the couch until he woke and insisted that they both go get in their own bed. Pistol was relocated to bedside proximity, dogs were on duty in the children's rooms, and all the doors were securely locked. He needed to rest. Tomorrow would be another full day, though Fridays were usually his day off each week. To compromise, he told Lanie that the two of them would work until noon so that anyone else wanting to throw stones at him before the weekend would have the chance.

Only a few had indicated they might stop by on Friday, so no one bothered to create a schedule for the visits. Matt planned to just conduct Friday morning with an open-door policy.

He let Lanie go home at noon as promised, but he stayed in the office another two hours putting the finishing touches on his sermon for Sunday morning. Since the office was normally closed on Fridays, the likelihood of anyone stopping by that didn't have an appointment was slim When he finally closed his Bible and laptop computer, he knew two things about his sermon. First of all, it would be brief since that seemed to be a big point of contention. Secondly, it would not be what many of them expected to hear. As far as he could guess, some who had been in the church for years fully expected him to either not show up Sunday at all or to show up only to announce his resignation. Instead, he would preach from the Bible a sermon about thankfulness, using a passage from the Apostle Paul's letter to the Philippians, Chapter four, where he wrote, "I have learned the secret of being content in any and every situation." He was amused with the idea that, just by using that verse, he might send some of the troops in search of stronger ammunition – especially when there was no mention of stepping down from his position. But, for now, the responsibility of preaching God's word to the South Mill Church was still his, and he was going to be faithful. He would then work in the office on Monday and Tuesday and be off the rest of the holiday week. Somewhere in its history, the church decided to close the office for three days at Thanksgiving. He was looking forward to some family time.

CHAPTER THIRTY-ONE

Abigail was big on sending holiday cards to a select list of friends and family members, and Thanksgiving was, after all, a holiday. Since they would not be going home to Texas to see Matt's parents or to Missouri to see hers, she felt it necessary to send both sets a festive card, complete with a Turkey and fall foliage adorning the front and a handwritten note from each of the children on the inside. She enclosed a recent photograph of each of the children, as well as one of the entire family. She also wrote a note saying how much they were looking forward to seeing all of them at Christmas and signed it *Matthew and Abigail*.

Matt's part of the mailing process involved dutifully obeying his wife and taking the cards to the post office on Saturday morning to mail. Abigail recently swore off putting anything in the mailbox at the house for the postal carrier to pick up. She imagined someone would snoop through anything going out or coming in, so she watched each morning for the postman to stop by with the day's delivery. By the time he was at the mailbox next door, Abigail was on the porch en route to get whatever had been left for them before anyone else could.

When Matt returned to the house, he sat in his truck a while listening to a sports broadcast on the radio highlighting the day's top NCAA football matchups. With the radio on, he did not hear the truck that pulled in behind his. When he clicked the radio and turned the ignition switch to off, he stepped out of the truck and was startled to the ground by a man standing at the edge of his truck bed.

"Don't shoot, Preacher! It's just me." As Matt absorbed the dew from the leaves underneath him, he looked up and noticed the man was wearing olive green coveralls and smelled like a chainsaw. Immediately, Matt recognized the lawn man that serviced the church properties, including the parsonage. He also landscaped and maintained lawns for a dozen or more church families, including the one Matt had been traipsing through in the darkness each night on his prayer runs. He smiled big and reached out a hand for Matt to grab, then hoisted him up to a standing position. "Didn't mean to scare you."

"Sorry, I zoned out listening to predications about all the games today." As Matt dusted himself off, pealing a wet leaf from his backside, he looked again at the man, whose name he couldn't remember at the moment, and asked, "What brings you by?"

"Oh, I just wanted to come get up some of these leaves. I'm taking off next weekend to go huntin', and I didn't want to leave you folks with a mess on Thanksgiving."

"Well, that's nice of you," Matt said, even though he knew the church was paying for his services so, nice or not, it was expected.

"I won't be long. Just gonna run the mower over 'em and bag 'em up. Hope I don't wake the kids."

"They're up, "Matt told him. Then, thinking he was probably being paranoid but wanting to rule out any other possibility, Matt turned and said, "Say, Al..." suddenly remembering his name, "Why'd you say 'Don't Shoot?'"

Busted, the yard man held his mouth wide open for a few seconds with nothing coming out of it. When he finally did speak, he could only speak the truth. "Awww, I was just jokin', Preacher! Brother Heath warned me that you had yourself a new firearm, and you don't wanna go sneakin' up on a man packin' heat." He then tried to start a conversation about guns since he, himself, owned more than thirty. But the exchange sent Matt over the edge when he said, "Yeah, Smith & Wesson makes a good one. Nine-millimeter . . . right?" Matt smiled politely and thanked him for coming and then abruptly turned and marched from the truck to the house, across the porch, through the front door, and into the kitchen where Abigail was clearing syrupy plates from the table.

"Did you tell ANYONE about our purchase in Columbia?" he was almost yelling.

Abigail whirled around to face him and shook her head from side to side vigorously. "No! I wouldn't tell anyone. You know that! Why are you asking?"

Heath knows we have it, and he's telling people.

"So, we have a gun," Abigail asked the wrong question, "what's the big deal?"

"THE BIG DEAL," Matt *was* yelling now, "IS HOW IN THE WORLD DOES HE KNOW?" Calming slightly, he said, "There's no way he could have seen it or even opened the lock box, and we paid cash for it, so someone must have been digging around in our personal papers and found the bill of sale!"

"Oh..." Abigail let the gravity of the situation settle on her as Matt sank into a chair at the kitchen table. He placed both hands across his head, stretching his thin fingers down to the base of his skull and began massaging. Abigail pulled a chair up beside him and tried to take over. "It'll be okay, Matt! Maybe since they know, they'll be scared to come back around. Or..." and she hesitated a moment, "...maybe we should think about buying our own place and getting out of the parsonage."

Matt didn't respond, but he did hear her. The idea had merit, but they had not been there a year yet. Even if the church were happy with him at the moment, the decision makers would never go for letting him leave the parsonage. Besides, he would need an increase in his salary to make up for what they afforded him by letting him live in the church's house for free. He knew it was not a possibility. For now, that was one area of his life that they did, indeed, control.

For the rest of the morning Matt roamed from room to room in the house, went outside and sat on the porch, and reclined on the couch rubbing a dog's head until the dog could no longer stand it and leapt down to wander the house a while himself. When cartoons were no longer interesting to Maggie, she suggested that they all play a game of Go Fish. Matt, rising slightly from his slump, thought that would be a good distraction. After losing one game to M.J. on purpose and another to both Maggie and M.J., Matt was in the middle of asking if Maggie had any sixes when Abigail came down the steps with her cell phone to her ear and asked Matt if they had any plans for dinner. He looked directly at her but gave no answer. He didn't want to answer until he knew who Abigail had on the phone. "Who is it?" he asked.

Abigail sometimes gave her cell number out much more freely than Matt, and church members had been known to call hers to get through to him. He wanted no part of dinner plans in which he would have to defend himself, discredit his nemeses, or listen to stories that implicated him in some carnal behavior.

Abigail muffled the phone and answered, "It's Jenni."

"Who?"

"Clack's wife!"

"Oh!" Matt was suddenly energized. "That Jenni!"

"She got a letter from Clack this morning, and she wants to know if we'd enjoy a ride up to Cardelville for an early dinner?"

"Anything to get outta here!" Matt said emphatically.

Abigail went back up the stairs and continued the call. Jenni was worried because of what Clack said in his letter about some people not being very happy with Matt right now. She did want to talk to Matt about Clack, but she was sincere in her concern for them, too. She had considered coming back to church again on Sunday, but the Methodist Church in Cardelville needed her to fill in there for a day.

Abigail, glad to have someone to confide in, filled Jenni in on the situation at South Mill. With the new knowledge, Jenni was even more insistent that they come. She gave Abigail the address of a restaurant called Dusty's and warned her it wasn't a fancy place – just a little family restaurant. She didn't bother telling Abigail it was literally her family's restaurant.

At 3:00, the dogs were corralled into the kids' bathroom with food and water bowls filled. The family piled into the minivan, the same Disney movie was loaded into the DVD player, and the Hardy bunch zipped up the road out of South Mill with haste. On several occasions, Matt slowed down just to let the car behind him pass because he was concerned that someone might be tailing them. Abigail did not accuse him of being paranoid.

At five, Dusty's opened for dinner service, and Jenni came out to welcome the Hardys. Hugs were followed by an introduction to a cousin who ran the place. A table was set for them in a corner away from the crowd that would gather. Jenni admitted that she wasn't much on cooking these days, so she chose something close to home cooking instead. Matt and Abigail found Dusty's to be a great choice. They ordered from the menu of comfort food and sat around talking like they really were at a family table. When dessert was ordered, Jenni slid her chair around to talk more quietly to Matt. She did not want her real relatives to hear her talking about Clack. First, though, she wanted to know that Matt and his family were okay. Matt tried to be convincing as he said they were, but Jenni's face revealed her doubts. When they finally discussed Clack, she said, "I'm probably a fool for asking, but is he really doing okay in this therapy place? He said in his letter he is, but he's said that before."

Matt flashed a genuine smile and said, "He's doing great! He really is!"

"So, he's still there?"

"He came home Wednesday night as a reward for his progress, and I took him back up there first thing Thursday morning." He then added for Jenni's assurance, "He wanted to go back."

"You're really good for him, Matt!"

Abigail joined the conversation. "Clack is good for Matt, too! He needs a friend who isn't one of his church members right now."

Jenni continued her line of questioning until she almost believed that Clack did, indeed, want to change his ways. Then she asked, "Do you think I should go see him?"

Matt thought it would be a great idea and almost jumped out of his seat when she asked. "If you want to go tomorrow, I can call ahead tonight and let them know you're coming."

Jenni shook her head and said, "I'm playing at the Methodist church in the morning and for a community Thanksgiving service there in the evening." Nervousness attached itself to her voice as she almost whispered, "Let me think long and hard about it, but I think maybe next Sunday..."

Matt was still ecstatic over the news. "Yes!" he cheered, "Next Sunday is great." Then, he thought of an even more exciting prospect and blurted it out without even consulting Abigail. "Of course, he'll be at our house on Thursday for Thanksgiving dinner. You should join us, too!"

Jenni smiled but politely declined saying, "Clack and I don't have the best track record for holidays, and I would hate for something to go wrong and ruin yours."

Shortly after her uncle had died, the family sold the Edisto house. Jenni's cut had just been more money sunk into Clack's failed business. Since then, she dined with Mary Ellen's side of the family on Thanksgiving, and, even after she passed away, the new tradition continued. "My family actually does Thanksgiving here in the restaurant. Did I tell you this was my aunt's place?"

Matt shook his head, but Abigail said that she had noticed some pictures of Jenni on the walls. She especially admired the one of Jenni in a long white gown standing beside a handsome man in uniform, but she thought it might be best not to mention the wedding photo. Perhaps Jenni didn't remember that it was there.

Jenni thanked them for coming, walked them to the parking lot, and wished them a Happy Thanksgiving. Everybody hugged everyone, and Matt made sure the kids had fastened themselves into their car seats while Jenni and Abigail babbled on about this and that. But Jenni walked with Matt to the driver's side of the vehicle with something still on her mind.

"I need to tell you something," she said.

"Okay. I'm all ears."

"I'm sure you didn't know what all you were bargaining for when you went to Clack's rescue a few weeks ago and..." Jenni's eyes glistened. "...you know that he and I have been through hell together..." Her voice dropped as she choked back tears, and Matt reached out and held her hand. She continued, "I thought for a long time that I hated him for what he put me through. But over the last few weeks I have realized that, divorce or no divorce, I guess I will always love him. And I know without a doubt that he will always love me."

Matt smiled and kept himself from saying something cheesy. Jenni continued – and the gravity of her words pressed hard against Matt's soul. "He's just loyal like that...to a fault some would say, but it's not a fault. It's a gift. Use it!

Matt was intrigued and wondered what she meant. Jennie explained, "I know my husband, Matt, and if there is one thing you can count on, it is that Clack will have your back no matter what you are facing back there in South Mill. He's never been the church-going type, and I'm as shocked as I can be that he is now, but he can be a blessing to you. So let him!"

When she finished speaking, she let go of Matt's hand, gave him a big hug, and said, "Now y'all get going. Tomorrow's a busy day for you!" As they drove home, Abigail and the kids sang songs, but Matt stayed silent taking in nothing but the road ahead. He felt like Jenni's words were almost prophetic, although he had no idea why. Still, he replayed them over and over in his head.

Just before 9:00, Matt turned off the headlights of the minivan and walked around it to carry a comatose M.J. into the house. When he reached the top step, he noticed a newspaper rolled up and lying against the front door. The paper did not run on Saturdays, so Matt assumed a neighbor had found one and thought it was theirs and tossed it onto the porch. Without much thought he kicked it inside the house and planned to toss it in the trash after he unloaded his bundle into his own little bed. Abigail followed Matt and Maggie upstairs to give kisses and say goodnight.

When Matt came down to discard the newspaper, he noticed some big, bold, handwritten red ink on the front page. He rolled the rubber band down the tubular shape and spread the edition out on the kitchen cabinet. Without much creativity to their artwork, someone had scratched through the date on yesterday's paper and written the upcoming Monday's date over the top of it in red marker. Below it was a similarly scratched out headline about a new underground waste water system being built in South Mill, and in its place a new handwritten headline read: SOUTH MILL'S PASTOR HARDY RESIGNS! In the margin, a note was scribbled in the same red ink that said, "Can't wait to read this headline on Monday morning." The stairs creaked and startled Matt, but it was just Abigail coming down. Quickly, Matt tore off the front page and folded it into the pocket of his jeans. He flipped through the rest of it quickly and, finding no more red ink revisions, wadded it up into a ball and tossed it in the trashcan. He could wait to tell Abigail.

CHAPTER THIRTY-TWO

The Sunday morning church service had never been more packed. It looked more like an Easter crowd than one gathered for the Sunday before Thanksgiving. Ushers had to put out chairs in the back for the latecomers, but, in the end, everyone got a good seat. When the announcements, prayers, choir anthems, and congregational singing were over, the Reverend Matt Hardy took the pulpit to deliver Sunday's sermon. All eyes were on him – waiting for something out of the ordinary. His insides were a jittery mess, but his demeanor was cool. He was unaware, from all outward appearances, that so many had come expecting a show. Instead of giving them one, he read scripture, prayed for God to speak through him, and preached an eloquent and inspiring message on contentment and Thanksgiving from the fourth chapter of Philippians. And he did it in all in just under twenty minutes . . . a new church record.

When the church sang the closing hymn, a family that most of the congregation did not know stepped out of their pew and joined Pastor Matt at the front of the sanctuary. People peered around taller ones in front of them and leaned out into the aisles to see what was transpiring at the altar. It really was not an unusual sight, as it is the tradition of most Baptist churches to give an altar call or invitation for anyone present to come to the front. Regularly, someone would walk the aisle to give his or her life to Jesus, to pray or repent in response to the sermon, or to join the church membership and be spontaneously *voted* in. When the song was over, Reverend Hardy asked the congregation to be seated for a brief moment and motioned for the family to stand beside him at the front. A broad smile created dimples that had not been as prominent recently as they once were. He read from a card that the family had filled out, though he didn't need any assistance knowing their names. "I'd like to introduce you to some friends of mine," he said proudly. "This is the Weller family: Toby and Christa, and their children Jacob and Christopher. You may remember them from our prayer list a few weeks back when I asked you to pray for Jacob here," Matt smiled bigger and put his arm around Jacob, certain that no one remembered and almost as sure that no one besides him had actually prayed for him. He continued, "The Wellers have been attending South Mill for a while now, and today they have come to say they want to make this their church home." Even saying the words, Matt wondered why. "So, if you are excited to welcome them into the South Mill family, say Amen!" A half-hearted *amen* went up from the congregation as Matt tried to scan certain faces to see if their lips actually moved. It was a weird tradition, and, though there was no "yea or nay" vote, the Wellers received a unanimous affirmation to their request to join the church. Matt wanted to say, "And just like that, you're now part of the nightmare." Instead, he welcomed them into the loving and faithful fellowship of believers and invited them to remain at the front after the service to shake hands with and be "officially" welcomed by *the loving and faithful believers* of South Mill.

Matt was satisfied that he had faithfully executed his duties for the morning. He had even given those hoping for something remarkable a short, short sermon to talk about. If, however, that did not fulfill their hopes, maybe his next trick would. With still a minute-and-a-half left before the magic hour of noon, at which time the whole crowd wanted church wrapped up so they could head to lunch, it was time to close in prayer, but Matt had other plans. Suddenly sounding more like an evangelist than he ever had, Matt closed the service by saying, "We've sung praises to God this morning. We've prayed together. We've heard the gospel preached. And we've received a beautiful new family into the life of this church. *This* is good news!"

Then, reaching inside his suit coat pocket, he whipped out the front page of a newspaper and held it high for the congregation to see. With a slight of hand move that would rally a real illusionist, he shoved it back inside before anyone could have read even one word from it and said, "Unfortunately, nothing that has happened here today will make tomorrow's headlines." He made eye contact with a couple of wide-eyed conspirators and then concluded, "...but good news seldom does!"

No one moved right away, unsure whether or not there was more to come. Realizing the awkwardness of his benediction, Matt threw his hand high in the air, began walking up the center aisle to take his position at the back door, and said much louder than was necessary, "God bless you all! Happy Thanksgiving!" The Sunday morning worship service at South Mill was over, and, while it had been a very good day by typical measure, a portion of those in attendance went home disappointed.

The foyer traffic was light, as Matt expected it to be. Very few chose to exit through his doors and, instead, participated in the obligatory handshake with the new church members and made their way out one of the two side doors at the front of the sanctuary. Some of those who did come past the preacher ignored him completely, walking with someone else nearby with whom they faked important conversation or amusing laughter. Miss Mabel, of course, came his way, pulled him in close and kissed him on the cheek and told him, "You did good today, Preacher! Don't you worry!" As she shuffled out the door, she turned back and said, "And I'm looking forward to my Thanksgiving dinner at your house on Thursday!" Matt smiled and said he was also. *Why couldn't they all be like her?*

When the room was clear, Matt kicked the doorstops and closed up shop. He cut back through an empty sanctuary, grabbed his Bible from the front pew where he had left it, and ran by his office before meeting Abigail and the kids for a low-key Sunday lunch at home. Public appearances in restaurants were not the best move for a few weeks. When he reached his office, the door was unlocked and opened. Brother Heath had let himself in. Matt took a deep breath and prepared himself to say, "May I help you with something?" but Heath cut him off and led the confrontation.

"That was an impressive service, Preacher!" Stephen spoke derisively.

Matt recognized the sarcasm but thanked him anyway.

Then, with a haughtiness that exceeded any Matt had personally seen from the man before, Stephen waved his hands in the air in mock celebration and said, "Woohoo! Four new members. I guess you're pretty proud of yourself, huh?"

Matt had no response. He did not know what to say.

"They can't join fast enough to save you here! And, besides, they never last!"

Matt knew what to say then. "Ever look in the mirror and ask why?"

Heath took a deep, slow breath and then another one before barking, "Young and dumb! Do you not realize that God has plans for this church that don't involve you? We gave you three days, Brother Matt! Three days to figure this thing out."

Matt's anger burned for the old man when he asked, "Don't you mean three days to write a resignation letter?"

"Three days to prayerfully consider your options!"

"What options?" Matt wanted to ask, but he knew there were none. Besides, he had a much more pressing question that, in the heat of the moment, didn't seem like it could possibly make the situation worse. So, letting his eyes shout for him, he gazed deep into the old man's pale green eyes and quietly asked, "How do you know what goes on in my house?"

Heath backed up a step and rested the back of knees against the wingback chair where he had sat for a thousand of his daily visits with pastors over the years. His mouth wanted to smile but seemed too exhausted to convince his lips to curve upward, so he forced dry breath through his yellow teeth and said, "I already told you that ain't your house. All these things you keep calling yours are just things we let you use!"

"So, since the church owns the house, you can come and go when you want? Day or night? By invitation or by intrusion? You can just break into the home where I try to keep my family safe from people like you and plunder through all of my personal belongings?" Matt noticed how loud he was speaking and quickly lowered his voice in case others were listening nearby, which would come as no surprise.

Feigning offense, Heath snapped back, "I've never broken into anybody's house, and why would I care to go through your personal stuff?"

"I don't know, Brother Heath. Maybe so you could warn the groundskeeper to beware of…oh, I don't know…maybe a Smith & Wesson nine-millimeter?"

Heath's face turned blue, and his lips quivered. He tried to step backwards but fell into the wingback chair behind him. He sucked the air from the room. For a moment, Matt thought he might need to call for medical attention. And when Heath looked him square in the face, Matt thought he was about to ask for help. Instead, with a jerking movement, Stephen threw his arm sideways and extended an old, crooked finger toward the door and, in a venomous and gravelly whisper, demanded, "Get out of my office!"

Matt squelched any possible concern he had for the health of the old fart, and he certainly felt no sympathy for him. He grabbed his Bible and coat from his desk and stormed out. Heath spoke one more time before Matt was out of earshot and said, "You have one more week." Matt stopped cold in his tracks before choosing to ignore the warning. Then he left without locking any doors behind him.

After lunch, the kids and Abigail dozed in and out of afternoon naps. Matt slipped into his tiny home office and placed a courtesy call to Casey Briner, the chairman of the deacon board. Casey was cordial and even complimented Matt's sermon before Matt got down to business. He briefly recounted his unpleasant interaction with Brother Heath and then admitted that he was aware that some were expecting him to resign at any time. He explained to Casey his commitment to the church, which was, in his opinion, part of his faithfulness to God's calling on his life. He shared that he had no intentions of being run off by a few threats and nasty rumors. Matt suggested that, if Casey felt the need, they could call an emergency deacons' meeting for Monday evening to get everything out in the open. Casey indicated that he was not very supportive of meeting on Thanksgiving week when so many folks might be headed out of town. After concluding the call, Matt assumed his naptime position on the couch, but wide eyes and a racing mind kept sleep far from his afternoon. That evening, he did go on his run, but he found his covert prayers to seem empty and meaningless, reaching no higher than the pine branches that hung over his hidden head. He still saw no movement inside the house and wondered if the old man might still be sitting in the wingback chair in *his* office. On the trek back home, Matt questioned the futility of the exercise and considered whether he would ever even do it again.

The two-day work week was fairly uneventful. A few folks meandered into the office to drop off this or that, and Matt strained to hear every interaction with Lanie or Trudy. Most steered clear of his office altogether, although a few did stick their head in his door and wished him a Happy Thanksgiving. He smiled amiably and returned the sentiment. He made a hospital visit on Tuesday morning to see the elderly mother of a less elderly church member who had developed some fluid around her heart. He found it drudgery to knock on the door of a hospital room where his presence might not be welcomed. Fortunately, the family was out, and the old lady, who would not know him anyway, was asleep. Quietly, he jotted a note on the back of his card and left it where the family would find it when they returned. He searched the parking lot for Brother Heath's car, but evidently this visit was not significant enough to merit the old man's attention. When Tuesday came to an end, Matt had a sermon ready that would be the first in his Christmas season series, and he had no plans to touch his notes again until Saturday. For the next four days, he was done with South Mill Baptist Church. Except for Miss Mabel, of course.

On Wednesday, Abigail ran into Christa Weller at the grocery store and learned that, with their extended family so far north in Pennsylvania, it would just be the four of them on Thanksgiving, and they were going to eat out...maybe at a Cracker Barrel. Abigail wouldn't hear of it and invited the four Wellers to join the four Hardys and a couple of other guests at their home.

That evening, Abigail placed her mom on speaker phone to guide her through the family recipe for cornbread dressing while Matt drove to the church to pick up two long tables and some folding chairs to accommodate the Thanksgiving crowd they were hosting. He had not asked any committee for permission to borrow them, so he imagined the comments like *there he goes again...misusing church resources.* As he pulled out of his driveway, a Global Air van zoomed past him coming from the direction of the park, and he said out loud for no one to hear, "Hey, follow me! I have your helium tank!" But the van turned right at the highway and headed in the opposite direction.

When Matt reached the church, he pulled under the portico at the fellowship hall where the tables and chairs would be easily loaded. He didn't normally check the mail, but with the church staff off for three days, no one would be checking it until Monday, so he thought he should. At the edge of the parking lot, he opened the mailbox door and grabbed what had been left that morning in a bundle and carried it with him into the church. He walked up the hallway to the office to drop the mail on Lanie's desk, but as he placed it there, he noticed a beautiful golden colored envelope with a Hallmark seal on the back. The front was addressed to *Rev. and Mrs. Matt Hardy and Family*, but there was no return address. He tucked it into his back pocket to take with him, pleased that someone had sent his family a Thanksgiving card. When he had loaded the tables and chairs in the back of his pickup, he sat behind the steering wheel and opened the envelope. The front of the card was a nice photo of a family gathered around a table for Thanksgiving. He read the words to himself: WHEN WE COUNT OUR BLESSINGS AT THANKSGIVING... He opened the lovely card to read the rest of the message which said: YOU ARE AT THE TOP OF THE LIST! The words *THE LIST* were circled in bright red ink and underlined three times, and there was a newspaper clipping inside. Immediately, Matt's heart began to race with the realization that the card was not intended to be a blessing. Unfolding the clipping, it was Tuesday's front page and, once again, the headlines had been crossed out and rewritten. The new red one said: GAY LOVE TRI-ANGLE INCLUDES SOUTH MILL PASTOR. Underneath the headline was glued a black and white photo of Matt hugging Doc Figgins. He recognized the occasion right away as the night Abigail cooked dinner for Doc and Corey. Corey was also in the photo, but other important elements were not. The picture was some-what grainy, taken from some distance by a camera with a mediocre telephoto lens, but the intent was clear. Corey was standing behind the pastor looking down at what appeared to be his butt. In reality, Corey had been looking down at the small, three-foot-tall M.J., but he, of course, was cropped out, as were Abigail and Maggie so that it seemed Corey's eyes were focused on the pastor's derriere as just the three men stood together in a compromising situation. *Appearance of Impropriety.*

Matt's chest heaved as he tried to breathe. There had been no moment in his life that he had experienced the cocktail of anger and sadness that had just been served to him. He was not gay, but he did love Corey and Doc, and, in someone's sick attempt to smear him, he could not bear the idea of somehow disrupting the happy home they had made together. Abigail had been wrong. Whatever immunity had been granted these classy gentlemen by everyone in the church up until now had been removed because hurting Matt held more value than protecting them. He sat with the engine idling trying to decide if he should go immediately to the Figgins farm and show the couple what some camera-carrying jackass had done. Un-consciously constant in his lifelong practice of putting others ahead of himself, his own reputation was the least of his concerns at the moment. But after thinking through the motives behind the camera, he concluded with a fair degree of certainty that whoever had done it would not actually involve the other two men right away. Matt was the target, not Corey and Doc. He would not rush over.

Instead, he flung the transmission into drive and pressed the pedal to the floor leaving tire tracks on the pavement under the portico. Rather than turn left to head home, he peeled out of the churchyard to the right and drove three miles south while totally ignoring all speed limit signs along the way. When he reached Boggus Drive, he swung the wheel left and departed the highway on two wheels. A quarter of a mile down the road, he pulled a set of keys and a wadded up black windbreaker he seldom wore from his truck's center console and exited the vehicle. After unlocking what was becoming a familiar gate, he left the truck where it was and walked the dusty driveway to a rickety handrail. In the glow of his headlights still shining from the gate, he fidgeted for another key on the ring and disappeared behind a white mobile home with silver trim. Exactly six minutes later, longer than he had intended to take, he returned, clamped the lock on the gate, and gently placed the rolled-up windbreaker into the truck's console, carefully laying the set of keys on top of it. He drove back the way he had come, this time cautiously obeying all traffic laws. When he arrived at home, his demeanor was calm, and he seemed excited about Thanksgiving dinner on Thursday.

Abigail had finished the dressing and stored it in the refrigerator for the night. She would cook it tomorrow. She looked around the kitchen for any remaining dishes and then said she was headed to bed. Matt followed close behind. He had to be up early the next morning to go get Clack. There would be no nighttime jog. Abigail asked if he thought Clack would be okay with the Wellers joining them. He assured her that Clack would be the perfect gentleman. Upstairs, Matt rambled in the closet for a moment before carrying the small biometric lockbox to the bedside drawer. Abigail was used to the nightly procedure by that point, and, until they had a house of their own with a security system, she slept soundly knowing that they were well protected.

CHAPTER THIRTY-THREE

At 7:28 a.m., on Thanksgiving Day, Matt said good morning to a dapper Clack Collins. Wearing pressed khaki pants, a starched blue pinpoint Oxford cloth shirt, and brown leather driver moccasins, he looked like a Kennedy vacationing on Cape Cod. They shook hands, loaded Clack's suitcase into the back of the truck, and zipped back down the road toward South Mill. Clack told Matt of the progress he had made in both his therapy sessions and on the construction projects. He admitted that he was enjoying himself a little too much and that it was time to really consider returning to life in the real world. That raised the first comment out of Matt since they hit the road. "Are you ready?"

"Blake says this weekend will be the tell-all. I did fine on my one-night-out, and I think I will this weekend. I mean, I'm not going to slip, but if I can manage it without too much frustration and temptation, I should be able to show up Monday, attend an exit panel, and come home to stay. I think that'll motivate me."

Matt was happy for Clack, although his face did not show it. He was having a hard time listening to his friend discussing plans for the future when his own seemed so compromised at the moment. He was twenty-eight years old, and, if folks around him had their way, his career would soon be over. Clack finally pulled his left leg up into the seat, which allowed him to turn his entire body toward Matt and say, "What the hell is wrong with you?"

Matt did not want to put his troubles onto a man who had just testified of his victory over his own, but there was no one else to talk to about it. Seeking permission, Matt turned to the giant beside him and asked, "Can we talk about me for a minute?" The minute turned into the next seventy-five. Matt relayed to Clack every detail of what had been doled out by those on the other side in the tug-o-war. When he pulled out the photo of him and Doc with Corey looking on, Clack became the big brother wanting to hunt down the playground bully.

"We don't know who took the picture," Matt explained.

"But we know who the ringleader is," Clack snorted.

"Right!" Matt agreed. "But it's Thanksgiving, and we can talk about this later. We're home, and I have a lot to do before everyone else arrives. You can help!"

Before they exited the truck, Clack took one last look at the photo and said, "Well, look on the bright side."

Matt's eyes widened, and he asked, "What bright side, Clack?"

"The picture does show off your nice ass!"

Matt laughed out loud for the first time in a while, and then he became embarrassed that he found that comment funny. "You're insane!" he told Clack.

"Not according to the fine folks at Respira de Nuevo."

When Matt and Clack walked through the front door, Abigail did a double-take. "Matt," she called, "you'd better hide the turkey because a fox just walked into the henhouse." Matt had to admit that Clack did clean up nicely. Clack's past as an officer and a socialite did not seem like such ancient history at the moment. He was clearly committed to being on his best behavior for Thanksgiving. He put out the folding chairs, set the table, and even taught the kids to fold napkins into the shape of a turkey. It was like he had been part of the family for years. Nothing about his presence made anyone tense, and all indications were that he had found the man he used to be, and everyone, especially Clack, could give thanks for that.

Miss Mabel arrived with a car load of delicious homemade treats and one rutabaga pie. The Wellers came bearing desserts straight out of their Pennsylvania Dutch heritage. The apple dumpling filled the air with an aroma fit for autumn, and they amused one another trying to pronounce the other dessert, *melassichriwwelkuche*. When no one could, Toby got a laugh when he said, "Of course you can. Repeat after me . . . shoo-fly pie." The children played well together. Jacob, the oldest of the four, took on the responsibility role and kept everyone safe and out of trouble, but Maggie was clearly the boss. Everyone ate too much, laughed a lot, watched lots of football and stayed much longer than they intended. It was a fun day, and, when everyone had gone except Clack, Matt excused himself to the upstairs bedroom for a few minutes where he broke down in tears and told God how much he wanted to stay at South Mill.

Clack finally said he, too, should head to his place for the evening, and Matt gathered his sweater and truck keys to drive him. Clack hugged Abigail and then patted M.J. and Maggie on the tops of their heads. "You'll be back tomorrow for dinner?" Abigail asked. He nodded and said he would.

"But y'all don't have to babysit me all weekend," Clack said with a grin. "I'm really going to be okay."

"We're not babysitting you," Abigail jabbed back. "We may want you to babysit them," as she wagged a pointing finger back and forth between her two kids. Everyone laughed, and Clack said that was something he would enjoy. He said goodnight again, and he and Matt stepped through the front door onto the porch.

Clack saw it first. Another newspaper had been tossed up onto the porch. He picked it up and said knowingly, "It's awfully late for the paper to arrive."

Matt reached a hand out, and Clack placed the rolled up, banded paper in his hand like a baton in a relay race. "There's no paper on Thanksgiving Day in South Mill," Matt said with the same sour look he had when he forced down a piece of Miss Mabel's pie at dinner. "Come on, we'll open it in the car."

With trembling fingers, Matt removed the rubber band and unfurled a copy of Wednesday's local paper. It, too, had the red markings, and the new headline read: PASTOR'S WIFE CHEATS WITH OLDER LOVER! The headline took Matt's breath, and when he looked at the attached photo, he screamed and began beating the steering wheel with his fists. Clack called his name several times, but Matt bounded out of the truck and ran in no particular direction, pinging from a tree to the minivan to the shrub at the front porch and then finally to the center of the yard where he fell to his knees and wept. Clack knew to let him have the moment and remained seated in the passenger seat until Matt was still. Slowly, he stepped to the center of the yard and knelt beside Matt. Reaching for the newspaper with one hand, he placed his other around Matt's shoulder and waited for Matt to release his grip. When he let go, Clack read the headline and dropped to a sitting position. In the faint moonlight, he could see a picture of a woman snuggled up to another on a sofa. In an attempt to ease Matt's pain, Clack said, "I can't even tell who they are."

Matt reached into his pocket and pulled out his cell phone, illuminated the flashlight app, and shined it on the photo for Clack to see. In the light, one woman was clearly Abigail, and the older woman was, without a doubt, Jenni. Clack produced a pair of reading glasses from his pocket to get a better look, and Matt began to explain, "Jenni had cried over you for the better part of a Sunday afternoon, and Abigail slid over on the couch to comfort her." Pointing to Jenni's head resting on Abigail's, Matt said, "There's nothing there except a Christian lady ministering to a hurting spouse of an alcoholic...no offense."

"None taken," Clack said as he shined the light on the photo again. "It doesn't look like anything more than that. So relax."

"Clack, in the right hands it's anything they want it to be. And they were right outside of my front windows when they took this picture...or inside. Who knows?"

Clack thought for a moment and then said, "Look, tomorrow we strategize for a fight or a surrender or whatever you decide. But tonight, we're both tired, and we need some sleep before we make an emotional decision. Trust me; I'm the king of emotional decisions."

When Matt and Clack finally arrived at Clack's trailer, Matt pulled up to the gate and reached into the center console and patted around on his soft windbreaker until his fingers touched the keys to Clack's gate, trailer, and truck – the set Matt had been carrying since last week when he took Clack back to Altaville. Before getting out, Clack asked to see the photo one more time. Matt showed it to him reluctantly, and Clack studied it soberly. A goofy grin began to grow across Clack's face, and Matt asked, "What are you smiling about?"

"I'm just thinking," Clack said, "We've got some fine-ass wives, don't we?" Matt looked shocked, but Clack didn't stop. "I mean, it's kinda hot, the two of them, don't you think?"

Even if he was a pastor, Matt couldn't help himself and busted out laughing at the inappropriate humor this guy always came up with. After a few more comments from Clack followed by more laughter, Matt told Clack that he would check in on him in the morning. Clack assured him he was fine and made a plan to meet up tomorrow afternoon. "I'm going in the house to hunt my cell phone. I haven't seen in since I went to the hospital. I'll text or call you when I find it, and you call me if you need anything!"

"Okay! Good night! And thanks!" Matt spoke in broken phrases that were choked off by tears.

"It's going to be okay. You'll see!" Clack promised as though he had the whole solution already figured out. He closed the door, placed one hand on the gate, threw his suitcase over and then leaped over it himself without ever opening it. Matt aimed his headlights at the railing to the back porch until Clack was out of sight. When an inside light flicked on, Matt knew he was in for the night, so he backed out and headed home. He was oddly calm the whole drive there. Somehow, Clack had brought peace to the turmoil.

Back at home, Matt hoped Abigail would never have to see the fake headline and photo he buried in his dresser drawer before going back downstairs to hold her and watch the evening news. With both feeling edgy, the loud engine startled them when it pulled into their driveway, and fear paralyzed them momentarily from even moving to see who it was. Seconds later, a gentle knock coaxed them from their cushy sofa to the front door to see that Clack had returned and was standing at the door with a suitcase, blanket, and pillow. Matt snatched the door open and stared up at the friendly face, noticeably more subdued than Matt had seen it recently. "You okay?" He asked.

"Yeah," Clack replied. "Are you?"

When standing there gawking at one another felt weird, Clack looked at Abigail and said, "I'm sorry for barging back in like this, but I..." he hesitated, "... was missing the dogs, I guess, and I was wondering if I could crash on your couch for tonight."

Abigail and Matt exchanged glances, each waiting for the other to answer. Finally, since the question had been posed to her, Abigail said, "Of course, Clack! Come in." Matt quickly cleared the extra sofa cushions and offered Clack something to drink – a safe offer from a Baptist preacher's kitchen. When everyone had settled comfortably, Abigail called it a night and went upstairs. Matt asked Clack again if everything was okay, and Clack assured him it was. So Matt, too, announced he was going to bed but would first bring the dogs down for Clack.

"No, that's okay," Clack refused. "Let them stay with the kids. I'm feeling better now."

Clack clicked the remote and kept the television on another hour after Matt went upstairs. When SportsCenter was over, Clack used the light from the set to arrange a pallet between the bottom of the steps and the front door. No one would cross that path in the night without him knowing it. Obviously, the dogs had nothing to do with his return, but he would be up early before anyone else became aware of that fact. He slept off and on, albeit restlessly, but he didn't mind. He was on guard duty.

CHAPTER THIRTY-FOUR

Matt woke to the smell of bacon and coffee and found Clack in the kitchen cooking breakfast. Clack had already drained one pot of coffee, but there was another one brewing. When Clack pulled a pan of golden buttered biscuits, made from scratch, from the oven, Matt said, "Is there anything you can't do!"

Clack shrugged then struck a serious posture and spoke, he hoped, directly to Matt's heart. "I can't preach a sermon or love people the way you do." When the thought seemed incomplete, Clack finished it by saying, "But maybe I can make sure you get to keep on doing that."

"Okay, that's way too heavy this early in the morning," Matt dismissed Clack's comment. He told him to save the sentimental stuff for later in the day and excitedly bit into one of Clack's biscuits and savored a hot cup of strong coffee. Clack already had the newspaper spread out on the table and assured Matt it was the real one and the only one on the porch when he stepped out there at sunrise.

After breakfast, Matt asked Clack to help get the tables and chairs back to the church before anyone noticed they were gone. While Matt changed, Clack took it upon himself to load them up in the back of his truck. When they arrived at the church, the mail carrier was just pulling away from the church's box, the first on her daily delivery route. Matt was compelled to check it, and he was relieved to find nothing more than a few advertisements, which he tossed in the trash, and a ministerial journal to which he subscribed, which he decided to drop off in his office. Since Clack had never been further than the fellowship hall, Matt invited him up to see the office suite, but the tour ended before it began when Matt saw that his office door was wide open. He walked slowly around Lanie's desk and stopped in his own doorway. The office was empty. The wingback chair was gone. The desk and credenza had vanished, too. Where they sat, Matt's files and drawer contents were piled on the floor. The couch had disappeared, as well, and lying where it used to sit was the helium tank that Matt had rolled underneath it a week ago. The phone that usually sat on Matt's desk was on a shelf, and Matt headed straight to it, picked up the receiver, and began pushing buttons. Clack held off with any questions, expecting answers to come by way of the phone call Matt was making.

When Dorothy Heath said hello, Matt told her to put Stephen on the phone. She said he was resting, but Matt said it was urgent, so she reluctantly obliged him. When the old man picked up, Matt's fury spread like wildfire. "Where the hell is my furniture?"

"Oh, do you have some furniture missing?" Heath smugly replied. "If you're referring to those nice items from the church office, those are mine. I bought them years ago, and I've been loaning them to the church ever since. But my son has started a business, you know, and he needed some office furniture. Rather than go out and buy new, I figured...well, you know."

"You self-righteous son-of-a-bitch," Matt burned on. "This ends now! You call off your posse, and I'll take you on, one-on-one, man-to-man. But you leave my wife and my friends out of this! Do you hear me?"

Silence! Then a click. The old man hung up.

Clack stood by shaking his head, not believing that someone who called himself a Christian, much less a retired pastor, could do something as heinous as what was being done to Matt. Matt explained how he didn't believe he was the first in the church's history to deal with Heath or someone like him, and he dug from his files the card about funeral flowers that was left behind by someone. But who? He studied it for a moment, showed it to Clack, and returned it to the file.

When the men saw no benefit to staying any longer, Clack hoisted up the helium tank and said, "Let me take care of this for you." He hauled it to the bed of his truck and promised to return it to Global Air. He knew where their office was and said he was headed that direction later in the day. Matt was in no mood to argue and thanked Clack for getting rid of it.

Clack stayed with Matt and his family through lunch and even dozed with them as the afternoon sun warmed the living room. The mail came later than usual on the day after Thanksgiving, but that was to be expected. When it did arrive, Abigail trotted outside to retrieve it. When she returned, she called excitedly to the children that the first Christmas card of the year had arrived. Everyone gathered around to see it but let Maggie do the honors of opening it. It was a beautiful card, with a wooden white church covered in a blanket of snow on the front, and it read: IN THIS MOST BLESSED SEASON OF THE YEAR... No one read the rest of it on the inside because when Maggie opened it, she said, "Look! It's M.J."

Chills shot through Matt's chest as he bounded for the table. On a glossy white page, someone had created something that looked like a real estate brochure. It was doubled over to fit in the card, but, unfolded, it was a tri-fold collage of photographs taken from inside the parsonage. On one page, M.J. lay sleeping in his bed with Chop tucked under his arm. On another, Matt stood on the back porch shining a flashlight toward the woods. On another flap was Maggie, sound asleep in her bedroom with Felix resting his chin on the footboard of her bed. And another picture stopped short of capturing Abigail in her Friday night routine of a relaxing bath. But the candles around the garden tub were lit in the photo.

"Who took those pictures, Daddy?" Maggie asked with a concern that no one her age should feel.

"I did, Honey!" It was a lie, but he had to think quickly. "I was testing out a camera for your mother's Christmas present, and I asked the man at the camera store to send them to me." Matt was impressed with his fast thinking and looked sharply at Abigail imploring her to go along with the gimmick. "I didn't like it," Matt said, as he folded the pamphlet and then folded it again and then again. "I decided to buy her something else." Needing to shift her attention, Matt said, "Have you and M.J. made your Christmas wish lists? Why don't y'all go get a pencil and do that now? You can write M.J.'s down for him." When the two scampered off to find paper and pencil, Abigail burst into tears.

"What is that?"

"It's us. And it's our children." He was answering Abigail's question, but he was looking at Clack when he spoke. "And someone was in our house taking pictures of us all." Clack's expression was pained, and he nodded slowly back at Matt.

Then, to Abigail, he said, "And it's the end of a very bad nightmare. I promise!"

He left the room and returned with the three headlines that had been delivered in one way or another to him over the last week. He then told her about his standoff with Heath on Sunday, and about the office furniture, too. With every blow, Abigail became more inconsolable. Matt, oddly, was not emotional at all. He shared everything slowly and calmly and just let Abigail wail. When she suddenly pounded her fists on the table and said, "Give them what they want!" Clack stood up and politely excused himself. "Resign Sunday!" Abigail cried. "Don't even preach! Ask them to let us stay in this haunted house until we go home for Christmas, and we will go in a moving van and never look back."

Matt looked at Abigail and smiled sweetly then kissed her cheek and said simply, "Okay."

CHAPTER THIRTY-FIVE

By 7:00 p.m., it was obvious that Clack was not returning, so Matt convinced Abigail to let him go check on him. Selling the idea wasn't easy. Abigail had been looking out the windows and doors since the sun began to set, and she was paranoid that someone was out there with a camera or worse. Matt rambled around in their bedroom closet for a long time and then came out with the lockbox, brought it downstairs, and sat it on the coffee table in front of her in plain sight of the children. There was, however, no need to explain it to them. "You know how to use it," he told her, "so use it if you have to." She stared expressionlessly at it, but nodded that she did and would.

Matt backed the truck out of the driveway and headed right toward Clack's house. He drove all of twelve feet and stopped. His truck was now hidden by thick pines to anyone looking from the house to the road, yet it was parked right outside the house giving the appearance that he was home. He stopped, cut the lights and engine, and ran around to the passenger side. He opened the door, retrieved his black "jogging" clothes that he had taken out of the house with a bag of garbage an hour earlier. He shimmied out of his khakis and yanked the black sweatpants up to his waist. He traded his plaid shirt for a tight-fitting black nylon tee shirt. He placed his stocking cap on his head and gently removed the black windbreaker jacket from the center console of his truck, unrolling it carefully so that nothing fell out. Wrapped in the jacked, he was fully suited for the occasion and jogged to the park just like he had done on other nights before, this time keeping his right hand in the pocket securing what hid inside.

At the dugout, he ducked into the pines and emerged into the now leafless lawn of Stephen and Dorothy Heath. Her car was not in the garage but was, instead, sitting in the driveway just in front of the house. At precisely 7:20 p.m., Matt ducked low as the front door opened, and Dorothy stepped out. She spoke to someone inside, "Are you sure you're okay for me to leave you?"

The old, slow, familiar gravelly voice answered back, "Yes. Go!"

Dorothy closed the front door and lumbered down the steps with a casserole dish in one hand and a pie plate in the other. When she had placed the food securely on the back floorboard, she closed the back door, opened the driver's door, and shoved her thick body inside. The engine roared, the lights came on, and she was off on her nightly delivery. When she was gone from the driveway and out on the road, Matt thought he saw movement in the house, a silhouette or a shadow moving swiftly. He dismissed it as his imagination. Heath could never move that quickly.

From his familiar hiding place, Matt began his prayer by first apologizing to God for being there. Then, he offered up excuse after excuse for his sinful attitude and actions. He prayed that nothing Stephen Heath had done nor anything he, himself, was about to do would come back to hurt his beautiful wife and darling babies. Then, he finished by praying for boldness for what came next. From somewhere in his memory, some line from a play about a "damn spot" danced through his thoughts. He knew it was Shakespeare, but he could not name the play.

He had let more time pass than he intended, and Dorothy would not be gone forever. So, rising to his feet, Matt stood up straight, emerged from the shrubs, and walked purposely up the front steps to the door of the Heaths' home. He turned the handle; Dorothy had not locked it. He entered the foyer and scoped out the formal living room to his left. He'd been there before, so he knew Stephen would be in the den. He could hear the television blasting almost deafeningly. He paused for a moment before opening the door to the den, counted to three, took a deep breath, and then burst into the room. Heath didn't notice him. Didn't speak. Didn't move. But someone else was in the room, and he did move – with such speed and agility that Matt didn't notice him come from behind. And before Matt could scream or run, he was jerked backward and lifted off the ground with one unseen hand and muzzled with another. He wrestled to get free, kicking the air, until the hands that held him lowered him to where his ear was level with his assailant's mouth. And when the mouth spoke in a whisper tone, Matt froze in terror.

"Shhhhh, Matt! It's me, Clack." Clack put the preacher's feet back on the floor and turned him around fully to face him, still keeping one hand over his mouth. "We have to get out of here! Okay?" Matt shook his head to say no and reached to remove something from his jacket pocket, but Clack's enormous hand stopped him short as he whispered, "He's already dead! We have to go!"

Matt's eyes widened and his shaking head shifted to a nod, and Clack spoke again. "I'm going to uncover your mouth, but you can't say a word. I have to get something, and then we have to get out of here before the wife gets back." Again, Matt nodded. With Clack's hand gone, Matt expected it to be easier to breathe, but he was mistaken. A heater was blasting in the corner, and Matt noticed that Heath was bundled up in blankets. Had Clack created an oven and baked the old man? Matt was frozen, spellbound by the old man sitting there silent, still – peaceful. Even as Clack busied himself behind Brother Heath, Matt could not break his stare. Finally, Clack knelt down and then heaved a familiar tank up into the palm of his hand. He carried it resting on his shoulder like a rifle. In the other hand, he held a small green bag. "Follow me!"

Matt obeyed, and the two exited the house through the back sun porch door and took a hard left into the same wooded pines that had shrouded Matt on his nightly adventures. They ran breathlessly without speaking until they reached the park. Clack paused at the dugout to see if anyone was around, and when the coast was clear, he motioned for Matt to follow on. In the parking lot, Clack fell to his knees, lifted the cover off of a manhole, and pointed for Matt to drop in. Once Matt's head was out of sight, Clack lowered the helium tank to him, and crawled in behind it. When he descended the ladder, and he and Matt were both standing on the ground, Clack said, "I know there's a lot to talk about, but we need to move right now." Clack lit a battery-powered lantern that illuminated their cavernous passageway – the new, clean, yet-to-be-used waste water system the city was still completing. They clipped along for about fifty yards when Clack pointed to another ladder and said, "Up we go!" Matt led the way, lifted the manhole cover with surprising ease, and emerged onto a street one block over from his own. Clack followed and, after replacing the cover, pointed to his truck that was parked in front of a vacant house with a "For Sale" sign in front of it. Clack threw the helium tank in the back, the two men jumped in the cab, and Clack gunned it to Matt's house.

Matt motioned for him to pull in the driveway, and Matt bolted from the door to his own truck and quickly changed out of his black clothes. Clack, too, performed a quick change beside his own truck while Matt wheeled his around in the street and parked beside Clack's in the driveway. Calling to Abigail as he approached the porch to keep from startling her and potentially being shot, Matt announced that he had found Clack.

Clack led the conversation once inside the house by saying to Abigail, "I'm sorry to worry you both. My truck wouldn't start (which was a lie), and I still can't find my cell phone (which was the truth). Abigail yawned and said she was drained, both physically and emotionally. With two strong men in the house, she thought she could sleep and went to bed. She kissed Matt on the lips and then Clack on the cheek. When she had disappeared up the steps, Matt listened for the bedroom door to close and then motioned for Clack to move to the kitchen table. When both were seated opposite one another, Matt let out the question he had held with his breath for the last fifteen minutes.

"WHAT DID YOU DO?"

"I saved you from making a huge mistake, and I saved your family from even more pain, and..." Clack continued with a casualness that irritated Matt, "... I probably saved your job."

Matt shook his head trying to process any part of what Clack said. He stammered for a while, trying to speak words but only making sounds unable to decide which words to say. He had questions, but where to start? "You killed him?" seemed like a good place.

"His best years were behind him," Clack flippantly said.

"No, Clack! That's murder."

"I prefer to think of what I did tonight as preventing a murder."

Matt was appalled at the way Clack was talking about it as if it were some sort of business transaction. "What do you mean you prevented a murder? You said he's dead!"

"Well, when you put it that way, I guess it is unfortunate for the old man that the outcome is the same either way."

"Why, Clack?"

Clack stared at Matt before cutting him to the core with his response. "So that you didn't."

"I was just there to talk to him, Clack. I wasn't going to murder him."

Clack's lips formed a calculating smile and then said, "Where's my gun?"

Matt was stunned. He hesitated and Clack repeated the question. Slowly, Matt walked across the living room and out the front door and returned with his black windbreaker jacket. He unfolded it and reached into the pocket and handed Clack the .38 that he had saved him from a month earlier.

"Now, see," Clack spun the pistol like a top on the table and calmly explained, "we'd be needing to dispose of this pretty piece of hardware if it was a murder weapon. Thankfully, it is not."

"How did you know?" Matt sank back into a kitchen chair.

Clack launched into a long but important explanation so that both he and Matt were clear on all that had led their current set of circumstances. "When you took me home Thursday night, I noticed that my pistol was gone. I actually expected it to have been removed before I came home last week for my one-night-out, but no one had been in the house, and everything was just as I had left it. So, Thanksgiving, after that evening paper arrived on your porch, you took me home, and that's when I realized it. You were the only one who had a key to my place. I was afraid of what you might be planning. Of course, I hoped you were just keeping it for protection, but I couldn't know for sure. So I came back to spend the night so that if you got some crazy notion to go out and do something stupid, I would be here to stop you."

Matt sat and listened like a schoolboy to the fascinating story Clack told.

"When the Christmas card came today, I saw your face, and I knew the plan you were sitting on had hatched. So, when I disappeared, I did a little planning of my own, took a few walks past the park, scoped out the underground system, bought a few supplies, and made damn sure I was there ahead of you."

"By the way," Clack interrupted himself, "there are much better hiding places in those people's back yard than where you camp out every night."

Sensing he had told enough, Clack finished by saying, "Anyway, I waited for the wife to leave, and I slipped in through the door on the porch. They really should keep their doors locked."

Matt was taking it all in, but still had unanswered questions. "How?"

"Oh, I'm sorry, Clack responded sarcastically, "I thought that heavy helium tank I was hauling around was obvious."

"You hit him with the helium tank? Are you nuts? Now we have a much bigger murder weapon to get rid of."

"There's no murder weapon, Matt!" Clack actually laughed. "And this is the ingenious part." Matt was engulfed again in the story.

"You've heard about how dangerous it is for SCUBA divers to resurface too quickly? Well, what happens is gas finds its way into the bloodstream through a tear or something smaller than a pinhole in a blood vessel and ends up cutting off the blood flow to the brain. It's basically the same thing as a stroke. The person dies because of an obstruction in the blood vessel caused from inhaling pressurized gas. In other cases, the gas simply crowds out the oxygen and the person dies from asphyxiation. Hard to tell, really, which one took the old dude out, but I'm betting on the second one. Either way, autopsies are hardly ever conclusive in these cases. There will be no questions. No investigation. No murder weapon."

Trying to recreate the events in his mind, Matt asked, "How did you get Heath to inhale helium?"

"I told him it would be fun to hear ourselves laugh and talk funny, you know, like a couple of kids sucking the helium out of a balloon."

Matt looked mortified.

Clack reached across the table and smacked some sense into his head. "No, you idiot. I conned an oxygen mask and some tubing off a lady at the medical supply store . . . " Clack made air quotes with his fingers and continued, "...for my father, who is here for Thanksgiving, you know, and is quite confused these days and left his supplies at home in Kentucky."

Matt's eyes widened and he raised his thick black eyebrows in amazement. Clack went on. "Add a little tape to help hold the tubing in place on the regulator, and the hard work was done. He never saw or heard me come in, and I'll spare you the details, but with a couple of deep breaths he was gone. I actually thought he might be trying to outsmart me for a minute. No one goes that quickly." Then, as an afterthought, Clack began to nod as he said quite matter-of-factly, "His health must have already been compromised."

Matt stood from the table and began to pace. Clack reached out and braced Matt's shoulders and, for the first time seemed gravely concerned. "Look at me and listen, Matt! This is the most important thing I've said in a long, long time. Ever heard of the Just War Theory? *Jus Ad Bellum* and *Jus in Bello* and all that jazz?"

Matt nodded and said, "Yeah, in Seminary . . . ethics class."

"The military teaches that too," Clack continued. "Study it again sometime. Our cause was just. All diplomatic attempts were exhausted, the action was proportional, and the intention was to produce a good outcome for innocent people."

Matt felt like he was listening to a great philosopher. Clack squared Matt's shoulders like a dad lecturing a son and finished his lesson by saying, "*You* were not there when Heath died. You did not know I *was* there. You had no knowledge of *my* plan. So *you* were not even an accomplice. Forget what you went there to do. You did nothing! No one ever has to know that you were there."

Matt began to cry, and Clack pulled him to his chest and held him tightly. He canopied Matt underneath his own broad torso and whispered in his ear, "You're innocent, Matt. You're gonna be okay." And to make sure it sunk in, he repeated it over and over again. Matt reached one arm around Clack and then the other and held on as he understood the troubling gift he had been given. Two men had gone to commit a dastardly deed that night – one in anger and hatred for an enemy, and the other in love and sacrifice for a friend. Clack, though guilty, was, in Matt's summation of the night, the more honorable of the two.

Suddenly, his gratitude gave way to worry about the wellbeing of the best friend he had ever known, and he pulled away and looked Clack in the face and said, "No one ever has to know you were there, either."

Clack nodded and turned to the refrigerator. Scanning the selections before him of cola, juice, tea, and milk, he said to Matt, "Boy, am I in the right house tonight!" Holding a can of Pepsi in his hand, he said, "I really need a drink, and this is the strongest thing you've got."

The two had been sitting on the sofa drinking Pepsi and silently staring into a blank television screen for half an hour when a knock on the front door shot both of their hearts into their throats. Clack swallowed fast and said, "Answer the door." Matt was beginning to panic and asked who Clack thought it could be, and Clack told him that it didn't matter - they could not be tied to anything that had happened in South Mill that night. "Just play it cool."

And though Clack was right, playing it cool was difficult when Matt saw Sergeant Andrews, of the South Mill Sheriff's Office, on the porch. Matt opened the door, and the officer removed his hat and began to speak. "Good evening, Preacher! I'm sorry to disturb you. Looks like you may have company..." His voice trailed off as he looked in Clack's direction, but a broad smile crept across his face and he said, "Well, look who it is!"

Clack raised his can in the air to say cheers. "Good evening, Officer! Nothing in this can but Pepsi. Would you like one?"

"No, no! I'm good. Thank you anyway." It was clear by his jovial mood that he was not there looking for any murder suspects. To Matt he said, "I'm on my way over to Brother Stephen Heath's house. I'm sorry to tell you this – I know how close y'all are – but Brother Heath has passed away. Miss Dorothy called the station and asked if I could let you know, and I didn't think a phone call was in order. She's hoping you'll come to the house with me."

"Why?" Matt was suspicious. Why would Dorothy want him to know? Why would she want him to come to the house?

Finding the question odd, the officer said, "Well, I'm sure partly because you are their pastor. But I will tell you that he passed away in the den, and she wants someone to help move him to his bed before their children arrive. Thinks it'll be a more dignified presentation." Then, turning his attention to Clack, he said, "In fact, Colonel Collins, would you mind coming and helping us? Brother Heath's a pretty big man."

"Call me Clack! And I'll be glad to. Do you think his wife will mind? I've never met them." Matt was trying to get used to how calm Clack was and how casually he was chatting it up with the deputy.

The Sergeant assured him it would be fine – that everyone in South Mill was just one big family anyway.

Clack shrugged at Matt, and Matt shrugged back. Looking at Officer Andrews, he said, "Let me break the news to my wife, and I'll be right there." He told Abigail only that Dorothy had called to say Stephen had died and needed him and Clack to come help move him for the kids' sake. Abigail was groggy when she said, "Oh no! I'm so sorry for his family." But as Matt left the bedroom, she said, "When no one is looking, kick him once for me." As Matt closed the door, he thought out loud, "we're all going to hell."

Matt drove and Clack rode shotgun as they followed the flashing light of the patrol car. No siren. Neither spoke, except when Clack said, "Now even our finger prints inside the house would make sense if anyone was looking."

When they arrived and stepped out of the car, Clack patted Matt on the back and said, "Okay, Pastor Matt – go do your thing." Matt stepped slowly up the front steps, turned the knob and went in without knocking. When Dorothy saw him coming through the hallway to the den where Stephen remained, she began to cry and fell on Matt in an embrace. Matt embraced her right back and said, "I'm so sorry, Dorothy! He'll be missed around here!" Then Matt pulled back, introduced his friend, Clack, who was visiting for Thanksgiving and had come with him and Officer Andrews to help get Brother Stephen to a more comfortable setting. She was nothing but hospitable to all three and asked if they would mind if she left the room while they moved him. They didn't mind but rather preferred it, as there would be no graceful way to manage moving a man his size through doorways and a narrow hall. She said she'd be in the kitchen and offered to fix them a cup of coffee or a cold drink. With Clack taking the upper half of the body, Matt and Andrews each supported a leg, and in a clumsy mess, they took Stephen Heath to his bed for the last time ever.

Matt stepped back and the officer went to let Dorothy know they were done as Clack pulled the sheet and blanket up to Stephen's chest. When Matt turned to position himself at the foot of the bed in proper mourner fashion, he was shocked to see a rack of oxygen tanks, green in color and each stamped with the words SOUTH MILL RESPIRATORY SERVICES: A DIVISION OF GLOBAL AIR. When Dorothy entered, Matt politely asked, "What's with all the oxygen?"

Dorothy responded, "He would hate for you to see these." She then explained that six months ago, right about the time Matt had arrived, Heath was diagnosed with pulmonary fibrosis or interstitial lung disease. She told how most patients with it last anywhere from three to five years, but no one knew how long Stephen had had it. Three weeks ago, they had been to the doctor, the same day they saw Matt from a distance in the parking lot, and the doctor said it had progressed rapidly. Suddenly the blue lips and the pale face and the running out of breath made sense. "We still didn't know how long he had," Dorothy continued, "but we never dreamed it would be this quick." Clack's face became animated at the news, and he fought the urge to blurt out *I told you so.* Thankfully, only Matt noticed.

"I had no idea," Matt admitted.

Letting her emotions go again, Dorothy spoke between sobs, "I guess after having the whole family over for Thanksgiving, he thought it was a good time to just let go and go home to Jesus." Matt placed his arm around her and, though his hypocrisy stared him in the face, he said, "Why don't we have a prayer?" So the four of them joined hands, and Matt led a touching prayer, giving thanks for Brother Stephen and the life of service and ministry he had lived. Somber faces then filed out of the bedroom, and Matt offered to stay until the Heath's children all arrived. Dorothy did not find that necessary, especially when some were driving several hours to get there. She promised to call if she needed anything, and Matt promised that he would check in on her in the morning. He knew that her pleasantness would wear off with the shock by then, but he would call or come by just the same.

Bidding goodnight to one another, Sergeant Andrews walked to his patrol car, and Clack and Matt made their way to the truck. At the driver's side door, Matt paused and took in the immensity of the man climbing in on the other side. For a moment he was breathless. Then, he turned and walked slowly toward a grove of azaleas, where he stood and stared upward, looking beyond the tops of the tall pines and into the cloudless, starlit heavens that alone knew the truth.

CHAPTER THIRTY-SIX

The South Mill Baptist Church held an overflow crowd on Tuesday morning at 11:00 a.m., as had the Brewer-Hampton Funeral Home the night before. Visitation had gone on for three hours Monday night, and on Tuesday morning at 10:40, after praying with the family around the casket, Matt ducked into his minivan, because it was the nicer of their cars, and watched the Heath family continue to visit with even more relatives and friends. Finally, the funeral director insisted that they, too, load into the funeral cars – two brand new Cadillac limousines with leather seats and tinted windows – for the procession to the church. The Heaths planned to receive friends again in the foyer of the church when the service concluded before going to the cemetery. Dorothy, who was clearly over the initial shock of Stephen's passing, was no longer sweet to Matt, but she was cordial, and that was acceptable to him.

Abigail attended the funeral reluctantly as the dutiful pastor's wife, but M.J. and Maggie stayed home under the watchful care of their two chief babysitters, Felix and Chop, who were supervised by Clack and Jenni Collins. It was an odd way for the two to reconnect, but the kids kept conversation topics from becoming too heavy. And they would have plenty of time to work on whatever was next for them after Clack finished replacing a staircase at Respira de Nuevo. He was honest with Matt and admitted he probably needed a couple more weeks there in light of all that had recently transpired...but that he was going to be fine and home, hopefully in Cardelville, in time for Christmas. He wanted both of his significant others to visit him weekly until then.

Jenni had a contact who was a breeder, and a litter of baby Samoyeds was going to be ready for weaning and a new home just in time for Christmas. Until their two replacements arrived, Chop and Felix would stay in South Mill.

Lanie had been quite busy on Monday, printing the program for the largest funeral service the church had ever seen. Trudy, too, had been diligently working the books to set up a designated receipts fund for Stephen Heath Memorial Contributions and working the phones to schedule herself a face-to-face meeting with the Briners, Jim Pethel, and anyone else she felt needed to be put on notice. Somehow the two secretaries also managed to find time to scour phone books, contact other churches, and Google a list of name for hours. They were tireless in their efforts to make contact with some folks they thought would want to attend the service, or at least know that Brother Heath had died. When the funeral was over and the family was in another receiving line out back, another group gathered near the front of the sanctuary around Matt. Lanie did the honors of introducing seven former pastors of South Mill Baptist Church to the current minister. Matt was blown away – he never thought they'd return. One of them, number five, welcomed Matt to the club and congratulated him on being the only one of them who had survived the reign of terror. Another, number six, said, "Now, you get to be the one who sees what we all knew this church could be!" They all left their phone numbers and addresses with Lanie to share with Matt, and each said he would be glad to return for a visit anytime now, at Pastor Matt's invitation of course.

Just before continuing the procession from the church to the cemetery, Matt was left alone with Lanie at the front of the sanctuary surrounded by sprays and wreaths and potted plants, all beautifully adorning the pulpit area in honor of the church's founder. Matt thanked Lanie for all she had done to make the day special for the Heaths and for him. She produced the same sweet smile that greeted him every morning. Lanie was inhaling the aroma of a gorgeous full orchid when the funeral director signaled for Matt to rejoin the family. As he started up the aisle, he almost tripped when he heard Lanie say, "Funeral flowers really *can* be quite fragrant." He looked back at her only for a second as confusion gave way to clarity. As he turned to walk away, a crooked smile raised on the left side of his face forcing the same eye into a narrow squint as he said quite simply, "Amen!"

Author's Note: While I have spent a lifetime in small towns like Cardelville and South Mill, the characters within this book are fictional people I made up to help tell a story that I hope you have enjoyed. My respect and reverence for churches and their leadership is a passionate conviction for me, and I in no way wish to discredit the life-change that comes from engaging in the devout practice of one's faith. But I do suspect that there are times when even the best of church leaders is pushed beyond his or her limit.

Furthermore, I have no direct knowledge of things that took place in the Vietnam conflict, nor of helicopters like the "Quiet One." I am forever thankful for the U.S. personnel that served in Vietnam, and I believe that each of them is a hero. If in my attempt to tell a good tale, any accurate information I accidentally included surrounding Clack's military career comes from articles and non-fiction books I've read along the way. Of particular interest is one article written by James R. Chiles, in Smithsonian's *Air and Space Magazine*, in March 2008. I highly recommend it as an accurate investigation into the aircraft used by our heroes in Vietnam.

****

A **Word of Thanks** to the helpers along the journey. For my assistant, Mary Rich, who proofread a million times and met with me during COVID, against her better judgment, to give me her notes. For the insight of Rachel, Jeremy, Jane, Dennis, and finally Ashlie – you guys were a great team. Thank you for being honest with me and helping to refine the story. Finally, thanks to Anne, Andrew, and Elizabeth – my home team! I love you, and I hope you'll finally read this thing.

VENGEANCE IS MINE, a work of southern fiction, is the character-driven story of Clack Collins, a larger-than-life Vietnam veteran and former success in the homebuilding industry, for whom the 2008 recession destroyed everything, including his marriage to a former U.S. congressman's daughter. It, too, is the lamentable struggle of Matt Hardy, a fresh-out-of-school preacher in the rural South Carolina town where Clack has retreated to both find work and drink his demons away. When the politics of a small southern town, spearheaded by one of Matt's own predecessors, work to derail the young cleric's good deeds and destroy his sweet family, he is pushed beyond what any good man can withstand and resorts to a plan that will forever invalidate his holy reputation. It is, however, the unlikely and often humorous friendship with Clack, a man guided by his own compass of justifiable war, that becomes Matt's own salvation.